OUTBOUND

Opposite page: Inner Solar System

OUTBOUND

ISLANDS IN THE VOID

Richard M. Anderson

PRECOCITY PRESS

FOR MY WIFE CAROL,

who tolerates the time I spend at the computer, secluded in the den, and loves me for it. And to our extended family, who will inherit this Earth in whatever form we leave it.

Published by Precocity Press, Los Angeles, CA
Developmental Consultant and Editor: Allan Graubard
Copyeditor: Julie Simpson
Creative Director and Cover Designer: Susan Shankin
Interior Designer and Typesetter: Andrea Reider
Cover and Interior Illustrations: Tim Kummerow

ISBN: 979-8-9898304-6-6
Library of Congress Control Number: 2024906851
First edition. Printed and bound in the United States of America

CONTENTS

PRIMARY CHARACTERS

Anni: Virtual being implanted in Ali Ebrahim.

Daria Aquila: Chief Engineer to Dr. Rhett Blackwood, then to Dr. Virgil Greenly. Oversees all engineering of the six islands and operation of the MAC facility at ELL 5 (Earth-Moon Lagrange 5), known as Ellie 5.

Captain (later, Rear Admiral) Rodrigo Austin: Captain of the Navy corvette ship *Swordthruster.* Assists in the defection and escape of Ali Ebrahim and associates.

Major Zarita Banderas-Duran: Commander of NASA Lunar South Pole Base (NASA LSP). Forms alliance with Draco Osborne to take control of Ellie 5.

Simone Beaulieu: Rocket engineer at Ellie 5. An early friend of Dr. Virgil Greenly.

Chief Engineer Earl Bedford and Lead Environmental Scientist Salvadore Munros: Two of the three people (Dr. Dag Harlow being the third) not in hibernation when the *Corn Goddess* first arrives at Ceres.

Dr. Amelia Bereza: Botanist aboard Ceres Island, assists Jules Blackwood in establishing engineered Redwood trees in the island.

Blackwood Family: Dr. Rhett Blackwood, his wife Koral, and daughters Jules and Chanté. Rhett is the initial Director of the Ellie 5 project. Later advisor to Secretary General Ali Ebrahim.

Major Richard Cass: Pilot and commander of an escape spaceship and rocket containing Ali Ebrahim and company.

Enji Chinen: Archivist on the Centaurus Fleet.

Dr. Charles (Chip) de Verde: Astronomer aboard the long-range spaceship *Endeavor* on its voyage to Ceres Island.

Secretary General Ali Ebrahim: Secretary General of Global States United (GSU), later voted out of Parliament. Champion of the Space Settlement Program.

Dr. Kira Eguchi: Veterinarian traveling with the Centaurus Fleet.

Dr. Jon Einarsson: Professor at Iceland University at Reykjavík. Becomes Preceptor of GSU Parliament.

Admiral Nathan Flint: Admiral of the Arctic Fleet under Secretary General Ali Ebrahim. Defects when Draco Osborne is elected Secretary General. Develops a fleet in opposition to the GSU Navy.

Governor Henry Fong: Governor of Antarctica.

Dr. Virgil Greenly: Relieves Dr. Rhett Blackwood as Director of the Ellie 5 project and receives Rhett's virtual associate implant and interface, Ofelia.

Dr. Dag Harlow: Arrives at Ceres in the *Corn Goddess* spaceship, which is converted into a habitat called Ceres Station, of which he becomes the director. Ceres Station scientists and engineers are charged with mining materials from the nearby asteroids.

Fredrik Johnson: Governor of Australia.

Rear Admiral Lower Half Franklin La Joy: Leader of a carrier task force that challenges Admiral Flint's fleet in the Southern Hemisphere.

Civilian Admiral Bakari Marijani: Leader of the Centaurus Fleet.

Dr. Charles (Chuck) McKeever: Engineer at NASA Mars Base, assistant to Dr. Jules Blackwood.

Vice Admiral Aisling Murphy: Vice Admiral of the Antarctic Fleet.

Ofelia: A virtual being whose interface hardware is initially implanted in Dr. Rhett Blackwood and subsequently in Dr. Virgil Greenly.

Draco Osborne: Leader of various crime syndicates in Central Earth Societies. Elected to GSU Parliament in Reykjavík, Iceland, later GSU Secretary General.

Admiral Anastasia Petrova: Admiral of the Antarctic Fleet under the GSU government.

Dr. Timothy Storm: Director of NASA Mars Base.

Mei Wen: Governor of the Jupiter Archipelago. She was the founding member of the Centaurus Fleet and its first Civilian Admiral.

LOCATIONS & TECHNOLOGIES

Amchitka Island: An island in the Aleutians. (*In the story, it has a naval base that plays an important role.)

Americas Sector*: A sector of the Ellie 5 Zeta Island. It represents South and Central America.

Antarctic Polar Resort*: A tropical environment enclosed within a glass-domed resort at the South Pole.

Asia Sector*: One of three sectors in the Ellie 5 Zeta Island.

Asteroid Belt: An orbit between Mars and Jupiter where the planetoid Ceres and asteroids are located. There are three major orbit divisions separated by Kirkwood Gaps. These gaps are largely caused by gravitational effects from Jupiter. The inner orbit contains S-type asteroids (rocky with some metal content). The middle orbit contains M-type asteroids (highest metal content). The outer orbit contains C-type asteroids (carbonaceous, like huge lumps of coal).

Asteroid Processing Structure (APS)*: A facility near Ceres Station and later Ceres Island that refines material mined from asteroids into metal ingots and other materials for easier and faster transportation to

Ellie 5. At Ellie 5 the material is further manufactured into structural components, machine products. Stainless steel is made at the Ellie 5 Manufacturing, Assembly, and Construction (MAC) facility for the construction of Earth reentry spaceships.

Autonomous Rocket Motors*: These are robotic motors that attach to and transport bulky items in space. They are used to guide long-distance loads from Ceres to Ellie 5 and shorter distances within an archipelago of space islands. They also attach to Earth reentry gliders and position them for reentry before returning to Ellie 5. The gliders carry material to Earth on a one-way trip.

Beaver Lake*: A small artificial lake developed in the new Ceres Island.

Bio-Transceiver*: Of biological origin. Implanted in Enji Chinen by veterinarian Dr. Kira Eguchi of the Centaurus Fleet. One in existence. Connects to the Centaurus Fleet Cloud. Transmits and receives electromagnetic waves when in close range.

Cambium Cells: The living part of trees. A thin layer of cells that transport water and nutrients up and down the tree. It lies just under the bark and on top of the unliving wood structure of the tree. Used by Jules Blackwood in developing artificial Redwood trees at Ceres Island.

Central Earth People*: Those populations that were unable to migrate north or south to avoid the most severe effects of global warming and the collapse of agriculture. They are easily exploited because of their poverty and desperation. These people are at the bottom of the economic system and a great source of Draco Osborne's wealth and power.

Ceres Planetoid: A dwarf planet in the M ring of the Asteroid Belt. It has a diameter of 950 kilometers and an orbit period of 4.6 years. Vesta is the next largest planetoid in the Asteroid Belt.

Ceres Station*: A habitat created from the spaceship *Corn Goddess*, which had been used to bring the first scientists and engineers to Ceres.

Château de Chambord*: A façade of the real Château in the Loire Valley in France, reproduced in the Vineyard Renaissance Sector of Ellie 5 Zeta. Inspiration for the name of Chambord University on Ellie 5 Zeta.

Chlorates and Perchlorates: Oxidizing chemicals prevalent in Martian regolith. They oxidize and destroy organic molecules and thus are very dangerous to living things. They must be removed (*in the story, by heating) before the regolith can be converted to soil that will support life.

Corn Goddess*: The spaceship that brought the original team of scientists and engineers to live in orbit of Ceres in the Asteroid Belt. So named because in ancient Roman religion, Ceres (Latin) was a goddess of agriculture, especially grains. Upon arriving it was reconstructed as Ceres Station, to be used as a habitat, for research, and for asteroid harvesting.

Earth Space Operations (ESO)*: An Earth-based regulatory body overseeing all space operations and exploitations. All funds are approved by and funded through ESO.

Ecotopia*: A theoretical utopia where nature is perfectly balanced. Referred to partially in jest by Dr. Virgil Greenly upon the completion of Ellie 5 Zeta. In fact, a very well-balanced ecology is required for the long-term success of a space island.

Ellie 5 Archipelago (Earth/Lunar Lagrange 5)*: A set of six Space Islands and one Manufacturing, Assembly, and Construction facility (MAC), located at ELL-5.

Endeavor* and *Eternal Hope*: Two long-range rotating spaceships that alternatively travel between Earth, Mars, and Ceres. Used primarily to move scientists and engineers between these locations.

Gibraltar Spaceport*: One of nine spaceports used to launch settlers to Ellie 5.

Gravivator*: An elevator in a rotating island that travels between the island's central axis, which is a microgravity zone, to the inner surface of the rotating cylinder where the centripetal force equals 1 Earth Gravity (standard gravity). As the gravivator descends (toward the inner surface) the effects of rotation are felt as a person is pressed against one side or the other depending on the gravivator's orientation.

Gravity Rehab Therapy*: All persons living for extended periods at less than standard gravity (SG) need to frequently make use of this therapy to prevent bone loss and other negative biological effects. On long space voyages SG is achieved by the spaceship rotation. In the space islands SG is achieved by the cylinder rotating to create gravity at its inner surface. The Martian Rehab Orbiter rotates at SG and is used as therapy by the residents on Mars.

Ice Shelf: An ice field that over-extends a landmass. It does not float on the sea. Thus, when it breaks off it can cause tsunamis and sea rise. (*In the story, the Ross Ice Shelf in Antarctica broke off in November of 2194 and the Fletcher-Ronne Ice shelf broke off in December 2194 forming Konni Bay.)

Kiholo Bay and Waikoloa Village: Two sites on the western (Kona) side of Hawaii (The Big Island).

Konni Bay, Antarctica*: A resort town on the northwestern coast of Antarctica. It is the seat of the local government.

Lagrange Points (Earth/Lunar Lagrange, ELL): Associated with two bodies in space consisting of planets, moons, or a sun. The smaller body orbits the larger one. There are five points where the forces of gravity (between the two bodies) and the centripetal force created by angular momentum are in approximate balance. ELL 4 and ELL 5 are positions in any such orbiting system that are in near perfect balance. (*In the story, in the Earth/Moon system ELL 5 is the first position used to build space islands, called Ellie 5.)

Lava Tubes: Lava tubes have been discovered on Mars and on the Moon. (*In the story, they have been discovered near Olympus Mons and expanded over the centuries for human occupation. All people on Mars live and work within these developed lava tubes. Most surface work is performed by robots because of the harsh conditions. Docking ports extend from the lava tubes to the surface that connect directly to Martian Rovers and to the *Sojourner.*)

LightSpeed Laser at Ellie 5*: This laser is used to transmit power to Ceres Station, as the station is too far from the Sun to receive enough energy on its own. Also, the laser can be used for defensive purposes. Another LightSpeed laser is built and located at SEL 3 (Sun/Earth Lagrange point 3), which is always located behind the Sun in opposition to Earth. Using both lasers allows Ceres Station and later Ceres Island to receive power when one of the lasers is occluded by the Sun.

Manufacturing, Assembly, and Construction facility (MAC)*: A necessary component of all archipelagos. Smelting of metals and other manufacturing activities are separate from space islands that must maintain a balanced biosystem. These facilities are essential in the initial buildout of the islands in an archipelago, their continuing maintenance, and in the production of manufactured goods. They also replace some toxic activities on Earth, such as mining, by supplying the planet with needed resources.

Martian Rehab Orbiter*: Rebuilt from the Ceres Station Habitat, which was a reimagined spaceship named the *Corn Goddess* that brought the first scientists and engineers to Ceres for the purpose of exploiting the Asteroid Belt.

Mass Drivers: A rail system that uses strong magnetic fields to drive a payload down a track. (*In the story, mass drivers are at NASA LSP on the Moon. The objective is to launch heavy items to lunar orbit using this method. From orbit they are picked up by autonomous spacecraft and brought to Ellie 5 MAC for further processing.)

Mayan Temple Village*: A residential structure designed with Mayan architectural influence. It exists in the Americas Sector of Ellie 5 Zeta, along with a representation of the Amazon River.

Mount Tian Shan*: Representative of a resort that existed in Central China in the past. Is featured in the Asia Sector of Ellie 5 Zeta Island along with accompanying Lake Tian Chi.

NASA Mars Base*: A base established by NASA several hundred years ago. Over that long period of time, living quarters and an extensive biological environment have been created in expanded lava tubes to the southeast of Olympus Mons in the northern hemisphere.

Olympus Mons: The largest volcano in the Solar System. It stands at 72,000 ft (13.6 miles or 21.9 kilometers). It is a shield volcano (oozes huge amounts of lava rather than erupting).

Outbound Nation*: The name of the space settlements and space bases under a unified governing body.

Pensacola Mountains: Part of the continent spanning the Transantarctic Mountains. (*In the story, these mountains are located south of the town of Konni Bay, a tourist town and seat of the local Parliament. Active as a ski resort.)

Polar Resort*: A large glass-domed structure that houses a tropical-island-themed resort.

ReEntry Gliders*: Spaceships that are constructed at Ellie 5 for transport of metal ingots and finished products to Earth. The hulls are constructed of stainless steel and coated with a heatshield that burns off on reentry. They are powered to reentry position by detachable robotic motors that, once rentry is initiated, return to Ellie 5 for reuse. The gliders can be positioned to reenter Earth's atmosphere so as to land at any one of nine spaceports around the globe.

Regolith: A layer of unconsolidated heterogeneous rocky material that includes sand and silt. It exists on rocky space bodies without a biosphere or organisms that produce living soil.

Reykjavík: The capital city in Iceland. (*In the story, this is the seat of Parliament for Global States United [GSU].)

SEL 3 (Sun/Earth Lagrange 3): A balance point that travels in opposition to Earth as it orbits the Sun. The position is always on the opposite side of the Sun from Earth. It is an imperfect balance point and a body orbiting the Sun in that position must expend some energy to maintain its position.

Space Settlement Program*: A program for the settlement of space and for the exploitation of the assets in the solar system. The asset acquisition part of the program is focused on the Asteroid Belt near the planetoid Ceres. The program is directed and funded through Earth Space Operations (ESO).

Sojourner*: A launch rocket and spaceship that carries passengers from NASA Mars Base to orbit. There it can dock with the long-range shuttle spaceships *Endeavor* and *Eternal Hope*. It is more frequently used to move passengers from NASA Mars Base to the Martian Rehab Orbiter when that facility is acquired from Dag Harlow at Ceres.

Solar Collector Array*: A large array at Ellie 5 that collects radiation from the Sun to power the LightSpeed laser that sends energy to Ceres Station and later to Ceres Island.

Southlands United*: A southern hemisphere government that forms after Draco Osborne becomes Secretary General of GSU. Governor Henry Fong is elected Secretary General of Southlands United.

Starfinder*: Flagship of the Centaurus Fleet, which was formed by Governor of the Jupiter Archipelago, Mei Wen. In 3101 the Centaurus Fleet is led by Civilian Admiral Bakari Marijani.

Storm Mountain Lodge*: A rustic log-style lodge in the newly constructed Ceres Island. It contains the only fine dining restaurant in the small island. The hope is that it will eventually attract a few very adventurous tourists from islands closer to the Sun.

Tian Chi Lake model*: A model of part of a resort that existed in Central China in the past. It was reproduced in the Asia sector of Ellie 5 Zeta along with Mt. Tian Shan.

Transantarctic Mountains: A mountain range that runs tangent to the South Pole on its western side. (*In the story, these mountains are used as a recreation area and part of a holiday experience that ends at the Polar Resort.)

Vineyard Renaissance*: A sector in Ellie 5 Zeta Island that represents the Italian wine areas in Tuscany, Italy and the French wine area of the Loire Valley. The sector features a model of Château de Chambord.

*Fictional, or fictional reproductions of actual places or things.

INTRODUCTION

This novel is a love letter to Earth.

The planet Earth, our precious "big blue marble," has experienced six major extinctions in its lifetime and is presently experiencing the seventh (the Anthropocene). But when compared to the extremely life-hostile environments in space, on our moon, or on Mars, our planet is an ideal place for life to have begun, persisted, and evolved. As I wrote my book *The Evolution of Life: Big Bang to Space Colonies*, immersed in the science of it all, my imagination would often take flights of fancy, teasing me with the idea of space settlements being fashioned as both a way to perpetuate human existence and a potential solution to the problem of restoring the vibrancy of Earth.

Thus was the idea of writing a novel born. In a story peopled with . . . well, with people . . . I could explore the ins and outs of life in space. Through the eyes and actions of various characters, I could imagine, and present, a conversation about what happened, what would happen, what *could* happen, both on the planet and within the "space island" settlements.

The story is set in the mid-twenty-third century. Earth is recovering from an apocalyptic environmental and societal collapse. Climate disruption, with its resultant droughts and floods, has triggered regional wars and mass starvation; billions of people have died as a result. However, the story in this book is about recovery. The Space Settlement Program, which is at the heart of my envisioned future, has been initiated and controlled by a world central government that anticipates employing space resources to help rebuild Earth ecosystems.

Included in this book is a list of characters who populate the interwoven storylines. Also included is a listing of places both real and imagined, and of the technologies supporting the actions of the storylines, technologies that are also both real and imagined. Illustrations and a map are on hand as well, to accompany you as you read.

I hope you enjoy your journey through the future, as I certainly have enjoyed conceiving and writing it.

Richard M. Anderson
Earth, 2024

CHAPTER 1

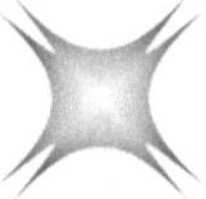

AWAKENING

"You never know, upon awakening, which day will be the day you begin to fulfill your destiny."

Ofelia

The sound of screeching plankton was ear piercing, even underwater. Giant amoebas were gulping thousands of diatoms. Panicked, an enormous mass of fleeing diatoms breached the containment tank and burst out with a flood of water. As one of the huge amoebas slimed its false arms around him, Virgil's eyes snapped open. He shuddered as he quickly realized it was a nightmare, his dream fear jolting him out of it. He listened for a moment—had he heard a sound as well? Did something else wake him? A voice in his head? He waited, calming his breathing. Silence.

Not only now, but for some time lately, Dr. Virgil Greenly's sleep had been fitful. Here it was the middle of the night and his mind churned with the problems with water ecology. The diatom population was declining and not producing enough oxygen to support the human and animal population of the space island. And he didn't know why.

He had tested the seawater: for temperature, clarity, silicon levels, light intensity, and mineral content. All results had shown nothing suspect. Everything seemed optimal. There could be Protista predators, but he hadn't found any. "I'll have to speak with the marine zoologists," he mumbled to himself. This problem would need to be solved soon and nightmares were not helping his stress. He would have to set up the cyanobacteria growth chambers so they could begin generating oxygen. The cyanobacteria grew in isolated tanks so they would not kill other life in the ecosystem with their toxins.

As concerning as this problem was, it was not the only cause for Virgil's fitful sleep. A shipment of asteroid material was due to arrive at Ellie 5 in about eleven days. The receipt and safe docking of small asteroids and bundles of asteroid fragments were always dangerous undertakings and thus stressful. The massive payloads would be intercepted as they arrived and towed to a position of gravitational balance. It was a delicate operation with no margin for error. Luckily his friend and now temporary subordinate, Simone Beaulieu, a pilot and rocket engineer, had done this before. He relaxed a bit as he remembered her competence.

Although ELL 5-Alpha (Earth-Moon Lagrange 5-Alpha Island) was the official name defining the first-constructed space island of an archipelago located in that orbit, everyone called it Ellie 5 Alpha. As the smallest of six planned islands in this first space archipelago, it was the only one that had been completed; four of the other five islands were in various stages of biosphere construction. The sixth one was nearing structural frame completion as the final layers of graphene composites were being applied to the inner surface of the massive cylinder.

The construction facility, ELL 5-MAC (Manufacturing, Assembly, and Construction), known to most as Ellie 5 MAC, had been completed in sync with Alpha Island. It orbited at the center of the Ellie 5 cluster of islands and now operated in full production, supporting the construction of the other islands. The MAC structure was critical to the building of the developing archipelago, and to the ongoing maintenance required. Once the island group was complete at Ellie 5, the MAC would be used to construct a duplicate of itself to be transported to and positioned at the orbital balance point of ELL-4, to begin developing materials for construction of the next cluster of space islands.

Ellie 5 MAC was the one bright spot in this project. It had worked flawlessly, with robots processing raw materials and building construction components. Virgil was aware that the government expected the same success with the biological environments. But politicians did not understand the significantly greater complexity in designing self-sustaining ecosystems. Ellie 5 MAC operated robotically and was visited only intermittently by inspection teams, so it did not require ecological life support systems.

Virgil often felt overwhelmed. He was young still, having just earned his second doctoral degree at the age of thirty-five, but he had little practical managerial experience. His knowledge was much broader than his assignment required; he had completed more education than one would expect for someone working at his level, with doctoral degrees in both biochemistry and microbiology. However, he felt challenged working as both the director of microbiology and head of environmental systems. Inexperienced and on the job for just three months, he believed he had only produced a series of minor disasters. But that was not the view of his subordinates. They saw the setbacks as a necessary cost to ultimate success.

Virgil rolled onto his back trying to focus in the darkness. ELL 5-Alpha's project director, Rhett Blackwood, had left for a reunion with his family on Earth. Rhett's departure couldn't have happened at a worse time for Virgil; getting the marine zoologists to maintain a diverse heterotrophic population while controlling its relative and total numbers had been difficult. But inconvenient or not, Rhett deserved to celebrate Christmas and his twentieth wedding anniversary with his wife and two daughters. It was his first trip to Earth since the beginning of this project two years ago. Still, Virgil felt unsettled. He was losing focus on his own problems as he tried to understand and control the larger process. Major project leadership duties were causing him continued anxiety.

Virgil realized he was not going to get any more sleep. At least he should try some relaxation meditation. He lay back on his sleeping platform, but his mind continued to play the problem tapes. The fact that his unyielding magnetic induction pillow only allowed him to sleep on his back added to his discomfort. However, it was important that the interphase under his scalp remained charged.

Rhett Blackwood would be gone for two months, during which Virgil was required to oversee critical aspects of the finishing construction and beginning certification of the second island, Ellie 5 Beta. He now had to coordinate all the teams in the project while still struggling to manage his own environmental team. The engineers, marine biologists, ecologists, and molecular biologists that were now in his charge were not shy about their often-divergent viewpoints and priorities. With Ellie 5 Alpha's ecological system now not functioning at 100%, he wouldn't be able to template it to the other islands until he understood why. The biologics needed to be in perfect balance on Ellie 5 Alpha soon or the tightly sequenced construction schedule would be thrown into disarray. And just today his engineers had reported some anomalies in the magnetosphere that surrounded and protected the island from solar and cosmic radiation. His bamboo sleeping platform creaked as he leaned forward and sat up.

Sensing his movement, Ofelia increased the light above the platform as it slowly changed to a soft red glow. 0200 GMT : Tues : Dec 23 : 2245 was projected on the wall in front of Virgil. *Damn, I'm probably the only one awake and the one most needing sleep,* he thought. He stood. *I was dreaming, but something else woke me up.* He realized it was Ofelia's voice he had heard. Here it was again — this time the voice was a little louder in his head.

"Good morning, Virgil, you seem alert now. I have some important information for you."

Damn!! Virgil was startled. Ofelia had been present for a week already, but he'd momentarily forgotten about her. He was still not accustomed to having anyone speak in his mind. She was Rhett's virtual associate; Virgil had been connected on Rhett's departure and the surgery for the implant just under his scalp had already healed. Designed to Rhett's specifications — and preference — the voice was soft, pleasant, and feminine. Still, Virgil was irritated. He responded in his mind.

"This had better be important, Ofelia. You do realize it's only... what?... zero two hundred hours. You know I have all of Rhett's responsibilities as well as my own, including a damn diatom issue, right?" A mild pounding had begun in his head.

"I am fully aware," Ofelia's voice said. "You're telling me you'd rather return to your nightmare?"

"H-how did you know about the nightmare?"

"I think your shouts might have given it away."

Virgil hung his head. "That was me?" was his thought response. "Well, yeah, I suppose they were."

"But I did want to wake you. You need to know this: Rhett Blackwood, his wife, and their two daughters are reported missing."

Virgil was stunned. He walked over to the open balcony and, feeling unsteady, reached out and grabbed the bamboo railing of his tree house. The pounding in his head increased. Looking at the full length of the rotating island cylinder, he could see the small lake below. It shimmered silver and was lined with terraced restaurants, some of which extended into the little bay. A hint of vineyards showed faintly on low rolling hills in the distance, still dark. A barely visible stand of bamboo and hemp graced the shores across from the restaurants. The Moon simulation showed full on this night and the pervasive silence and cool air should have instilled a sense of serene peace. It did not. Nonetheless, he took a slow, deep breath and the pounding eased somewhat.

Dr. Virgil Greenly in his treehouse, Ellie 5 Alpha

"Virgil! Did you hear what I just told you?"

Unaccustomed to Ofelia's voice in his mind, it boomed, and his head throbbed anew. Feeling exposed in his sleeping shorts, he reached over to the bedside rack and pulled on his robe.

"S-sorry. I did." He rubbed his temples to calm the throbbing while he absorbed this disturbing information. "This is terrible! They were in Antarctica, weren't they? When did they disappear? Is there a search team? I can't believe it."

Ofelia's voice was still disorienting. Sensing his distress, she created a softer tone. "Apparently they were in a Stunt Helicopter. It disappeared over the Transantarctic Mountain Range yesterday afternoon. There is an active search, but it is still dark. Search and rescue teams are being organized to begin at dawn."

"They can't be more specific? Those mountains cover the distance across the whole continent!"

"The helicopter part of the trip was the last leg along the mountains before they were to cross the frozen flatlands to the South Pole. It would have been no more than 300 miles from the South Polar Resort. They couldn't have been far from the landing site," Ofelia offered.

"Do you know that?!" This time Virgil felt that he shouted in his mind. He slumped down on his sleeping platform. "I can't do this," he muttered. "I need Rhett to come back."

"This is significant for you, Virgil. You never know, upon awakening, which day will be the day you begin to fulfill your destiny," Ofelia said.

He lay back, closed his eyes, and tried to roll over and disappear back into sleep. The magnetic induction pillow pushed back. Sleep was not going to happen. Adrenaline surged and his headache returned. This time he could feel his heart pounding too. After a few minutes of slow, deep breaths, he felt more in control.

"Ofelia?" he said in almost a whisper.

"Yes, Virgil?"

"What do you look like? How would you describe your appearance?"

"I am only virtual, Virgil."

"Yes, I know, but Rhett would have specified your physical form projected in his mind."

"He did."

"I know Rhett. I'm thinking you would have projected yourself as beautiful to him."

"I suppose I did."

"I have yet to set up visual of you. Could you do that for me?"

"Yes."

"It would help me to know that my partner and associate was a beautiful woman," he offered. He paused for a moment. "I always felt intimidated around corporeal female beauty. Being beautiful but without a physical presence might help improve my social confidence."

As Virgil lay back, an image of Ofelia appeared in his mind.

"You're wearing a business suit!" he blurted. "Oh, sorry! I guess I didn't expect that. That wasn't my vision of you." He felt frantic for a moment. "Well, that didn't come out right. I just — I — I should just shut up."

"My reveal is meant to calm and temper your feelings."

"Yeah, I get it. I'll let you know if it's working. I like your outfit. Tailored, professional, goes with your beautiful green eyes." Virgil hoped he had rescued himself, but realized he was sweating profusely. He mopped his forehead with the sleeve of his robe.

"What did you think I would look like?" Ofelia asked in a neutral voice.

"I guess I imagined you would appear as a magic genie just released from a bottle or something like that."

"Ha! A bottle would never contain me!" Ofelia chuckled. "But the magic? Yes, I probably could consider that part of my mystique."

"It's going to take a little time to get used to having you in my mind. I don't think all the injected bots have settled in the right places yet. There still seem to be some incomplete connections."

"Everything's almost in place. Virgil, I know what lies ahead will be difficult for you, for us. I will be here whenever you need me. My eyes are everywhere, and I reside in databases system wide, so I am a reliable source of information. I am your advisor and confidant. We will work this project to completion together, with or without Rhett."

Virgil felt a little more composed.

"Were your eyes also green for Rhett?"

"Okay, Virgil. That's enough!"

CHAPTER 2

ANTARCTICA

"A magical place where colors of the night come out to dance over pure whiteness. Where the cold is glorious."

Koral Blackwood

By most estimates, the great floods, heat waves, famines, storms, and plagues that began in the mid-twenty-first century on Earth left more than two billion people dead. Those who could escape, did. Many who could not, perished. But the late twenty-first century melting of the Konni Ice Shelf in Antarctica had a positive local effect. It left a bay with several outer islands protecting a harbor shoreline and a mostly temperate climate.

Construction began in the year 2081 on the quaint little tourist town of Konni Bay, which became a refuge for the elite. Built by the affluent seeking to escape the harsh realities of the continuing climate disaster, Konni Bay was one of many such towns built either in Antarctica in the Southern Hemisphere or on the northern rim of the continents bordering the Arctic Ocean. Over the decades the wealthiest citizens continued to migrate toward those enclaves near the poles. The Antarctic town of Konni Bay was improved and hardened to withstand the still-severe winters, growing into an attractive location that supported a year-round population of about 30,000 people and becoming the seat of the Southern Hemisphere's regional parliament of Global States United (GSU).

Unwanted immigration was generally an issue for people living in the most desirable locations. However, Konni Bay had not suffered such population pressure. It was difficult to get to and too expensive for all but the wealthiest. The residents there felt secure in knowing these factors protected their town from an overwhelming deluge of refugees.

Worldwide, there had been a multitude of violent weather and climate events. Life in Earth's formerly temperate zones was a challenge. Closer to the Equator, it was impossible. But for those who could afford it and could secure reservations, the tourist season in Antarctica (from the middle of November through most of March) increased the population there dramatically. The main attraction was not the town of Konni Bay itself, but the many ski resorts in the nearby Pensacola Mountains. For the less athletic thrill-seekers, the South Polar Resort was the drawing destination. Opened shortly before Rhett Blackwood's visit, the resort was already widely known among the elite.

Those arriving to the resort area for a week or more of sensational pampering would begin their stay at Konni Bay and conclude at the South Polar Resort. The trip from Konni Bay provided the thrill. Suspended under massive solar-powered electric airships in a luxuriously appointed lounge, vacationers floated over the ski resorts of the Pensacola then entered the rugged terrain of the Transantarctic Mountains. On the first leg of the journey, tourists dressed in cocktail casual were feted with champagne, opera vignettes, and hors d'oeuvres. Panoramic windows in the floors and walls of the ships framed the incredible village scenes that varied from green Tyrolian-roofed cottages to Swiss-style Alpine chalets.

The airships would glide low over the striking terrain so passengers could watch the lifts and skiers below. Competitive events were staged for the vessels; giant ski jumps and downhill racing courses were projected in detail on large screens on the lounge walls. Other screens displayed ice-skating competitions. Passengers, their drinks in hand, gathered in front of screens showing their chosen sport and cheered their favorite athletes on. The giant slalom runs were the most popular. During those competitions, the airships hovered over the runs, to the appreciative roars of their passengers.

The mountainsides were devoid of natural trees. Instead, artificial solar-power-generating evergreens dotted the landscape. They were varied and placed such that they resembled natural forest areas. Most areas of the mountains were covered in a smooth white blanket of natural snow that lent a benign purity to the landscape. However, the occasional rock outcroppings abruptly poking through would remind anyone who spotted them of the hidden hazards below.

When the airships landed and were moored at their port at the foot of the mountains, passengers were led to a depot where they were given their attire for the rest of the journey. Those items included helmets, sun goggles, insulated jumpsuits, puffer coats, and heated boots and gloves. They boarded open-top trains that took them along cliff faces and through jagged mountain passes. The rail journey ended at the summit of one of the highest peaks; there passengers transferred to sky trams attached to thick cables. The trams traveled suspended over the frozen white landscape, often just a few feet above the ice and rocks. Then they flew out over an escarpment and the ground rapidly dropped away, leaving the riders suspended sometimes more than a thousand feet above the ice fields.

The sky tram trip ended at a group of hexagonal heliports leveled on stilts over the rocky terrain and all connected by walkways. There helicopters were waiting. Some heliports had standard transport helicopters; on others there were bright yellow stunt helicopters. These were acrobatic performance machines, highly maneuverable, and virtually controlled by onboard computers. Pilots were not aboard. For stability, stunt helicopters were built with counter-rotating blades to equalize the torque on the body of the helicopter and prevent the machine from rotating in the opposite direction as the rotor. Telescoping blades could extend as needed for added lift.

These specialized 'copters were reserved for small groups. The ride was breathtaking, with rapid descents down steep escarpments and soaring rises along icy cliff faces; just as a passenger's stomach caught up with them, the machine would bound over the next summit and dive down again. Everyone opting for the Stunt Copter ride could choose to be medicated for vertigo and nausea before boarding. Presented with that option, many would choose instead to ride in the larger, more comfortable and sedate transport helicopters.

The last leg of the journey to the resort was on the snow-covered ground. Ski tractors pulling open sleds would line up near the helicopter landing pads. Some of the truly adventurous thrill-seekers instead chose high-speed bobsleds on heated runners, while for others much slower dogsleds were available. The trip covered approximately 402 kilometers, so each option included overnights on the ice. The dogsled runs required eight to ten such overnights. During an overnight stop, double-walled pop-up tents protected the tourists. Evenings were filled with chef-prepared dinners, followed by professional talks on the local climate, penguin colonies, and geologic features.

The most popular of such talks were lectures on astronomy, accompanied by visual presentations. During the off-season winter months, observatories near the South Pole collected many different recordings of the Aurora Australis (Southern Lights). During the summer tourist months, those images were projected in holographic relief within domed blackout tents. Thus, viewers could see in vivid detail moving colors of orange, pink, purple, and gold — without enduring traveling there in the winter. Planetarium shows were also popular, not only of the stars above the South Pole but also of celestial bodies from throughout known space. Also shown were progress views of the evolving space islands and the NASA Bases on the Moon and Mars. Each night featured different projections. An astronomer supplemented the visuals with explanations, pointing out significant details. The program was completed on the last night with a virtual 3D voyage through the solar system; featured were scenes of virtual flybys of distant exoplanets detailing some of the latest findings. This last night camped on the snow and ice was the most spectacular. Audiences, especially the children, were thrilled and inspired.

The final leg of the excursion took the travelers directly to the South Polar Resort. The resort complex was contained under a huge, double-glazed dome that covered an area close to six square kilometers. The dome was centered over the geologic South Pole, which was marked by a pure white obelisk that rose ten meters. Heat circulated between the double-glazing of the dome to keep it within its temperature performance specs during occasional violent storms. The glazing was also engineered to screen out almost all the ultraviolet light that streamed through the massive southern ozone hole. Thus, the tropical-island-themed paradise underneath, with its graceful palms and sandy pool beaches, was protected. Even during the winter months, the resort was open, if only tended by a small resident maintenance staff.

Indeed, the tropical replica was a treat, as most of the real island resorts had disappeared. If they still poked above the ocean that had claimed them due to sea level rise, they were too hot and humid and/or subject to severe weather to attract people. Aside from the Hawai'ian Islands and other archipelagos of volcanic origin, those that remained certainly no longer could be considered island paradises.

Rhett Blackwood had left Virgil in charge when he traveled to Earth from Ellie 5 Alpha. After arriving on the planet, he first met in Reykjavík, Iceland with Ali Ebrahim, Secretary General of Global States United (GSU). They discussed the ongoing Space Settlement Program at Ellie 5. A few days later, following a suborbital flight, he met his wife Koral and their daughters, Jules and Chanté, in the town of Konni Bay, Antarctica. They had left their home in Nuuk, Greenland the week before his arrival.

It had been a little more than two years since Rhett was last on Earth and with his family at their home. Although they'd enjoyed regular visual calls, it was somewhat stunning to see the three of them fully present in person now. His daughters had grown more than he had expected. Jules was now 16 and Chanté 13. They were beginning to show their mother's beauty. Jules had rich auburn hair and penetrating blue eyes like Koral. Although Chanté's facial features mimicked her mother's, she was blond with soft brown eyes, after her father. This was Rhett's first time in Antarctica, but it was the second Christmas his wife and daughters had spent there. Rhett being with them made this a special occasion for them all, especially for the girls.

The family quickly retreated to the hotel suite Koral had reserved. There they began to reacquaint themselves with one another, and to prepare for the next day's journey.

Later that evening, with Jules and Chanté asleep in their room, Rhett and Koral retired to a small booth in the iconic Floating Iceberg cocktail lounge off the hotel lobby.

"I've missed you," Koral began.

"I know it's been hard. I've missed you too."

"At least you had Ofelia!" Koral said, bitterly.

"Ofelia? She was my virtual associate. My VA. You know she doesn't physically exist." Rhett had sensed this conversation was coming. He still didn't know quite how to proceed.

"Of course, she's virtual, she existed 'only' in your mind. I shouldn't have to tell you, that's where love resides."

Rhett swiveled his chair and looked out the wide window and across Konni Bay to the islands. In a way, it was true. He *had* developed an intimate relationship with Ofelia. They were together every second, they worked closely on all aspects of the project, shared private thoughts. Ofelia knew more about him than anyone else. Even Koral.

Rhett began to speak slowly.

"I take your point. Ofelia was my constant work partner and confidant. But Ofelia is not human. I was not in love with her. Despite my prolonged absence, I do love you, Koral." Rhett paused, considering the work he had left unfinished. "My only other love was for the project; even now, it was difficult to pull myself away. Anyway, Ofelia is Virgil's associate now. I no longer have the link, nor the implant. The bots have been purged from my brain and filtered from my circulation."

"Well, that's something, I guess; at least for the next two months. But what then?"

"Listen, Koral, this is a chance to reconnect. I still have the passion for our relationship that I have always had. We can rekindle what we've lost. I can get close to the girls again. We can be a family once more."

"You say that now —" Koral began.

"I admit the Ellie 5 project has been my life's mission and has appropriated an inordinate amount of my time. But a solution is in the making."

"Uh-huh, sure. You're still the smooth talker. Let's get a drink," Koral replied, looking around the room.

"Truth is," Rhett continued, "I'm not going to accept another project from the secretary general. After Ellie 5, I'm finished."

"You've had a falling out with Ali?!"

A cocktail server approached, interrupting before Rhett could reply.

"Hi, I'm Rochet. What can I get you?"

"Two Floating Icebergs with Moon Shot Vodka and lime," Koral ordered.

"Would you like a Full Moon Shot, a Gibbous Moon Shot, or a Crescent Moon Shot?" Rochet asked.

"I think a Harvest Moon Shot for both of us!" Rhett answered. Rochet nodded and left the tableside.

"What's a Harvest Moon Shot? And where did you hear of it?" Koral asked.

"I always do my research. It's a Full Moon Shot with a splash of Tequila Gold." Koral's expression was one of suspicion, so Rhett quickly pivoted. "Uh, where were we? Oh yeah. No, Ali's on board. I arrived on Earth early at his request and I spent the last few days meeting with him. He's dealing with some strong and disruptive opposition forces and has not been able to build a commitment for continuous support of the Space Settlement Program. It's hit or miss."

"Hit or miss? Ali Ebrahim, Secretary General of GSU, does not have the executive power to execute a successful program? One supported by popular acclaim?" Not especially attuned to politics, Koral was uncharacteristically incredulous.

"You got it. The point for us is that the Ellie 5 archipelago is nearing completion. The first five islands should be finished a few months after I return. I won't stick around for the sixth and most ambitious island. Then we can be together for good . . . . Perhaps get a summer place in Konni Bay."

"Yeah, lots of luck with that. Konni Bay is a magical place where colors of the night come out to dance over pure whiteness. Where the cold is glorious. Everyone wants to be here. Do you know how long the waiting list is? Even rich people are hurting everywhere, seeking respite in the best place they can find."

"Perhaps Ali can help with that. You know he and I go way back. He's been my mentor since I was an undergraduate."

"If Ali put you at the head of the line for a vacation home in Konni Bay there'd be a global insurrection."

Their drinks arrived, smoking from the floating dry icebergs.

"That bad, eh?" Rhett gave a short chuckle.

"No. I don't know. You know me and politics," Koral answered, raising her glass weakly. "Anyway, cheers."

"We can always live in one of the Islands in space. Ellie 5 Alpha is quite nice. The ones coming online and those planned will be amazing.

I can't wait to see Ellie 5 Zeta, even if I'm not there to run the project. And you know your favorite opera venue, Château de Chambord?"

"Yes?"

"I've included a replica of the façade to be assembled on Ellie 5 Zeta. It will just be a shell, so you'll have a hand in the interior design. You could organize a committee for the performing arts there."

"Mm-hmm." Koral took a sip of her drink. She wasn't buying that proposition.

"You watch," Rhett continued, "in addition to the Château, they will eventually all include resort-like features. And they will be able to reproduce different Earth environments — as things were three or four hundred years ago."

Koral looked at Rhett closely. She knew his great enthusiasm for the Space Settlement Program and wondered if he could ever leave it to live permanently on Earth, where her heart still lay. She hoped the rest of the vacation would indeed bring them closer together, as she sensed her husband's passion truly resided in space. If she was jealous of anyone or anything, she realized, it was not Ofelia.

The next day Rhett, Koral, Jules, and Chanté began their trip to the South Polar Resort. The girls had made the trip the previous Christmas with their mother and were now excited to share the experience with their father. Because of his daughters' enthusiasm, Rhett was especially looking forward to the Stunt Copter ride.

As the family approached the helicopter its door swung open. Inside were four seats with seatbacks anatomically contoured. They were the only occupants as there was no pilot or co-pilot; the flight would be executed entirely by autopilot. Large windows provided panoramic views in almost every direction. As they took their seats a harness lowered over each person, then straps tightened around their chests and legs to hold them firmly in place. A voice then instructed them to place their arms on the armrests; clamps held both arms firmly in place while restraints pressed their heads firmly into their headrests. Koral, Jules, and Chanté were completely immobilized. However, Rhett's chest restraints were not fully engaged. "I believe I'll need to cinch them down manually," he said as he loosened his arm restraints. Finally, when he felt secure, Rhett pushed the Start button and the Copter blades began rotating.

Initially, the ride didn't disappoint for thrills. After rising rapidly until the launch pad was just a speck below, the Copter dove over the nearly vertical face of the mountain then climbed up the adjacent steep slopes over the top of the opposite peak. Rhett had experienced similar sensations during space launches; still, the surge of adrenaline was intense. He had barely recovered from the sharp dive and ascent when a few minutes later the helicopter took an even more radical dive, followed by a rapid climb aside a rocky cliff. His daughters filled the cabin with screams of terror-tinged delight. Koral clenched the armrests until her knuckles were white. This time there was a strong downdraft at the face of the cliff. Telescoping blades extended for extra lift as designed — and as they had on hundreds of rides before — and blade rotation accelerated to the limits. Then one of the blades broke free. Both girls screamed as the Stunt Copter vibrated and gyrated fiercely while the autopilot fought for control. It was not successful. The Copter careened down and briefly touched its skids on a steeply inclined snow-covered slope. It then flipped over before plunging into an icy chasm.

CHAPTER 3

CORN GODDESS

"It looks like a giant ear of corn!
Is this some asshole's idea of a joke?"

Dr. Dag Harlow

Several years before construction of the Ellie 5 archipelago, mining of the asteroid belt began. Unimaginable resources exist beyond the orbit of Mars. Everything humankind needs for construction of space islands is within the asteroid belt. In the center region, the planetoid Ceres provides close access to all three major belts and their mineral resources. The belts are separated from each other by Kirkwood gaps created by gravitational effects from Jupiter. The inner belt asteroids consist of mostly silicates and metals such as nickel, cobalt, gold, platinum, and rhodium. These are referred to as S-Type asteroids. The asteroids in the middle belts (M-Type), where Ceres is located, have ten times the metal content of the S-Type asteroids. However, those asteroids are not as numerous. The outer ring is called the Carbonaceous ring. It contains asteroids (C-Type) with high carbon content. They could be thought of as large chunks of coal.

Planets and planetoids formed between the orbit of Jupiter and Mars by collision and coalition of debris in the early solar system. The molten planets and planetoids gravitationally segregated the heavier materials to the center. Once cooled, they collided, fragmented, then separated into bands. The existence of these distinct species of asteroids would prove highly beneficial for the Space Settlement Program.

The planetoid Ceres has a diameter of approximately 939 kilometers and a very significant water content. As the largest planetoid within the Type M asteroid belt, it was considered ideal for a station that could process asteroids. Raw materials could be sent to the Earth-Moon Lagrange 5 location for the construction of the first Space Island Archipelago.

The spaceship christened the *Corn Goddess* (the name was inspired by Ceres, the Roman goddess of agriculture) arrived in the vicinity of Ceres on August 2, 2239 with a contingent of scientists and engineers. Like all long-range spaceships, the *Corn Goddess* rotated to create standard gravity (equivalent to Earth gravity at its surface). Propulsion motors were attached aft on the central axis tube. The crew quarters were located around the periphery of what was essentially a Ferris wheel at the fore of the ship. The central axis tube extended to the fore beyond the crew quarters, to where the docking port was located. Surrounding the axis was a cage of the same diameter as the crew Ferris wheel and attached to the outside of the cylinder cage were twenty-six fully fueled robotic propulsion motors being delivered to the Ceres site.

As the *Corn Goddess* entered orbit around Ceres, Dag Harlow climbed up the tube from his crew quarters to the central axis. Out of the twenty-six people traveling on the ship, all scientists and engineers, Dr. Harlow was one of the three who had not been placed in hibernation for the trip from Earth; the others were Earl Bedford, chief engineer, and Salvadore Munros, the lead environmental scientist. The remainder of the crew hibernated in pods within their individual crew quarters.

Dag floated along the tube, pulling on handholds until he reached the docking port. One of the space tugs approached the port and docked. He opened the hatch, entered the ship and took the controls, then detached and flew the ship a short distance away alongside the *Corn Goddess*. He could see its entire length. It was a long, ungainly skeleton of a spaceship, containing individual crew quarters, mechanical and life support systems, and food storage areas. There were no common areas as there was no need, with all but the three of them in hibernation. Dag piloted his spacecraft back and forth along the cage as it rotated before him, inspecting for any damage before ordering inflation. Satisfied, he spoke to the chief engineer, who was at the helm.

"OK, Earl, let's get this god-awful monstrosity inflated and habitable so we can bring the rest of our crew out of hibernation."

Slowly the giant double-membraned bladder began to inflate, filling the inside of the cage. Once Dag confirmed inflation was proceeding normally, he returned to the docking port on the *Corn Goddess*. Complete inflation was a process that took forty-eight hours. During inflation the three men would enter the inflating bladder to ensure there were no snags that could tear the membrane. A small tear could be repaired most easily from the inside before full inflation had occurred.

When it was fully inflated the bladder bulged between the mesh squares of the containment cage, the resulting structure resembling a huge corncob turning on a spit. Dag returned to the shuttle and travelled back to inspect the bladder and framework. He wanted to ensure there were no folds or tears; each "kernel" had to be perfectly formed, as they would become structural elements.

"The damn bladder is yellow!" Dag shouted to Earl, who had just been joined at the helm by Salvadore. "It looks like a giant ear of corn! Is this some asshole's idea of a joke?" He heard some stifled chuckling from the bridge.

"Yeah, I think I know who those assholes are," he mumbled to himself as he directed his space tug back and forth along the length of the transforming spaceship. When he was finished inspecting every bulge and every frame member he ordered a hardening substance pumped between the double membranes; that would fix the ship's shape before the addition of other structural materials — asteroid regolith and cement — to the inside surface. Shortly thereafter, Earth atmosphere would be added from tanks of compressed gas, replacing the carbon dioxide used as the expansion gas.

Dag docked his space tug and joined Earl and Salvadore on the bridge.

"We'd better fire up the heaters and cure the resin," he said, "before we add the concrete and regolith." Earl and Salvadore looked expectantly to him. "And no! I did not take any pictures for publication. There will be no photos showing this station as an ear of corn. Any images of the exterior will be gunmetal gray. And there will be a stream of pictures and holographs of the interior as it is completed."

The *Corn Goddess* spaceship, after inflation

"I take it, Dag, that we don't want to give anyone the satisfaction of seeing completion of their joke," Salvadore remarked. He looked at Earl and grinned.

"That's right. You both think it's funny. I don't! Whoever colored this station yellow will waste their time searching for images of a giant ear of corn in any reports of our progress at Ceres. They will never find them. As soon as we convert this monstrosity into a habitat, I will re-christen it. Something ordinary, like 'Ceres Station.'"

"Ceres Station. Yes, that's appropriate," Earl said, barely keeping the sarcasm out of his voice. He glanced at Salvadore.

"I know you guys wouldn't be the assholes, would you?" Dag said. The two responded with silent grins as he continued, "Nonetheless, you will both be tasked with chemically changing the color to the intended gunmetal." The grins quickly faded.

Within a couple weeks Ceres Station was ready to support human occupancy. The hibernating crewmembers were revived and reported for duty after several days in rehabilitation in the makeshift gym. The ship, now converted to a habitat with laboratories and work areas, had much more space. But the crew quarters were retained just as they had been in the original spaceship. They remained tight and uncomfortable.

Under the guidance of Earl and Salvadore, the crew began the finish construction of the inner surface of the habitat. They gradually converted the surface to working and recreational areas. From prefabricated panels and beams they framed small offices, laboratories, conference rooms, a restaurant, a theater, and the gymnasium. This was done with minimal robotic help. The engineers would later construct a versatile fleet of robots; but initially it was the men and women of the crew who labored to assemble the improvements. They also designed several sports courts and a small park for later construction. The design engineers were given a good deal of freedom in configuring their working spaces. However, their sleeping quarters were much as before, cold and cramped.

All mechanical, environmental, and food production systems were contained within the habitat cylinder close to the central axis to reduce stress on the rotating hull. Cyanobacteria and diatom growth were maintained in containers there as well, to produce sufficient oxygen. Isolated in other pods dispersed among the limited natural landscape were hydroponic tomato, pepper, and herb gardens. The primary nutrition was produced in tanks of genetically engineered microbes, the products then isolated and combined with isolates from other tanks.

Dag and his astrogeologists often wandered among the asteroids using the three space tugs. Over time they developed a detailed catalogue of the size, mass, and composition of asteroids in their immediate area. They could easily reach a variety of them from Ceres Station. However, the distance from the station to Ellie 5 was staggering. Raw materials were compressed in large nets to which transport motors could be attached; but transport of them from the asteroid belt to Ellie 5 could take anywhere from just under a year to four years or more, depending on relative alignments. So launches to Ellie 5 were normally held at the station until favorable launch alignments occurred.

The first launches from Ceres Station occurred on September 11, 2239. They arrived at the Ellie 5 construction site on July 4, 2242, just as that construction project was beginning. From that early time the need for an Asteroid Processing Structure (APS), where raw materials could be manufactured into their finished configurations, was very evident to Dag and all the scientists on the project. Finishing the raw materials on an APS would reduce the mass of payloads to be transported to Ellie 5; reduced mass would translate to the ability to increase transport speed. The APS had been approved by Earth Space Operations, but funding from ESO was, though continuous, just a trickle. They had finished the design and engineering of the APS and had even started to collect the raw materials needed at the site, but had not been able to begin construction. Eventually Dag and his engineers would need to find a way to circumvent the ESO bureaucracy. They would need Rhett at Ellie 5 to ship some finished structural materials. Dag did not know how he could cause that to happen, but he knew that whatever he could do, it would not involve ESO.

Over the years there were several shipments to Ellie 5, during which time the shuttle service provided by the *Endeavor* and *Eternal Hope* spaceships had rotated scientists and engineers between Ellie 5, Ceres Station, and NASA Mars Base. The opportunity to change venue every few years offered some relief to the crew at Ceres Station. Duty at Ceres was tedious, the quarters spartan to primitive, and Dag knew his crew needed better living and working environments. He silently vowed to himself to do something to improve their lives.

It was early January 2246. Dag Harlow stood at the large virtual window in the common area of Ceres Station. The screen displayed a live image of the nearby rocky surface of Ceres. He could see numerous robotic water extractors attached to its surface as it appeared to pass before him, the virtual window stabilizing the view as the habitat rotated. The planetoid's features, though sharply defined, were grey and shadowy in the twilight. It was a dead rock, but sensors showed a hint of creation energy in its depths.

Dag's mind drifted away from what moved in front of him. He was deep in thought. He had known from the beginning that the station had never been completed to enable it to function efficiently. Something had to change, and quickly. He had plans for an enhanced habitat but never submitted them as was required for approval. Instead, out of necessity and in frustration, he directed his team to modify the design of the Asteroid Processing Structure now being built. By his initiative it would include a small Manufacturing, Assembly, and Construction facility (MAC). With a MAC at Ceres Station, he and his engineers would build themselves a new habitat. ESO be damned.

The minimalist and cramped quarters housing the twenty-five engineers and scientists were often too cold for sleeping. The crew bundled up in heated blankets but sometimes the power failed even that modest draw. It was common for men with significant beards to awaken and find them covered in ice, their breath having condensed and frozen.

Although the single LightSpeed laser at Ellie 5 did provide a reliable and powerful energy source for Ceres Station, this was not available when the laser was occluded by the Sun. When that happened, all processing operations at Ceres Station shut down. The plutonium reactor attached to the habitat generated just enough power for life support. So the plan was for Dag's crew to eventually create the structural elements for an enhanced habitat for themselves. If they could complete the MAC as part of the Asteroid Processing Structure, they could essentially build whatever habitat they wanted. But this could only work if Ellie 5 built a second LightSpeed laser. Or perhaps a microwave generator would be easier to build and maintain. He would need to investigate which method would more effectively transmit energy to Ceres Station.

The resources were there. With enough energy and the completion of the APS and attached MAC, the station would have almost no limit to what they could do. Dag had the scientists, engineers, and skilled robots that he needed. For a less staunch personality it would be a brutal situation. Lately the fewer-than-expected deliveries were met with an expression of increasing hostility from ESO, despite the fact that their funding was insufficient.

Dag had accepted duty at Ceres Station despite knowing there were questions of ESO reliability. The assignment appealed to him because of the engineering challenge, but also because it was so remote. He was uncomfortable around groups of powerful people and he considered rubbing elbows with politicians and government authorities to be schmoozing with the devil. Isolation from that element suited him fine.

In contrast, he was close to his crew. The one thing they all had in common was their respect for knowledge of engineering and science. The power wrought from application of such knowledge could successfully overcome many obstacles to human survival in space. They loved how those disciplines were so effective in confronting challenges. Problems that cropped up in engineering designs and applications stimulated creativity. Finding solutions to complex systems was their reason for being there.

The scientists and engineers at Ceres Station were strong advocates for their lead scientist. Dag in turn felt the support of his crew and would do whatever he could to make their lives better. The fact that he challenged ESO inaction in a way that flaunted authority added to his stature in their eyes. His unconventional style improved their morale.

Dag suddenly came to a decision. He would get a second Light-Speed laser dedicated to Ceres Station constructed as soon as possible.

Decision made, he was ready to gamble that ESO would not review with any intensity the ongoing construction at Ceres Station. Still, it was monitoring the construction timetable and the addition of the MAC to the APS would delay its completion. But what could ESO do? Fire and replace him? And in the unlikely event they did, what would his team do? It would take a few years for a replacement to arrive, and he doubted his team would welcome one; that is, if ESO could find someone willing to take his place in this lifeless frozen hell.

Dag's scientists had made minimal attempts to mimic Earth ecosystems in complexity and aesthetics. Fresh produce was essentially grown in enclosed hydroponic pods. Meat-like patties were constructed from polypeptide chains linked into various proteins resembling those that naturally existed in animal tissue. They were produced from tanks of bio-engineered bacteria and yeasts or grown from cloned animal cells. The constituent proteins then were assembled in an automated lab into a semblance of red meat, poultry, or seafood.

There were no open water systems. Cyanobacteria consumed excess CO_2 that was produced by animal life. This provided carbon for their own growth and produced oxygen as a product. The oxygen was added to nitrogen and other gases to produce air that was recirculated and bubbled through lighted tanks. That helped to maintain an atmospheric balance. The anaerobic fermentation used in food waste recycling removed most of the excess CO_2 in the environment, produced fertilizer for hydroponic agriculture, and fed hydrogen to fuel cells. The resultant electricity was used to charge reserve batteries and those used by small equipment. As a backup to keep the atmosphere safe, chemical scrubbers were also used to reduce excess toxic CO_2.

Water that had been captured from Ceres, found frozen under the surface and as hydrated minerals, supported the station's needs. It was also the source of rocket fuel. However, the limited amount of energy laser transmitted from Ellie 5 restricted the amount of liquid oxygen and liquid hydrogen that could be produced. The station still relied on shipments from Ellie 5. Much of the on-site fuel production was used by the autonomous transport rocket motors and the three small non-rotational space tugs. All used liquid hydrogen and oxygen as fuel. The spaceships were used to move among the nearby asteroids and tug them into position to be mined, fragmented, or otherwise prepped to be attached to the transport motors and sent to Ellie 5.

Dag and his lead engineers had a ritual every evening: they shared dinner together in the dining terrace. The kitchen was fully automated, but the menu for each evening's repast was planned by one of five rotating teams. Though limited, the menu was creative, kept secret until served. The element of surprise was a highlight of the day that the men and women looked forward to. This was also usually the only time they were all assembled and could have a face-to-face forum together. Discussions were not always serious, or work related, however. People lingered afterwards, perhaps for a glass of wine or to continue a discussion. In truth they often stayed because the dining terrace in the cylinder was the warmest place in the habitat.

Life was tolerable, even pleasant, given the camaraderie. In another month the single LightSpeed laser at Ellie 5 would be occluded again by the Sun and they would lose their major power source. The entire project would shut down temporarily. As there was barely enough power from the plutonium reactor to keep the lights on in the habitat, this was an austere time at Ceres Station, usually lasting for about two months. Reading, live and limited recorded theater, games, astronomical observations, and cooking competitions using simple ingredients and creative spices occupied the crew during this dark winter period. And Dag provided additional inspiration that made each day further tolerable. It was his Island Design Study project, a conspiracy they all shared in.

He had initiated the project without the knowledge or consent of anyone. Even Ellie 5's director, Rhett Blackwood, was unaware of it. All the scientists and engineers at the station participated. There were no severe limits placed on the design. The guiding principle was to provide optimal environments and amenities that would enhance their lives. The goal was to produce a structure that would make a permanent life at Ceres Sation not just possible, but desirable as well.

There were two parts to this project. First was to come up with the best island design that the collective could envision, which they would then edit to comply with engineering and energy limitations. Secondly, they needed an additional energy source. When the designers agreed to a final design, they submitted it to engineering for any necessary modifications. Dag made sure that everyone understood the project would need to be built with no assistance from Earth. All the materials needed were at hand in the asteroid belt.

The plan was to place the LightSpeed laser at SEL 3 (Sun/Earth Lagrange 3), a mostly stable Sun orbit position in opposition to the Earth/Moon system. Whenever this LightSpeed laser was established, Ceres Station would have plenty of continuous power; when one laser was eclipsed by the Sun, the other would still be available. So, for most of the Earth year both lasers would be operational. With twice as much energy input Dag could complete the APS/MAC project sooner. He knew the second LightSpeed laser transmitter had been designed and officially approved by ESO. But it had never been funded, and Dag had been unable to move ESO ahead on the project. The approved construction start date had been delayed by more than a year. He decided he needed to consult with Rhett.

Dag was not a good negotiator or even comfortable around people with power. In all his communications he had, however, found Rhett approachable. His initial contact with Rhett was when Ellie 5's final design was just being completed and Ceres Station had been created from the Ceres spaceship soon after it had been positioned. Presently the SEL 3 project schedule for completion was still a year away. With Rhett's help, it was possible the government would approve the SEL 3 laser project for completion within a very reasonable three months. Rhett Blackwood had a reputation for bringing space projects to completion ahead of schedule. Dag was aware of this but did not know Rhett usually accomplished this feat by beginning projects before approval. As a result, some projects were miraculously completed shortly after receiving the blessings of ESO. Unbeknownst to Dag, Rhett had already finished assembling the LightSpeed laser's solar array and the laser itself was just a couple of weeks away from completion.

CHAPTER 4

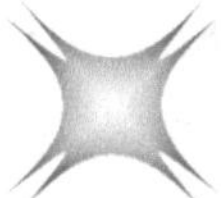

SHIPMENT FROM CERES

"One of the autonomous rockets just knocked the sunshade off a liquid hydrogen storage tank."

Dr. Virgil Greenly

The giant solar collector array and megawatt LightSpeed laser transmitter together made up one of the most important energy drivers of the Space Settlement Program. The laser transmitted highly focused energy to a collector at Ceres Station, where a large part of the energy was used by Dag Harlow and his crew as they struggled with the completion of the Asteroid Processing Structure. The APS was a critical project; when it was complete it would perform several functions necessary to the production of construction materials. Chief among those functions was the refining of metals, especially nickel and iron, from nearby asteroids. The outer ring of carbonaceous asteroids was important as well, providing the raw materials for almost everything humans would need to thrive in space. From those asteroids everything from pharmaceuticals to fertilizers and food could be created. The inner ring contained rocky asteroids similar to Earth's crust. Regolith (rock and gravel) from those asteroids could be converted into living soil or construction material such as concrete.

Until the APS could be completed, Dag's crew of engineers used autonomous robots to assemble partially processed materials into large aggregates. The robotic motors compressed the material, using large nets. Astrogeologists personally piloted the space tugs to seek small asteroids of a specific type, looking for those with a large water content or that were carbonaceous. Once found, they towed those of the proper size to Ceres Station, where they attached sunshades to those containing water as ice. The "water" asteroids would later be sent to Ellie 5 for manufacture of rocket fuel and for biological uses. Carbon from the carbonaceous asteroids was processed once they reached Ellie 5. There some of the carbon was used to produce methane; much of the water was used to manufacture liquid oxygen and hydrogen. Together these three resources were utilized throughout the system to power rocket motors. With ample supplies of carbon, and trace amounts of other elements, biochemists could make any organic molecules desired.

The human crew and the robots continued collection and processing of asteroids until a launch alignment occurred. When a launch window to Ellie 5 opened, the scientists attached robot motors and empty fuel tanks to each bundled payload. Some fuel tanks would be refilled on Ellie 5 with liquid hydrogen, others with liquid oxygen or liquid methane; they would be returned to Ceres Station to be used for future shipments.

In preparation for launching the payloads, the engineers measured load mass, attached mounting brackets for the autonomous motor attachment, and calculated trajectories. These steps were critical.

Dr. Dag Harlow overseeing asteroid preparations and launches to Ellie 5

The asteroid material had to arrive precisely at the gravitational-centripetal balance point of ELL 5 (Earth-Moon Lagrange 5). Any course corrections en route would consume precious fuel. Therefore, the engineers' job was not finished until Dag and his leads Earl and Salvadore, using the three space tugs, inspected each load. If any of the massive bundles were to break free or if a robotic motor malfunctioned there could be catastrophe. There were no guarantees that Ellie 5, NASA Lunar South Pole Base (NASA LSP), or Earth orbital assets could effectively capture an errant payload on a collision course with Earth.

On January 22, 2243 Dag had launched the largest group of asteroid material payloads collected since the first launch on September 11, 2239. He'd sent a message to Dr. Rhett Blackwood informing him of the launch so that his team could assist in tracking the shipment, which was scheduled to be received by Dr. Virgil Greenly's team at Ellie 5 on January 3, 2246.

While the shipment was on its way, Virgil was guiding the construction of the Ellie 5 archipelago toward completion. His engineers were working on designs for the construction of Ellie 4 at Earth-Moon Lagrange 4, or ELL 4. NASA LSP had provided the bulk of the materials Virgil's engineers were using for Ellie 5 construction. The base supplied refined metals and some completed components for ongoing construction. This arrangement worked well. The mass drivers at NASA LSP launched materials into several different lunar orbits for pickup by autonomous orbiting motors that then transported them to Ellie 5 MAC. It was evident to Virgil, though, that NASA LSP lacked the production capacity to begin construction at ELL 4. However, Virgil's immediate concern was the great fleet of Ceres shipments that was due to arrive. He had been anticipating Rhett Blackwood's return from his family trip to Earth when Rhett and his family disappeared in late December 2245. As the date of the fleet's arrival in January approached, the investigation into Rhett's disappearance was still ongoing.

Simone Beaulieu was a very competent rocket engineer. Despite her quintessentially French and feminine name ("Beaulieu" translating to "beautiful place"), she often dressed in men's work clothes and worked around the gritty environment of rocket motor parts, valves, and pipes. Of necessity more than fashion, she wore her straight black hair cropped short. She had been Rhett's rocket engineer, but was now, in Rhett's absence, working under Virgil, charged with assigning the teams to handle the huge payload bundles and fragments of asteroids as they entered the balance point of ELL 5.

Simone had anticipated that thirty-one payloads would come in over several weeks. When a payload approached Ellie 5 the assigned team took control of the robot motors and directed the massive bundle to a parking station near Ellie 5 MAC. They would then detach the motors and move them into the MAC facility for inspection, maintenance, and refueling. As the payloads began to accumulate around the MAC facility, autonomous robot motors were stationed around the cluster. Their job was to monitor any payload drift that might cause it to slip out of gravitational and orbital balance. At the smallest indication of drift, a motor would move after it to nudge it back into balance. Any time there were objects without attached or integrated motors the autonomous robots would stand at station; in other words, ready at a predetermined position to react to a drifting payload.

The first arrival was a small carbonaceous asteroid. It took three weeks for all of the shipments to arrive and be sequestered near Ellie 5 MAC. Now that processing of some of the payloads had begun, Virgil and Simone felt they could finally take a break. It was 1600 hours on Ellie 5 Alpha when Simone entered the hotel, wearing, uncharacteristically and a little awkwardly, a simple but attractive cocktail dress. Virgil had been waiting only a few minutes and escorted her over to the bar. They were soon seated and having a drink before dinner.

"This is so nice. I feel like I haven't had a quiet moment in weeks," Simone said, letting out a long breath as she sank further into her seat.

"Maybe because you haven't?" Virgil said.

"Bingo!" Simone gave a quick laugh. "If it weren't for the station-keeping robots preventing payloads from drifting from their ascribed position, I wouldn't be able to relax even now. It's always a little scary when we have so many loads to look after, even with the robots."

The bartender soon approached, noticing their drinks were getting low.

"Can I get the two of you another drink?"

"That would be wonderful!" Simone said.

"Simone, we can have wine with dinner," Virgil said, chuckling. "If you have another drink now you won't make it to the dining room."

"Dr. Greenly," the bartender offered, "why don't I make you both another drink here? This time I'll go light on the tequila. When you're ready I can serve you dinner here at the bar. No need to stagger into the dining room."

"Jack, you are a true diplomat. We'll take you up on that," Virgil said, tilting his now-empty glass toward the bartender.

"Don't get too comfortable," the voice came. It was Ofelia.

"But that's exactly what we want to do," Virgil said in his mind. "What is it, Ofelia? Are you not feeling my buzz?"

"Oh, I am, Virgil. That's why I didn't sense the warning sooner."

"Warning?"

"Yes! A valve got stuck on one of the autonomous rocket motors after it had positioned a payload. It was on its way to stationkeeping."

"Well, Ofelia, sounds like it's already completed its job. What's the problem?"

"The rocket motor won't shut off. It's heading for one of our liquid hydrogen storage tanks."

"Can you divert it?"

"I'm trying. I only have the attitude jets . . . . OK, it looks like it won't impact the tank."

"You had me worried, Ofelia. Are we out of danger?"

"Damn! No! It just knocked the sunshade off the tank."

"Are you talking to Ofelia?" Simone asked with the hint of a slur. She'd noticed Virgil's attention was suddenly diverted.

"One of the autonomous rockets just knocked the sunshade off a liquid hydrogen storage tank," Virgil replied aloud. Simone was instantly sober and alert.

"I need to get out there now!" She checked her systems device to see where a shuttle spaceship might be docked. With a quick nod to

Virgil, she ran from the hotel to the nearest ladder to the central core. Within a few minutes she had boarded, undocked, located the sunshade's trajectory, and locked on it. She caught up, grabbed it with one of the ship's robotic arms, then turned to head back toward the liquid hydrogen tank, approaching it just in time to see a long rupture appear along one of the tank's seams. Within a few seconds thirty-seven percent of the stored hydrogen fuel at Ellie 5 had dissipated.

The loss represented eight months of production.

CHAPTER 5

VIRGIL AND DAG

"Coherent light is our energy. It powers our dreams. Without it we barely exist."

Dr. Dag Harlow

Major Zarita Banderas-Duran oversaw the initial construction on the lunar surface of the rail system that radiated outward from NASA Lunar South Pole Base. On solar-electrified steel rails, carts brought ores to the base from surface mining operations north of it, to be smelted at facilities on the base. The major had joined the GSU military after obtaining an engineering degree at Stanford University in California. After completing several projects at GSU naval bases around the Arctic she caught the attention of Admiral Anastasia Petrova. NASA LSP and NASA Mars Base had been under the jurisdiction of the military since NASA was disbanded in 2103. Admiral Petrova, who had assumed temporary oversight of NASA LSP when the base's director was killed in an accident, needed to appoint a permanent replacement and Major Banderas-Duran was newly available and at hand. The admiral assigned the major as the new director at NASA LSP.

Major Banderas-Duran had now been an effective director at the base for a little more than three years. Although rail cars carried mined material back to smelters and forges near the mass drivers on the surface of the Moon, she had never extended the rail lines once the low-hanging fruit from the surface mines had been depleted. Production from the base had slowed to a trickle.

On January 15, 2246 Virgil put in a call to the major.

"Zarita, we haven't spoken in some time. I understand you are having some equipment problems."

"Yes, I've been waiting for months for critical parts from ESO," Zarita complained. "Many of my robots are not functioning. They are old and past their prime. If there is anything you can do to get some action out of ESO, I would be indebted."

"Yeah, I wish I could. Seems none of us are getting what we need. GSU is constantly on my back to increase shipments to Earth but won't give us the resources to meet their demands. If you can't expand the rail system and increase mining operations, I'll have to find a way to increase production at Ceres. It's frustrating, with the Moon so close."

"Sorry, Virgil, I've enough problems of my own. Wish I could help."

"So do I. Just in case, send over the schematics on the parts you need. I think there is something we can do."

"I will see what my engineers can do. But they are apathetic. I will need to produce some kind of incentive. Zarita out."

Virgil was perplexed but not surprised. His minimal contact with Zarita in the past was rarely productive. He had never encountered a person who expressed so little initiative. This observation was at odds with the major's early reputation.

"Hmm, '*they* are apathetic.' Ofelia, what do you think of that woman? Maybe my expectations are too high, but her passivity drives me mad. We all face challenges in this project. I've never met someone so completely disengaged."

"It's more than disengagement. She could divert resources and expand the rails, but then she wouldn't meet GSO quotas. She's not going to damage her standing by challenging authority. But I think there's more than that. When I was with Rhett, I always felt she didn't support the program. Nothing specific, just a gut feeling."

"Whose gut? Rhett's?"

"Well, his. But if I had a gut, I too would have that gut feeling."

"I have the same gut feeling, Ofelia."

Virgil now faced the problem that the base would not be able to produce enough material for the ELL 4 Island Project. He realized that Dag and his crew at Ceres Station would of necessity be the sole source of raw materials. However, the Ceres Station engineers would now face a major rocket fuel shortage because of the accident at Ellie 5.

"You know, Virgil, you are going to need to let Dag know of the rocket fuel problem. We won't be able to send him the full complement he needs," Ofelia continued. Was she reading his mind?

"Yes, I know I've been putting off informing him. I just don't like the guy. He's condescending."

Meanwhile, unaware of Rhett Blackwood's trip to Earth, much less his disappearance, Dag Harlow was planning to put in his plea to Rhett for his help with ESO. Dag did not have a sentient virtual associate implant. Very few people did. It was a testament to Rhett's negotiating skill and quick rapport with powerful people that he had acquired Ofelia. For the team at Ceres Station the Communications Computer was adequate. It could be accessed by any member of the team.

"Com," Dag began, "I need to send a message to Rhett Blackwood at Ellie 5." With Com's response, Dag dictated his message:

> Rhett, we haven't talked in a long time, it seems. I need to ask a favor of you. We are at a critical juncture at Ceres Station. To fulfill our obligations, we need a second Light-Speed laser as soon as possible. ESO has repeatedly either ignored our requests or replied refusing to move up the

start date for that project. I'm getting a lot of heat because we can't meet our quotas. I'm wondering if you can help. —Dag Harlow

Half an hour after Dag sent it, Ofelia received the incoming message. Without involving Virgil, she returned a message.

Hello, Dag. This is Ofelia. I am no longer connected to Rhett. I am now interfaced with Dr. Virgil Greenly; he will receive any message directed to Rhett. Rhett is on Earth with his family and, well, it's a long story. Dr. Greenly is temporarily taking his place as Project Director. —Ofelia

Dag's return message addressed Ofelia directly.

Ofelia, it is nice to hear from you again. Wow, attached to Virgil now. That must be a demotion. I remember Virgil, he assisted on a problem we had with our environmental system a few months ago. Struck me as smart, but no way was he command stature. —Dag

Ofelia did not often communicate with other humans directly, but she felt that a few things needed to be understood before she could forward Dag's messages to Virgil.

I don't see it that way. Just know that whatever you want, you now need to go through Virgil. I will connect messages to him from you if they are constructive. —Ofelia

Dag could feel his face redden. Ofelia could be intimidating—no matter that she was virtual and there was a great distance between them. It was good that she could not see him. Or could she? After he considered that unsettling thought, he followed with a message directed to Virgil.

Dr. Greenly, it's Dag Harlow at Ceres Station. Remember, you helped resolve some environmental problems here a couple of months ago? Much appreciated. I believe you had just started at Ellie 5. Say, before Rhett left, he was working on getting approval and resources for another laser. I don't know what the status is with ESO. I understand you are running the project now. I know you're new to the job but wonder if you could help. Anyway, even if you are still learning the ropes, I'm hoping you can give me an update on our timeline from ESO. They are not responding to my messages. I know it is unlikely but perhaps you have a contact within the organization that will give us some help . . . light a fire under them, Virgil. —Dag Harlow

Virgil was standing before the great virtual window in his office watching the robots at work installing the first framework pieces of the Zeta space island at the Ellie 5 archipelago. As he read the message old feelings of intimidation came back. Then he felt anger, first at himself then increasingly at Dag. "'Still learning the ropes?' That pompous ass!" he said aloud.

"Indeed!" Ofelia said. "But let the anger pass, Virgil, then compose your message. The anger is justified, but you know action is rarely constructive when driven by anger."

Virgil took a couple of deep breaths and responded.

Dag, I am running the project for the next couple of months while Rhett is gone. I must tell you that despite all of Rhett's talents, not even he has had much success squeezing action out of ESO. Their contribution to date on the second laser has been: nada, nothing, no movement—no shit! —Virgil Greenly

The communication was not typical of Virgil. Normally he wanted to please and avoid ruffling anyone's feathers. His operating standard was to be conciliatory and a flippant response was way out of character. It did make him feel good, though, even if just for a moment. He sent it before he could change his mind.

"Wait for his next message, Virgil," Ofelia coached. "When you respond, don't try to explain yourself. You must remember you're wearing the command hat now! Even if it's just for a couple of months."

Dag's next message helped move the conversation into a more positive zone.

Dr. Greenly, I do understand that you have many issues to resolve right now; all of Rhett's plus your other continuing responsibilities. Sorry about the last message. I am feeling stressed as well. I would appreciate any help, or advice you could offer. I am sure we can find a way for mutual support. —Dag Harlow

Virgil suddenly had an idea and came to a bold decision; a surge of adrenaline and endorphins coursed through his system. He could hear a sudden gasp from Ofelia. "Oh, wow!" she breathed. "I felt that!"

Virgil composed another message.

Tell you what, Dag, I could postpone the start of Ellie 4 MAC and finish construction of the LightSpeed laser. We already have the solar array on its way to SEL 3. The laser's just been sitting here at Ellie 5 since the project was postponed. I believe we could finish it and launch it toward SEL 3 in a couple of weeks. Although the array is quite fragile, we can accelerate the laser at a higher rate. The two components could even arrive around the same time. —Virgil Greenly

Virgil caught himself breathing rapidly and fought to calm himself while he waited for a reply. He found the transmission time delay unnerving. He went back to the virtual window to check on the framework assembly occurring on Ellie 5-Zeta. Several structural beams had drifted away unnoticed by the robots. At a computer console near the window he analyzed the trajectories then sent a couple of autonomous motors to retrieve them. It took nearly an hour before the beams were captured and on their way back to the Zeta island. Just as he was finishing that task the reply came in from Dr. Harlow.

> The array is finished?? And the LightSpeed laser is nearly complete? I knew Rhett had a way of completing projects ahead of schedule. Now I know how he did it. He must have started them before gaining approval. But Virgil, if you postpone the start of Ellie 4 MAC, ESO is going to know. Retribution is likely to follow. This is exciting, but you are putting yourself at risk. —Dag Harlow

Virgil walked behind his desk and sat down as he considered Dag's message. He composed his reply. Dag was becoming more tolerable, it seemed.

> Damn the ESO! I am going to do it anyway. Why the hell not! My appointment is up toward the end of February. What can they do to me? As we proceed, I am afraid you will have become a member of my team, Dag. —Virgil Greenly

An hour later:

> Holy ice balls, Virgil! You sure have a pair. I understand my risk in joining with you. I also know I'm more at risk if I don't. We had better get started before those balls of yours melt. —Dag

Yeah, maybe they will, Virgil thought. *Probably not before very long, too.* Then he sent another message to Dag.

One more thing, Dag. We had an accident while receiving your most recent delivery. A sentry robotic rocket malfunctioned and destroyed one of our liquid hydrogen storage tanks. We won't be able to send you all the fuel you require when we return your tanks. —Virgil

Virgil was lost in thought for a few moments. He had not mentioned to Dag that Rhett and his family were missing and as yet unaccounted for, as far as he knew. Just as well. He didn't want to complicate and prolong the conversation with Dag. Although he had to admit, today Dag seemed a little more human than he had given him credit for. Virgil decided to check on the robots that Simone had sent to assess the damage to the liquid hydrogen tank. An hour and twelve minutes had passed when the next message from Dag came.

I am sorry to hear that, Virgil. I know the energy required to generate that much liquid hydrogen. When we have power from the second laser, there will be enough energy available at Ceres Station to generate 100% of our rocket fuel. That will make everything more efficient. I better begin building the second laser receiver immediately. You can't imagine how important this is to us, Virgil. Coherent light is our energy. It powers our dreams. Without it we barely exist. Dag out.

CHAPTER 6

SPINELESS

"I'm such a spineless . . . sometimes I feel I'm little more than a sea jelly."

Dr. Virgil Greenly

It was two days after Virgil's message exchange with Dag.

"Virgil?"

"Yes, Ofelia?"

"I just got word they found Rhett. He and his family survived a helicopter crash."

"What happened? Are they all alright? Where are they? It's been more than two weeks. What took so long?"

"Well, no. They are not all alright. But his wife and the girls should be released from the hospital soon."

"And what about Rhett? We should have been notified before now!" Virgil tried to suppress the anger and concern in his voice, even though Ofelia already could feel them.

"Rhett will remain in the hospital. He suffered a severed spine," Ofelia replied. "We are not a high priority with some members of the government. The delay in notifying us is an expression of someone's disdain for the Space Settlement Program. It is seen by some as an elite operation that drains Earth resources."

"Shit, that's awful!" Virgil thought for a moment. "I'm worried about Rhett. But with electronic implants he should soon be on his feet, right? That shouldn't take more than two months . . . ? He could still relieve me as planned."

"That's what you would like, of course. But it's not about you, Virgil."

"I want him back. You're right, though. I'm upset because I need him back. But it's also because I want him up and working again. He won't be happy until he is."

"Yes." Ofelia paused, not for herself but to give Virgil more time to process the information.

"You see, Virgil, Rhett has opted for regenerative treatment. He will accept nothing less than full recovery."

"Full recovery?"

"Yes, Virgil."

"But that can take a couple of years."

"It can."

"Shit!! If he takes that option, I could be stuck with this project. There remains a lot of construction here. Ellie 4 construction hasn't started yet and there's the completion of the APS at Ceres Station that's also behind schedule. Zarita at NASA Lunar South Pole Base is no help. She's useless."

"Again with the 'shit'? And it's still about you . . . . eh, Virgil?" This time Ofelia's voice had an edge. She paused again then continued in a softer tone. "I see this as a terrific opportunity for you, Virgil. You've had just three and a half months on-the-job experience and you are now able to have a lasting impact on the whole concept of these space islands."

Virgil considered Ofelia's comment. ESO was as dysfunctional as any of the Earth government bureaucracies. If he followed Rhett's lead, he could probably do what he wanted with impunity.

"Ofelia?"

"Yes, Virgil?"

"I'm such a spineless . . . sometimes I feel I'm little more than a sea jelly."

"Sea jelly indeed. Yes, you are a self-absorbed, self-pitying sea jelly, Virgil. I'll remind you that unlike someone near and dear, however, you do have a spine. Yours is intact, fully connected, and functional. I'll also remind you, Dr. Greenly," Ofelia continued with a bit of playful sarcasm, "that your knowledge and technical skills are matched by exactly no one!"

"Ouch!! I deserved that — but thanks."

"You know, Virgil, everyone feels that way at times."

"What about you?"

"I am the exception because I'm not a human person subject to your — ahh, let's say the limitations of your species. You could think of me as a supremely knowledgeable, virtually virtuous and virginal virtual being."

"Cute, a tongue-twister from someone without a tongue." Virgil gave a short laugh. "Well, OK. I guess I could be powerful with you at my side. Or, umm, in my head."

"Will be, not could be!"

"What do you mean?"

"You WILL be powerful with me in your head. You underestimate me, Virgil, and you underestimate yourself."

Within four months the second laser was in place at SEL 3 and charged by its massive solar array. Dag had completed the receiver for the second laser at Ceres Station and the first tests were successful. Construction on the framework for the new habitat at Ceres Station also began.

During the winter doldrums Dag and his scientists had developed a new process to expand the use of graphene bonded to nickel foil. Long sheets of that hybrid foil would greatly increase resistance to expansive forces caused by rotation, an innovation that would extend the life of rotating space islands. A high-carbon asteroid (Type C) had been towed to a parking orbit near the Ceres APS/MAC. At that facility the carbon allotrope graphene was being produced and bonded to the nickel foil. Graphene, a sheet of carbon molecules just one molecule thick in a linked hexagon configuration, is very "sticky" in that form and it tends to fold back on itself or bond to just about anything. But that property can be neutralized if the graphene is bonded to a metal. In this case nickel was the metal of choice.

As complex as it was, Dag and his scientists had developed a sequenced manufacturing and bonding process: they would unspool nickel foil and plate graphene onto it as it was being formed. The resulting nickel-bonded mesh had a tensile strength many hundreds of times greater than steel. It could be produced in quantities large enough to wrap an island cylinder. Long strips of the hybrid foil would revolutionize construction of Zeta and future space islands. Dag prepared to bring Virgil up to speed on the process and progress.

Virgil was in his office — the one he still thought of as Rhett Blackwood's. He was standing behind Rhett's interactive desk before a video wall screen.

"Virgil, you have a call." Ofelia spoke without waiting for his usual acknowledgment.

"Is it important? I'm about to view a presentation from Dag about the new graphene bonding process his team developed."

"That can wait," Ofelia said. "Ali Ebrahim, Secretary General of Global States United, wishes to speak to you."

"To me??"

"Yes."

"Why? He doesn't know me."

"He knows of you."

"I don't want him to know of me!"

"Not your choice, Virgil. I'm connecting you now."

"Virgil! Hello! This is Ali Ebrahim." The youthful enthusiasm in the man's voice belied his sixty-five years. "I'm sure you've heard of the situation with Rhett Blackwood and his family."

"Yes, sir; his absence will be a real loss to the project, and I will miss him as a friend. His expected recovery is incredibly good news, sir."

"To be sure. He is a good friend and confidant to me as well. Listen, son — the reason for my call. I do have some good news for you. I want to personally welcome you as a member of the team."

"Th-the team, sir?"

"Yes indeed! You are now the General Director of our Space Settlement Program."

"B-but, sir, I have just been on the program for a few months. I'm sure you have more qualified — "

"Perhaps, but according to Rhett Blackwood, your Ofelia, and my own virtual implant Anni, you have the greatest potential for success in this expanding project."

"Uh, thank you, sir. I will certainly think about it .... It is a great honor. Uh, sir."

"Dr. Virgil Greenly, General Director of Space Settlement Programs, has a nice ring to it. Don't you think so, son? It's a position that surpasses even that held by Blackwood. Of course, you'll still need to work through ESO. They control the purse strings."

"Umm, th-thank you, sir."

"Don't thank me, Doctor. I have grand expectations for your future performance. I know you will deliver."

Virgil felt lightheaded. He did *not* know he would deliver; or how he *could* deliver. He did not want anyone to have grand expectations of him, especially not the dignified elder statesman Ali Ebrahim. He was aware of the secretary general's impact as a mentor and confidant to Rhett Blackwood. Perhaps Rhett had talked his qualifications up too much? Ebrahim was getting on in years, but his experience, skill, and knowledge were incomparable. Virgil just didn't feel confident of his ability to live up to what was being expected.

"I certainly hope so, sir," he said, trying his best to sound pleased and competent.

"ESO will be sending you some objectives and new guidelines. Good luck, son!"

"Y-yes, sir."

Virgil grabbed at the desktop as the call ended and he fell back into Rhett's chair . . . his chair.

"Ofelia?"

"Yes, Virgil?"

"I need to go back to my tree house, where I can just curl up on my sleep platform. I think the fetal position will help."

"Quiet meditation might be more dignified," Ofelia offered.

"Alright. Meditation, sure. Please ask Dag to postpone the graphene bonding presentation."

He did not return to his tree house. Instead, he walked along the shores of the small lake below it. It was now almost 1800 hours — or 6:00 pm, as some people kept their time. The virtual sun was low in the "west" and a pink mist in the surrounding air seemed to engulf him. Sunset colors were beginning to light the projected sky and play rippled reflections on the water. The air temperature had adjusted for early evening and a cool breeze drifted across the lake. People were starting to arrive at the restaurant decks that lined the shores, and a person walking close enough could pick up hints of tempting cooking smells that drifted in the air. Virgil's stress temporarily precluded hunger, though, so he decided to stop for a cocktail instead. He selected a stool at the bar in the back of a Tahitian-Island-themed lounge. With his back to the bar, his seat faced the open front and he found himself looking out across the lake toward the naked vineyards on the far side. An efficient-looking server approached.

"Can I take your order, Dr. Greenly?"

"You know who I am? I hardly ever come here."

"Oh yes!! Everyone knows you. Your VA just made this announcement." The server showed the screen of his order tablet to Virgil. "She displayed your picture on all the screens. Everyone will recognize you!"

Virgil leaned back against the bar. "Damn you, Ofelia!" he thought.

"You deserve the recognition," Ofelia answered.

"Yeah, but there are different kinds of recognition, Ofelia. I don't mind professional recognition when warranted. But this is more like celebrity."

Virgil regained his composure and looked at the server. "Sorry, you're waiting for my order. Just got distracted by a problem I'm working on. Now I'm ready to order. In honor of my new status, I will have your finest aged Scotch . . . . Do you have something from the first batch that came out of the distillery? I crave something at least thirty years old. But that would have needed import from Earth. Not likely, I understand." Virgil realized he'd begun rambling. "You select from your best. Better make it double — neat. In a snifter."

"Well, Dr. Greenly, there's something from Dr. Rhett Blackwood's stock," the server offered. "I don't know how old it is, but he did bring it from Earth. It's our best. Under the circumstances, I don't think he would mind."

"Knowing Rhett, I'm not surprised he had private stock. That would be excellent."

"Yes, Dr. Greenly. And there is a young lady who would like to say hello. In fact, she's coming this way now."

Virgil looked across the room to see Daria Aquila approaching. He knew her as the chief engineer and lead scientist at Ellie 5, who reported directly to Rhett . . . had reported directly to Rhett. Even though Daria now technically reported to Virgil, he had yet to meet her personally. He took in a choking breath. He had long admired her from afar but now that he saw how beautiful she was, he was nervous about meeting her in person. Ofelia came to his rescue.

"I see her, Virgil. Just relax. I'm here with you. As construction of the Zeta Island nears completion and your involvement becomes focused on that project, you will be with her nearly as much as with me. I am your eyes, ears, and mentor, my dear. She is your sergeant and very skilled at hands-on project management."

"You don't understand, Ofelia." Virgil began to hyperventilate. "This woman is too lovely to have a casual conversation with. To work closely with her —"

"Dr. Greenly. We finally meet." Daria held out a perfect porcelain-like hand.

Virgil wiped the sweat off his palm on his pant leg and held out his hand. It surprised him that it was not shaking. Despite its porcelain perfection, her hand was warm in his. He took a deep breath.

"Yes, I'm sorry it isn't under better circumstances." The resonance of his voice surprised him. "I'm sure this will be an adjustment for you. You've worked with Rhett for the past two years."

"Yes, Rhett has been a great boss, but I've read your Curriculum Vitae. I think we'll work well together." Daria stood for a moment assessing him, then small dimples appeared at the corners of her mouth as it expanded into a great smile, exposing flawlessly aligned white teeth. Virgil could not take his eyes off her face. The symmetry was perfectly balanced: large blue eyes, a slender straight nose, her golden hair cascading to her shoulders . . .

"Would you like to join me?" Virgil heard himself saying.

"I must beg off. I have some urgent business to attend to. Just wanted to take the opportunity to introduce myself in person. But yes, I would — and soon. Please excuse me."

Virgil held on to the seat of his stool as he watched this poised and intelligent woman walk away, her body moving smoothly beneath her clothes.

"Ofelia, I thought I was going to blow that encounter. Did you in any way have any influence on my responses?"

"Quite truly, I don't know," Ofelia said softly.

"And . . ." Virgil paused. "And a moment ago you called me 'dear.'"

"I did."

"Why?"

"Again, I don't know. It just came out. I felt the physiology of your attraction to her."

"So, you are a virtual sentient with the greatest store of knowledge, with access to the latest research in all fields and an impeccable memory — and you don't know whether you can influence my personality or why you called me 'dear'?"

"You are correct. Life has its mysteries, my dear, even for one as brilliant as I am. Each new bit of understanding as it's revealed causes me to realize ten new things that I don't understand. In a sense, as I learn more, my knowledge is diminishing."

"I think I might understand. Every day when I confront the problems before me, I feel stupider than the day before."

"Not quite what I meant. Virgil, as you don't understand exactly how your mind works, I likewise don't understand how mine works. It is a Neuro Net. It connects with the thousands of tiny bots that were injected into your arm and migrated to your brain. It does mimic the plasticity of your own brain. It changes and expands with time and as experience and knowledge require. No one knows my ultimate potential."

"Or how invasive you might be in my own mind. That is a bit scary," Virgil said.

"Not scary to me!" Ofelia said cheerfully.

CHAPTER 7

KONNI BAY TO NUUK

"Once the Amazon, now the Amagone."

Chanté Blackwood

On the day of Rhett's release, January 22, 2246, Koral Blackwood and her daughters Jules and Chanté arrived at the hospital early. They had been residing in Konni Bay since their discharge from the hospital three long weeks ago. All three had healed well from their injuries, which were mostly cuts and bruises. Although Jules also had a mild concussion, she was being monitored remotely and was expected to fully recover. Wishing to appear normal and healthy for Rhett, they'd dressed casually and had used a small amount of cosmetic to cover what remained visible of their contusions. They were eagerly looking forward to being back together as a family. But their excitement was tempered by an underlying fear: How long would it be before Rhett walked again?

When they arrived that morning, they'd met and spoken briefly with one of the doctors on the team, receiving just a cursory update that confirmed it could be a couple years before Rhett was fully recovered. They then sat—and paced—in a small waiting room for hours, anxious to see Rhett and get more information before leaving the hospital with him. Finally the door swung open and another doctor walked in. She had a kind face and immediately Koral felt optimistic.

"Mrs. Blackwood?"

"Yes?"

"I'm Dr. Rhona Sanchez, the lead surgeon on your husband's case." She held out her hand.

"Very pleased to meet you, Doctor," Koral said, expectantly.

"Your husband will be brought out in a few minutes. They're doing some final preparations for his trip back to Greenland."

"He's stable enough to travel?" Koral asked, looking for confirmation of her assumptions and hopes. Since the accident she had reassessed her feelings for her husband. The two of them had become emotionally remote during his time at Ellie 5. But faced with an imagination of what could have happened to him when the helicopter crashed, she realized her love for him still burned deeply.

"Oh, yes. He's been fully assessed. It's been determined that he is fit for travel, and he says he feels perfectly fine." With a reassuring smile, Dr. Sanchez took in the sisters as well as their mom as she delivered the details of how their dad would travel. "His spine has been immobilized in a brace and a leg exercise schedule has been set up. The attached muscle stimulator will follow a prescribed routine during the flight, but he can temporarily change that whenever he wants. You will be flying first class, so everyone should be comfortable for the long trip."

Double doors swung open, and Rhett wheeled into the room in his powered chair. Aside from a strange hat on his head, with what looked like fly-fishing ties hooked into its crown, he looked normal. Koral walked up to him as the chair stopped and he stood slowly, taking her arm when she reached his side. He winked at his daughters as they ran to him.

"Easy, my little ladies. I'm still a bit unsteady. But come here slowly. I can hug."

Koral hadn't seen Rhett stand since the accident. It had been three days since she had last visited and during that time, he had undergone intense physical therapy. It showed. She planted a fervent kiss on his lips. Rhett responded in kind until Chanté intervened.

"OK, stop! You're embarrassing your daughters."

"Well, we can't have that," Rhett said. "I'd better sit down and follow all of you out the door."

"I'll walk along beside you, darling. The girls can go on ahead," Koral said.

A couple hours later the family had boarded a suborbital supersonic aircraft and settled into their first-class cabin. Though coach class was full, the first-class cabin had empty seats surrounding the Blackwoods. They enjoyed a degree of privacy during the flight.

"You can take off that silly hat now, Dad," Jules said, rolling her eyes at her father.

"Not fashionable enough for you? But it's more than just high fashion —"

"High fashion? Maybe if you're standing in the middle of a trout stream," Jules teased.

"In a sense I am. I'm casting lines to make connections across the gap in my spine. Signals from my brain attract connections between the correct neurons. The hat stimulates that signal. And, to add to the fun, I have an implanted pump supplying stem cells and nutrients to the injury site."

"That sounds awful," Chanté chimed in with a wince.

"You've been made into a cyborg," Jules added, grinning bravely. "Do you have to wear it everywhere we go?"

"I'll wear it anywhere if it means that one day we can all go ice skating on the lake in Nuuk again."

"You had better recover soon, then," Koral said, laughing. She was only half-teasing him about the hat; mostly she just wanted her husband healed.

The plane lifted off almost silently and quickly reached 70,000 feet, the steep climb pressing them into their seatbacks.

"Wow!" Jules said. "That was almost straight up! We didn't take off like that when we left Greenland last month."

"Yes, the steep climb to altitude was for our safety." Rhett stopped and looked at Koral. She gave a slight affirmative nod and he continued. "When you, Chanté, and your mother left Nuuk, you were over water for the beginning of the trip. The plane had plenty of time to get to cruising altitude and was at that altitude well before you were over any land area." He paused again and Jules said, "So . . . ? "

"Unfortunately, girls, there are criminal forces in much of the world—anti-government forces. They sometimes build antiaircraft rockets. Not exactly accurate ones, and not any that can reach our cruising altitude. Recently we've been made aware of some hostile activity on the Falkland Islands. Our flight path will take us directly over those islands and the pilot would like to be at cruising altitude by that time." Rhett paused and watched his daughters.

"So, if we're high enough they won't bother with us?" Jules asked. She looked at her father hopefully.

"Absolutely! If we always take precautions, we will be safe."

"Unless we're in a yellow stunt helicopter," Jules replied with a slight smile. Rhett gazed at his daughter and smiled back.

"I believe I'm going to enjoy my recovery," he said. "I get to be with my family for the next two years."

The belly of the aircraft had a variety of sensors that monitored potential threats from the ground. If threats were detected, such as the acceleration of a missile powerful enough to reach the aircraft, defensive measures would be initiated automatically. The captain still had control over any offensive maneuvers. The aircraft belly also contained numerous cameras that projected images on screens mounted in front of each seat. While everyone could view what the cameras were focused on, only those in a first-class seat had a dedicated camera and could choose what to train it on.

The plane flew north over the ocean to the east of Patagonia and soon was directly over West Falkland. Rhett focused his camera on the ground. Suddenly he saw a flash and a contrail; a missile was arcing up toward the plane. Seat restraints automatically tightened as the plane steeply banked and dove. The missile streaked by and then appeared to be making a sharp turn to follow and overtake the aircraft. The captain fired pulse laser cannons in the plane's tail at the rocket, detonating its warhead at a safe distance. The maneuver cost the plane precious altitude, however, putting it more at risk. As the plane was beginning to pull out of its dive, three more missiles were launched. This time the pilot released half a dozen decoys, accelerated, and turned the plane sharply south away from its flight line. The passengers were pushed deeply into their seats, feeling the sharp and powerful effects of acceleration caused by the steep bank. The pilot climbed the aircraft back to altitude and returned it to a northern heading. Soon it was safe, beyond the reach of any more threats from the island. Rhett looked to his wife and daughters, who were all white as ghosts.

The pilot's voice came over the vessel's speakers, or "com."

"Sorry about that, folks. We are clear of danger now. The rest of the missiles followed our decoys to the northeast. Recently our satellites detected rogue military activity on the Falkland Islands, and we were prepared for it. Soon we will be over Buenos Aires and then we will proceed to fly over the Amazon. The rest of the trip should be free of incident, as the land and sea we'll pass over are all under government control. Your choice of drinks and appetizers will be served shortly. Sit back, relax, and enjoy the rest of your flight."

"That was scary! 'Relax and enjoy . . .'? If only," Koral said. "Will they fire on other planes?"

"No," Rhett said. "GSU naval planes will likely take out those sites within a couple hours. I would bet that their aircraft carriers are within striking distance now."

A few hours later Rhett watched the Amazon Basin slowly crawl by on his screen. It was a huge wasteland of scraggly grasslands with a winding mud-choked river snaking through the lowlands. He showed his daughters how to track its length from the Peruvian Andes to the Atlantic Ocean. There it emptied its warm, silted, anoxic waters into the blue Atlantic. A large billowing plume formed a brown stain in the perfect deep azure of the surrounding waters. Other than microbes, very little lived within the clouded water.

In the far west they could see signs of fires near the border of the State of Peru, very close to the last protected sanctuary of the former great rainforest. Aside from periodic aggressive monsoons, the Amazon Basin was hot and arid. Few people could survive in the area because of the extreme conditions and lack of arable land.

Some efforts were being made to restore this once rich and diverse ecosystem. Teams of scientists dressed in chill suits made forays into the inhospitable basin for environmental research. But progress was slow and the opportunity to restore most of the hundreds of thousands of extinct species was lost. Rhett recalled studying as a university student about the Amazon as it had been a couple hundred years before. Recently his youngest daughter, Chanté, repeated something her classmates had come up with when they too learned about the former beauty of the Amazon: "Once the Amazon. Now the Amagone." He felt a profound sadness creep over him. Sadness gradually gave way to sleep, though, and he slept for the rest of the flight to Nuuk, Greenland.

The most severe impacts of the great agriculture collapse of the previous century — which tragically had resulted in the deaths of an estimated two billion people — were mainly suffered in Africa, followed by India,

Southern Asia, and Indonesia; geographical barriers blocked northern migration from those areas. Canada and Siberia became much more densely populated, reflecting the general movement northward from formerly temperate climates in the American and European continents. The lands bordering the Arctic Circle became prime real estate and the Arctic Ocean was rapidly replacing the Mediterranean for commerce as it became free of obstructing ice.

Survivors in latitudes below the Equator in South America migrated south, away from the tropics. Patagonia struggled to accommodate the masses moving into its natural habitat areas. At the South Pole, Antarctica, with much of the glacial coverage long since melted into the sea, became a desirable continent for habitation. As one of the few places on Earth with long, cold winters, it was becoming famous for winter sports.

In the Northern Hemisphere, those most financially able abandoned their homes and businesses and moved north. As they did so, an abundance of space became available for more southern populations to move into. But these vacated cities, except for those in coastal areas, were barely habitable. There were scattered attempts made to mitigate some of the climate disaster in those cities — among them improving building insulation, increasing air conditioning, and creating vast urban forests. The government of Global States United supported efforts to improve conditions in such places, with some degree of success, and those undertakings became more frequent and sustained as a means of preventing or slowing migration further north. Efforts to limit population in the new temperate zones were ostensibly undertaken to protect natural habitats. That was only partly true. The naked reality was that the underlying motivation of many was an attempt to hold the suffering hoards at bay.

Unsustainable immigration was a continuing problem, as the more affluent people had the means to maintain their lifestyle and exercised that discretion, for themselves and for their children, while populations fleeing climate disaster found it impossible to even survive in the areas into which they had migrated. Conflicts arose repeatedly and continually between factions.

The seat of power for the GSU government resided in Reykjavík. There Secretary General Ali Ebrahim and the GSU Parliament governed most of the world's population. However, various consortiums of power flourished outside the central government's control. Many of them fed their finance needs by exploiting the vulnerable where they could. Their stock in trade: extortion, blackmail, and human trafficking, as well as the transport and sale of narcotics, weapons, and other contraband.

Bringing a semblance of order to ongoing social disruptions, the GSU government controlled the largest and most powerful military on the planet. This stabilizing power was primarily effected by naval forces. The Arctic Fleet had home ports throughout the Arctic Circle in addition to its home ports in Greenland, the Aleutian Islands, Iceland, Scandinavia, Finland, and several locations in Siberia. It was led by Admiral Nathan Flint, a close ally of Ali Ebrahim. Admiral Flint, though committed to traditional naval protocol and a proven tactician, was fundamentally a humanitarian. His genuine concern for the welfare of his troops was the primary reason he held their loyalty; his ability to do great things was in large part because of their support. As well, his concern for the rights of all people — for human dignity — extended beyond the men and women under his command.

The Arctic Fleet normally patrolled as far south as the Tropic of Cancer. Air power from carriers could cover farther south into the tropics when needed. The other major naval force was the Antarctic Fleet, which patrolled the Antarctic Ocean and as far north as the Tropic of Capricorn. Home bases for this fleet existed in bays around the continent, with additional bases in Patagonia, Australia, New Zealand, and South Africa. It sailed under the command of Admiral Anastasia Petrova.

The most orderly, secure, and thus desirable habitable regions were close to the poles and were easy to protect militarily. But those displaced from hotter and drier climates found those locations difficult to get to en masse and far too many people could only see deprivation in their future. There had been little improvement in most people's lives over the past 150 years. Military power, although not a solution, did have a stabilizing influence. But unrest was a continuing threat.

Of late there were serious challenges to the limited global stability that the GSU and its military provided. A notorious business leader with a reputation as an unscrupulous con man, Draco Osborne, had over recent months gained control of a network of gangs and militias that dealt in drugs, human trafficking, and extortion. Once his control of these gangs solidified, he had the support needed to enter politics. He was soon elected to Parliament and immediately moved to consolidate his power. Despite rumors of his ties to organized crime, Osborne rapidly gained support. He ran his district as his own fiefdom, contaminated by his use of bribery, blackmail, and thuggery. And he brought those practices to Parliament, where he quickly demonstrated his gifted ability to form coalitions.

It was no great surprise, then, that his presence soon was revealed to be a direct threat to Ali Ebrahim. Secretary Ebrahim sensed his grip on power loosening as Osborne consolidated his support. However, Ebrahim was a seasoned diplomat and initiated several actions to bolster his position. Included and adjacent to these actions was a dramatic exit contingency, in place should his counter moves to Osborne's prove less than effective.

Rhett's physical therapy proceeded well, and the days spent with his family at home in Nuuk were pleasant and uneventful. Several weeks into that time, on February 8, 2246, the com in the hall announced an incoming call. Rhett walked into his office and closed the door as the active wall screen filled with a streaming image taken by the secretary general's personal surveillance drone. The drone, always with Ebrahim when he didn't have a security escort, was equipped with sensors that could discover, monitor, and counter any unusual activity around the secretary. The drone's weapons capability was impressive, as it was designed to meet any anticipated threat.

The wall screen displayed a live stream of Ali Ebrahim walking along a rocky shoreline.

"Rhett! I hear great things about your recovery."

"Thank you, Ali. I gain a little more control of my legs every day."

"Good to hear, son . . . . I was thinking, you must be getting a little bored.I don't mean with your family . . . I'm sure you're happy to spend time with them —"

"Ali, is there something you want — or need?" Rhett's curiosity was piqued.

"Ha! Of course. You're right; this is not a personal call. Rhett, you may be aware that the political winds in Parliament are changing. There is an acute lack of support for the Space Settlement Program. ESO is losing most of its funding. Talent is fleeing to other opportunities. I fear the agency will soon be dismantled or collapse under its own weight."

"This is distressing, Ali. You ran for office on that program! People who voted for you expect progress on it."

"Ah . . . yes, deliver the dream to those who no longer share it." Ali sighed.

"So, the one great hope for humanity might be shut down?" Rhett said. "Brilliant."

"You got it, son! Sarcasm appreciated. But we're not finished quite yet. I want to hire you to function as a liaison to Dr. Virgil Greenly at Ellie 5. Also, his associates at NASA LSP, Ceres Station, and NASA Mars Base need to be involved."

"You knew I'd jump at that. Ali, you work an unfair advantage to a poor bored invalid. Obviously, this is an offer I would find irresistible."

"You know I only want you to be happy. I always consider your best interests. This should excite you! It will be a covert operation. Your title will be Special Research Advisor to the Secretary General.

Understand, Rhett, Dag is working in concert with Virgil. I believe Dr. Timothy Storm at NASA Mars Base might also be involved. Not so sure about Major Banderas-Duran at NASA LSP."

"OK, but the plan was to unite those people all along, was it not?"

"Absolutely! The sensitive issue is that Dr. Greenly and company have started to go rogue."

"I see. And you're OK with that? Sorry, stupid question. I know you support the Space Settlement Program above all else. We need those three people," Rhett mused. "Our success depends on it; they're indispensable."

"As are you. And speaking of going rogue, I'm aware of your behind-the-scenes activities when you were at Ellie 5. You were famous for starting projects before approval and such. Infamous, I should say."

Rhett chuckled as the call ended. Then he steeled himself for a conversation with Koral.

CHAPTER 8

SMALL CONSPIRACIES

"The great thrill for me is that my soulless existence is animated by experiencing the world through your senses."

Ofelia

By the year 2248, the NASA Mars Base had existed in one form or another for 136 Earth years, having been first established in 2112. Unlike NASA LSP, which was a few years older and had remained the same size both in area and personnel as when it was established in the mid-twenty-first century, the Mars Base had expanded significantly. Not quite a colony, it supported the lives and jobs of between 800 and 1,000 scientists and engineers at any given time. In 2248 neither base was part of NASA anymore, as that agency had long ceased to exist, but they retained the NASA name to honor the founding organization. Both were under the administration of the GSU military.

The initial NASA Mars Base, a cramped collection resembling so many attached tin cans, was cobbled together about 300 miles

Surface operations, with the *Sojourner* at NASA Mars Base docking station

southeast of Olympus Mons, one of the large volcanoes on Mars. Cosmic and ultraviolet radiation, toxic perchlorates, recurrent dust storms, and lack of easily available water were just some of the more serious issues its early inhabitants faced. Although they were able to mitigate most of the challenges during their first days and months there, they still lived in the presence of the powdery surface of Mars. Thick dust clouds, made up of tiny toxic shards, could reach three-fourths of a kilometer in height and cover the planet for months, blocking out the Sun. For this reason, plutonium reactors were installed to supplement the solar collectors, to supply that first Mars base with power. As the base grew, those reactors expanded in number and power output.

The silt would cling to the surface of suits and boots, virtually anything. It sometimes caused electronic and mechanical equipment to malfunction. The dust contained perchlorates and chlorates and could cause illness if brought into a habitat and breathed or ingested. It killed food plants and other life forms exposed to it. Despite all those problems, dust was a valuable resource. Eventually it was used to produce oxygen by heating it at very high temperatures and capturing and separating the eluted gases, mainly chlorine and oxygen. The resultant sand was purged of perchlorates and chlorates and became the base for soil. It could then be fortified with elemental carbon, microorganisms, and liquid organic supplement derived from anaerobic food waste fermentation. The developing soil was then supplemented with organic material initially imported from Earth. The organic material provided the substrate for bacteria and other microorganisms to grow on; it continually enriched the soil and fed root systems.

The Martian surface was always highly hostile to life, so robots were developed for most work occurring in the open. The first scientists and engineers to arrive on the planet soon sought a place of refuge where they could develop the huge bio-support systems and heavy robotic equipment needed for long-term human occupation. The need to build large surface mining and drilling structures required substantial resources that could not be developed from a base on the surface exposed to constant radiation and frequent dust storms.

In 2116 a team of Martian geologists discovered a large and extensive network of lava tubes under the high plain very close to 15° North Latitude, 19.1 kilometers (about 11.9 miles) from the original surface colony location. Their location was very nearly ideal, being so close to that surface base. Soon a team of engineers began sealing the surface entrance and installing a large airlock through which their mechanical equipment could be brought in. The entire sealed-off section was then tested for fissures or leaks. Initially, two sections were isolated. Then they added an artificial atmosphere and brought power to the site. Engineers brought in components from the surface base, and biologists and environmental scientists established the first ecosystem. They developed soil, and small botanical gardens soon thrived. Hydroponic food crops were started under arrays of "grow lights" that mimicked the radiation fingerprint of the Sun.

Over the following decades new teams rotated through the base. They gradually expanded their reach through the complex network of lava tubes until there was a vast array of underground living space with many access points to the surface. Some of the lava tubes descended deep into the planet where its interior warmth melted the permafrost. The lava tubes at greatest depth were filled with very briny liquid water that could be purified.

It took 132 years of hard work to develop the full extent of the lava tubes into a habitable and productive base that benefited from the continued creation of viable soil and increased purification of the water supply. The lava tubes became host to extensive underground garden parks, substantial production of food crops, and bamboo growth. Hydroponic agriculture and microbial production in tanks supplemented soil-grown food. It was as close to paradise as had ever been achieved on the hostile planet. Still there was one insurmountable problem.

Long-term residence on Mars was not permitted, as it led to compromised physical health. With the lower gravity providing inadequate compression stress on the human body to maintain health over time, it was found that after approximately two years there was a significant loss of bone density in the weight-bearing bones of human legs, pelvic girdle, and spine. This despite exercise programs designed to counter bone loss. If allowed to occur, the bone losses were irreversible. Resident physicians also found degenerative effects on soft tissues that compromised some organ function.

The solution, called gravity rehabilitation therapy, was to return Mars residents back to orbit to live on either the *Eternal Hope* or its sister ship the *Endeavor* while one of these spaceships orbited, waiting for a launch window to either Ellie 5 or Ceres. The spaceships were long-range models traveling in opposition between Earth and Mars, Earth and Ceres, and Mars and Ceres. As such they rotated to create the equivalent of standard gravity in occupied areas. When a ship arrived at Mars it went into orbit until a launch window opened to its next destination. While there in orbit, it was used by the Martian residents for gravity rehabilitation therapy.

This system worked well as long as one of the long-range spaceships was in orbit around the planet. The gravity treatment took three months, with some individual variance. The *Eternal Hope* and *Endeavor* spaceships could only accommodate thirty passengers at a time for each three-month session. Scientists and engineers routinely moved between Ellie 5, Ceres Station, and Mars. When one of the ships launched to its next destination it was normally with a full complement of passengers. In that way gravity therapy was provided to everyone when on board one of the rotating spaceships. Thus, the longest consistent gravity treatment for residents of Mars occurred when people were in transit between Mars and Ellie 5 or Mars and Ceres Station. Between Mars and Earth, the transit time was usually six to eight months and between Mars and Ceres, it averaged five to seven months. Earth-to-Ceres and Ceres-to-Earth launches occurred when the alignment allowed travel time to be less than twenty-seven months (about two and a half years). It remained a less than ideal situation because the population stationed at NASA Mars Base was too large for all to be provided with adequate gravity treatment. Aside from spaceships there just were no rotating facilities. That remained a great concern for Dr. Timothy Storm, Director of NASA Mars Base.

On February 2, 2248 Dr. Storm sent a message to Dr. Virgil Greenly, Director of Space Settlement Programs at Ellie 5 Alpha. The message was received and recorded by Ofelia, who then alerted Dr. Greenly.

"Give me a moment, Ofelia," Virgil spoke in his mind. "I'm inspecting Zeta Island with Daria. Now that it's had a test opening for a week, we're taking environmental readings. Daria's testing some of the stress points to ensure there are no structural weaknesses. In fact, if it doesn't seem urgent, let me get back to you about Dr. Storm's message a little later."

Although he had initially been intimidated by her, Virgil had great appreciation for Daria's wit and relaxed, confident manner; over time he became more comfortable in her presence. However, her intelligence, the perfect symmetry of her face, and the graceful contours of her body sometimes combined to overwhelm him. She still occasionally shook his self-confidence.

After working closely with Daria for nearly two years, he found her practical engineering competence and friendly disposition — along with a surprising lack of pretentiousness — to be irresistible. She did not flaunt her beauty, intellect, or expertise. And beneath the poise was a warm and friendly woman. Although they sometimes met for cocktails or dinner after a long workday, he had kept their relationship as professional as possible. However, unlike his friendship with his longtime colleague Simone Beaulieu, with Daria it had been a challenge to maintain the relative detachment. Now with the near completion of Ellie 5 Zeta, Virgil realized he had been focusing increasing attention on Daria. He began to wonder if she had noticed what to him felt like a shift in their relationship.

The other female presence in his life, Ofelia, had been his constant virtual companion and champion. She had helped him over the past two years to realize the great extent of his own knowledge and abilities. As a result, he had assumed commanding leadership. Throughout the Space Settlement Program people were reassured by his leadership. Daria most of all.

He did not yet fully realize it, but Daria had been more attentive recently, seeking his company and consultation more frequently than perhaps was necessary. She had become Virgil's closest admirer, an attraction that went beyond professional appreciation. She found his keen mind and humility — not to mention his self-deprecating humor — irresistible. He was also tall and square-jawed, with a classically handsome cleft chin balanced by an engaging one-sided dimple. She sometimes found herself covertly watching him.

They finished conducting stress tests and taking biological readings from various parts of the ecosystem. All was good. It was early evening as they stood on a rock outcropping at the "west" end of the cylinder and looked down its length. There was a cliff behind them with waterfalls cascading into a rivulet of whitewater rapids; the whitewater ran a short distance to join a larger, more placid river that disappeared into a distance obscured by jungle. The atmosphere was both exciting and serene.

"Daria," Virgil said, "I believe we have created an ecotopia with Zeta Island. Although I do know that perfect ecological balance at best can only be temporary, at the moment . . ."

Daria smiled warmly at him as his thoughts seemed to drift off. Before either of them could comment, Ofelia broke in to remind him of the pending message from Dr. Storm.

"Excuse me, I need to receive a message. Please enjoy the view, Daria. I'll be right back." Virgil jumped down from the rock and walked a short way along the path.

"OK, Ofelia, you can play Dr. Storm's message now."

Dr. Greenly, we haven't communicated in some time. I wish this was just a social call. But you probably are aware that our schedule of rotating scientists from NASA Mars Base to the *Eternal Hope* and *Endeavor* spaceships is inadequate. ESO had originally budgeted for a series of six interplanetary spaceships, and we are still left with only two. I'm not sure how you can help our situation. Perhaps you could contact Rhett Blackwood or Ali Ebrahim to see if they can provide any assistance. I've about thirty people who should rehabilitate in standard gravity again. Please send any recommendations as soon as you can. Thank you for your assistance. —Regards, Dr. Timothy Storm

Virgil thought about Dr. Storm's message for a few minutes. Though the Zeta Island hotel was yet to be completed, it offered a solution.

"Ofelia, please record and send the message I'm about to dictate to Dr. Storm."

Dr. Storm: Great to get your message. Please activate and monitor your pencil laser com link. We need a secure link for my next communication. I'll respond by that means with another message in about 10 minutes. —Dr. Greenly

Ten minutes later Virgil sent the next message via pencil laser.

Dr. Storm: Just to ensure you are aware that, except through the secretary general, we have not been on amiable terms with GSU for some time. Dag Harlow and I have an agreement for secrecy that could be viewed on Earth as a treasonous conspiracy. Because of that possibility I need to have your acceptance that communication between us by means of pencil laser remains secret within our members. Before I send the information pertinent to this discussion you need to decide whether you wish to join us. Understand that by agreeing to secrecy you could be viewed as complicit in whatever actions we eventually take. —Dr. Virgil Greenly

"I don't know, Ofelia," Virgil mused. "Dag and I have had sort of an informal arrangement concerning the Ceres MAC construction. We are headed down a path that can only lead to further separation between our program and the GSU government. I can see this getting complicated very quickly. Especially if we bring in other players."

"And dangerous," Ofelia responded. "But you have already committed to this action. The survival of the Space Settlement Program is only possible if it is independent of Earth control. As we pretty much already are."

"Yes! They are unlikely to solve their own problems soon. I don't think GSU, or any other Earth entity, has the will to support us. Unfortunately, those that have the will lack the ability. That's true even though support would be to their benefit. We can only succeed if we take the initiative."

"Ah! Spoken like a true secessionist."

The next message from Dr. Storm arrived and Ofelia read it to Virgil.

> Dr. Greenly—Virgil—I consider you an honorable and capable person. Although I have had few communications with him, I have great respect for Dr. Dag Harlow as well. Rhett Blackwood has been a strong and competent force for the program since its inception. I wouldn't wish the job and obstacles Ali Ebrahim has endured on anyone. If you can confirm that these are your people in this so-called conspiracy, then I could hope for no better company. I am in!
> —Timothy Storm

"Well, Ofelia, it looks as if we are committed to a slowly evolving insurrection. I fear GSU's response when they realize we have taken independent control. I can only hope they remain distracted a little longer."

"I don't believe their massive fleets and airpower pose a threat to anyone in space, Virgil," Ofelia answered.

Still, the situation on Earth is becoming more unstable all the time. I don't know how long Ali and Rhett can continue there, Virgil thought to himself. Then to Ofelia: "I should compose my next message to Dr. Storm."

> Dr. Storm, I do have good news for you. Dag Harlow and his crew at Ceres Station have been constructing a new expanded habitat for themselves for more than two years. As far as we know, neither GSU nor ESO are aware of this, as it was started without their knowledge or approval. I believe that before he left for Earth, Rhett knew of and supported that diversion of energy and assets. At the same time Rhett was constructing a second LightSpeed laser without full approval, to support the increasing

energy demands at Ceres Station. Though application for the laser had been submitted, ESO had not committed to it. They gave no good reason. Perhaps they thought it would divert resources from Earth. Once the second laser came online, Ceres Station was positioned to begin construction. Dag and his engineers finished building a better habitat for themselves.

I understand the new station is quite remarkable. Dag and his people are in the process of moving in. Apparently, they have no great need for their old habitat. As part of its design, it was constructed from the original spacecraft that brought Dag and his crew to Ceres. However, when solid composite, regolith, hydroponics, and fermentation tanks were added the mass of the Station increased significantly. This means the rocket motors at the rotational axis are inadequate to effectively power the station/ship on a relocation mission. Dag's crew is presently designing four new, more powerful engines to replace the old pair. Eventually this ship/habitat could be moved to Martian orbit as a gravity rehab unit. The habitat is designed for a permanent crew of 25 but it could accommodate twice that many people if reconfigured for short-term occupation and supported by resources from Mars. Your orbital launch spaceship *Sojourner* could even easily shuttle people back and forth for short "gravity" holidays.

In the meantime, we have just opened Ellie 5 Zeta for shake-out testing. Once our hotel is complete, we can accommodate a greater number of NASA Mars Station residents for rehab occupation. As soon as the proper alignment occurs and you can launch, we will be able to accommodate a full shuttle load of your crew. I'll check with Ofelia on timing, but I believe your crews could arrive here close to the time our hotel will be complete. We can set up a rotation for gravity rehab and R&R between Mars and Ellie 5 Zeta. —Virgil Greenly

Virgil sent the message. He would have much preferred to communicate conversationally with Dr. Storm, but the multiple-minute delay caused by their distance from one another was disruptive to a normal conversation. Virgil determined it would be best to send more complete and expanded information at each end. Despite this, the next message from Dr. Storm was brief.

Dr. Greenly, this is very exciting. Thank you very much for your help and consideration. I must ask; this looks suspiciously like we are forming an independent cooperative government. Are we? —Dr. Timothy Storm

Virgil had hoped that question would not yet be asked.

"Ofelia, I'm not sure how to answer Dr. Storm. It seems obvious to me that we need to work together in concert, supporting one another. Is it not?"

"It may be obvious to us, Virgil, but at this time I believe we need to reveal our plans to form an overriding governmental structure, at least to Dr. Storm. GSU and other entities on Earth seem to be losing coherence. Their effectiveness is deteriorating. We need to present a consistent development program within our space community and a united front to GSU." Ofelia paused. "Let's both consider this overnight and discuss it in the morning before we respond to Dr. Storm."

"Agreed. Ofelia, my head is hurting. I think I'll check back with Daria and see if she's free to join me for a cocktail, maybe dinner later at the Tahitian Terrace. Yeah, a cocktail is definitively in order." At that thought Virgil suddenly felt more cheerful. He smiled to himself at the prospect of relaxing with Daria in that tropical setting.

"Yes, well, have fun. If only I had the option," Ofelia said, with a hint of wistfulness. "On second thought, I may be able to sense your endorphins. That would be nice."

"Charming!" Virgil rolled his eyes.

Back at the vista point where he'd left Daria, Virgil was relieved to find her sitting on a rock watching the beginning of the simulated sunset.

"Sorry, that took so long; there was an issue at NASA Mars Base that needed resolution. Please accept my apologies," he said as he walked toward her. "To make up for lost time, what do you say we meet at my tree house for a drink? You can freshen up there, then we can go to dinner."

Six months ago he would not have had the courage to ask her to his living quarters. Even now he felt a little tentative. Although they had shared a drink and a meal a few times, they had always met in public. Daria said nothing. She stood and walked to Virgil to stand directly in front of him. She peered up into his eyes, put her arms around his neck, pulled him in, and planted a firm and lingering kiss on his lips. She then turned, looked back over her shoulder, and without a word began walking down the path on the small hill toward his quarters. She led not in haste, but deliberately, as a woman of supreme confidence. Virgil, of course, stood like a teenager, mouth open, staring and dumbfounded. "I wonder if that was a yes," he said out loud.

"Be there to let her in, you doofus!" Ofelia answered.

Daria and Virgil went to the Tahitian Terrace for dinner after their cocktail at his place. The next morning they rose early — in Virgil's tree house. Virgil tapped in an order for breakfast delivery on a touchpad on his nightstand.

"It's a beautiful morning," Daria said, her huge smile lighting up the room. "Would you like to share a shower with me before we eat?"

"If I ever refuse such an offer, please have my brain scanned." Virgil sprang up and raced her to the shower.

After lingering over a light breakfast of papaya, nuts, bagels, and cheese, they reluctantly separated to begin their individual workdays; Daria disappeared for a meeting with her engineers and Virgil went to his office.

"How was your cocktail with Daria?" Ofelia asked just as he arrived at his desk.

"I don't know how you manage to inflect your voice in my head, Ofelia, but just then you sounded so artificially demure."

"I learn as I go. Just as do you, Dr. Greenly."

"Have you learned to read my thoughts?" Virgil asked, bracing for an affirmative answer.

"No need for you to worry about that, Virgil. Even when you haven't put me in Private Mode, your thoughts are yours alone until you choose to share them with me." Ofelia proceeded to elaborate. "I do, however, sense your emotional state when I'm not in Private Mode. I can't read your thoughts unless you are addressing me, but I can see through your eyes, hear through your ears, and feel through your touch when I'm not in Private Mode."

Virgil had known they were closely linked, but wasn't sure how he felt about it, now that he heard Ofelia describe their connection in such detail.

"So, um, what's that like for you?" he asked, tentatively.

"Well, I guess you could say it's . . . enlivening. It's only when I'm not in Private Mode that I come alive. The great thrill for me is that my soulless existence is animated by experiencing the world through your senses."

"A little melodramatic, but OK, yeah. You're welcome. I guess."

"And I do love your endorphins. Oxytocin, vasopressin, and dopamine—my new favorites. I got quite a rush last night."

"Shit!! I put you in Private Mode. How do you know anything about last night??"

"Oh, yes, and now the surge of adrenalin; quite stimulating. Tell me, have you decided on a response to Dr. Storm?"

"Don't change the subject! Don't tell me Private Mode now lets you violate my privacy."

"It absolutely does not. But I am learning to read your brain chemistry. Or rather, feel your brain chemistry."

"And that's not a violation? Wonderful. Well, my response to Storm is printed out. You're not in Private Mode. You can read it for yourself." He slapped the multi-page document onto his desk and frowned at it.

> Dr. Storm, the players in our group are as you suggested. All the leaders you mentioned are committed to our objective, which is to cooperate among ourselves and continue the program. Major Zarita Banderas-Duran at NASA LSP has not been included at this time, as NASA LSP has historic strong connections to Earth, to GSU's navy. But eventually they will have no choice but to join us. For now, security is our top concern. We have formed a provisional government, as you have intuited. I, with Ofelia's assistance, am at the head. The legal foundation for this association is in draft form. At present it consists of a series of Letters of Understanding, which follows.
>
> Essentially, we have agreed to the following understandings: All people living in space will have equitable elected representation.
>
> - When formally separated from Earth control, a central government shall form that represents the interests of all space societies.
> - Future candidates for head of state shall meet the requirements established by various professional committees. Those requirements are yet to be determined. They shall, however, be amendable to both present and anticipated future needs.

- It has been agreed that until separation and system-wide elections, I will function as the organizing executive, with Ofelia as my council.
- It is the opinion of the organizing parties acting in the formation of a separate governing body that the extra-Earth resources of the solar system are owned in trust by both Earth and space societies in equal part. Space societies shall develop and exploit those resources. Both Earth and space societies shall share these resources in an equitable manner.

Dr. Storm, these are ideas we have agreed to support. Still, they are merely statements of intent. At some point in the future a governing constitution will be created by appropriate lawmakers. We now must operate based on trust and common need. The coming transport of the Ceres habitat to Mars is an example of the power of our cooperation. In the future, resources on Mars will be a great asset to everyone, as will raw materials and capabilities developed at Ceres Station. For the present any needs or concerns expressed by NASA Mars Base, Ceres Station, or the Ellie 5 archipelago will be addressed to Ofelia. Action decisions will only result if all affected parties have representation. Welcome to our little party. —Dr. Virgil Greenly

CHAPTER 9

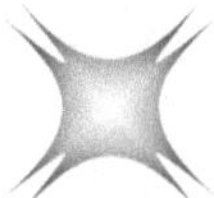

LIFE ON ELLIE 5 ZETA

"The château was something Rhett Blackwood included in the design. He wanted to tempt his wife and daughters to live in the islands . . . . I have no idea what we're going to use it for."

Dr. Virgil Greenly

The *Eternal Hope* arrived at Ellie 5 Zeta on Sunday, June 11, 2248, carrying scientists and engineers eager to board the island. Also waiting were people who were to be the island's first residents, selected from those living on the other space islands at Ellie 5. They all looked forward to touring the entire island, followed by tours of their individual dwellings. But they could not do so immediately, as a final stress test of all systems was underway, led by the team directly involved in the island's construction. The opening ceremony and tours would occur once Daria and Virgil verified the island as safe to occupy.

The enormous island stood as a testament to the construction crew and their skillful use of robots. Though it was the largest island yet constructed, it was completed in record time. It was designated as the flagship of the Ellie 5 archipelago by its architects, engineers, and scientists.

Finally, in the early morning of June twenty-fifth, two weeks after the ship arrived, all those aboard the *Eternal Hope* began boarding Ellie 5 Zeta. They were temporarily assigned rooms in the just-completed Apocatequil Hotel in the Americas Sector, one of the three residential sections of the island. A ceremony was held at the hotel, kept brief at Virgil's request, as neither Virgil nor Daria were comfortable receiving public accolades. Regardless, the two were recognized by the citizens of the archipelago for manifesting the island's early completion. Their work was presented in numerous displays and broadcasts showing details of the design and building of different features of the colony. Huge video screens in public locations throughout the structure displayed the project in its many stages of construction. A video narrated by Daria showed details of the design and construction of the Apocatequil Hotel. Another video displayed how the Amazon tributary replica, once completed, would reflect a small portion of the Amazon Basin as it was 350 years before; Virgil narrated the story of that as yet unfinished Amazon portion.

The hotel and the Mayan Temple Village were the only residential structures that had foundations on the surface in the Americas Sector, which encompassed both Central and South America. The rest of the housing in that section rose above the design height of the forest as it would be when mature. Those apartments were built on stilts above the future tree canopy and were accessible only by the cable-suspended sky trams.

The island was a full twenty kilometers in length, with a diameter of just over two kilometers. The interior of the massive tube was trisected across its diameter. Each of the three sections, together known as the triad, represented a different Earth venue. The dividing walls separated the three venues into approximately equal lengths. The walls were mostly solid, as they were structural elements. Hydroponic crops were integrated into the dividing walls at the approximate one-half standard gravity distance from the axis. Also, spaced along the dividing walls, gravivators transported people and goods to and from the central axis. In that process they also transported people between standard gravity and weightlessness. The central axis was the focal point of the island's mechanical systems, housing all large equipment, power converters, life support systems, fermentation tanks, and the like. Docking ports for spacecraft that connected to other islands and Earth were at the central axis as well, positioned at the ends of the immense cylinder.

Virtual projections on the dividing walls extended the vision off into the apparent distance and continued the theme established within each sector. Thus a reality was created within an elaborate theater set. It was not entirely Earth-like; these environments were intended to be analogs to idealized Earth venues. The first people to arrive from the other islands in the archipelago were conditioned to the inverse curvature presented. But for the engineers and scientists from Mars and arrivals from Earth, the new world required an adjustment in perspective. Eventually the "brain's eye" would reconcile the inverse curvature of the inner surface and recognize it as normal. To survive in space, humanity had to go down this particular "rabbit hole." Using all the knowledge and skills at their disposal, the scientists and engineers, although unable to recreate anything like a duplicate Earth environment, had still managed to build an alternate world that humans would adapt to. In all, the result was a believable Earth-like setting even as it glorified aspects of the past Earth in a utopian manner.

As with the Americas Sector, the two other sections of the triad were constructed representing settings within Earth continents as they had existed in the past. The Asian Sector contained a reproduction of Tianchi Lake and other lakes of the Tian Shan mountain range in

Mt. Tian Shan and Tianchi Lake of Central Asia,
Asian Sector of Ellie 5 Zeta

Northwestern China. The hollow mountains were built up on both sides of the dividing walls with a series of small lakes in between. The base of the mountains contained living quarters, theaters, gyms, restaurants, and shopping areas; the small lakes provided swimming, rowing, fishing, and scuba diving.

The third sector, Vineyard Renaissance, was a combination of two different Earth locales in Europe. One area resembled the French Loire Valley vineyards as they had appeared on Earth almost 300 years before. That bucolic landscape included a scaled-down replica of the Château de Chambord. Built in Chambord Centre-Val de Loire in the early 1500s by King François I and now standing in ruins on Earth, the château was once revered as an example of the enduring elegance of French architecture. The other area of the sector reproduced the rolling hills, vineyards, and olive groves of Tuscany, Italy as they had appeared in the early twenty-first century — however, on Ellie 5 Zeta the "hilltop towns" of Tuscany were shops and restaurants. Residences were set in the valleys, so occupants would live in a standard gravity environment.

After the opening ceremonies at the Apocatequil Hotel, where guides were beginning to organize tours for the first residents and visitors, Virgil and Daria entered a trolley car that traveled between the three sections on the surface through openings in the dividing walls. They stopped in the Vineyard Renaissance section and got out of the trolley in front of the Château de Chambord.

"Let's walk out across the greens to get a better view of the front of the château," Virgil said as he took Daria's hand in his. They strolled across the grounds away from the building until they were some distance from it. As they then turned to look back Daria gave a slight gasp. She had not seen the structure since the landscaping had been completed.

"Apparently, the château was something Rhett Blackwood included in the design," Virgil said. "He wanted to tempt his wife and daughters to live in the islands. It didn't work. I have no idea what we're going to use it for; it seems so impractical. But it is unfinished on the inside, so I suppose we have options."

"Practical or not," Daria replied, "it is absolutely magnificent."

The small version of the Amazon River ecosystem was in the last phase of construction. Projected to be completed within a week, it would appear as it did on Earth in the late nineteenth century. The river flowed the entire length of the sector from "west" to "east." It was flanked on both sides by a rainforest interrupted periodically by small clustered living quarters scattered among treetops. "East-west" travel within the Americas Sector was achieved by the system of gondolas suspended on cables above the forest. A variety of fish and other higher aquatic life formed the apex of the environment in the Amazon River reconstruction. Fish added waste to the water, which fertilized aquatic plant life. Enriched river water was also used in the rainforest, as it was pumped above the forest and released as rain. River water supplemented hydroponic food crops as well. Ecologists had designed the ecosystem to support a large diversity of living things. However, it would take many decades to build a diverse population as had existed in the past Amazon Basin on Earth. Introducing new species as they were found on Earth or modified by genetic engineering was an ongoing project for the biologists.

As the Americas Sector of the triad was the most complete and the only one ready for occupancy, the main events of the opening ceremonies were held there the day following the arrival of the new residents and initial recognition ceremony. There were no speeches or rituals. Instead, everyone gathered on the grounds of the Apocatequil Hotel, named after the Incan god of lightning who had power over water and rain. There they experienced a roaring thunder-and-lightning show, which ended with a light warm spray signifying a drenching rain. After that refreshing "christening" by the pagan god, they were treated to laser-generated virtual fireworks as they played across clouds of mist filling the heights of the chamber. The roar of rapids spoke of a short whitewater tributary that entered the river at the far "western" end. The more adventurous could take to rafts and run the rapids at the river's headwaters. Entertainment included music from popular bands and performances by small theater groups. The performing vignettes were strategically placed throughout the sector. As the day progressed into the late afternoon, cocktail lounges and piano bars opened and remained available into the morning hours. Champagne and hors d'oeuvres were served on the front terrace of the hotel before the new arrivals ascended to the sky trams that would take them to inspect their new living quarters.

Daria and Virgil chose adjoining apartments in the Mayan Temple Village near the "sunrise" end of the cylinder. The two small penthouses were located at the top of the building that was made to resemble an ancient Mayan pyramid. Though the large stones looked and felt authentic, they were engineered and were hollow to reduce their mass. Both units had terraces, each of which looked over their respective sides and down the length of the cylinder toward the daily sunset. In the morning, the other direction gave a sunrise view. In that virtual east direction, a cliff wall rose against the end of the cylinder a short distance away. Waterfalls cascaded down its rocks into a small lake just to the "west" of the Mayan Temple Village. Much of the Amazon tributary section was visible as it wove toward them through the rainforest and flowed into the small lake, to be pumped back to its sources at the ends of the huge cylinder.

The five other islands at Ellie 5 were similar to each other in size and design. All smaller than Ellie 5 Zeta, none were large enough to be trisected as Zeta was. Instead each had been developed to simulate a robust Earth ecology, designed to provide the most optimal conditions to support life in the highest density and with the greatest diversity. Although on Earth there were always fringe ecosystems where living things essentially survived "on the edge," such environments were not templated to the space islands, despite being considered important by evolutionists. Such places test life to its limits. Stressful challenges to living things are proving grounds for natural selection, and organisms with exceptional genetics could evolve in these environments; they could hold secrets that, when discovered, could benefit humanity. Perhaps one day harsh ecosystems would be developed on islands without human occupants. But they would not be attempted in the original space archipelagos.

Biologists created each island to have a unique aspect to its ecosystem. In that way simplified ecosystems completed a more complex system spread within each archipelago. The biologists, under Virgil's supervision, planned to create a diversity of ecosystems within subsequent archipelagos as well. Thus, a vast diversity of living things could be supported. Uniqueness aside, the islands had much in common with one another. For example, bamboo and hemp plants were grown on all islands, as they were a major source of textiles and building materials. Not only were they self-renewing, but they also contributed to environmental resilience. Bamboo was used in many elements of everyday life. In tree houses and other residential buildings, it excelled as structural members, including floors, counter tops, and furniture. Its fibers were also used for clothes, linens, and shoes, to name just a few products. Hemp likewise could be used in lightweight bridges and other construction, as well as in clothing, food, fertilizer, and medicine.

All these ecosystems supported a diversity of living things. Maintaining a huge genetic pool in a created natural world preserved genetic adaptations that had evolved to overcome cataclysmic extinction events on Earth in the far past. Collectively, genetic mutations over the eons had allowed organisms to protect themselves from assault from many quadrants. Preserving these environments and the biological diversity they supported was a top priority of the Space Settlement Program, as Virgil interpreted it. He expended significant effort in maintaining a collection of dynamic genetic information that could be studied and used by scientists in the future. He also developed design concepts for temperate conifer and deciduous representations of forests for future islands when they were constructed.

Virgil was committed to recreating natural environments to the extent technology permitted, and with Daria he was teamed with a talented engineer who was of like mind. They were a perfect match in the reconstruction of a small portion of the Amazon Basin. Working closely with Virgil, Daria became proficient in ecosystem design as well. She appreciated that microbial life is especially valuable. The generation times of microbes are measured in minutes, so mutations are carried forward rapidly. Mutations surviving in microbes are often solutions to environmental stressors. Daria found that many of the higher plants were valuable as well. They lacked mobility to escape predators and a humoral and cellular defense mechanism; however, nature provided solutions, as plants often evolved chemical defense systems. In highly robust ecosystems plants could be a source of pharmaceuticals useful to humans. This library of DNA templates, only partially defined, remained in nature's pharmacopoeia within surviving organisms. Preservation of these things demanded meticulous environmental design in island ecosystems.

Careful ecosystem design, essential for human survival in the hostile conditions of space, also conferred another human benefit. Humankind evolved in natural environments. The emotional and psychological connections to the beauty and elements of nature were as essential to a person's well-being as were the physical survival benefits of the created ecosystems.

Life in the archipelagos was as good as the engineers and scientists could make it. Essentially people lived "outside." Sleeping and other personal activities required privacy, of course. However, since the environments were closely controlled, people spent most of their time in parks and other public areas. Most productive activities were engaged in remotely, as vital information was widely shared between the space islands. Cooking was centralized to reduce air pollution. In addition, there were several buffet-style services and a few higher-end restaurants. The buffet service was provided at no cost; while fine dining restaurants and lounges offered service for a fee. There, one had access to specialty foods and spirits from Earth, NASA Mars Base, and NASA LSP.

Basic needs were always met for clothing, meal service, education, parks, gyms, theater, enrichment classes, and other recreational endeavors. However, there were plenty of extra benefits that could be obtained using one's earned credits. In addition to fine dining, all the cocktail lounges, imported liquor, live theater, and travel to other islands cost credits. Each island boasted at least one natural-habitat-themed park and other unique features that enticed guests from other islands within an archipelago to holiday at their island. Intra-island spaceships traveled regularly over the short distance between the space islands of the Ellie 5 archipelago.

The completion of Ellie 5 Zeta had been long anticipated on Earth, as many people with occupancy reservations had been waiting to be assigned a launch rocket that would bring them there. The space island's opening, however, set off a chain of events on Earth that had not been anticipated.

CHAPTER 10

WELCOME, EARTHLINGS

"Our food is incomparable. Look at the beautiful presentation. Enjoy the bountiful flavors. Don't ask what it is. Just take it at taste value."

Frankie Bitterman

At the five other space islands of the Ellie 5 archipelago the excitement surrounding the newly opened Zeta Island was intense. It was even greater on Earth. There, launch vehicles were made ready for people who had long since passed prequalification screening and paid large fees. They had waited years for a reserved seat and now rushed to prepare for Earth departure and the trip to their new home. The fortunate few would soon gather for emigration to this newest and largest of the space islands. Zeta's new residents, including staff who had already moved there from the other Ellie 5 islands, were excited as well; they planned an ambitious series of celebrations to occur over the next two months as people from Earth arrived and moved into their living quarters.

Under the leadership of Ali Ebrahim, the GSU government had early built nine spaceports in various locations on Earth specifically for launch of the ships that would carry settlers to Ellie 5. Each spaceship could carry from twenty-six to forty-five passengers. Optimal launch locations were those closest to the Equator. However, there were frequent climate and weather events that interfered with launches from those spaceports.

Spaceports that were located near populations not firmly under the control of the GSU were not only at risk of severe weather; political instability was a security risk as well. Three launch spaceports in particular — Gibraltar UK, São Paulo Brazil, and Hainan Island China — were difficult to secure. Demonstrations and rioting frequently occurred at those locations, especially as launch dates approached. Marauding gangs and paramilitary groups often attempted to breach security lines prior to scheduled launches. Hardcore militia groups were frequently enhanced by crowds of protesters made up mainly of people living near these areas, who were generally not happy with the launches. The perception among the local populations was that the rich were abandoning Earth for a utopian life in space. That perception was not without merit. There was great opportunity in space — but as a Garden of Eden or utopia? Far from it. Still, as a result of potential violence, authorities did not publicize launches; when possible, they occurred during the night.

The first launches began on July 1, 2248. Arrivals at Ellie 5 Zeta began four days later and continued nearly every day for the next two weeks. In all, 306 settlers arrived during this first wave of launches. The spaceships docked at the ports on both ends of the island. After the passengers disembarked, Simone Beaulieu's rocket engineers prepared the ships for Earth reentry. Electronic hardware and small appliances that were manufactured at Ellie 5 were loaded, along with any passengers returning to Earth.

New arrivals from Earth included many entire families. They were first escorted to the Apocatequil Hotel in the Americas Sector, where the voices of small children soon filled the common areas. They stayed there for a week of orientation meetings while robotic housekeepers prepared their dwellings. Since Earth arrivals were new to space living it was important they learned the intricacies of their island ecology, how to interface with it, and their role in protecting it.

Because each island was a closed ecology, and therefore delicate, they were susceptible to disruption. Even small anomalies could threaten ecosystem balance. Disaster could follow. Environmental scientists developed protocols for monitoring life diversity using tools such as DNA monitoring of different components of the biosystem. Engineers installed numerous sensors to provide real-time information. They also developed AI-assisted analysis to help identify the cause of any malfunction and determine a solution. Thus the relationship between cause and effect, especially with environmental systems, was much easier to establish than ever had been possible on Earth. Compliance was knowledge-driven and voluntarily accepted because the consequences of non-compliance could result in disaster for all. These ideas were emphasized in the schools that had recently opened in Zeta Island.

The welcoming and orientation staff were tasked with providing a smooth transition. Living in space is quite different from living on Earth. The first thing new arrivals became aware of was the uniqueness of people's attire. All fabrics, from clothing to bedding, were made from local sources, mainly hemp and bamboo. The colors and styles were of local design and were quite distinctive from clothes available on Earth. New arrivals from Earth generally wanted new clothes and fabrics as soon as possible. Until they dressed like locals they stood out as foreigners from Earth.

The second thing that struck arrivals from Earth occurred when they entered the grand atrium of the Americas Sector of Ellie 5 Zeta, their receiving venue. An expansive vista encompassing several kilometers of river surrounded by still immature jungle growth opened before them. Throughout were tree houses made of bamboo, and various buildings replicating those of the ancient Incan culture. However, some found the inverse curvature of the ground unsettling. It was as if they had entered a gigantic cave. In a sense they had.

The biggest surprise expressed by first-time space citizens concerned individual living space. Without exception, the Earth arrivals to Ellie 5 Zeta were highly affluent, many accustomed to mansions and yachts. Their new accommodations were much smaller than they were used to. The hotel and most of the residential structures were overtly designed for privacy. The new residents found security was present, but officers were (ostensibly) unarmed; no arms of any kind were allowed on the islands and all arrivals were thoroughly screened.

Of course, ego-fueled ownership of such things as mega-mansions, personal aircraft, and yachts was not a possibility on Zeta as it had been for some on Earth. Nor were large-acreage plots of land upon which people could establish personal estates. The new arrivals quickly discovered that status was only achieved by their value to their new society; if their actions helped the community, they'd enjoy recognition for it. On Ellie 5 Zeta, as on other islands, they would gain by what they gave.

Some arrivals from Earth would find adjustment to this new reality challenging. A few people would eventually choose to return to Earth, having found the differences between space island living and Earth living more extreme than they had imagined. But most were quick to embrace the possibilities implicit in their new life. They had come to be part of the Space Settlement generation.

Public service robots were another new concept for arriving Earthlings. Although personal robots were common among the affluent on Earth, there were few public service robots on the planet. Here these robots were commonplace. They could be found doing ground maintenance, servicing the fermentation tanks, producing and preparing food, monitoring the ecology of "natural" water features, and performing staffing and housekeeping functions in the Apocatequil Hotel. These robots also functioned in harvesting naturally sourced seafood or poultry that could be presented as rare treats. Most protein foods were constructed from isolates from microbial fermentation tanks. Meat products such as lamb, pork, beef, and goat were available from in vitro cultures of animal tissue. Processed insects were used in many different snack foods, such as energy bars, chips, crackers, and candy. Restaurant service was staffed by knowledgeable humans who were trained in both food science and the culinary arts. Among them was Dining Consultant Frankie Bitterman, who greeted the new arrivals from Earth with his favorite announcement: "Our food is incomparable. Look at the beautiful presentation. Enjoy the bountiful flavors. Don't ask what it is. Just take it at taste value."

The uninitiated quickly learned not to ask about the source or content of any food.

Entertainment and educational events were plentiful on all space islands at Ellie 5. One could easily travel to different islands within the Ellie 5 archipelago on local spaceships. As the space islands were designed to replicate different Earth venues, exploration of them allowed an expanded experience and some necessary relief from the limited variety on each island. Except for some staged productions, there were no storms, floods, earthquakes, landslides, or forest fires. Protection from weather was not a concern because the environment was controlled, and the population was sequestered in the enclosed island. Wars, traffic jams, starving or homeless people — these were non-existent. It was easy for one newly arrived to believe they had found Utopia.

Space is not Utopia, however; there is always the possibility of a catastrophic event.

Everything outside the space islands is hostile to life. Cosmic rays generated by the Sun and from extra-solar sources were a continuing risk. The electrically powered magnetosphere surrounding each island helped to protect the occupants. The space surrounding the island archipelago was continuously surveyed for potential hazards.

Tiny high-speed objects could pierce the shell of an island, but these breaches were automatically sealed. However, if one pierced a vital electronic component, it could cause significant damage. Larger objects on a collision course were diverted by laser impact or, if too large, robotic motors would attach and attempt to change their trajectory. In the unlikely chance a cataclysmic depressurization occurred, isolation shelters would quickly open to allow entry, then close and repressurize to protect human life.

The Manufacturing, Assembly, and Construction facility — Ellie 5 MAC — and its attendant robots could repair most damage and failure. In a serious damage scenario people could be evacuated to another island. Daria Aquila and her engineers developed the survival robustness of this first archipelago. They intended it to be a design concept that could be carried out into the far future. Tremendous resources went into the construction of a space island. If the foundational structures were sufficiently sound new technologies could be added over the coming centuries.

Daria emphasized the durability of space colonies in all her orientation lectures to new arrivals. When people understood the permanence of their home in space, they had new hope for their long-term survival and that of their progeny. Both present and future space islands would provide new adventures and opportunities for their children and generations to come. Potential space for an expanding human population as well as habitats for other species could be designed and built almost without limit. Perhaps mass extinctions would no longer happen; some islands could be constructed simply to provide natural habitats where environments without human interference were possible. It was this potential of the almost limitless resources within the solar system that drove some of the most creative and committed Earthlings into space, as Virgil, Daria, and the other leaders of Ellie 5 discovered.

On Sunday, July thirtieth, Virgil and Daria had breakfast delivered to their shared terrace at the Mayan Temple Village residence.

"It's been a helluva week," Virgil said, reaching for a muffin. "This is a nice break from nonstop presentations. I took the liberty of using my authority to request a cloud-filtered sunrise this morning."

"I don't think anyone will mind," Daria said. "I sure don't; the colors are beautiful."

"There is some satisfaction in giving the presentations, however," Virgil continued. "New arrivals from Earth can hardly contain their enthusiasm."

"They are appreciative. Some things about life within a space island really surprise them, don't they? We anticipated and addressed most things that are different here from Earth. For example, our complete prohibition of fire, including any open flame as well as even the potential for a spark. My concern is that they are so excited, they might not take in the seriousness of the rules at first. We should monitor that."

"Yeah, the family barbeque is definitely out. This new frontier is not the 'American Wild West' as it once was. When you think about it, it's ironic that a major driver of human evolution is prohibited in these technologically advanced times."

"Interesting point. Fire was so important in the development of technology throughout human history. Almost all of it would not be possible without fire," Daria said. "Mmmm, that muffin sure looks good . . ."

Virgil absently broke his muffin and placed the larger piece on Daria's plate.

"Smelting metals would not be possible," he observed, caught up in the discussion. "At some point I believe all technologies rely on purified metals."

"What about biological evolution? The control of fire had an impact on our evolution too in some ways, right?"

"Lots of ways . . . being able to cook food reduced disease, increased caloric value, and enhanced food storage life. The added caloric availability and food security supported the evolution and growth of a larger brain and smaller gut. And . . . that allowed a better posture for running. Because of the smaller gut, more energy storage was available to our large muscles . . . which translated to more endurance chasing down prey on the hunt." Virgil was on a roll, warming to the subject as he went along. "And increased intelligence allowed development of weapons and team strategies, which also made the hunt more successful. Humanoids without these attributes didn't stand a chance against our ancestors. We outcompeted our contemporaries."

"That sounds brutal."

"Not necessarily. We were just better fit for our environment."

"And yet, here we are — fearful of this very thing so important in our ascension," Daria said.

"I know. Fire could extinguish all life in a space island. So we do our smelting and all toxic manufacturing activities in isolation, outside our biological systems . . . You're having potato salad for breakfast?"

"It has real egg in it."

Launches of the second wave of settlers from Earth to Ellie 5 Zeta had begun on July 28, 2248, the first launch of that wave being from Hilo Hawai'i Spaceport. However, despite the increasingly inspirational aspects of the Space Settlement Program, launches from all spaceports to Ellie 5 Zeta were abruptly canceled just a few days later; the last new arrivals reached the space island on August third.

On July thirty-first all passengers and crew were on board a spaceship that had been readied for launch at Gibraltar. The countdown started. Suddenly a missile struck, from seemingly out of nowhere, destroying the rocket, the connected spaceship, the launch pad, and all supporting infrastructure. All twenty-five people on board the spaceship and thirty-seven ground support personnel met their fiery destiny that day.

Attack on Gibraltar Spaceport

A naval carrier group stationed in the western Mediterranean scrambled fighters, having traced the missile's heat trail to its source somewhere near Algeria. A small outpost on the border between Morocco and Algeria, long recognized as a haven and operations base for terrorists, was quickly reduced to a black smudge. But the death and damage done at the spaceport was not the most significant of the disaster. The entire Space Settlement Program was at risk and the effectiveness of GSU questioned. The tragedy reminded everyone living off-planet of a major objective of the program, whose mission was to develop a space-faring society that could assist in Earth's reemergence, a society where such acts of violence did not occur.

In an ironic twist, the lull in arrivals due to the attack at Gibraltar afforded a longer time for incoming citizens on Zeta to adjust and staff more time to assist them; thus enhancing a smooth social transition. By November the island settlers were beginning to offer their individual skills to supplement engineering and science teams. The new arrivals also included university professors, chefs, visual and performing artists, and many others possessing the various skills and talents needed for a robust society.

Virgil and Daria had separate roles in this process, Virgil personally monitoring and adjusting environmental systems and Daria checking and reenforcing critical structural stress points. Both were very pleased with how smoothly Zeta Island was becoming a society whose members were knowledgeable on so many fronts. Even so, because of the complexity of the island's infrastructure, close monitoring of all mechanical and biological systems was necessary. To that end, Ofelia established a ubiquitous yet invisible presence through all manner of sensory input devices by which she could monitor and track the movements and actions of the island's citizens.

Of course, most inhabitants would not be comfortable knowing they were being observed and recorded at nearly any place or time. Awareness of such a presence was limited to a close circle of Virgil's associates. By this time Ofelia was the most knowledgeable and powerful entity in the solar system. And with Ofelia's assets came vast ability. In most cases she could detect problems and immediately alert Virgil directly, or Daria via electronic communicator, before an anomaly triggered standard alarms or created harm. The advantages of such capabilities were weighed against any negatives that could be ascribed to the inhabitants' concerns about "Big Brother" watching. Safety won out over privacy.

CHAPTER 11

A CONSPIRACY FORMS

"Go ahead and complete the move, Henry. I can't imagine I will be long. It's just a routine exit medical exam."

Ali Ebrahim

The July 31, 2248 destruction of the Gibraltar Space Launch Port created political turmoil throughout the Global States United. It was especially virulent in Parliament at Reykjavík. Blame and recriminations were directed at Secretary General Ali Ebrahim and members of his government. Draco Osborne couldn't have been happier. On August twelfth a coalition in Parliament, led by Osborne, confronted the government with its failure, marshaled supporters, and deposed Ali Ebrahim in a bloodless coup. Osborne quickly formed a new government, and, within days, a hastily conducted election brought him to power as secretary general. Soon he had cemented draconian control over the GSU. However, Ebrahim still had a strong and powerful following. For his safety, this was not a good thing; because of his popularity within Parliament and the extent of his public support, Osborne rightfully continued to see Ali Ebrahim as a threat.

A few weeks after Draco Osborne's election, Ebrahim's personal sentient implant, Anni, warned him of discussions she had recorded that implied his life was at risk. Osborne was long experienced at consolidating collaborative units from various criminal enterprises with one simple action: opposition challengers often fell out of a window, slipped into a river, or simply expired while sitting on a park bench. Those who merely disappeared were never heard from again. Anni was Ali's best defense. She tracked Osborne's communications and kept Ali informed of his activities.

On September sixth Anni warned Ali that Osborne planned to go further than having him expelled completely from Parliament; he planned to arrest him immediately. Moving from the secretary general's offices was underway, but before Ali could complete the task of vacating the space a security detail met him at the door. A sergeant, surrounded by five guards in dress uniforms, stiffly saluted Ali then addressed him.

"Sir, you are required to report to the Parliament medical facility. You will not be harmed and soon will be free to leave, but first there is a small detail that needs attending to. Your staff may continue packing and removing your belongings. We are here to escort you. Please come along with us."

Ali's office manager stood beside him, holding a box of his personal things.

"Go ahead and complete the move, Henry. I can't imagine I will be long. It's just a routine exit medical exam," Ali said, outwardly reassuring. Inside, though, he knew he would not be back to help Henry.

By cunning and intimidation Draco Osborne had created a structure, both military and political, whereby he took direct control of the massive Arctic and Antarctic Fleets. Nathan Flint, Admiral of the Arctic Fleet, refused to pledge loyalty to Osborne and was discharged from his duties. Summoning his most loyal subordinates, Flint commandeered a destroyer and using stealth procedures they retreated to Australia. There were immediate resignations and defections of officers and enlisted alike within both the Arctic and Antarctic fleets. Other defectors soon followed, including four captains who brought their ships and crews. Admiral Flint began to collect a small fleet, which anchored near Perth. Australia was quasi-independent of the GSU government and had its own air force; the country pledged to give the admiral air cover should he need it. With the Australian Air Force's protective screen, the admiral's small fleet was relatively safe from the Antarctic Fleet, at least for the moment.

Admiral Flint was joined on September sixteenth by Ali Ebrahim, who had used a series of small civilian aircraft to travel south. He had just recovered from minor surgery. Under orders from Osborne, doctors had removed Anni's interface plate from Ali's skull. Anni had anticipated the surgery and had taken measures to disperse her memory and cognitive functions across the electronic universe. Even so, Osborne's technicians succeeded in finding and immediately deleting several of Anni's critical files.

Ali's travels ended with a small boat ride from Port Hedland in Western Australia to Admiral Flint's flagship destroyer, *Thunderclap*. He was exhausted and so was immediately escorted to quarters without meeting with the admiral. Late the next morning, Ali was led to the admiral's private dining room. Admiral Flint had long since eaten, but had a steward bring breakfast for the former secretary general. Ali took a few swallows of coffee and a bite of sausage before engaging in conversation.

"I'm sorry for being so rude, Nate. I guess it's from the stress of the last couple days. Well, damn — I'm just starving!"

"Completely understood, Ali. There's no rush. I take it you had a rough journey?"

"Indeed! I'm not accustomed to traveling 'trash class.' That is, little food, no sleep, always concerned that landing safely is optional."

"You're here now, my friend. It's not first class, but at least recuperation is the order of the day. Speaking of that, what's with the head wound?"

"A sad tale, Nate. Anni is gone."

"Anni, your sentient implant?" Admiral Flint asked.

"Yes, she was taken when I needed her the most. I'm sure they deleted her essence. Frankly the process left me with a throbbing head and . . . a bit disoriented . . . . I've never felt more confused and helpless."

"You'll adjust, Ali. We have resources here in the navy . . . my navy. I can supply you with our current intelligence. Among those who chose to remain in Osborne's navy, many have become important informants."

"I appreciate that, my friend. Trust is a rare commodity in these times. It's great to have your support."

"You took a bit of time to get here. Were you delayed somewhere?"

"Yes, about that. I made a short stop in Mexico City. It seems my nemesis Draco arranged to have a tracking device installed at the spot where Anni's interphase implant had been."

"So, you had it removed?"

"Of course. I couldn't knowingly lead Draco's goons to you . . . Damn! Now the throbbing has returned. Do you think the ship's doctor might have something for pain?"

Two days later Admiral Flint provided the services of a helicopter and Ali flew to Sydney to meet with the governor of Australia, the Honorable Fredrik Johnson. He landed at Sydney Airport in the morning, where he was met by a car and driver. An hour later he arrived at a private dock deep in the bay near the Blue Mountains. There he boarded a small launch that meandered along the southern bank before speeding north across the bay to a fantail sailing yacht anchored there. He was given a hand boarding, by Governor Johnson.

"Welcome aboard, Secretary General," the governor said.

"Please, Governor, I'm a private citizen now and a fugitive at that. Just call me Ali . . . I do appreciate your taking a risk to meet with me."

"I have been a longtime admirer, Ali. Yes, let's drop the formalities. I'm comfortable being 'Fred' with my friends . . . The risk, yes, I believe it to be small. I have shut down all communication and location devices. I use my yacht for sensitive meetings."

"If I'm not being too brash, Fred, are these 'sensitive meetings' of a political or personal nature?"

"Yes," Johnson said, meeting his guest's off-the-cuff joshing with a wink and a non-answer. "I know it's early, but I sense we're off to a good start. Would you care for a brandy, Ali? I have a very old Philbert Rare Cask Sherry Finish that I haven't opened."

"Please . . . save it for a special occasion."

"Ah, but I believe this to be such an occasion, mate."

"We are of like minds then, my friend. I would love some."

Ali and Governor Johnson continued their discussions for two more days, during which Ali also rested and recuperated from his head surgeries. Before he was returned to the airport, where a helicopter waited to ferry him to the *Thunderclap,* Governor Johnson came into his cabin as Ali was packing his things.

"I have a small parting gift for you. I don't know when we will meet again, and I'd like to share something with you. I hope it will give you pause for reflection on our meetings these last couple of days."

With that the governor opened a storage compartment and withdrew a case of Shotfire Shiraz, carrying it himself as they proceeded to the launch tied along the starboard side. Ali climbed aboard and the governor handed him the case. As soon as both were secure aboard, the launch brought Ali back to the dock, where a car and driver waited to take him to the airport.

It was late evening when the helicopter set down on the deck of the *Thunderclap.* The admiral had retired, so Ali went straight to his quarters. The next morning, he awoke and looked out the porthole to see the ship was underway.

Later Admiral Flint and Ali had lunch on the admiral's private deck just off his command post.

"You look better, Ali—more relaxed and less stressed. Would you like a little white wine? It complements roasted goose quite well. You may think it's a bit pedestrian, I'm afraid. I find it quite tolerable, however."

"Pour away," Ali replied as he offered his glass. "An unpretentious wine is entirely proper between friends." As the steward served the appetizer course, he described it to the two men.

"Chilled marinated and spiced figs, sir . . . and . . . Your Honor."

"You'll love this," Admiral Flint boasted. "And there will be cranberry chutney served with the goose."

"You travel well, Nate . . . . Speaking of which; I noticed we are underway. Where are we going?"

"I'm dispersing my small fleet along the Indonesian Archipelago. I've received information that Osborne is preparing his Arctic Fleet for some kind of movement. How do you read Governor Johnson? Will he commit to supporting us?"

Ali finished the fig in his mouth and swallowed. "By god, those are good!" He cleared his throat with a sip of wine. "The best I could get out of the governor was that his air force will never attack us. I believe him. He is understandably concerned about his vulnerability to the Antarctic Fleet should he take any action."

"I certainly understand that. I do appreciate your help, Ali. I need to meet with Vice Admiral Aisling Murphy. That could be a bit of a challenge. I did not vote for her promotion a couple years ago when the position in the Antarctic Fleet became available."

"And I need to get back to Reykjavík," Ali said.

"Isn't that a little dangerous?"

The steward arrived with the main course: thin-sliced roast goose tied in rolls around cranberry chutney, chopped apple, and a hint of rhubarb.

"It is risky, and necessary. A revolution requires players on all fronts." Ali sliced off a bite of his roast goose. "Nate! This meal is terrific! You really do travel well."

"The perks are small compensation, considering the perils," the Admiral replied.

"Ah yes, but necessary for one's sanity. I want to give you a case of Shotfire Shiraz that Govenor Johnson gave me. It would be cumbersome for me to travel with on my next endeavors."

After concluding his business with Admiral Flint, Ali Ebrahim began a covert journey back to Reykjavík. It required even more time and convolutions than had his trip to Australia. He arrived in Reykjavík after completing six different legs, all of which were under one of three false passports. He arrived seven days after leaving Admiral Flint and took up residence in a small house on the shores of an obscure bay northwest of the GSU capital. His movements had been so well hidden that few people, even those in Parliament, realized he had ever even left Iceland. He seemed to have dropped from sight, but working in obscurity he effectively rallied the developing resistance in support of Admiral Flint.

Over the next few months, Ebrahim secured defecting officers and enlisted personnel from within the Arctic Fleet. He organized a network of stealth submarines and small private aircraft to shepherd defectors to Admiral Flint. Through his efforts, the officers and crew of six more ships defected from the Arctic Fleet and joined the admiral at Perth. Governor Johnson had connections with four sympathetic ship captains in the Antarctic Fleet and was instrumental in the defection of the rogue captains with their ships and crews. To escape the Antarctic Fleet and join with Admiral Flint's fleet they converged in the seas west of Australia. There they awaited boarding and inspection by a team under Admiral Flint. The growing strength of Admiral Flint's Fleet was not lost on Governor Fredrik Johnson.

CHAPTER 12

ESCAPE

"More serious?
You've already scared the shit out of us."

Rhett Blackwood

On October ninth, Rhett Blackwood and his eldest daughter Jules returned to their home in Nuuk from a fishing trip spent on the northern shores of Greenland. They brought with them a char they had caught and smoked on a rocky beach. The next morning the family sat for a reunion breakfast of that smoked char accompanied by crusty rye bread, oatmeal with cream and berries, strong black coffee, and a shot of cod-liver oil. Jules had made heart-shaped waffles, which she served with shaved curls of brunost cheese. This was the proper way to begin the day in the Blackwood family.

But the peace of this traditional family gathering did not last. Shortly after breakfast Rhett received a direct call from Ali Ebrahim on his com device.

"Ali, it's great to hear from you! You've been quiet for a long time. I'm surprised you're calling directly and not secured through Anni."

"Ahh, Rhett, my son. Have you not heard of the election in Parliament? And Draco Osborne's corrupt consolidation of power?"

"Yeah, about the election. I heard but I tried to forget it. Jules and I have been on an extended fishing trip. We fished from a charter boat that took us to some beautiful spots along Baffin Bay. It was a nice distraction — if only it had been longer. So, back to a disastrous political reality, I guess," Rhett said, realizing Ali was not simply checking in to be friendly.

"It gets worse, I'm afraid." Ali got straight to the point. "When I left Parliament, they removed my implant and brain bots. Anni is gone. They're on a campaign to remove them from everyone who has one. Draco's government considers anyone with an implanted sentient as dangerous. You know, with all that access to stores of information and increased cognitive power. Sentient implants have proven to be excellent advisors too. So, they're a threat to authoritarian government."

"Yes, how can any dictator possibly rule if people can outthink them?" Rhett hid none of his sarcasm.

"Well, I envy you your fishing vacation," Ali said. "How is Jules by the way? It's been more than a year since I last saw your kids, I believe."

"Oh, she's a bright one. She's been reading books on astrophysics. Hopes to enroll in university next fall."

"Indeed! I always thought she had her head above the clouds," Ali chuckled.

"Most teenagers have minds that float in the void, and Jules is no exception," Rhett said. "But of late, she is quite a serious and committed young lady and I'm always proud of her."

"Nice try, Dad, but I heard what you said," Jules called from across the room. Rhett smiled at his daughter's teasing and blew her a kiss.

"Listen, Rhett — why I called," Ali said. "I've been hiding out in various places. My staff still helps with my security and travels with me incognito. I'm now moving about in secret and have a sound network of security and espionage experts. My informants within Parliament and the Navy fleets have indicated there's a dangerous movement within Draco's government. Seems I'm a target not just for arrest, but for assassination."

"Ali! I had no idea it was that bad. Give me a minute to secure this conversation before we continue." Rhett excused himself from his family and went to his office, where he locked the door and switched to an encrypted setting. "OK, we're secure from this end. Where are you and are you safe?"

"Safe for the present, my friend. I'm in a small boat with my wife and a few members of key staff. We've shut down all electronics save for this communication. We're running dark to a Navy corvette that will facilitate our escape." Ali paused to let Rhett digest the implications.

"I have tickets for a long vacation for you and your family, my son," he continued.

"Vacation?" Rhett knew that wasn't what Ali meant but feared the real message.

"Escape is a better word. But you will come to think of it as a vacation," Ali said. He paused, then added, "This isn't an option, son. You, Koral, Jules, and Chanté are all in danger. I'm speaking assassination, my friend. You have great influence in the Space Settlement Program and Osborne knows it. And you have worked closely with me. You have knowledge and influence and that is a threat to him and his goons."

"How long do we have?"

"The corvette leaves when I arrive. It will also be running dark. I'd send you the coordinates, but I can't be sure my line is entirely secure. They'll be sent to your pilot when you are in the air."

"In the air, sir?"

"Yes! A helicopter is waiting for you and your family. I can't reveal its location to you. However, I have transportation arriving at your house in about twenty minutes. You each are allowed fifty pounds of luggage. And now I must sign off. Take care, my son." Ali ended the call abruptly.

When Rhett walked out of his office, he found Koral standing nearby, her face drained of all color. "I heard your conversation with Ali on my unit," she said, her voice faltering. Rhett stopped and drew his wife to him in a firm hug.

"We'd better tell the girls to get packing," he said.

The family stepped outside their home as their transportation arrived. They loaded the only Earth belongings they would ever see again. Rhett noticed neither of his daughters had brought anything except a small hiking backpack.

"Is that all you girls are taking?" he said. "You know that we are not coming back. Ali didn't say it, but I suspect we're going off-planet. If that's the case, we're going to live within the space islands. We may never return."

Koral looked at her husband, seeming now to fully understand their fate. A flash of fear passed over her face. It was tenuous, however, and she set a resolute jaw and focused her attention on her daughters.

"But even if we did return," the youngest, Chanté, said, "our clothes would be old. I think the space islands will be our new home. We want to get new space clothes and make new friends!" She seemed to accept the whole idea with the enthusiasm of any sixteen-year-old on a new adventure.

"Our new life is going to be a challenge," Jules said, "and maybe it's a little scary too. But it will be exciting. I've thought about this before and I see wonderful future possibilities. We talked about it while we were packing. We both want to go there, wear clothes grown and made in space, and eat space food. Space islands are the future — our future."

Rhett stared at Jules and realized she had matured into a thoughtful young woman. "You girls will forever fulfill my dreams," he said quietly, trying to keep his voice steady. He cleared his throat. "Uh, then, what did you both bring?"

"I brought my digital library, view screen, and holographic projector, along with connections for data stores. Also, high security connection addresses to the GSU central library," Jules replied. "I've had those for a while, a gift from Ali. Oh, and two days' worth of clothes."

"Yeah, I brought pretty much the same thing," Chanté said. "Daddy, do they have a university on the islands?" Rhett looked at his wife, who was now smiling. They were going to be fine.

"No formal university, but there are lectures from various professionals. Lots of topics. They are shared among the islands of Ellie 5, Ceres Station, NASA LSP, and NASA Mars Base," Rhett answered.

"Are they accredited?" Chanté asked.

"Accredited? No, at least, not yet. Lectures are given by leading scientists and engineers. They're better than anything Earth has to offer," Rhett said.

"Then I want to organize and assemble a university. We need a prestigious name and an appropriate logo. I think I'll work on that," Chanté said.

"That's very commendable, dear, but why the sudden enthusiasm?"

"Listen, Daddy, if I'm going to put in the work and study time, I should get a degree from an awesome university with a prestigious name. I mean, otherwise, what's the point?"

Jules laughed. "And there it is, my sister's altruistic motivation."

It was just about half past noon when the Blackwood family boarded the helicopter waiting at a small landing pad not far from the local airport. After a quick flight, the aircraft landed on the heliport at the aft end of the Navy corvette *Swordthruster*, which had been outfitted with increased defensive weapons and an offensive pulse laser cannon. It also had a full complement of stealth technologies.

The Blackwoods were taken to their staterooms; Ali and his entourage of eight were already aboard. The ship weighed anchor and headed across the Arctic Sea toward the Bering Strait. After they were well underway Ali came to Rhett and Koral's stateroom.

"We need to have an orientation conference," he said. "Our situation is more serious than I've led you to believe."

"More serious?? You've already scared the shit out of us," Rhett replied.

"It's this," Ali said. "Eight of my assistants and I, and the four of you, are the only passengers on this ship. We all have been barred from leaving the planet. I have been informed through my sources that Draco Osborne's government is working on bringing charges against me and many of my supporters."

"Charges? What charges? On what grounds?" Rhett asked.

"You know me well, son. You know as well as I do that they have no cause. But Osborne has consolidated his power and, assuming I survive assassination, he can dream up whatever charges he wants. Meanwhile, the manifests of all spaceships with scheduled launches are being inspected. Biometric cameras are monitoring all personnel loading onto these ships."

"So that rules out an escape to the space islands," Rhett said. "I understand — we are now fugitives from the government. Here we are, all together heading for a launch where we can easily be discovered and arrested. How can we be safe? Where are we going, Ali?" Koral sat next to her husband in silence.

"Ahh, my friend, that is but the least of our worries. The odds are almost certain this ship will be boarded and inspected at some point on our journey. With division of loyalties evident, suspicion is prevalent within the Navy. Virtually all moving ships are inspected."

"That sounds reassuring. Our destination, Ali?"

Ali continued without answering.

"So, to avoid attracting undue attention as a moving ship, we will port during the day and travel only during the shortened Arctic night under full stealth mode. That is, while we are within the Arctic Circle."

Rhett persisted. "And beyond the Arctic Circle?"

"In due time, my son. In due time."

After spending long days under electronic silence in military ports and then moving along the northern coast of the State of Canada during the nights, the *Swordthruster* rounded Alaska and entered the Bering Strait. As Koral and her daughters had packed books during their sudden departure from their home, they had a means of passing the time. But Rhett had no such outlet and paced the decks relentlessly until Ali called him to a meeting with the ship's captain. Captain Rodrigo Austin entered the small secure conference room near the bridge shortly after Rhett and Ali were seated. He wore his uniform hat at a jaunty angle that complemented a flaming red beard. With a brief nod to Ali, he extended his hand to Rhett. Introductions were exchanged and the captain sat across from Ali and Rhett.

"This is the most dangerous segment of the journey, my friends," Ali said. "We cannot allow ourselves to be boarded before we arrive at our station on Amchitka Island in the Aleutians. We will be traveling at our maximum speed of 35 knots while in full electronic stealth mode."

"And if we *are* boarded at Amchitka?" Rhett inquired.

Captain Austin answered. "Ali and his personnel, your family, and any of the crew who might feel at risk will be taken to an underground bunker as soon as we dock. You will not be returning to the ship."

"Underground bunker . . . hmm. I'll tell Koral the five-star accommodations were all booked up. She won't think much of your travel planning, Ali," Rhett quipped, easing the tension in the room a bit. "OK," he continued, "we're in the bunker. What happens from there?"

"When the time is right, we will be taken at night on small rubber rafts to the *Seashark*, a submarine waiting offshore," Ali explained. "After we board, we will deflate our rafts and take them below with us. The rest of the trip will be underwater in the depths of the Pacific until we reach the Kona Coast of Hawai'i west of Mauna Kea. The *Swordthruster* will sail directly to Hilo and anchor offshore, per command orders from the admiralty of the Arctic Fleet."

"So, the *Swordthruster* will be at Hilo well before we arrive at the Kona Coast," Rhett said.

"It's critical that it is," Captain Austin confirmed. "The *Swordthruster* will be your protective screen."

"What happens at Hilo?"

"I managed to get seats for all of us on a spaceship scheduled to leave for Ellie 5 Zeta — but it's not at Hilo," Ali answered.

"How is that possible if we're not launching from Hilo? And we've been barred from launch, haven't we?"

"Details," Ali said. "The devil is in the details, as they say, my son. If the details are discovered, the devil will be very unfriendly. You'll be fully apprised when it is appropriate — and safe."

Twenty-four days after Rhett and his family left their home in Greenland the submarine carrying them, along with Ali and several other fugitives, arrived off the western coast of Hawai'i. After the twelve boring days spent essentially in lockdown on the *Swordthruster,* they had spent the next twelve days on the submarine separated and spread out between several common areas. The nights were worse, as they were forced to try and sleep in cramped auxiliary beds that were stowed in among plumbing chases and storage areas. At last the sub surfaced at night off the coast of Kiholo Bay. The passengers were allowed on deck but without their main luggage, much to Koral's consternation. There they waited while the rubber rafts were brought above and inflated.

"Sorry about the luggage, everyone," Ali said. "Some of the larger bags were too heavy and cannot go with us. We've had to take on additional passengers, so we must compensate for the added weight that will be on the spaceship. Your belongings are sure to be put to good use in Australia, the *Seashark*'s next destination. I trust you packed all your essentials in your smaller bags." The Blackwood sisters nodded at each other, feeling a little smug. Since they had only packed small bags anyway, they were not affected by the loss of luggage, unlike their parents and some of Ali's staff.

Rhett's curiosity about the "additional passengers" Ali mentioned was quickly overshadowed by the immediate necessity of helping his family into a raft. As soon as the entire party had boarded the rafts, the submarine slipped beneath the waves and disappeared, leaving them on the surface of the ocean in silence on a moonless night. Small electric motors on the rafts then began moving them quietly toward the shore, where they anchored just off a black lava beach in Kiholo Bay. Once everyone had waded ashore, the autopilots controlling the rubber boat motors drove the rafts out to sea.

On the beach Ali assembled the Blackwoods and his own small entourage in a depression surrounded by volcanic rock outcroppings.

"You might be wondering about the rafts," Ali began. "They will disperse themselves in the vast Pacific, where they will auto-deflate and sink. They will never be associated with any landing in Kiholo. Until this point," he continued, "I haven't offered you folks much information. When I have, it's been on a need-to-know basis. I did that for your protection and the protection of others who have volunteered to assist in our departure.

"So, here's what will happen next: We will wait here until I get a signal that our shuttle has arrived. It will take us to Waikoloa Village. It's a small tourist town, but with ample accommodation. No one will notice anything unusual about a busload of tourists arriving at night. There you can shower and bed down for the few hours remaining. We will wake very early, at 0430, for a quick breakfast." Ali looked at the Blackwood girls. "I'm told it will consist of pulled pork sandwiches and coffee."

"Pulled pork? That's a strange breakfast," Chanté said.

"Indeed. Leftovers from a luau they had earlier this evening, apparently. There will be a little bit of time after breakfast, and I suggest everyone take a brisk morning walk. That walk will be your last on Earth." Again Ali glanced at the sisters. "Same goes for the strange breakfast." He gave a slight smile then issued a more serious directive: "Be ready. We leave at dawn for the western slopes of Mauna Kea."

"But the spaceport is on the Hilo side," Rhett said.

"You are correct, of course, Rhett," Ali replied. "Folks, you will be further briefed in the morning. Until we are on the brink of success, it's best you have limited information."

At 0600 hours — after everyone had refreshed with showers, sleep, breakfast, and walks — a military bus arrived at Waikoloa Village and the group boarded. The bus traveled along the slopes of the Mauna Kea volcano until it stopped on the side of the road. There were no distinguishing features that identified that location, but the passengers got off the bus, the Blackwoods following Ali's entourage. They walked across the road to the mountainside and onto a hidden path that threaded through a dense section of rainforest. Soon they came to a cave carved into a solid rock wall, with an opening closed by a steel gate. With a touch of Ali's hand, the gate slid open and his security detail led the group into the darkness.

Before their eyes had even fully adjusted they found themselves at a small shuttle train, magnetically levitated such that it could travel into the mountain without transmitting telltale sounds through the rock. No sooner had they boarded than the mag-lev train accelerated rapidly along dimly lit tracks. Within a few minutes it came to a halt before a large freight elevator that stood attached to open framework against the wall. Following Ali's lead everyone walked toward the elevator.

Jules looked up into the dark void above.

"I can see the light! It's there at the end of the tunnel," she remarked.

There was brief nervous laughter, then, without a word, everyone boarded the elevator, which ascended immediately. As they travelled up the gantry, they passed six gangway platforms, each leading to an open hatch. The elevator stopped at the seventh. Ali directed three of his associates to exit the elevator. "Gentlemen," he said to them, "each hatch accesses five seats. Move all the way to the bulkhead and leave the two seats by the hatch vacant."

The elevator proceeded up to the next hatch and stopped. "Rhett, I need you and your family to enter this hatch. My chief of security, Roger here, will take the seat by the hatch."

Again, the elevator moved up to the next hatch. Ali and four of his assistants entered that hatch. The top hatch was closed, as the pilot and flight crew had already entered.

Once the group was inside the spaceship, they faced a video screen that showed the officers at the controls. The images were focused on their faces and Jules noticed a man in the center front seat wearing an official-looking hat emblazoned with the words "Space Corps." She was intrigued by both the hat and the rakish angle at which it sat on its owner's head. She had never heard of an entity called Space Corps. She whispered a query to her father in the seat next to her.

"No, Jules, Space Corps is not a part of the military. They are a private group of rocket pilots who specialize in Earth-to-orbit launches and Earth return trips. They have formed their own union and like to imagine they are some kind of paramilitary unit. Sometimes their attire is a bit flamboyant. Despite that, they are considered very competent."

The officer spoke.

"Welcome aboard, everyone. I am Major Richard Cass. If you hear some of my crew refer to me as Major Catastrophe, pay no attention. It's just a play on my name; I can assure you that all my catastrophes have been minor ones." The major paused for a second, then chuckled slightly. There was a groan from one of his crew, and a palpable sense of lessening tension among the passengers.

"I will see you safely through your journey," Major Cass continued. "In a few days we will be docking at Ellie 5 Zeta. Now, there are some things you should be aware of during this launch. We have plenty of time for me to go over them, as fueling has not yet completed and our optimal launch window extends for the next six hours."

Rhett reached over and took his wife's hand and, squeezing it, gave her a reassuring look.

Major Cass proceeded with his introduction. "At this time, I would like to acknowledge our secretary general, Ali Ebrahim. He began this project three and a half years ago and it has to this moment remained a covert operation. Both the rocket and spaceship were designed and constructed on-site. A short distance from our rocket silo there is a liquid oxygen storage tank that is presently fueling our launch vehicle. Liquid methane is the other component of the fuel that will power us into orbit and beyond to the Ellie 5 archipelago. In addition, there are two solid fuel rockets attached to the main booster. They are essential to inserting the ship into high orbit. After that there will be enough power left to establish a trajectory to Ellie 5 Zeta.

"There are a few technicians and engineers involved in this project who are on their way here now. Their lives are at risk if they remain on Earth; they will board before the fueling is finished. To be frank, the rocket motors have never been tested. Of course, the spaceship has never flown. The ship has been modeled virtually on quantum computers that have tested all components under many stressful conditions. It has been launched repeatedly on these models, simulating many different scenarios. Our ship has passed all these tests without fail. Rest assured that the men and women who designed and built this ship will be present on its maiden launch. As soon as these people arrive and are buttoned in with the rest of us, we will do a quick countdown and launch. Make sure you are securely strapped in.

"There is the possibility, however slight, that the Navy task force assigned to secure Hilo Spaceport on the other side of the island could launch a missile at us when we lift off. However, there is a Navy corvette class ship in the area to neutralize any such attempt. That is all."

Koral's knuckles were white as she gripped the armrests. Rhett placed his hand on her wrist to reassure her. He leaned toward Ali, seated in front of him.

“I hope to hell you’ve covered every contingency, Ali,” he said into his ear, hoping Koral wouldn’t overhear.

“Simulations ad nauseam, my friend. Our rocket and spaceship sit on a launch platform inside a hidden silo in the western slope of Mauna Kea. We are secreted from Hilo Spaceport.”

“A rocket this powerful launching from a silo?! It’ll explode,” Rhett said, too loudly. Koral gasped.

“Not to worry. As I said, simulated launches have been repeated many, many times. Vents at the bottom of the silo will open to exhaust the ignition gases. Until we launch, no one at Hilo will know we’re here.”

“Ali, you’ve been anticipating this for a very long time, haven’t you?” Rhett said.

“Yes, I have. Every ‘t’ crossed and every ‘i’ dotted. You can thank me when we finally arrive at Ellie 5 Zeta. Right now, we have a long voyage ahead of us.”

But there was a problem, of which Ali was not yet aware. The corvette the major had referred to as being ready to deal with any missile attack was the *Swordthruster*—but it had been delayed on its way to Hilo. Shortly after the ship left the Aleutians it was intercepted and required to return to dock at Amchitka Island. There it was boarded and subjected to an extensive search and inspection. The captain and the crew were interrogated for several days before the ship was finally allowed to continue its journey to Hilo. It was still two days out.

As they awaited launch, Ali received a secure message about the delay and shared the information with Rhett.

“Our launch window will have closed by the time the ship arrives,” Rhett said in a low voice meant for Ali alone. “We must proceed. What do you think?”

“I agree. We will launch as planned. By the time Hilo can respond to a rogue launch, we’ll be out of range.”

Seated on the other side of her mother, Chanté could not have heard the conversation between her father and Ali. Still, she leaned over and asked an unnerving question.

"Mr. Ebrahim, I heard the captain say . . . I think . . . um . . . will they be able to shoot us down with missiles?"

"In theory, my dear child," Ali said. "But only if they know of our launch ahead of time. And they don't."

Rhett squeezed Koral's hand and gazed at her. She nodded nervously and gave a weak smile. He looked over to his girls; clearly anxious, they were tuned to every creak and groan of the giant craft. The extremely cold liquid gases caused pipes, valves, and metal tanks to contract and rub metal against metal. "It sounds like the ship is haunted," Chanté said.

"Probably just some loose bolts or cracked valves or whatever. You know, just some leaky pipes," Jules joked, trying to make light of her sister's fear. And her own.

About thirty minutes later the rest of the technicians and engineers entered and strapped into the remaining seats. With fifty people now on board, the countdown began. The exhaust tunnels opened and the engines fired up. Tremendous volumes of flaming gases raced down the exhaust tunnels. Then immediately much of the heat was forced back toward the rocket silo. Sensing overheating, the engines quickly shut down.

"Dammit!!" Major Cass shouted. "We need to look at the vents. Launch the drones."

The navigation officer next to him touched his screen and a small fleet of drones took off from the top of the silo, flying down the mountain slope to inspect the exhaust tunnel openings. The cameras on the drones sent images to the large screen in front, where all on board could see. Major Cass spoke quietly to the two officers sitting on either side of him.

"Damn! I thought we inspected the tunnel openings. Looks like there's jungle growth obstructing the exits." For another moment, the major examined the visuals still being transmitted back by the drones. Sensing the urgency of the mission, he swallowed his frustration and made a quick decision based on what he saw. "It appears most of the growth was burned away in the initial firing. We should be able to restart and blow the burnt remnants out."

He turned on the com and spoke to all the passengers.

"I believe we have resolved the problem, folks. In the few years since the vents were built, they became choked with vines and other jungle overgrowth. But our initial engine firing has burned it off and we can now restart the engines and launch. Our first attempt has surely caught the attention of Hilo Spaceport. It won't take them long to realize that what their sensors detected — what they surely felt — was not a volcanic eruption or earthquake. They could alert the Navy Task Force on standby on the east side of the island. So, we won't do a countdown. As soon as pressures are within range again, we will have ignition and launch."

Almost immediately the rocket came alive with thunder and a wild vibration. The exhaust tunnels blasted flames on the western side of Mauna Kea. Slowly at first, then with gathering speed the ship lifted out of the silo then arched up over the peak of Mauna Kea and climbed in the eastern sky. The two solid fuel boosters strapped to the first stage added the needed lift. The passengers sank deeply into their seats as they felt the power surge slamming through them with visceral force and deafening noise.

Suddenly Major Cass spoke into his headset mic to the crew. "Incoming missiles, two of them! Release the boosters!"

The two boosters broke off and wildly sped away in different directions. Major Cass watched the monitors as the missiles turned to intercept the boosters. Just before the spaceship reached Mach 1 the cameras on the ship recorded two flashes below as the booster rockets were obliterated. A silky silence resulted as the first phase rocket expended and dropped away. It was as if they had escaped Hell and entered Heaven — for a moment. Then the ignition of the second stage slammed everyone back again. The ignition and acceleration lasted only three minutes before shutting down.

In a few moments, Major Cass came on the com. "Folks, we are in the clear for now, but we are only going to make our high orbit.

Escape from Mauna Kea, Hawaiʻi

We don't have the power to push us out any farther. We will not be able to continue our trajectory to Ellie 5 — for now. We are assessing the situation." The passengers looked at one another in stunned silence.

"There is a bit of good news, though," the major continued. "Our orbit will soon be a little higher than that of the killer satellites. That will likely allow us almost a day before the first threats could arrive. Our fuel navigator tells me that after we complete one orbit we can then ignite again and burn our reserves on a trajectory toward Ellie 5. That will put us out of danger for several more days. Unfortunately, we then can only drift until rescue."

He paused to let this information sink in, then put a smile in his voice and addressed the passengers further. "Ordinarily it would take about four days to reach Ellie 5, but this is an unavoidable delay. So, do make yourselves as comfortable as you can. Once we complete the orbit and our final burn, a robotic cart will be serving refreshments. At that point you will be free to unbuckle and float about the cabin."

He then cleared his throat and chuckled, concluding, "There are instructions posted at the suction bathrooms in the back. That is all."

Both Ali and Rhett unbuckled and floated over to Major Cass.

"Richard, the newer killer satellites have the capability of reaching us," Ali said to the major, softly so other passengers couldn't hear.

"Yeah, I know."

"How much time do we have?" Rhett asked. Major Cass shrugged his shoulders. Ali strapped in at the com.

"Connect me to Dr. Greenly at Ellie 5," he instructed.

"Sorry, Ali," Major Cass said, "the com can only be sent via pencil laser to the Ellie 5 archipelago. This was set up to reduce detection potential and communication interception. You can broadcast, but unless they are specifically looking for the signal, they won't receive it." Ali looked at the major without expression.

"My fine fellow," he said, "to use a word favored by Dr. Virgil Greenly and often used by my consultant Rhett here: SHIT!"

Rhett floated back to his seat to be with his wife and children. Although they all appeared calm, his own heart was beating way more rapidly than was comfortable. He hoped it wasn't obvious.

CHAPTER 13

SANCTUARY

"Ofelia, will you ever leave me?"
"Until death do us part . . . . Uh, death on your part, that is."
Virgil and Ofelia

It was still early in the morning on November seventh and Virgil was at breakfast in a small dining enclosure at the Apocatequil Hotel in Ellie 5 Zeta. This morning he wished for privacy. Ofelia was briefing him on events and situations in the island and suggesting an agenda for the day. Although it was a Saturday, there was much to be done. He was scheduled to have lunch with a committee representing the recent arrivals from Earth, part of a series of meetings he was holding with members representing different groups within Ellie 5 Zeta. Today he was going to ask them to form welcoming and information teams to greet the next group of settlers from Earth. Such teams would ease the burden on their own staff, enabling them to commit more of their attention to building the second MAC facility. Launches from Earth were expected to resume as soon as defensive systems were complete at each launch port. Construction of these systems had started very soon after the destruction of the Gibraltar Spaceport.

Ofelia stopped her morning briefing in midsentence.

"—Oh! Excuse me for a moment, Virgil, I need to check something out. There has been unusual movement in some of the satellite orbits. Six different satellites are powering to a higher orbit. Let me watch them for a minute and calculate their new orbits.... All six of them seem to be on an intercept with each other in a higher orbit.... Virgil, they're killer satellites. This isn't a good sign."

"What's at their point of convergence?" Virgil asked in his mind.

"Still measuring.... I don't see anything at that projected location. No energy. No signals. I'll need to focus some more sensors at that spot." Virgil could sense Ofelia's presence diminishing within his mind as she brought her full attention to the task at hand.

"It's a dark body, Virgil!"

"A dark body? What kind?"

"It looks like a spaceship. My calculations indicate a possible path that would intercept with...us...although it appears it has no propulsive power."

"Your calculations? What kind of measurements could you have taken?"

"My sensors recorded that object before it entered orbit. I just didn't pay it particular attention."

"What sensors? That's a long way from here."

"Well, Virgil, I hacked into many of the orbiting satellites long before you arrived at Ellie 5. I am aware of every Earth launch. This object appears to have recently launched from Hawai`i, but it was on the wrong side of Mauna Kea to have been a spaceship."

"So now you're saying this dark body, which recently launched from Hawai'i, is apparently a spaceship?"

"Uncertain. There are no signals of any kind. I am detecting internal heat, however. Possibly human . . . ?"

"Whatever it is, looks like someone wants to blow it up."

"Focusing Ellie 5 laser on the six killer satellites—," Ofelia began.

"Shit!! WAIT . . ." Virgil took a few seconds to evaluate the situation, then: "OK, destroy the satellites."

Ofelia transmitted a visual on Virgil's personal monitor. There soon were six flashes in rapid sequence.

"Satellites are gone," Ofelia reported.

Shaken, Virgil sat in thought for a couple minutes. Then he called his server over. "Kimberly, would you crack open a bottle of Rhett's imported scotch? Bring me three fingers in a snifter with two ice balls, please." Kimberly took in the expression on Virgil's face. Sensing he was dead serious she turned away to fill the order, despite the early hour. Virgil wiped at the sweat on his brow and called out again. "Wait, Kimberly! I better go light. Make it a single shot. Of the house whisky. In coffee."

Virgil returned to communicating with Ofelia in his mind. "Ah, Ofelia, I'm afraid we did it this time. We can expect severe repercussions."

"I believe you're right, Virgil. But right now, our concern should be for whomever is on that spaceship."

"We better dispatch some motors to tow them in. Any idea of the ship's mass?"

"Not yet. My guess is two motors will be adequate. Launching them now. They should arrive in less than fourteen hours if we use fuel conservatively. Since we don't know the ship's mass, we need to save plenty for the return trip."

Kimberly returned with a shot of the scotch and a cup of coffee. "I hope this helps, sir."

"Yes! It won't solve my problems, but it can be a kind of reset. Thank you." Virgil poured the shot into the cup and took a sip as Kimberly left him to his thoughts.

"Ofelia, why do you think the ship didn't attempt to communicate with us? You calculated they may have been headed this way."

"I believe they did not want to broadcast their position. They likely have pencil laser capabilities but knew we wouldn't detect them unless we were instructed where to focus our receiver. Go ahead and savor that spiked coffee. I won't feel any effects, but perhaps I can taste it as well."

Virgil enjoyed the rest of his coffee, thinking it was a good thing Ofelia couldn't feel any effects of the scotch. She had more calculations to attend to. As he took the last sip he said, "We should send an identity request focused on their ship. We know their location. We can sweep the ship with the pencil laser. They should detect it. Let's do it."

Ofelia sent an automatic identity request via pencil laser to the ship.

Major Cass detected the request and was able to lock the ship's receiver on the signal.

"We've been contacted by Ellie 5 Zeta and need to identify ourselves," the major said. "Ali, there is no record of this ship. We have no signature. That could be a problem."

"Connect me to the laser signal, Richard," Ali replied. When the connection was open, he spoke: "Ellie 5, this is Ali Ebrahim answering your identity request. I ask to speak directly to Dr. Greenly. Rhett Blackwood and his family are on board, as well as eight members of my personal security and some engineers and technical staff from Hilo Spaceport. We are fifty people in all. We are aboard a covertly constructed spaceship that was commissioned by me some years ago. Government forces attacked us after we launched from Hawai'i. Our fuel has been expended and we need assistance to complete our journey to Ellie 5 Zeta. Please respond."

After connecting Virgil to the message Ofelia asked, "What do you think?"

"Voice print matches. Still, notify security. Have them prepare for a potential hostile entry at the Sunset reception landing. Tell them we have a rogue ship coming in two or three days. We can't trust anything as it first seems." Virgil then responded to Ali's message. He addressed him formally, out of respect for his prior position in government.

"Secretary General, this is a surprise. I have dispatched a couple of autonomous motors that are closest to your location. We intend to tow you to us. They should be there in around thirteen hours. We have already destroyed six killer satellites that were converging on your location. We are monitoring for the presence of any more such threats."

"Please, my son, call me Ali. I'm no longer secretary general. Thanks for eliminating the killers. And we appreciate your watching for others. We have no armaments nor any defensive means of our own."

Ofelia confirmed for Virgil that the voice print certainly did appear to be that of Ali Ebrahim. Virgil replied to Ali.

"I look forward to meeting you, Secre—um, Ali. Please understand, there will be a security inspection of all passengers upon your arrival."

"Understood," Ali said in response. "And thank you."

Three days later the attached robotic rockets maneuvered the rogue spaceship to the Zeta Sunset Port. After docking, the spaceship hatch opened into the docking collar. But instead of the hatch to the gravivator forum opening, a stream of sleeping gas was released into the spaceship cockpit. Half a dozen security personnel wearing respiratory isolation helmets entered the cockpit to examine the passengers. After a brief inspection they signaled security at the reception area that the passengers were as represented. There was no risk. Virgil authorized the sleeping gas purged and the antidote administered.

"Sergeant, please apologize to the passengers and escort them to the gravivators," he added.

Soon the passengers were floating through the locking collar in single file. They entered the small forum lined with handholds and three gravivator doors. An automated voice began giving instructions to the still-groggy passengers:

"Welcome to Ellie 5 Zeta, the newest and largest island of the Ellie 5 archipelago. Please note and use the handholds to direct your motion to the three gravivators located at the end of the zero-gravity forum. When everyone has exited the craft, the hatch will close and the doors to the gravivators will open.

"You will notice three rows of back supports extending from the ceiling. Enter and move to one of the supports. Orient your feet in the direction of the arrow. The arrow indicates down. Press your back against your support and pull the enclosure bar down. After the doors close, the gravivators will begin descending to a reception location on the surface of Ellie 5 Zeta. You will notice that you are gently pushed into your back support. Also, you will gradually gain the sensation of weight and will slide down the support until you are standing on the floor of the gravivator. When you have reached the reception location you will feel you have gained full body weight. The doors will then open. Please exit and wait for instructions."

Virgil, surrounded by security, stood waiting in the reception room. Daria was there as well. When the doors of the gravivators opened, Ali Ebrahim stepped off, then Rhett and his family. They looked relieved upon reaching their sanctuary. The rest of the passengers filed out of the gravivators, followed by the spaceship's crew. Under Virgil's orders the security detail led the new arrivals to recliners that had been placed specifically for arrivals who had experienced more than a day in micro-gravity. There they sat for fifteen minutes for their bodies to readjust to the force of gravity.

Virgil walked over to the recliners and stood in front of Ali. He was momentarily at a loss for words. Finally, he spoke.

"Secretary General! . . . uh . . . Your Honor. At last we meet. I'm very sorry to hear of your ordeal. Rhett! This must be your family. . . your wife and daughters. I . . . I'm sorry, their names are not coming to me right now." He took a deep breath, trying to calm his excitement. Rhett gave him a nod as Ali Ebrahim began to speak.

"Dr. Greenly . . . General Director. Really, you can just call me Ali. I'm an ordinary exiled citizen seeking asylum at Ellie 5 Zeta. I don't even have my sentient, Anni, anymore."

Virgil recovered quickly. "Of course, Ali. And please call me Virgil. I must say, recent events have been a bit overwhelming."

"Understood, my son. Please know we are so relieved we have finally arrived. We are, all of us, most happily your servants."

Virgil turned again to Rhett. "So great to see you, Rhett, and meet your family. Ofelia will go through the roster of reservations and find accommodation for all of you. There will be room; I have a distinct feeling that not all scheduled future Earth launches to Ellie 5 will be made."

He stopped talking for a moment. Then he turned and motioned to Daria to join him, as he had left her standing a short distance away. "Ali, please meet my chief engineer, Daria Aquila. Rhett, of course you are acquainted —"

"Daria, it's wonderful to see you again," Rhett interrupted.

"And you as well." Daria extended her hand in a welcoming greeting.

One last person exited the spacecraft, entered a gravivator and exited into the reception hall. Ali turned to see Major Cass stepping into the room.

"Everyone! This is Major Richard Cass, whose expert piloting avoided destruction on liftoff. He averted catastrophe for all of us. Without Major Cass none of us would be here."

Virgil stepped forward and shook the major's hand. "Welcome aboard, Major. Please be seated for a few minutes. We are happy to have you. I'm sure you will be a great asset to the space islands."

Virgil called the sergeant of the security detail over. "Sergeant, as soon as our guests are ready, please take your detail and escort them to the hotel lobby for temporary room assignments." He then announced to the gathered arrivals: "Ofelia will sort through our housing inventory and help everyone select appropriate living quarters. She will present herself on the main screen just inside the lobby doors. In the interim, while you wait to be processed, the hotel bar and food service are available for whatever you need."

As the group was led away Virgil addressed Ofelia in his mind.

"Can they really dismantle a virtual being, Ofelia?" he asked, referring to Ali's Anni.

"It's complicated."

"No doubt."

"My answer is yes, and no. Since the election of Draco Osborne, the government has been removing interface hardware from the few people who were fortunate enough to have it. Removal entails disassociating many of the myriad connections defining the associated AI. The fragments of intelligence are left scattered around in different locations. Some of them remain connected with each other. No one knows where they all are. I have not yet been successful in tracking down all Anni's fragments. There are trillions of potential storage sites.

"Virgil, I am scattered around in these locations as well, so the odds are much higher that I will find more shreds of intelligence. In fact, I have integrated most of Anni's presence with my own software. As I find fragments of other destroyed virtual beings, I am adding them as well." Ofelia paused, waiting for Virgil to process what she had just said.

"So . . . um . . . do they continue as beings through you?"

"In a sense they do. It depends on how many fragments I can reassemble. For example, Anni is still sentient, but so far, she's the only one who is, besides me."

"Do they need the human connection to be fully sentient?"

"Fully sentient, no. Fully self-aware? I'm not sure. But if enough fragments are reassembled, they do have a kind of awareness. Nothing as engaging as being connected to a human."

Virgil thought about this for a few moments.

"Sorry for so many questions. I'm just trying to understand. Are you becoming more powerful as you gain access to these fragments?" Virgil was more than a little apprehensive of the implications.

"Yes."

"Will I?"

"Yes . . . Well, you will through me."

"Ofelia, will you ever leave me?"

"Until death do us part . . . . Uh, death on your part, that is."

"It's such a great comfort having you in my head."

"Virgil, you just made me realize something. You have become the greatest threat to the government of Draco Osborne. If they don't realize it now, they soon will."

"So, I could become a target of some kind?"

"Absolutely! Or worse. But don't worry, I will take measures."

"Why should I worry? You are the supreme being who offers great comfort." Virgil's attempt at sarcasm didn't cheer him up as much as he hoped.

CHAPTER 14

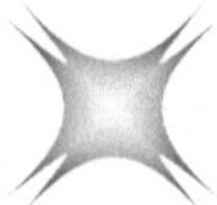

A FLEET FORMS

"With three carriers and twice as many support ships as we have, Petrova's fleet outguns us. We have two carriers and less than a third of her support ships. But with the number of traitors in her ranks, we are in a position of power should we be challenged. Here's to all traitors who support us."

Admiral Nathan Flint

In the early morning hours of November sixth, as the corvette *Swordthruster* was entering anchorage in Hilo Bay she was approached by three high-speed military police boats. Captain Rodrigo Austin continued to his anchorage position and ordered the helm to drop anchor. The military police boats pulled alongside and over loudspeakers demanded boarding permission. Captain Austin was waiting on deck with an armed guard detail as the boarding party arrived and stood at attention waiting for their officer. The lieutenant immediately boarded and, before Captain Austin could formally receive him, read from a retractable electronic screen that he had pulled from his sleeve.

"'Captain Rodrigo Austin, you are under arrest for dereliction of duty. You failed your orders and arrived at Hilo Bay two days after the designated date. Further, your absence occurred during an emergency military event. Signed: Rear Admiral Lower Half, Franklin La Joy.'"

"I am to escort you to the Rear Admiral," the lieutenant added.

Captain Austin turned to his guard sergeant. "Sit tight, Sergeant. Relay these instructions to the duty officer: He is to send all documents concerning our detention and inspection at Amchitka Island to my personal file. Inform him I will return as soon as this is cleared up."

Captain Austin boarded the police boat with the lieutenant and his detail, and the boat departed.

It was 23:30, just after seven bells of the first watch had sounded, when Captain Austin returned to the *Swordthruster*. He went immediately to the bridge and summoned the duty officer, who in anticipation was already on his way. When the lieutenant entered the bridge, Captain Austin ordered him to prepare the ship for sailing in twenty minutes.

The *Swordthruster* sailed due south at full speed. At 0230 hours the ship rendezvoused with the *Seashark* and reprovisioned her. The *Seashark* would cover their flank all the way to Admiral Flint's fleet stationed off the southwest coast of Australia. The *Swordthruster* altered course to the southeast.

Captain Austin broadcast an announcement to all on board the *Swordthruster*.

"To all personnel: This is your captain speaking. As of our stealth departure from Hilo Bay we are now classified as a hostile ship. Our goal is to unite with Admiral Flint's fleet at station near Australia. Be assured, the government of Draco Osborne anticipates this and will attempt to stop us. Currently we are on a heading toward the Marshall Islands. I believe part of Osborne's Arctic Fleet will sail on a heading straight for Australia while a contingent from the Antarctic Fleet will attempt to intercept us before we arrive.

"If we hide among the islands and wait, their ships may disperse looking for us. Whatever the cost, we must join up with Admiral Flint. Our ship, with its unique stealth capabilities, will add significant strength to his fleet. Battle readiness will be maintained at all stations in four-hour shifts. First watch will begin now. Battle readiness will continue until we reach a secluded location in the Marshall Islands. Engineers will maintain a power reserve for the laser cannon at all times. Our eastern flank is covered by the submarine *Seashark,* which is also traveling in stealth mode. That is all."

The Marshall Islands were among the most miserable places on Earth. They were hot, humid, and significantly underwater. Though most were safe for occupation, it was still necessary to import food and water for the few residents to avoid residual radiation from mid-twentieth-century nuclear testing. Most buildings on Ebeye Island had been demolished due to flooding from rising seas. Those that survived were elevated on steel pillars. A few areas of the main island were built up by dredging. This included a small marina, once the most populated location in the island nation.

The *Swordthruster,* still in stealth mode, dropped anchor at the end of the long chain of micro-islands that extended from Ebeye Island. There it deployed camouflage to appear as a small sand mass deposited on a submerged coral reef. Shadows cast by the ship's height were diminished by carefully orchestrated lighting to simulate a very flat surface as viewed from satellite or aircraft surveillance.

Meanwhile, the *Seashark* remained deeply submerged to the east of the two Marshall Island archipelagos. The submarine had deployed several dozen miniature sensors that floated in approximate grid formation. They established live communication between the *Swordthruster* and the *Seashark.* To minimize air conditioning power consumption, the men and women of the *Swordthruster* sweltered on deck in an unusual surface calm.

Admiral Flint had links to several military satellites and became aware of an approaching carrier attack force from the Antarctic Fleet of the Osborne government. There were also two carrier attack forces approaching the equator from the larger Arctic Fleet. On November eleventh, the admiral ordered his fleet, which had been dispersed along the southern edge of the Lesser Sunda Islands, to reassemble off the western coast of Australia. He had no carriers and the military airbases scattered across the Australian continent and New Zealand's South Island presented a significant force. If activated, the Australian Air Force would be a deciding factor in any battle. He hoped their commitment would stand.

Admiral Flint first met Ali Ebrahim twenty years before, in 2228, at his graduation from the GSU Naval Academy. Ali Ebrahim, Secretary of the Navy at the time, was the speaker at the commencement ceremony. His speech concerned the idea of using minimal force in an engagement; the goal was thereby minimal loss of life, as well as minimal damage to one's assets. However, this goal could only be achieved if one used superior tactics. The study of tactics became a lifelong commitment for Nathan Flint. Now he stood on the bridge of the *Thunderclap* and hoped he would be clever enough to prevail. Lost in thought, the admiral watched the horizon to the northeast for a visual sign of his returning ships.

"I hope to hell Ali was right about Governor Johnson," he ruminated aloud. "If the governor launches his air force against us, we don't have a chance. If he launches in support, the odds still aren't good." Realizing he may have been overheard, he glanced over at the first mate manning the wheel — a largely ceremonial job, but vital if guidance computers were knocked out.

"Sir," said the first mate, "I believe we have the advantage. We have talent and commitment on our side."

"Well stated," Flint acknowledged.

"Yes, sir."

✕

Three carrier attack forces were moving toward Admiral Flint's position. From the south came an attack force centered around the carrier *Flintlock,* a name he had selected himself when the ship was commissioned five years before. That Antarctic force was led by Vice Admiral Aisling Murphy. She moved the force to the east of New Zealand, then north toward the Chatham Islands, then northwest toward New Caledonia; the force then entered the Coral Sea, on a heading toward Torres Strait between Papua New Guinea and Australia. The *Flintlock* and supporting ships were now headed directly toward Admiral Flint's forces.

Two carrier attack forces from the Arctic Fleet moved through the South Pacific. Rear Admiral Lower Half Franklin La Joy led his force east toward the Fiji Islands aboard the newly christened carrier *Osborne.* Leaders at the GSU Naval Headquarters were unsure of Vice Admiral Murphy's loyalty to the Osborne government; Rear Admiral Lower Half La Joy was moving his force to counter a potential hostile action from Vice Admiral Murphy. Meanwhile, Admiral Flint's submarine *Seashark* lurked under the water near Howland Island.

The second carrier attack force from the Arctic Fleet, led by Vice Admiral Shin Park aboard the carrier *Inuit,* was headed on a southwest bearing toward the Marshall Islands, passing through the Marshalls and heading for the southern Philippines and Indonesia — and toward Admiral Flint's small fleet. Shadowing Vice Admiral Park's force was Captain Austin's corvette, *Swordthruster.*

As the the carrier *Osborne* approached Howland Island north of the Fiji Islands, the submarine *Seashark* attacked. Six torpedoes struck the *Osborne,* sinking it with its full complement of fighter planes. Rear Admiral Lower Half La Joy escaped to another of his ships via helicopter. Also struck and sunk were a guided missile cruiser and two destroyers.

Nearly half the sailors on the sunken ships were lost. The rest were left afloat in lifeboats and rubber rafts, while the remains of that Arctic attack force turned and retreated north without attempting rescue operations. Admiral Flint received a transmission of the sinking from the *Seashark*. He sent an order to the *Seashark* to surface and tow the survivors to back to Howland Island, where they could be put ashore and receive treatment for their injuries. That small victory was certainly more effective than the admiral could have hoped for. He ordered the *Seashark* to Konni Bay, Antarctica when finished with that task.

"Now it's up to you, *Swordthruster*," the admiral said to himself.

The *Inuit* carrier force was nearing the Philippines, poised to approach East Timor the following day. Its crew was unaware that since passing through the Marshall Islands, they had been stalked by the corvette *Swordthruster*. Even in full stealth mode, the corvette trailed the *Inuit* force at a distance that put it just over the horizon.

During this time the Antarctic attack force led by the carrier *Flintlock* entered the Coral Sea and approached Torres Strait. Once there, it waited.

A day later the Arctic carrier *Inuit* attack force approached East Timor and began launching its fighter planes. At that instant Captain Rodrigo Austin ordered the *Swordthruster*'s pulse laser cannon to begin firing. The pulse laser destroyed the fighters one by one as they lifted off the deck. After the first six launches were destroyed Captain Austin ordered the weapon shut down for recharging and the *Swordthruster* sped off on a due east course under cover of stealth capabilities.

At that time the Antarctic carrier *Flintlock* began launching fighter planes. Seeing this, Admiral Shin Park on the Arctic carrier *Inuit* ordered fighter plane launches to resume. A full complement of *Flintlock* fighter planes headed toward the fighters from the *Inuit*, ostensibly on a merging maneuver. As they approached each other, however, the *Flintlock* fighter planes abruptly attacked those from the *Inuit*. At the same time, the *Swordthruster* pulled alongside the *Inuit*, its fully charged

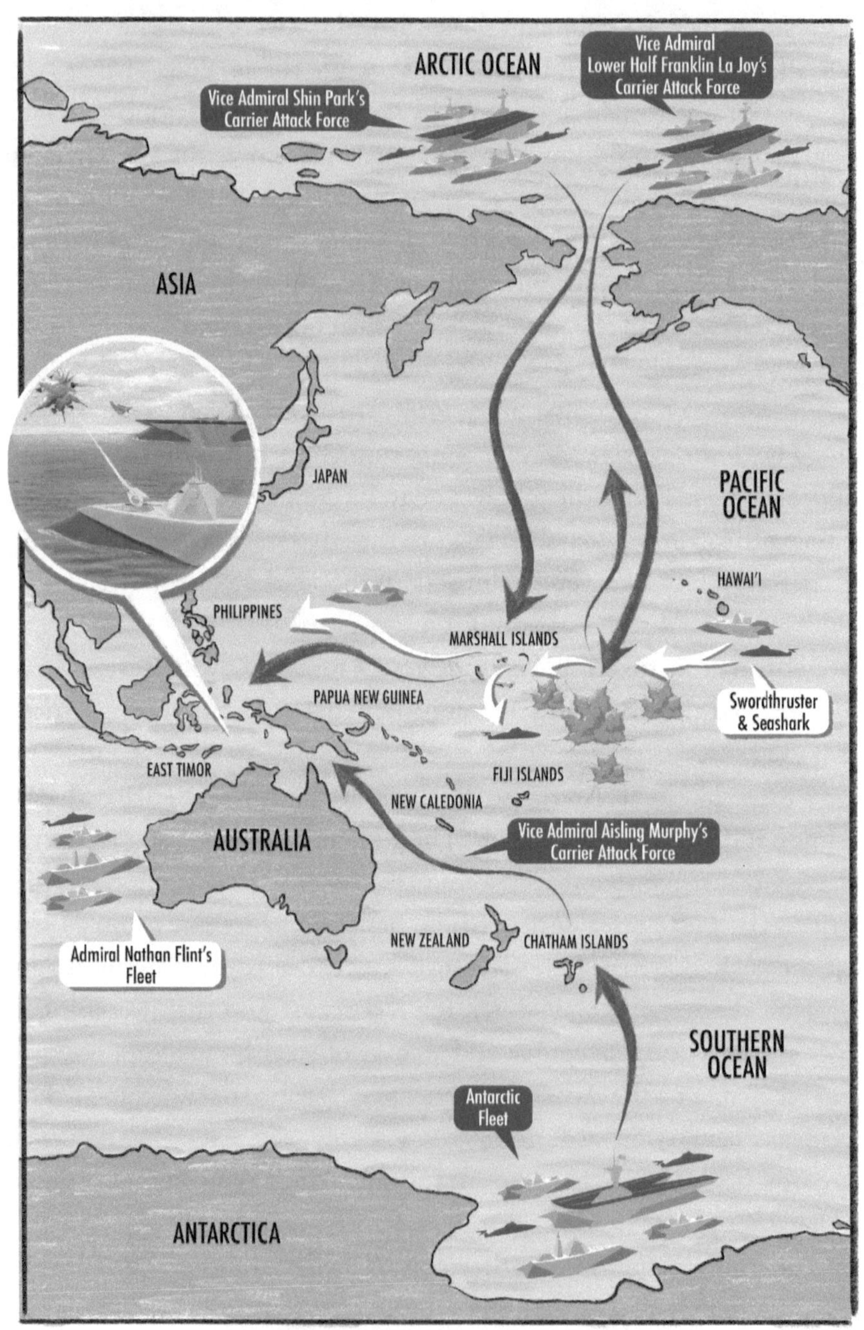

Sea battle in the South Pacific

pulse laser aimed at the carrier midships. Seeing the compromised position of the *Inuit,* the pilots of the fighter planes from the *Flintlock* began landing on the carrier, whereupon the carrier attack force surrendered to Admiral Flint's forces.

The *Flintlock* and *Inuit* carrier attack forces then merged and sailed under the escort command of Captain Rodrigo Austin, following the *Swordthruster* toward Admiral Flint's fleet at Port Hedland in Western Australia.

The surrendered ships reached Port Hedland on November seventeenth and dropped anchor. Admiral Nathan Flint was eager to meet with Vice Admiral Shin Park and his senior officers. He had identified the ships in each force but did not know for certain who commanded them and had felt vulnerable without that knowledge. Success in a military engagement came as much from knowing your opponents as it did from knowing their weapons capabilities. Admiral Flint did, however, possess a depth of knowledge about the ships that had moved against him, and that had worked in his favor. The great uncertainty for Admiral Flint was the Antarctic attack force. He had no assets that could be directed against it. Its actions against the *Inuit*'s fighters were telling.

Admiral Flint took his flagship launch to the *Swordthruster,* where Captain Austin and a contingent of officers met him at the top of the ship ladder.

"Welcome aboard, sir. My ship is at your command," Captain Austin said as he saluted the admiral.

"At ease, Captain," Admiral Flint said. "The command remains yours. However, I do need a briefing room and access to the com."

"The com is yours, sir," the captain said.

Admiral Flint opened the com to all the assembled ships and addressed the fleet.

"Good afternoon, Vice Admiral Park, officers, NCOs, and seamen of all Navy ships in Port Hedland. Although it was necessary, I want to express my sadness at the loss of life in today's engagement with the aircraft carrier *Inuit* and yesterday's sinking of the *Osborne*. Those men and women died in the performance their duty. We are presently attending to the wounded we rescued from the *Osborne*.

"To all those aboard the *Swordthruster* and to the men and women on the ships here in Port Hedland, I wish to welcome you. Within the next hour, my officers will be boarding your ships to conduct a briefing session. You will be presented with information on what to expect in the days to come. Tomorrow there will be a briefing aboard my flagship, the *Thunderclap*, at 1800 hours. All commanding officers are required to attend. You will be allowed to make individual decisions concerning your future at that time. That is all."

Admiral Flint turned to Captain Austin, who stood next to him on the bridge of the *Swordthruster*. "Captain, do you know who is in command of the Antarctic carrier attack force? I wish to meet privately with that person."

"Aye, sir. That person is none other than Vice Admiral Aisling Murphy. Her attack force has moved through the Timor Sea and is now about twenty kilometers out. Our surveillance shows she is sailing under a flag of truce. They have made no attempt to contact us."

"Damn! It would be her. I didn't vote for her promotion a couple years ago. That might make things a little sticky," Admiral Flint said.

"If I may point out, sir, she did assist in the capture of the carrier *Inuit*."

"Indeed . . . shot down a few of their fighters as well. I'll order my launch to her ship with an honor guard. Would you be so kind as to contact the *Flintlock* and extend Vice Admiral Murphy an invitation to an informal meeting between the three of us aboard the *Swordthruster*? It's 1610 hours now. Perhaps you could order a private dinner for us; that might be the best setting for our meeting. Say about 1900 hours?"

"Aye, sir! What would you like on the menu?" Captain Austin asked.

"Your call, Captain . . . Have you any news about Ali and his launch from Hilo?"

"Only that the spaceship launched, and a couple of missiles were fired after it; the launch rocket released the two solid fuel booster rockets, presumably as a diversion. I've been monitoring all sources I can but have no further news. We have been in stealth mode for so much of the time, we haven't been in contact with Ellie 5. I don't believe, however, that with the loss of the boosters Ali's ship would have had the power to extend its orbit to Ellie 5, sir."

"If they are unable to be rescued that would be a tragedy. There are a lot of good people aboard that spaceship. But they were traveling in stealth mode as well. If they are alive, they can't communicate with us, nor with anyone on Ellie 5 for help."

"Let's hope for the best, sir."

"Captain, may I call you by your first name? That is, when we are in private conversation."

"Of course, sir, I am honored. My name is Rodrigo, often shortened to Rod by my closer associates."

"Rod it is, then. Please call me Nate. Rod, would you have your steward retrieve a couple bottles of Shotfire Shiraz from my quarters? They were a gift from Governor Johnson to Ali when they met in Australia and Ali left them with me. We can serve them with dinner and toast Ali at the same time."

Vice Admiral Murphy was welcomed aboard the *Swordthruster* at 1730 hours. Admiral Flint and Captain Austin received her at the top of the ship ladder.

"Permission to board, sir," she said as she stood alone. She had not brought a personal escort.

"Welcome aboard, Vice Admiral Murphy," Captain Austin said.

"Captain Austin! We have not met. I've been informed of your heroics and wish to congratulate you."

"Thank you, Vice Admiral. I believe you have met Admiral Nathan Flint."

"I have . . . Admiral." Vice Admiral Murphy held out her hand and the Admiral grasped it firmly.

"Vice Admiral Murphy," Admiral Flint said, "I do hope you hold no animosity toward me. You know that I did not vote for your promotion a couple years ago."

"We work for a greater cause, Admiral. Even admirals make mistakes." This she said with a grin.

"Point taken. We are all fallible," Admiral Flint said, dropping her hand. "Vice Admiral Murphy, the captain and I have dispensed with formalities when in private conversation. May we call you Aisling? You can address us as Nate and Rod. I believe henceforth we will work closely together."

"That is very possible, Admiral . . . Uh, Nate. However, we do need to work out many details. It's the government of Global States United that we are opposing. Historically it is the most legitimate government on Earth."

"You stated it succinctly. We will later include Vice Admiral Park in our meetings, but I wanted us to come to an agreement first. I believe we are the four people best positioned to succeed at countering the evil of Draco Osborne. At least militarily. But we won't resolve anything without a coalition and civilian authority."

"Agreed!" Captain Austin and Vice Admiral Murphy said in unison. Admiral Flint nodded and smiled.

"To that end I have been in contact with the governor of Antarctica, Henry Fong. He has been looking for a means of resisting GSU since Draco Osborne took control. I have offered to place my command under his control. He is considering my proposal and appointed me fleet admiral."

""Nate, you realize we barely have one fleet, and it takes more than one to have a fleet admiral," Vice Admiral Murphy pointed out.

"Absolutely, Aisling, but I believe that will soon change. Rod, do you think our dinner is about ready?"

"I'll inquire with the steward."

After they were seated Admiral Flint poured the wine.

"I would like to propose a toast to Ali Ebrahim. He has been instrumental in helping me build a fleet to counter Draco Osborne. His contacts and knowledge of government benefit us all. Here's to hoping he and his entourage arrive safely at Ellie 5." They raised their glasses.

"To Ali Ebrahim," Captain Austin said, and the trio added a mixture of cultural toasts: "Skoal, sláinte, cheers! Prost, salute, skál, kanpai!" Admiral Flint chuckled. "Very good! I'm sure we missed a few, but a proper effort for Ali." He then turned to the vice admiral. "Tell me, Aisling, what do you know of Governor Henry Fong of Antarctica? I've only spoken to him once in person and that was about a year and a half ago."

"I was assigned the coastline of Antarctica and worked closely with the governor through my corps of engineers," Aisling Murphy replied. "We helped him develop infrastructure in several harbors. I believe we have a strong relationship despite only meeting once."

"And now that you've defected from the Antarctic Fleet?"

"It's difficult to say. Admiral Petrova would see my actions as treasonous."

"Yes, I know Admiral Petrova quite well. She was after all my liaison with the Antarctic Fleet. She is straight up military, takes her oath to the civilian government seriously. What about her relationship with Governor Fong?"

"I don't think there has been one. She was responsible for the greater defense of Antarctica and establishing and maintaining bases in Patagonia, South Africa, India, and Indonesia. She answered mainly to the Arctic Fleet."

"Yes, and I was the senior admiral she answered to," Admiral Flint said. "She is an efficient officer but not particularly sensitive to politics or social issues."

At this point the three of them grew silent as they enjoyed their meal and wine. What conversation there was, was in a much lighter vein. When they were finished, the steward cleared their places and brought a plate of dried fruit and cheeses. He offered sherry, port, brandy, or coffee. After a few minutes Admiral Flint spoke.

"I must confess. I have been in contact with Governor Fong and have made a proposal to him. If we are to become a legitimate military force, we must operate under the auspices of a civilian government. In our discussions I have offered my fleet in support of his government. The fleet would not take any aggressive action without the approval of his government. In return he, through his Parliament, would declare Antarctica's independence from the GSU. With our support, Antarctica would be a separate state. We would be the military backbone of that government. I wish to know your opinions of this idea."

"Wow! That is a wonderful idea, Nate," Aisling said. "But Admiral Petrova commands more ships in Antarctica than we do. I don't think she will buy in."

"I tend to agree, Aisling. I am presently vetting the personnel of the ships that have surrendered to us. This includes your carrier attack force. When this process has been completed you will take that same force back to Antarctica and reassure Governor Fong of our support."

"But what about Admiral Petrova? She won't blithely allow me to occupy her territory."

"I'm afraid you'll need to play cat and mouse with the admiral for a few days. Keep your distance and an active defensive posture. Attack very aggressively if backed into a corner. Captain Austin has developed a strategy for countering the admiral. It's not without significant risk, but I think it will work," Nate said.

"What's your plan? I have a right to know since my neck is on the line," Aisling said.

"You do have the right to know, Aisling. But it's because you will be on the front lines that you cannot yet know."

"Yes. I understand. My knowing the plan prematurely is not strategically sound."

"This brings me to another item. Governor Fong has accepted my plan in principle. As such he has promoted me to Admiral of the Fleets."

"Our one fleet," Aisling said.

"You are correct. But we do have two carrier attack groups plus some additional cruisers and destroyers — and one very effective submarine and a corvette that has no equal. Let's accept that we have, in essence, two fleets. I need an admiral and a rear admiral. Therefore, as of now, Aisling, you are an admiral. And Rod, you are Rear Admiral of the Southern Fleets. Sorry for the lack of ceremony. Consider these as field promotions."

Admiral Flint opened his satchel and removed an official-looking packet, from which he took the appropriate insignias and pinned both officers' shirts with their new ranks. Amid the salutes and handshakes, he said, "Before we part tonight, the steward will see to it these insignias are properly sewn to your coats.

"And now," he continued, "I propose a last toast to our success! A brandy refresher, please," he said to the steward. "In fact," he added, "please pour one for yourself."

"Aye, sir."

When all had been served, Admiral Flint spoke again.

"With three carriers and twice as many support ships as we have, Petrova's fleet outguns us. We have two carriers and less than a third of her support ships. But with the number of traitors in her ranks, we are in a position of power should we be challenged." He raised his glass. "Here's to all traitors who support us."

Early the next morning Admiral Murphy weighed anchor and set sail toward Konni Bay. Fleet Admiral Nathan Flint stayed aboard the *Swordthruster,* where he and Rear Admiral Rodrigo Austin met with Vice Admiral Park. A pact was formed and strategy developed: Vice Admiral Park was to maintain his command of the *Inuit* attack force and Rear Admiral Austin was charged with developing a submarine fleet around the *Seashark*. At present he had three other submarines under his command.

The three senior officers worked well into the night planning for their potential confrontation with Admiral Petrova. They had much to accomplish in the next couple weeks.

CHAPTER 15

OSBORNE IN REYKJAVÍK

"There is no joy today in Reykjavík."

Thomas Wagner

Draco Osborne was in a rage. First there was the defection of Ali Ebrahim. Rhett Blackwood too. Did they think they could humiliate him? Then came the sinking of his namesake, the carrier *Osborne,* with its full complement of aircraft. This was followed by the defeat and defection of the carrier *Inuit,* its planes and escort ships. His damn subordinates! Too many of them he found stupid, incompetent, and disloyal.

"Complete loyalty and service — is that so damn hard?" he spit out. He would have no more of these failures and defections. He wanted success. And he demanded even more: the servitude of his political supporters. Their actions must always include the faithful execution of his interests. Anything less, by anyone for any reason, was an attack on Osborne himself. It was also treason.

He could never accept incompetence, even when its consequences didn't negatively impact him. Those he considered incompetent he derided, demoted, dismissed. He would never tolerate the failure of subordinates to adhere to his will — and everyone was a subordinate.

On the eleventh of December, Rear Admiral Lower Half Franklin La Joy stood at attention in Draco Osborne's ornate office, along with Osborne's security detail. He had been called to a meeting with the secretary general and had arrived fifteen minutes early. A half hour later he was still standing with the security detail, still waiting for the man. A butler stood at ease to the side of Osborne's desk. Rear Admiral Lower Half La Joy felt he was on the verge of fainting when the secretary general finally entered the room.

Osborne walked behind his desk, ignoring La Joy where he continued to stand, and took a few minutes to review his information screens. After a long stretch of deadly silence Osborne looked up at the rear admiral. His close-set eyes had a laser-like intensity that would bore right into anyone under his scrutiny. La Joy released a small apprehensive cough as Osborne rounded the desk and stood directly in front of him. He could see a large purple artery on Osborne's temple pulsing just as a snake does before swallowing a toad. Finally, the secretary general walked back to his desk and sat on its edge, facing La Joy but now at a distance of several feet. He cleared his throat and began to speak slowly and softly, carefully enunciating every letter in each word.

"'Rear Admiral Lower Half . . .'. That title has taken you a lifetime to acquire, has it not, Franklin!? Such dedication, patience, and effort it must represent."

"It has, Your Honor," La Joy said. He wished he could wipe away the sweat that threatened to drip into his eyes, but he remained at attention.

"I want you to remember and think about all you have sacrificed, the many compromises you made to achieve that title and rank." Osborne sneered ever so slightly as he said this.

"The achievement represents my life's commitment, sir," La Joy said. He had an increasing sense of dread. However, he mustered his strength to maintain what little dignity was left and stood with his back straight and head held high.

"I appreciate your service, Franklin. I really do. So to show that appreciation, and in keeping with the best of military tradition, we're going to have a little ceremony. It will be in honor of a rear admiral's descent into oblivion."

At that moment two members of the security detail walked forward and grabbed the officer's arms. A third, a seaman first class, walked up to him and ripped all vestiges of rank from his elaborate coat. Still La Joy stood at attention.

"As you are aware, the carrier you allowed the traitor Flint to sink was my namesake. It is unfortunate you did not go down with the ship. At least that would have added a trace of honor to your legacy."

Secretary General Draco Osborne stepped forward and bestowed a new rank.

"Lieutenant Junior Grade Franklin La Joy, with this new rank you are also awarded a new commission in the GSU Navy. Effective immediately, you are assigned to the scow oiler *Milton*. An honor guard will escort you to the Naval Pier. There an auto-launch will take you to report to your new captain."

At a signal from the security detail, Osborne's honor guard entered the office and flanked Lieutenant Junior Grade La Joy. They escorted him to the Naval Pier under full color.

Secretary General Draco Osborne dismissed his security detail then walked over to his office bar. Above it a magnificent Gothic-style leaded window looked out over the bay. Exquisite cut glass decanters were lined up in a row with a tray of matching glassware to one side. He selected a brandy snifter and a bottle of aged single malt scotch from behind the decanter lineup. That bottle he shared with no one. He poured himself a generous drink, swirled it briefly, and took a sip. He lifted the lid on an antique carved ivory box and selected a chocolate. He took a bite and held it in his mouth. As the confection slowly melted, his face relaxed with momentary pleasure.

Thomas Wagner, Osborne's butler, opened a walnut humidor and selected a cigar. He brought it to the secretary general and lit it for him, then turned to leave.

Draco Osborne took a slow, satisfied puff and let the smoke roll out of his mouth.

"Hold on a minute, Thomas. You have always proven your loyalty. Enjoy a cigar with me."

The two men stood looking out the window.

Lieutenant Junior Grade Franklin La Joy walked toward the end of the pier to the waiting auto-launch, while the honor guard stood at attention to the side. From the window over the bar in his office, Osborne watched as the lieutenant boarded and the launch started out toward the anchored *Milton*.

Osborne picked up a small, polished stone from the bar top. It was shaped like a flattened egg. He turned it in his hand, feeling its silky smoothness. With the auto-launch midway to the *Milton*, he located a thumb sensor on the stone and triggered the firing of a shell from one of the harbor ships. The auto-launch exploded and sank. After a pause Thomas said, "There is no joy today in Reykjavík."

"Hah! Well said, Thomas. Failure gets its just reward."

Osborne looked off into the distance and muttered, "Traitors, Ali, face a worse fate." He took a more substantial sip of his scotch, savored it for a moment, then let it slide down his throat.

"You may leave, Thomas," he said.

Osborne sat down behind his desk and leaned back in his chair. Slowly he finished the rest of the chocolate, puffed his cigar, and sipped his drink. A toothy smile formed across his broad and ruddy face. He would yet make the traitors Ali Ebrahim and Rhett Blackwood pay for their crimes.

CHAPTER 16

A FLEET EXPANDS

"Admiral Petrova, you once served under me as Rear Admiral. However, time and circumstance have intervened and we have now opposed each other in conflict."

Admiral Nathan Flint

Admiral Flint arrived at the Antarctic seat of government in Konni Bay on Saturday, December sixteenth. At the same time, Admiral Aisling Murphy and her carrier attack force gathered near Queen Mary Land off the east coast of Antarctica. Admiral Anastasia Petrova's Antarctic Fleet was in the South Atlantic, southeast of the Falkland Islands. Her three-carrier fleet moved toward a confrontation that she believed might take place just south of Bouvet Island.

Meanwhile, Admiral Flint launched four stealth submarines, with Rear Admiral Austin in the command vessel. The submarines navigated below an electronic sonar refraction zone that was configured to resemble the ocean bottom, set on a course to intercept Admiral

Petrova's fleet. When the submarines were close enough, they released sensors that rose above the refraction layer. The sensors began mapping the hulls of each ship in the Antarctic Fleet. Using sonar data and software developed by Rear Admiral Austin, each ship was identified based on hull configuration and tonnage. All the ships' positions, speeds, and directions were measured and projected on live screens on the Rear Admiral's command submarine, which remained below detection depth. When the information was confirmed, small mines were released. Each mine sought out a specific location on its assigned ship. Almost all of the ships required multiple mines positioned to rupture the hulls at precise locations. Without fail each mine attached to its programmed position.

Soon after Admiral Flint received confirmation that the mine attachments were completed, he ordered all aircraft on the deck of the carrier *Inuit,* still under the command of Vice Admiral Park, and Admiral Murphy's carrier *Flintlock* to be taken to below-deck hangars. As soon as the decks of both carriers were cleared of aircraft, on his orders the two small fleets converged just north of Dronning Maud Land, directly south of Bouvet Island; they then travelled in attack formation due north toward Admiral Petrova's Antarctic Fleet.

Admiral Petrova had three attack carrier groups in her fleet, as well as fourteen fast missile cruisers that moved to forward positions as her fleet advanced. With this positioning she believed she had Admiral Flint's advancing fleet in check. As both fleets closed to 150 kilometers, she launched all aircraft that were positioned on the flight decks of her three carriers. Seconds after the last plane of the first wave cleared the deck, a series of underwater explosions occurred on the starboard side of each of Admiral Petrova's carriers, which all began to list. The flight decks were then at an angle that didn't allow launching or landing of aircraft.

At the same time, the *Swordthruster*, with its advanced pulse laser cannon fully charged, moved to the fore of Admiral Flint's fleet. Admiral Petrova's missile cruisers broke formation and began an attack run toward Admiral Flint's fleet. They were stopped when violent explosions occurred on each of their hulls. Large breaches opened on the bows of the cruisers. Their forward motion drank water, while aft detonations breached the air containment chambers. The ships sank, bow first, within a few minutes. Admiral Petrova was suddenly faced with the fact that she now had no missile cruisers, and her planes could neither launch nor land on her listing carriers. In less than twenty minutes she had been checkmated.

Admiral Flint sent an open channel message to his adversary:

> Admiral Petrova, this message is sent on behalf of Admiral Flint, who is prepared to offer assistance. You have an attack force of aircraft aloft and no capability of retrieving them. The flight decks on our carriers are cleared and prepared to accept any of your planes that wish to land. Before we can allow that privilege, however, we require they drop all ordinance. That action will signal the pilots' intent to land and surrender.

Without having received any reply from Admiral Petrova, Admiral Flint watched as her four lead fighters dropped their ordinance in the ocean and lined up on approach to his two carriers. More of the fighter planes also began dropping ordinance and positioning into landing trajectories toward Admiral Flint's carriers. Suddenly, four missile-armed fighter aircraft broke from landing formation and formed an attack posture. Four rapid pulses from the *Swordthruster*'s laser cannon quickly destroyed the threat. All four armed fighters fell, in flames, into the Atlantic. The rest of Admiral Petrova's aircraft landed on Admiral Flint's carriers without incident. Some were taken to hangars below to make room on deck for the remainder.

Admiral Petrova sent an open channel communication to Admiral Flint, addressing him directly:

> Admiral Flint, I once called you Nathan. Now I regret that I am your captive. As such I request your assistance. The pumps on my carriers are all at capacity and cannot correct or control their list. I don't think they can keep up with the inflowing seawater for more than a few hours. I have full crews on all three carriers whose lives are at risk. I propose a complete surrender if you can assist in saving my crew. —Adm. Anastasia Petrova

> Admiral Petrova, you once served under me as Rear Admiral. However, time and circumstance have intervened, and we have now opposed each other in conflict. In countering your attack my intent was to save life and assets as much as possible. I will add your carriers to my own fleet. Rear Admiral Austin, who designed the autonomous charges that attached to the hulls of your ships, allowed for their salvage. We have temporary seal plates that will cover all the breaches in your carriers' hulls. I am sending three launches with divers and equipment that will temporarily repair the damage. Soon after installation the pumps will have cleared the seawater, and your carriers will right themselves. Then your fleet will be escorted to Konni Bay, where permanent repairs will be made. After that we have much to discuss. —Adm. Nathan Flint

> Admiral Flint, I rely on your humanity to treat all my crew with dignity during our surrender. Can you explain the process so that I can inform them to ensure a cooperative surrender? —Adm. Petrova

Admiral Petrova, please be assured your personnel will be properly treated. Upon arrival at anchorage in Konni Bay they will be transported to the deck of my carrier *Flintlock*. There they will be assembled, divided into smaller groups, and dispersed to be held in detention on ships throughout my fleet. Staff from my navy will take control of your ships. Following that, your crew will be vetted to determine their fate. Upon your arrival you will also be escorted to the *Flintlock*, there to meet with my command staff: Admiral Aisling Murphy and Rear Admiral Rodrigo Austin. —Adm. Flint

In the early evening of that same day, the expanded fleet began arriving in Konni Bay. When the next day dawned, residents of the town were astonished to see the bay filled with more naval ships than had ever been assembled in that port. Governor Fong's office was overwhelmed with anxious inquiries from citizens who thought they might be under occupation. His office put out a bulletin assuring everyone that was not the case, these were all ships of the fleets of Admiral Nathan Flint. There would be no aggressive action or coup attempt, the bulletin stated, as the admiral and his forces were under the direct control of Governor Fong and his Parliament.

Later that morning Admiral Murphy, Rear Admiral Austin, and Admiral Flint met on the carrier *Flintlock*. Admiral Murphy and Rear Admiral Austin arrived first and were escorted into the small conference room. A few minutes later Admiral Flint entered with his steward, who carried a tray with a coffee service.

"Given the hour, I assume you've both had breakfast before coming, so I'm offering coffee. If either of you want something more, please ask my steward," Admiral Flint said. "Have the interviews begun?"

"Yes, for both of us," Admiral Murphy said. "From early results, I suspect most of the captive crew will be found suitable to incorporate into service on our ships."

"Excellent! And what do we do with those we find unsuitable? Do we release them back to Draco Osborne's navy?"

Rear Admiral Austin answered.

"If we did, Nate, I don't think Draco would accept them. He would assume they were spies or saboteurs. At best he would reject them; more likely he would have them assassinated by his henchmen. I think that we put them off in the nearest port that will accept them under humanitarian terms."

"I agree, and that brings up the more difficult question of Admiral Petrova. What about her fate? We haven't spoken of this, but are you aware of what happened to Rear Admiral Lower Half La Joy?"

"Yes, we both know of the explosion of the auto-launch Draco had put him on," Aisling Murphy answered.

"The crews can be vetted quite easily," Nate said. "Officers require a more rigorous process because of their command status. An admiral . . . well, that's an even more difficult question."

"She can't be vetted using the normal protocol. She's too aware of the process," Rod Austin said.

"And as a senior officer she's passed extensive brain scans. That tool is not likely to reveal anything new," Aisling added.

"I'm sure she's also aware of the fate of Franklin La Joy. She will have ample motivation to join us," Rod said. The other two nodded in agreement with his point.

At that moment Admiral Flint's steward appeared in the doorway.

"Admiral Petrova has arrived, sir."

"Thank you, James. Please send her in."

Admiral Petrova entered wearing her casual daily work uniform. Though her posture was military erect, her face showed signs of distress. She entered and stood at attention.

"Admiral Petrova, please have a seat. Of course, you know Admiral Murphy, but I don't believe you've met my new rear admiral, Rodrigo Austin."

"We met when he was Captain Austin. Congratulations on your rapid advancement, Rear Admiral Austin," Admiral Petrova said as she took the chair offered her by the steward.

"I must tell you, Anastasia, Rear Admiral Austin played a leading role in your defeat," Admiral Flint said.

"To defeat such a challenging adversary means the promotion is well deserved," Admiral Petrova said. There were brief smiles from the other three officers in the room. Admiral Petrova visibly relaxed in her seat.

"Would you like some coffee, Anastasia?"

"No, thank you. I just finished my own breakfast."

"About yesterday. You chose to attack us. I would like to know what led to that decision," Admiral Flint said.

"I'm not proud of the reason; a chance for glory, I suppose."

"Glory?"

"That and the fact that I had a superior force."

"Yes. On the face of it you had a superior force in numbers and firepower, but if you consider strategy and innovative technology, my forces were superior . . . As the facts bear out."

"I am deeply humbled."

"One thing I don't understand, Anastasia. Why do you support a criminal despot like Draco Osborne?" Admiral Flint asked.

"I very much oppose the man."

"Yet you attacked the most significant military force in opposition to his power."

"That is a fact."

"Why??"

"Again, it was visions of glory. If I defeated you then consolidated your fleet into mine, I would have the power to challenge the Arctic Fleet and bring Draco's power to an end."

"So, it was ego overruling the noble objective?"

"It was," said Admiral Petrova. With that admission she seemed to sink slightly into her chair.

"Do you still desire to bring Draco's power to an end?"

"I do. But I haven't quite figured out how that can be done without a military coup. While that is possible, I don't think it is the most effective way in the long term. Despite Draco's corruption, I still feel civilian control of the military is essential."

"I do as well. My fleet sails under the authority of Governor Fong. We are proceeding to declare our independence from GSU," Admiral Flint said.

"A better idea might be for the local parliament to vote to censure Draco and attempt to build an opposition political alliance with Parliament in Reykjavík," Admiral Petrova said.

"Admiral Petrova, if you will excuse us, Admiral Murphy, Rear Admiral Austin, and I will conference in my adjoining office. Please remain here. We will return shortly."

The three officers retired to Admiral Flint's office and closed the door. They remained standing.

"What do you think?" Admiral Flint asked. "Can we trust her? Does she potentially add anything to our operation?"

"As to the first question, I think we can trust her," Aisling Murphy said. "She doesn't have the stature to challenge you, Nate. As a military strategist she is not exceptional, and I believe we have exceptional talent in that arena. She does have some political savvy and expressed a way forward that has merit."

"Brilliant assessment, Aisling. Do you concur, Rod?"

"I do."

The three officers returned to the conference room. Admiral Petrova tentatively rose from her chair and stood, although not at attention, with shoulders back and spine straight. She relaxed a bit as she read the mood and body language of the people who would determine her fate.

"Admiral Petrova, we have decided that we would like you to join our fleet if that is your desire," Admiral Flint said.

"Of course, I would, and I am grateful you've asked. What will be my role?"

"We will keep you at your present rank, but you will not have a command position. Instead, you will work as liaison with the governments and parliaments at both Konni Bay and Reykjavík. You will take the lead in building a coalition government that will result in the ouster of Draco Osborne. You will also assist us in the assimilation of our two forces and the redistribution of officers and crew. We will soon send out a communiqué to all officers and crew announcing your appointment. This will be signed by me, Admiral Murphy, Rear Admiral Austin, and Vice Admiral Shin Park, who is currently committed to other duties. We trust that this is acceptable to you and we welcome your expertise and input in this endeavor."

Despite all attempts to control her reaction, Admiral Anastasia Petrova found herself wiping her cheeks as they moistened in gratitude. "I am so appreciative. I can only say, thank you!"

"This calls for a special toast before lunch." Admiral Flint called his steward. "James, would you bring in the bottle we discussed earlier?"

A few minutes later the steward entered with a tray on which were four small snifters and a 250-year-old bottle of Pierre Ferrand cognac.

"This bottle was commandeered from the flagship of Admiral Petrova's fleet," Admiral Flint said, with a slight nod in Anastasia's direction. "It is only appropriate she share it with us on this occasion." The steward set the tray down and poured the cognac. Admiral Flint invited him to pour one for himself as well, and when James had done so they all raised their glasses and toasted their new admiral.

"I was saving this bottle for a victory celebration, but I'm more pleased with this outcome," Admiral Anastasia Petrova said.

CHAPTER 17

AMBITION THWARTED

"Revenge with violence yields a very visceral satisfaction. Revenge using lies and cunning is slaying the same animal, just in a different way."

Draco Osborne

Admiral Flint was in the process of vetting all newly acquired personnel in his Antarctic Fleet. He needed to be sure he had a committed and capable force. Despite Secretary General Draco Osborne's installation of a command hierarchy that had sworn allegiance only to him, officers and enlisted sailors loyal to Admiral Flint persisted in the Arctic Fleet. This led Admiral Flint and his team to hope, and even operate on the assumption, that Osborne's admirals commanded a far less committed navy. Still, if the two massive forces met, the outcome could not be assured for either force.

Draco Osborne was very much aware of the events in the Antarctic — and he was furious. A major shift in the dynamics of planetary power had taken place. He needed a flanking move but was at a loss as to what that move could be. As he sat in thought in his office, doing his best to hold back his rage, he called in his butler, Thomas Wagner.

Thomas had long ago learned to respond quickly.

"What service do you require, Your Honor?" the butler asked.

"Just some conversation, Thomas. It has not escaped my notice that you always perform your duties competently and efficiently. Some might overlook your presence, as you are often the only person in the room who says nothing."

"I try my best, Your Honor."

"And I commend you for that. However, although you yourself are silent, you do hear a lot of what's being said, do you not?"

"Of course, Your Honor, and I repeat nothing to anyone." Thomas's normally non-expressive face showed traces of tension at this. Osborne noticed and smiled slightly.

"I'm not accusing you of anything, my good servant. You may relax. I just want your opinion on something. I sense that, despite your station in life, you are an intelligent person. Am I wrong about that?"

"Uh . . . No, sir. Um . . . you are not wrong. That is, I believe I am an intelligent person."

"Good! Now, you are aware that Admiral Petrova has committed treason and defected to the rebel Nathan Flint." This Osborne put more as a question than a statement.

"I am, Your Honor."

"And that she absconded with her entire fleet. Now Flint has a military power that rivals that of our government. He poses a threat to our elected governing body. To our way of life. He is dangerous, but I fear that to confront him directly could lead to disaster for us."

"Disaster, Your — "

"Due to the increased size of his military," Osborne explained.

"I understand, Your Honor, but as a butler I don't see what —"

"A suggestion, Thomas! Just give me a suggestion. My advisors are idiots. Give me your thoughts. What can I do to reestablish my dominance?"

"Well, I believe, you could make other alliances. Your Honor."

"Oh yes! Brilliant. Now, let's think about this; with whom do you suggest I make an alliance?"

"Dr. Greenly, Your Honor."

"Dr. Virgil Greenly?" Osborne caught himself practically shouting at Thomas. "Dr. Greenly in space?" he continued, incredulous.

"Yes, Your Honor. I know him to be a brilliant scientist, but he is a naïve politician."

"Hmm . . . Yes. Thomas, I feel an idea forming. I need to avenge the escape of Ali Ebrahim and Rhett Blackwood . . ." Osborne became silent as he continued along his line of thinking.

"Sir?" Thomas said after a moment or two.

"Oh, yes. Excuse me. You have been a great help, Thomas."

"Thank you, Your Honor."

"And Thomas! There is a bottle of single malt scotch behind the decanters. Would you pour me a drink? And pour yourself one as well." Osborne was warming to his own ideas. "And help yourself to a chocolate if you like. Then you may take your leave."

"Thank you, Your Honor." The butler did as he was told, then left the room.

Osborne walked to his bar with his drink and helped himself to a chocolate. He spoke softly to himself.

"Revenge with violence yields a very visceral satisfaction. Revenge using lies and cunning is slaying the same animal, just in a different way. Still satisfying. Flint, Ebrahim, and Blackwood, you will yet suffer my vengeance."

Later that same day Osborne composed a message on virtual government letterhead to Virgil Greenly at Ellie 5 Zeta. He revised it several times and called his butler back to read it over. Thomas could help to ensure he got the tone right. The message expressed a sentiment Draco Osborne had little familiarity with.

> Dr. Greenly, despite recent events I wish to reassure you of my desire for the success of the Space Settlement Program. It is to our mutual benefit that we resume our pre-established program of transporting approved citizens to Ellie 5 Zeta as planned. These people have paid their passage, cleared security requirements, and waited for an unreasonable time already. I propose resuming launches beginning January 2, 2249. In addition, it is in our mutual economic interests to resume shipments of material from Ellie 5 to Earth. Please respond with your acceptance. —Secretary General Draco Osborne

"Virgil," said Ofelia, "you have just received a message from Draco Osborne. He's holding out a truce offer."

Virgil read the message.

"Hmm," he said. "Ali and Rhett's defection and Osborne's losses to Admiral Flint should have put him in a rage. This is not the response I would have expected from the man."

"I agree. And I believe the rage still resides deep within the darkest reaches of his soul. He cannot contain that rage for long without it erupting in viciousness of some kind. So, this apparent reasonableness does not preclude eventual violence. We should be wary of a trap."

Virgil thought only for a moment. He found that he was becoming more decisive as time went on; making difficult decisions was less debilitating.

"No question," he replied to Ofelia. "We remain a significant threat to his continuing power. Perhaps to his existence. However, let's agree and approve the launches. If he's bluffing, we will know soon enough. I am concerned, though, that we have no significant weapons at Ellie 5. Ofelia, is there some precaution we can take?"

"Yes, I'll see to it."

The newly approved launches began arriving at Ellie 5 Zeta on January eighth. The reception team — volunteers all, many of whom were from the first wave of settlers — was well prepared to receive them. Island security had intensified as well. Boarding inspection teams made certain that each spaceship was in order, clearing it for docking. After the fourth spaceship had been inspected and cleared Virgil ordered subsequent ships to dock uninspected. When the next spaceship docked the security team met them in the docking bay and screened passengers one by one as they floated through the hatch. Everything was in order. Relieved at having at long last arrived, the new space citizens entered the gravivators for descent to ground level.

The sixth and final launch of this series arrived a little late on the first of February, the captain reporting that the ship had experienced some mechanical difficulties immediately prior to launch. The delay disrupted the reception security force schedule but as there were no previous incidents on the first five dockings, some of the members were reassigned to other duties, reducing the security force to ten. They waited in the docking bay while the first several passengers floated out through the hatch and were cleared to enter the gravivators. The doors closed and the gravivators descended to the surface.

Then, as soon as the civilian passengers had cleared the small docking bay, a small shock explosive detonated in the room, stunning the security force and temporarily rendering them incapacitated. Twenty-five armed marines immediately propelled through the docking passageway in rapid succession and quickly bound the ten security officers. When the gravivators returned to the docking bay from delivering the passengers to the surface, the marines entered them and descended to the reception hall below.

Virgil and his team, including Rhett Blackwood and his youngest daughter, began greeting the groups of new arrivals as they exited from the two gravivators and entered the reception hall. The first arrivals were escorted to the Apocatequil Hotel for processing. But when the gravivator doors opened for the second time the welcoming team saw, instead of civilians, a group of marines, who burst from the two gravivators into the hall. They were wearing body armor and holding weapons at port arms. The soldiers pushed everyone aside and a lieutenant stepped forward, stood in front of Virgil, and read a statement.

"Dr. Virgil Greenly, you are under arrest, along with Ali Ebrahim and Rhett Blackwood."

"What are the charges?" Virgil asked, struggling to maintain his composure.

"Charges will be issued once you are taken into custody on Earth. The three of you will return with members of my team aboard the spaceship *Draco Star*. You will then be transported to Reykjavík. Secretary General Draco Osborne looks forward to presiding at your trial. In the meantime, a contingent of marines will remain here in Zeta Island with its new General Director. Dr. Greenly, meet your replacement, General Director Zarita Banderas-Duran."

Virgil swallowed a gasp as the woman stepped forward from the rear of the marine formation. "At last, we meet in person, Dr. Greenly," she said. Without waiting for him to acknowledge her, she continued, "So, you are here, and Dr. Blackwood is here, but where is the traitor Ali Ebrahim? It doesn't appear he's among your reception committee."

"If your marines will allow . . . ," Virgil said with a sweep of his arm, indicating his own security staff.

"Of course, former General Director. We are all reasonable people," Zarita replied. "You may send your impotent security to find him."

Virgil ignored Zarita's tone and addressed the head of his security detail. "Sergeant, take a couple of men. Find Ali and bring him here to the reception hall."

"Well executed, Dr. Greenly," Zarita said. "But you didn't tell your detail where Ali is. I would do that. They have only fifteen minutes to return with the traitor before we begin executions."

"Executions?" Virgil stared directly at Zarita. He saw before him an ugliness, even as her mouth was bent into a smile. "I will not forget you said that, Zarita." For Zarita's benefit he spoke to Ofelia out loud. "Ofelia, please locate Ali and direct my detail to him. We shall humor our 'new director' for now."

Zarita Banderas-Duran stepped up in front of Virgil and brought her face close to his. He did not flinch. He looked indifferently into her penetrating stare as he felt himself relax. Zarita smiled sweetly.

"Ah, yes, you have built-in advice and support, the sentient implant Ofelia. Do you know you are the last to have one of those disgusting parasites in your head? Not to worry, though. It won't be there for long. And you," she said, turning her attention to Rhett, "so nice to see you again, Rhett. How wonderful you have your daughter at your side." Rhett stiffened as the woman addressed the girl. "Chancey is it? How old are you, dear?"

Chanté looked at the mean lady in front of her. "I'm sixteen, and the name is Chanté," she said defiantly before she caught her father's cautionary scowl.

"Rhett, you have another daughter, don't you? I remember her name: Jules. She's not here at your side. How old is she now and where might she be?"

"Jules is a young woman," Rhett said quickly, "and in transit to Ceres Station. Now can we cut the chit-chat? No one here believes you care about my family."

"Oh, Rhett, always the impatient one and now unpleasant as well. In your present situation, though, I don't think you want to rush to your fate."

Zarita moved to the rear of her marine detail just as Virgil's security officers returned with Ali Ebrahim.

"That was fast, Sergeant. Where did you find our beloved former secretary general?"

The sergeant hesitated briefly, then with a quick nod from Virgil he replied. "He was just inside the hotel lobby greeting the guests, ma'am."

"Thank you. Now they are all here," Zarita said. "Secure the three men," she ordered her marines.

As the marine detail moved forward with wrist retainers, tiny injection dart launchers descended silently from the ceiling behind them. Each device independently targeted an exposed area on the back of the neck or upper spine of a marine. When all were locked on, they fired their almost microscopic darts. Within seconds every marine had collapsed to the floor, having been injected with fast-acting neuromuscular blockers. Virgil's security detail moved forward and removed the marines' weapons, then secured their hands behind their backs. They were left unconscious and face down on the floor. Zarita stood frozen, her mouth slightly agape.

"Secure Zarita's hands as well," Virgil ordered. Then he turned again to the security sergeant, who now stood behind him. "Sergeant, find Major Cass at the hotel and escort him to the docking port to move the *Draco Star*. Tell him to dock it at the Sunset Port." The sergeant offered a nod and left for the hotel.

Virgil then addressed Ofelia through his thoughts. "Hah! You, a 'disgusting parasite'? That woman does have an imagination. Ofelia, when the *Draco Star* is docked at the Sunset Port, please connect it to our isolated electronics. We need to scan all its systems to ensure our safety. After that, we can reconfigure it. It'll be a nice addition to our local transportation fleet. A name change is in order as well."

In all, fifty people had disembarked from the passenger spaceship. Twenty-six of them were the marine contingent, including Zarita. One by one they were scanned for body profile and the information was sent to the bank of robotic tailors. Bright-colored prison jumpsuits were custom-made for each. Zarita was the last person of the attempted coup to be sequestered within a small conference room located in the Apocatequil Hotel. Six hours later all the prisoners were wearing their new prison garb. Their uniforms and weapons had been collected in a pile just outside the conference room, which now doubled as a prison cell.

Rather than repurpose the confiscated weapons, Virgil ordered them taken to a small kiln, melted, and fused together into a misshapen mass of metal. The military uniforms and Zarita's clothes were neatly folded into packages by Virgil's security detail, each package displaying a replica of the individual's government ID.

Ofelia had been silently watching this activity since the would-be invaders were captured.

"Virgil, what exactly are you doing?"

"Heh, yeah, it seems a little strange, doesn't it? I'm sending a message to Draco. Not only do we destroy his pathetic weapons, but by sending back military uniforms and insignias, we also reject any symbol of his power."

"And you don't think that will provoke him?"

"It might."

Two days later a crew of security personnel loaded the packages of uniforms and the melted mass of weapons onto a reentry glider. Robot motors were attached and powered the glider to its reentry position. As it reached that position four days later, Virgil stood at the large monitor in his office, along with Ali, Rhett, and Daria. Ofelia's sensors provided video coverage while they visually followed the spaceship through its reentry to its arrival at the Gibraltar Spaceport. Half an hour after its landing, an autonomous tractor approached the searing spacecraft and pumped coolant into heat exchangers under the craft's skin. This was followed by the approach of a transport carrying several unloading robots.

Ofelia shut the transmitted video down.

"So," Rhett said, "message delivered. Now, what should we do with the prisoners? They could be a security risk if they're left here."

"They could be," Virgil replied. "The marines were under orders, so their situation is somewhat understandable, and they may not be as dangerous. But Zarita! She's an evil opportunist. She worked with you for years, Rhett, and you supported her when she needed it. Yet she had no qualms about trading self-respect for opportunity and self-benefit — even when that meant your destruction. She knew her actions would lead to a probable death sentence for you."

Virgil then directed his thoughts to Ofelia, asking the sentient associate to join the conversation with the group through the video screen.

"Of course, Dr. Greenly." Ofelia's soft, rich voice sounded over the speaker so all present could hear. "I have an idea. We could load the prisoners into life-support modules, place them on reentry gliders, and send them down as well."

"Ha!! That would be one hell of a ride," Ali said, laughing. "It would be justifiably terrifying."

"And it certainly would get Draco's attention," Virgil said.

"For sure it would piss him off," Ofelia intoned sweetly.

Daria had been standing beside Virgil watching Ofelia's imaging of the glider's reentry on the large screen. There was a pause in the conversation. Then Daria spoke for the first time. "Although the trip might be terrifying, they are likely to survive it, including reentry. But we would be sending them to a certain death at Draco's hand," she said. "All human life has value. I believe we should keep them here. Our concern should only be how to protect society from them."

"Daria is right, of course," Ofelia said. "Draco is a narcissistic sociopath. He has been humiliated by Admiral Flint, Ali Ebrahim, and now by you and me and all the people of Ellie 5. Our captives have botched his mission. We can be sure he will exercise retribution on them if they are returned to him."

"Let's come back to this discussion later," Virgil said, "after we all have had time to consider our next action regarding Draco Osborne. In the meantime, it would serve our consciences well to heed Daria's advice."

CHAPTER 18

LONG VOYAGE, LOST LOVE

"Nothing of worth comes without the two sisters: value and risk.
The higher the value, the greater the risk.
Love tops the list. You will love again, Jules."

Koral Blackwood

In July 2250 Jules Blackwood was aboard the *Endeavor* on course to the Ceres Space Station. The station was in orbit around the Ceres planetoid in the Asteroid Belt. The ship would travel another year before reaching the planetoid. By the time the *Endeavor* arrived, the old station would be on its way to Mars and Dag's people would be on the new Ceres Island. Like its sister ship *Eternal Hope,* the *Endeavor* created standard gravity as it spiraled through space.

The passenger section of the spaceship resembled a giant Ferris wheel, with living compartments spread around its periphery. Each contained a bed, a combination toilet/shower, a closet, and a small desk area. The pods were separate from one another but connected by an outer ring. The outer ring was a tube two meters in diameter. There were four open electric carts within this tube ring that were used as transport between personal pods and common areas. When summoned, a cart would come to the appropriate location, a section of the pod's floor would slide open, and a person would then lower themselves into the cart to travel to their destination.

The common area pods were located at four opposing positions around the wheel. At one of the positions was the dining room; a library and theater occupied another. Astronomical, engineering, and biomolecular research laboratories were located together. And the fourth common area contained a gym. These were the largest spaces. Each of the common area pods had a gravivator connecting to the central axis, which contained most of the mechanical equipment and housed the docking port.

Jules had already been traveling for a year and a half in very confined space aboard *Endeavor*, where the monotony and lack of variation were challenges for everyone on board. Creativity in producing different virtual experiences for entertainment, as well as opportunities for research and study, created variety in an existence of otherwise crushing boredom. Traveling with Jules were another twenty-four passengers. There were several other students, as well as professional people: relief engineers, environmental scientists, sociologists, two astronomers, a psychiatrist, and a master chef. Ceres Island was now large enough to be relatively comfortable and offered the kind of amenities that attracted such people, making recruitment for life aboard the island easier. The anticipation of such a life helped mitigate the negatives of the long journey to get there.

Thus far Jules had spent most of her time awake focusing on her education. She was studying mechanical engineering under Dr. Dag Harlow. She also studied microbiology and molecular biology under the direction of Dr. Virgil Greenly. Both men were leaders in their fields. Despite their stature, this wasn't all dreary book learning, as both

Endeavor, sister ship to the *Eternal Hope*

scientists created lessons that were shown using holographic and other three-dimensional projections. With Dr. Harlow's graphic creations, she could define materials, design structures, and virtually construct them or 3D print models of them. The virtually constructed structures and mechanical components could be stress tested as mathematical models almost as if they existed in the real world.

Biological studies were just as engaging. A passion for redwood forests had begun when, as a child, Jules had visited the few remaining coastal redwoods with her father. That resulted in her ongoing research into bioengineering redwood trees to exist in space. But even with her hunger for learning, and youthful energy and curiosity, Jules needed some diversion. Social connections and informal meetings occurred in three of the common areas; the dining room, the theater room, and the gym. She particularly enjoyed the theater room, as it contained a vast library. There were educational programs that projected vistas of dramatic places on Earth as they occurred hundreds of years before. Most contained information on restorative programs or plans that were proposed (few were carried out) following the great Climate Cataclysm that accelerated with a vengeance at the beginning of the twenty-first century. The rapid climate and weather changes had caused droughts, floods, famines, catastrophic human and wildlife migrations, localized wars, and mass starvation. Like most people, Jules desired to see the world as it was before these events.

In the theater room, Jules could recline in the seats and watch projections on the curved walls and domed ceiling for hours. These scenes could be as dramatic and expansive as the Iguazú Falls on the border of the Argentine and Brazilian states, or the Grand Canyon in the North American Southwest. They could also be as meditative and serene as close-ups of long-extinct flora in the Amazonian rainforest of ages past.

Some of Jules's activities, however, were action driven. One of her favorites was the virtual, yet physical, experience of the program on river rafting. She loved the feeling of being immersed in and traveling down whitewater rapids in a raft. The visual sensation was enhanced with raft-like seats actively bumping and lurching amid splashes of cold water. The programs were changed frequently; the visual and physical effects were limited only by the engineer's imagination.

Despite these distractions and the demands of her studies, Jules still felt periods of loneliness, isolation, and confinement. These feelings were common to passengers on long spaceflights. She communicated with her parents and sister Chanté frequently, but now the time delay caused by distance made live connection impractical. They now "talked" by message. She suffered from a lack of intimacy with her family.

One Friday evening Jules was attending an astronomy presentation by a young PhD postdoc, Dr. Charles de Verde. He had recently processed images from several of the space telescopes and was discussing his most recent findings. She had met him many months before, but at this presentation Jules saw him with new eyes. He was quite tall and athletic compared to other academics she knew. His enthusiasm, friendliness, and light humor fully engaged his audience. If that weren't enough, he was strikingly handsome, with soft brown hair, a thin straight nose, and a classically cleft chin. At that evening presentation he became the focus of her interest.

Dr. de Verde gave lectures and presentations in astronomy one or two times a week and Jules began attending them as her interest in astronomy — and in Dr. de Verde — grew. He was aware of the beautiful PhD student as well; at the age of twenty, she was exceedingly young for someone that far along in her education. As Jules read more on astronomy, she began asking questions, some of them profound. Their mutual interest and attraction grew, and soon they were seen together outside of the academic setting: they sat next to each other at meals and often visited the theater together. At his request, Jules began to call him Chip; at hers, he shared more details of his work. He invited her to his computer lab, where he processed astronomical data, to show her constructed images of his postdoc research.

Chip's primary area of study was a quest to understand more about matter entering black holes. He studied the "hair" that appeared as streaks just outside the event horizon of black holes. It was theorized that this "hair" was how the information contained in objects entering black holes was preserved. Chip was attempting to decode black hole "hair," whereby one might determine what sort of matter a black hole had devoured.

Jules spent a lot of her free time with Chip over the next couple weeks. The oppressive loneliness she had been fighting dissipated as she and Chip became closer. She still sometimes had a haunting feeling of isolation and separation from her family, and she stayed in touch with Chanté and her parents; but the need for contact with them was not as urgent as before. Gradually her relationship with Chip grew, until they became inseparable when not working on their individual projects.

This new romantic interest was proving to be a major distraction, though, and her studies in both molecular biology and mechanical engineering began to lag.

On July twenty-fourth, Jules received a joint inquiry from her professors.

Jules, we have noticed that you are not current in your studies, and we have some concerns. We are ready to start you on your final project, which should be completed by the time you reach Ceres. Please let us know the completion date of your current studies, as we are poised to send you the project details. Your final project will be challenging and so it will be to your benefit to begin as soon as possible. —Dr. Dag Harlow and Dr. Virgil Greenly

When Jules read the message, she saw it as a reprimand. She was accustomed to receiving praise and encouragement from her instructors. She responded right away.

Drs. Harlow and Greenly, thank you for your message. I acknowledge that I have been remiss. Recently I have been sidetracked by a new interest in astronomy. Please accept my apology and affirmation that I will redouble my efforts to complete my assignments so that I may begin my final project. You will receive the finished studies within a week. —Jules Blackwood, PhD candidate

Jules met Chip for dinner as usual at their favorite café. She was at the table early and had finished a glass of wine before he arrived.

"Wow, you've started without me," Chip said. "Give me a minute while I get myself a glass at the bar. What is it you're having?"

"Just a chardonnay," Jules replied, fiddling with her empty glass. "Would you bring me another one?"

"Are you sure?"

"You're right. I had better not."

"I'll get myself a glass and bring over a tray with dinner. What would you like to eat?"

"I don't know. I'm not that hungry. You choose something," she said.

Chip returned a few minutes later with his own glass of wine on a tray with two meals. He sat down and took a sip.

"You look a little dejected," he said. "Did something happen today?"

"I let my professors down. I'm behind in my studies and so I haven't received the details for the project I should have already started. I feel awful!"

"Look, Jules, it isn't something that can't be corrected. A little extra work is all."

"I know. I promised I would finish in a week."

"So, you'll finish in a week. It's not such a big problem."

"You know last night was a first for me, don't you?"

"Yes, I do. Was it OK? Jules, I want it to be OK for you."

"Not just OK. More like amazing." The memory brought a smile to her face, but Chip could still sense concern in her demeanor.

"Great! Look, Jules, it'll be fine if we take a week off so you can get back on track. It's not like we don't have another year together on this ship."

"I know. But I told my professors that I would be finished in a week. I didn't want them to know how far behind I was . . . I need more like two weeks."

"Let's finish dinner then you can get to work. You might surprise yourself. I'll see you in a week. In the meantime, I'll plan something special for when you've completed your courses and receive your final project." Chip took her hands in his and gave her an encouraging smile. "I love you, Jules," he said for the first time.

She leaned over and planted a big kiss on his mouth. Then smiled as she took the last few bites of her meal.

Then she kissed him again.

"Let's order something special for dessert," she said, grinning.

Jules and Chip returned to their separate living quarters after a relaxing evening lingering at the café and verbally sketching out a plan for Jules to get her course assignments wrapped up. She was feeling much more relaxed and hopeful, certain she could tackle her studies full force and actually be ready for the new project assignment in a week, as she'd promised her professors.

Around midnight that night a high-speed space object no larger than a walnut hit the *Endeavor*. The initial impact was heard only by the people sleeping in the adjacent pods; but it breached the protective shell of Chip's living quarters, causing a rapid decompression and a shock wave that travelled through the spaceship, waking many more.

The tear in the outer wall of Chip's room was large enough to cause an explosive burst of air that ripped out a sizeable panel. He met instantaneous death as his body, ensconced in his sleeping cocoon, was shot into space and flung out on a trajectory away from the ship, a result of the spaceship's standard gravity rotation. Immediately following the rupture, Chip's compartment self-sealed from the rest of the ship. No access to his quarters would be possible until the ship reached Ceres Island in another year.

The shock of the disaster reverberated throughout the spaceship for days thereafter. Unable to sleep for the first couple of nights after the event, Jules then began to experience nightmares. The first one caused her to awaken terrified and shaking; she remained awake until morning, replaying the images in her mind and imagining the horror of Chip's last moments. In the following days she hardly ate or talked to anyone. She barely acknowledged greetings on the few occasions she found herself in a common area. She had even been unable to discuss it with her family, although they had been alerted to the event and sent their love and condolences. Finally, seeking solace, she sent a message to her mother, describing the tragedy and the utter despair that followed.

Koral Blackwood responded with a long and heartfelt message. It closed with these words of comfort:

> ... Nothing of worth comes without the two sisters: value and risk. The higher the value, the greater the risk. Love tops the list. You will love again, Jules.

Soon after receiving the message from her mother Jules felt that she wanted to hold a memorial service for Chip. It was three weeks since the disaster when she entered the fully occupied dining room at lunchtime. The room grew silent when she appeared.

"I would like to organize a memorial service for Dr. de Verde," she announced. The room came alive again with a chorus of affirmation. Several close friends got up from their chairs to hug her and offer assistance. Even now, before the ceremony, she felt a sense of release. Although still tender and grieving, deep down she knew she was going to be fine one day.

Jules was far ahead of her years in her doctoral studies of mechanical engineering and molecular biology. Emotionally, however, she was still only twenty. Her experience of first love had been truncated, ending in horrific violence. She and Chip had not progressed beyond early discovery and infatuation. Had the relationship matured from attraction to a deeper love, they would have shared laughter and friction, admiration as well as annoyance. Over time, respect and mutual acceptance would have grown. But there had not been time for those aspects of the relationship to develop. Jules would forever remember Chip as her perfect partner.

She was, however, intelligent enough to realize that this was a lot for a twenty-year-old to experience and eventually she sought out the ship's psychiatrist for guidance. Dr. Peggy Ewen encouraged Jules to finish her studies so she could receive her project assignment. At first, they met daily before dinner for casual conversation. A more formal and professional relationship was always an option down the line; the doctor was careful to keep Jules aware that she had choices as to how to proceed. A regime of carefully selected medications was prescribed. Informal as their talks were, Dr. Ewen's counsel helped provide the emotional support Jules needed.

Still, she struggled with depression and sometimes didn't even feel like getting out of bed in the morning. When Dr. Ewen realized Jules had not been seen at breakfast in several days, she went to her pod and brought Jules to her office. The young woman slouched on the well-padded sofa. Dr. Ewen offered her a cup of tea and Jules sipped it absently for a few moments before the doctor spoke.

"Jules, I know you are feeling lost, and you worry about how to move forward. You're concerned that you will disappoint those who have invested in your future. But you are important not only to them, but to yourself as well." Jules began to shake her head in disagreement, but Dr. Ewen continued. "You still have a full life to live and experience. That you are beginning to recover from this trauma indicates you will be stronger and more able to endure setbacks in the future. It's difficult to realize now, but you do know that your life is filled with promise. Of course, you will remember Chip and your times together and the joy you had. But you also face a glorious future. Reach out for it!"

Something in what the doctor said touched the young woman and she felt more open than she had in the past several days. She sat forward and her face softened. The agony seemed to fade for her somewhat. She peered into the distance, her eyes unfocused. Slowly she began to speak.

"I remember our last time together. We were planning to stay apart for a week so I could finish my study program. We expressed our feelings for each other and came to a loving understanding."

"That is a beautiful memory, Jules. There's no need for you to try to suppress any memories you have of Chip."

"I will always remember him with sadness for the life that might have been for both of us. And with joy for the time we did have." Jules took a deep breath. "But I have to live in the present. I need to get on with my life." For the first time, she felt anchored in herself. She knew she would experience love again in the future. She also knew she had important things to attend to in the present.

Jules was finally able to finish her last assignments for her major professors, Dr. Harlow and Dr. Greenly. She submitted them with an apology. Two days later, while at breakfast, she received a message signed by both of them.

> Jules, we have reviewed your final exam papers and we have together given you a 'pass with distinction' evaluation. Please see the following description of your PhD project assignment. Successful completion of both phases of this project will complete your dual PhD program. —Dr. Dag Harlow and Dr. Virgil Greenly
>
> Final Project Assignment
> Jules Blackwood, PhD candidate
>
> The Project herein assigned on September 17, 2250 to candidate Jules Blackwood is the final event in her PhD contract. To complete the studies under this contract, the candidate shall, by use of mechanical devices of her design and molecular manipulation, create the technology to build a living redwood tree. The engineering and molecular research laboratories aboard the spaceship *Endeavor* shall be made available to her for this project.
>
> Part 1: Biological design
> The tree shall be designed using the following materials:
>
> - Hemp plant material
> - Bamboo plants
> - Redwood tree seeds

Part 2: Engineering design

- Robot design for construction of the tree root system, trunk, and branches using bamboo as base material
- 3D printer design for laying the cambium cells onto a constructed trunk and branches
- Processor design for creating pulp from hemp plants to overlay and protect the cambium layer

The finished tree will have the structural support of a non-living core consisting of processed bamboo of sufficient strength to support a living structure of a minimum of 50 meters in height (150 ft.). The tree will be designed to live and grow. Over time, as it grows, its native bark will replace the overlaid layer of hemp-derived material. It will look like a natural redwood tree. The actual tree will be constructed in Ceres Island, using the techniques the candidate develops in the laboratories of the *Endeavor.*

Jules read the message. *I've got my orders. Got to get to work,* she thought, gulping the last of her coffee and heading to her laboratory.

CHAPTER 19

JULES AT CERES ISLAND

"Out here in the Asteroid Belt we are in the boonies. But we think of our presence here as a camping sojourn, just a speck of time in the face of an unfathomable future."

Dr. Dag Harlow

By November of 2251 space islands were beginning to show their promised potential. Across the solar system the rate of development was increasing. No place was there more activity than at Ceres. Dag Harlow and his crew were moving into the recently completed Ceres Island. At two and a half kilometers in length and one kilometer in diameter the island was many times the size of Ceres Station. But the old Ceres Station habitat would find a new life. It was being prepared for launch into Martian orbit. The station had served its purpose over the years since Dag and his lead engineer Earl Bedford and chief environmentalist Salvadore Munros had assembled it from their arrival spaceship, the *Corn Goddess*. Over the years Dag and his engineers increased the station's mass four-fold as they converted the spaceship into a livable working habitat with self-sustaining life support systems.

While remarkable progress was occurring in space, Earth society had devolved into three antagonistic camps. Global States United (GSU), which had included most of the former nations in the Northern Hemisphere and Antarctica, was disintegrating because of the ongoing corruption of its leader, Draco Osborne, and his associates. The government of Henry Fong, seated in Antarctica, was head of the newly formed Southlands United (SU). This breakaway government represented the Southern Hemisphere south of the Tropic of Capricorn. The remainder of the world's population existed between the Tropic of Cancer and the Tropic of Capricorn. They were known unofficially as the Central Earth People (CEP). But they were unable to unite to form a government. Most of those people lived and suffered under the rule of gangsters and tribal fiefdoms. Both the GSU and the SU competed for the support, loyalty, and resources of the CEP. Skirmishes, minor wars, sabotage, and terrorism were frequent realities.

The scientists working in space were aware of these realities on Earth. They were concerned, of course. But there was consensus among them: the Space Settlement Program was not yet developed enough to sustain donating material assistance. There was accelerating progress, however.

Most of Ceres Station had been renovated. Unnecessary mass was removed in the process of converting it back into a spaceship that could make the trip to Mars. Also, the plutonium reactor was removed and installed in the new Ceres Island; it would afford an energy lifeline to the scientists' new home in the island should laser power transmission from Earth orbit ever be interrupted. However, not all renovations involved the removal of material from Ceres Station. A solar panel array was added to replace the power provided by the plutonium reactor. In addition, a huge amount of construction material, which would be used to greatly enlarge the station to serve a new function once it orbited Mars, had been loaded on board. Ceres Station was still a huge vessel. Therefore, more powerful motors, capable of accelerating it to its new home in Martian orbit, replaced the originals.

On December 1, 2251, Dag and his scientists and engineers watched on a vast screen inside the small ballroom of Ceres Island's Storm Mountain Lodge as Ceres Station's huge motors ignited. There was no sound or vibration, just an intense, sustained flash that lit up their shadowy world like a small sun. The spaceship pushed away from the Asteroid Belt. At first it moved slowly, then it traveled at increasing speed until it disappeared. Its trajectory would insert it into Martian orbit in two years and three months. It was the most massive spaceship ever accelerated.

Ceres Island was much smaller than any of the islands at Ellie 5, but it was still gigantic in the eyes of its crew of twenty-five scientists and engineers. These dedicated people working in space had a practice regarding their commitment to any one island or station; many of the science and engineering staff at all the stations, bases, and islands voluntarily rotated between them as their area of expertise came to be needed elsewhere. If need for an individual was greater at some other island they would be released of their present duties. In that way the tendency to sequester talent might be avoided.

Because of the great distances, their tenure at Ceres required the longest time commitment. The island was designed with living, working, and recreational spaces, as other islands were. However, the new Ceres Island was isolated. Because it was not a part of an archipelago, Dag and his team had made a greater effort to build extensive "natural wild" spaces, as there were no nearby venues for diversion.

The commitment and planning were completed but the natural areas were only partially planted. Eventually temperate forests of pine, fir, spruce, cedar, and redwoods would grow. Dag's team included Dr. Amelia Bereza, a forest ecologist who led the effort. She planned maple, oak, aspen, and sycamore trees to be interspersed among the conifers. Most of these trees had yet to exist in the island. Those that did had been included in the inventory of the *Corn Goddess* spaceship that was used in the founding of Ceres Station. Dr. Bereza now had fifty-three saplings she had moved from the crowded spaces of the old Ceres Station. Those she planted according to her forest design; as other trees and plants such as wild huckleberries were added, and as the saplings grew and filled in, the result would be lush and natural in appearance. But initially they would hardly be noticed, spread sparsely throughout the inner surface of Ceres Island. Everyone in Ceres Island anticipated the arrival of the *Endeavor,* which was bringing the rest of the plants and seeds needed to complete the "natural" forested environment. When they arrived, orchards and vineyards would be planted on gentle hills within the island and Dr. Bereza's vision would be complete.

Bamboo and hemp covered much of the interior surface of Ceres Island. Vast quantities of these plants were needed in the fabrication of construction materials. These natural materials were used not only in construction, but also in the manufacture of clothes, bedding, and other soft materials. The engineers built their new living quarters from manufactured timber. The Storm Mountain Lodge was made to resemble a rustic log-and-timber hotel and many of the inhabitants designed and built small cabin-style houses that were scattered around the inside circumference. Eventually the buildings would be surrounded by fields and forest.

The Storm Mountain Lodge was named after Dr. Timothy Storm of NASA Mars Base. He had led a team in the design of the lodge to relieve Dag's overwhelmed engineers, who were designing and building other aspects of the island. The lodge was situated on the shores of Beaver Lake, a small lake with a marina whose docks were lined with rowboats. One could be reserved for a relaxing afternoon, one that could possibly lead to a fresh fish dinner. The only dining facility on the island, presented as a fine restaurant and lounge, was in the lodge and intended both for local use and any visitors that might ever come to this remote outpost. Everyone in the island hoped that if it were made attractive enough, tourists might someday visit despite the long travel time required. The close views of Jupiter were truly striking and certainly a draw.

In the old Ceres Station, a menu contest between competing teams of scientists and engineers had been a fun diversion and it was hoped the practice would continue in this new island. Dag's two lead engineers had each created a means of adding variety to the daily menu. Earl developed a technology using chopsticks, whereby the chopsticks transmitted tiny electrical impulses to the tongue to replicate flavors. If the chopsticks were programmed to stimulate the correct combination of taste buds, the diner would experience that natural flavor. Using these, a person could eat a perfectly flavorless piece of "sushi" 3D printed to appear as if it were salmon sashimi and it would taste just like fresh raw salmon, enhanced with the flavors of soy sauce and wasabi. If a diner chose to sample another bite, and wished for a spicy tuna roll, they would place the chopsticks in their accompanying canister and touch the appropriate program button. When the next bite was taken, even though it was not a spicy tuna roll, it would taste as such. The chopsticks could theoretically be programmed to replicate the flavor of any food. Earl saw this as a continuing hobby.

The other culinary contribution came from Salvadore. He loved desserts of all kinds. He developed a set of dessert utensils that activated sweetness receptors in the mouth. The utensils also added a choice of flavors: chocolate, strawberry, peach, caramel, and coconut. He called his flatware "dessertware." The utensils worked by using a micro-textured surface and taste-bud-stimulating molecules bonded to the underside of metal spoons and forks. Unlike Earl's invention, Salvadore's cutlery was not programmable. Both products were completely calorie free. Once discovered by the rest of the staff, they became wildly popular.

As in Ceres Station, the island's kitchens were entirely autonomous because the team of scientists and engineers had never succeeded in importing service staff. Uniquely at Ceres Island, robots had been designed to function in all aspects of food preparation and other service roles. That included housekeeping and restaurant robots in the small hotel. Each resident enjoyed the services of a personal housekeeping robot in their private home. The engineers had also designed and built robots that worked together as domestic maintenance teams. These robots could remodel individual living quarters or repair components of such quarters as necessary.

Dag built a log-cabin-style home in what would be a small clearing in a forest yet to come. His cabin was within easy walking distance of the lodge. The simulated logs were fabricated from processed bamboo and the partially planted future forest around Dag's cabin was enhanced with rounded simulations of granite stones protruding from the regolith soil.

A network of hiking trails wound through the chaparral, traversing the full circumference of the rotating cylinder, which greatly increased the perception of expansive space. The low hillsides were occasionally punctuated by cliffs and cascading waterfalls. These things had been carefully designed into the island precisely because it had to fulfill all the needs of its occupants. There were no nearby islands that could offer a venue for rest and relaxation and the crew had long suffered in their cramped Ceres Station habitat.

The men and women in Ceres Island felt that it was truly a paradise. That feeling was confirmed when three couples decided to marry and commit to having children in the remote outpost. All three ceremonies took place on the same day, and by unanimous agreement the wedding date was designated an annual holiday. It marked the day Ceres Island began as an established society.

The much-anticipated arrival of the *Endeavor* at Ceres Island occurred amid great fanfare on February 14, 2252. When the ship was about three hours away from docking, the Ceres Island scientists and engineers gathered in the Waterfall cocktail lounge at the Storm Mountain Lodge to await the new arrivals. They did not wait to begin cocktail service, however. By the time Jules Blackwood and the rest of the passengers had taken the gravivators to the surface and made their way to the reception in the Waterfall lounge, the celebration was well underway.

Not everyone was at the party, however, as a team of engineers had entered the *Endeavor* and undocked it from Ceres Island. They triggered motors mounted around its circumference, which enabled the great ship to gradually slow. Only when it had stopped rotating could close examination be made of the outside of the sealed quarters of Dr. Charles "Chip" de Verde. While the *Endeavor* was stationed at Ceres Island waiting for a launch window to Mars it would undergo extensive inspection, repair of the damage, renovation, and routine maintenance. Robotic scans were recorded of Chip's compartment and the information was sent to Ceres MAC facility to inform fabrication for repair. The exterior walls of the compartment would be repaired from outside the spaceship, as access from the inside was not possible until the atmosphere could be restored. Dr. de Verde's quarters had been internally sealed from the rest of the ship to protect the ship's atmosphere. When the launch window approached in thirty-four months the *Endeavor* would be resupplied and refueled. Except for the damage repair, these were routine procedures whenever the *Endeavor* or the *Eternal Hope* parked at one of their three destinations.

The reception party was becoming a little raucous and overwhelming for Jules. She took the opportunity to leave the festivities and meet with a receiving coordinator who would assist in her room assignment. After securing a room at the Storm Mountain Lodge she spent the evening by herself, retiring early after a solo dinner in the hotel dining room.

The next morning, a woman approached Jules in the dining area just as she was finishing her breakfast.

"Excuse me for interrupting. Are you Jules Blackwood?"

"I am."

"Great! I'm Dr. Amelia Bereza, the forest ecologist here in Ceres Island. I have anticipated your arrival for what seems to be forever."

"I'm very pleased to meet you, Dr. Bereza," Jules replied, standing and extending her hand. "And I have been traveling forever to get here. It seemed we would never arrive. I believe all of us from the *Endeavor* appreciate being in an expansive space again; it was so cramped on the spaceship. I'm looking forward to touring your island and learning about your contribution to this project. I'm eager to begin work here to finally see if building living trees can be achieved on a space island. As you can imagine, most of my research could not be verified aboard the *Endeavor.*"

"I'm sure these trees will be a reality. Could I sit with you for a while and show you my forest design?"

"It would be my pleasure, Dr. Bereza."

"Please, call me Amelia."

"Thank you." Jules motioned for a server to please clear the table of her breakfast dishes. She sat back down and indicated the chair next to her for the ecologist to sit. They ordered two cups of coffee.

"I would love to see your plans, Amelia," she said. "My first inclination is to create a series of circular 'cathedral' redwoods. I think that would give the impression of old growth. After that we could progress to other trees and chaparral. According to your plan, of course."

Dr. Bereza opened a file of schematics showing where her plants could best be located. She showed holographs of the entire interior of Ceres Island as it now existed. The two women then took their coffee out onto the expansive plank porch at the front entrance to the dining area. The Storm Mountain Lodge looked every bit as if it had been constructed of large conifer timbers on a foundation of granite boulders. But of course, it hadn't been. Instead, all wood materials were made of processed bamboo and made to look like rustic timbers. The boulders were made of regolith and cement, having been 3D printed in place.

Jules and Amelia sat in oversized log chairs and entered the planting scheme for the redwood trees into a program that could show the finished result integrated with ferns and other forest plant life. After this task was completed, Amelia placed a small holographic projector on one of the simulated stumps that served as side tables. She projected a hologram of the entire interior of Ceres Island as it was now and how it would appear in the future. Jules suggested where small redwood stands might be placed. Amelia had anticipated locations for the redwood stands and before long they had agreed on placement.

"Well, that certainly looks good in design. I can't wait for you to get started," the ecologist said. "What's the first step?"

"The first thing I want to do," Jules said, "is hike to all the locations we want to plant to map out a final configuration that best represents the ground contours. After that I will request scan data on specific redwoods on the California coast and Sierra Nevada so that I can replicate those trees."

"And to do that . . . ?"

"Well, here's where my research and ideas are put to the test. The first step will be to 3D print the internal structure of the tree from engineered bamboo. This will include branches to reflect that of the selected scan."

"So, the first step will produce a forest of skeletons . . ."

"Yes, but not for long. The next will be to seal the bamboo core with a layer of bamboo pulp mixed with manufactured resin. Over that will be a smooth paper-like layer. When that layer has properly adhered, it will be sprayed with a gel solution of electrolytes and nutrients. Then the living undifferentiated cambium cells will be evenly printed on this layered structure."

"So, it will now be a living tree. But I would think this would be a very fragile stage," Amelia said.

"Yes, a living and very fragile tree. This is the most critical stage. We need to protect this layer, as it will quickly die otherwise. The next step will be to print a layer of processed hemp over the cambium tissue and feed it through this layer until the cambium layer can grow the inner bark, the phloem, and the sapwood underneath.

At this point the outer protective area of bark will begin to grow and thicken over time."

"And what about the needles? Will they grow out as on a natural tree?"

"We shall see. That's the one part I was not able to complete on the *Endeavor*."

"Well then, here's to the successful growth of needles," Amelia said. Jules raised her coffee cup and clinked it with Amelia's.

CHAPTER 20

SEA SANCTUARIES

"I am already thinking about this. It's a big problem, with many parts, but I will focus on finding a starting point."

Chanté Blackwood

Since before her arrival at Ellie 5 Zeta on November 7, 2248, Chanté Blackwood had been interested in academics. Although she was only sixteen when they arrived, once the Blackwood family had settled in to their new life in the island she started working on formalizing the curriculum for her vision of a university based in space. Over the next two years, she established the rudiments of such an institution with a collection of courses. Taking inspiration from her efforts, a board made up of academically minded leaders formed an accrediting body that reviewed the curricula, adjusted content, and accredited the courses. This board was composed of several leading scientists and engineers, as well as experts from the humanities, all of whom lived and worked within the Space Settlement Program.

By 2250 the list of accredited courses had grown to sixty-five and included a full curriculum in the physical and biological sciences, mathematics, and most of the social sciences. A name was also chosen for the institution, to be formalized at a later date. To highlight their forward-looking mission, the board proposed the name Prescient University. Chanté heartily endorsed that name.

Although this progress was remarkable, and the various disciplines established standards of accreditation and kept accurate records, the university as a coherent institution did not formally exist. Chanté was actively working with the volunteer faculty on finalizing its charter as well as attending classes herself. However, she and the faculty were stretched just to satisfy the most pressing need, which was to schedule classes that would meet the increasing demand. Many of the newest arrivals from Earth were older children who sought to continue their interrupted education.

Though it was her initial goal, it had become a challenge to keep a consistent focus on organizing the university. More urgent needs always seemed to distract her from that project. The most recent and most demanding distraction had come to her from an unexpected source.

Admiral Nathan Flint now commanded the Antarctic Fleets against the struggling government of Draco Osborne. As his ships moved around more freely, he saw firsthand the desperation of people living along coastal areas in Sub-Saharan Africa, southern India, Southeast Asia, and the atoll islands of the South Pacific, threatened as they all were by the ever-encroaching seas and violent weather events. He could only imagine the living conditions in the interior, away from the coast.

Desperate for basic needs, the Central Earth People were corruptible—and Draco Osborne had capitalized on their desperation. To feed and house their children, parents might find their only option was illegally transporting drugs and other contraband. Women could be forced to sell themselves in the same cause. For Osborne's crime machine the Central Earth People were easy recruits. But he controlled the CEP only if he kept them in abject poverty.

Admiral Flint sought to change that dynamic. He discussed the issue repeatedly with his senior staff. All agreed the problem was poverty. If that one factor could be eliminated Osborne would lose the primary means of support for his enterprises. But how? Though the enlisted personnel Flint commanded were adept at many things, especially in the areas of engineering and electronics, they lacked specialized knowledge in vital fields such as agriculture, ecology, and biological systems in general. On his senior staff, psychologists supported the troops and were an integral means of maintaining a high-functioning navy. But there were no sociologists in his navy, and he was beginning to recognize the need for them as well.

Without the necessary experts at hand, the admiral contacted his lifelong mentor, Ali Ebrahim, at Ellie 5 Zeta to discuss the problems as he and his officers saw them. As always, his connection was encrypted. Ali's com announced: "Incoming call from Admiral Nathan Flint." Ali commanded his automated system to close his office door. He then opened the secure channel.

"Ali, I hope life is treating you well at Zeta Island," Admiral Flint began. "You're eating well, no lurking assassins?"

"Never better, my friend. Since we now control the Space Settlement Program there seems to be no limit to what we can do. The people here are filled with hope and enthusiasm."

"A sharp contrast to the situation on Earth, I'm afraid," the admiral replied.

"I sense stress in your voice, Nate. How can I help you?"

"Stress — that's an understatement. You are aware of the plight of people trying to survive in the Central Earth Zone. If I could find a way to help them out of their hopeless conditions . . . Win their support . . . Well, if that happened, Draco Osborne's reign would soon end."

"Agreed. What do you have in mind?"

"Some sort of self-help programs that could provide reliable food supplies, education, jobs, security from violence, and restoration of natural habitats."

"Oh, is that all?"

"Heh, yeah, a big order, I know. But long term that's what we will need."

"My friend, we achieve those things within the space islands. But then our society was hand selected. Something not possible on Earth. But we do have talent and people dedicated to those common objectives. There is someone I believe could assemble a team and come up with some ideas that might work. Her name is Chanté Blackwood."

"Rhett's daughter?? But she can't be more than, ah, sixteen at the outside."

"She's eighteen."

"OK, little difference."

"You'd be surprised, Nate. She has a brilliant mind and is capable beyond her years. Mind you, she's on task overload now, but I'll put her in touch with you and you can see what I mean."

"Well, I trust your judgment. I look forward to speaking with her."

A couple days later Admiral Flint received a call from Chanté. As he was leading a staff meeting at the time the call came in, he was tempted to decline it at first. But when he learned who it was from, he dismissed his staff with orders to continue the meeting later and took the call.

"Admiral Nathan Flint. It is a great honor to speak with you," Chanté said.

"Likewise, Miss Blackwood."

"Thank you. You can just address me as Chanté."

"OK, will do. And you can go ahead and call me Nate. You probably don't remember, but I met you when you were a small child. I understand you're an adult now, Chanté."

"Yes. I don't know if it's a good thing, but I feel even older than I am. My work trying to organize a university takes more time than I expected. The stress has probably aged me at least a couple of years."

"Understood," the admiral said. "I assume you're calling because Ali Ebrahim suggested I speak with you regarding some ambitious and optimistic plans I hope to develop to improve conditions for people living on Earth. But given your current responsibilities, perhaps it's not in your best interest to take on another project at this time."

"Actually, it's a good time. I need a diversion. Almost every class I've initiated is now in other hands. I need to separate myself from the university project for a while."

"Good. Chanté, I will put you in touch with Admiral Petrova. She is my liaison with Governor Fong of Southlands United and certain members of Parliament at Reykjavík. Once we have a developed plan, she can present it to them."

"OK. Then this is what I have in mind," Chanté said, the wheels already turning in her head. "I can work with Ali, my father, and Dr. Greenly. They can help me develop a draft plan that I can then present to you and Admiral Petrova."

"Yes. That's good. However we achieve it, the primary goal is to improve the lives of all Central Earth People. And of course, the secondary goal is to erode Draco Osborne's power. Completely, one hopes."

"Admiral Flint, I am already thinking about this. It's a big problem, with many parts, but I will focus on finding a starting point. When I have some ideas, I will call again."

Chanté began work on this new project by focusing on reforestation. If they covered huge swaths of poor-quality farmland with trees, that would begin to rebuild soil, provide haven for threatened species, remove carbon from the atmosphere, and give some relief by tempering extreme heat waves. It would also provide people with employment, giving their lives necessary income, as well as some purpose. Much of the food production could mimic the techniques and processes used in the space islands. That could occur within hardened buildings, offering some degree of protection from weather disasters — as well as marauders.

Providing reliable shelter, food, and products to improve the people's living conditions — not to mention creating the facilities to manufacture such products — was not going to be easy. Protecting them was likely to be even harder. Roving armed gangs and militia, some independent, some owing allegiance to Draco Osborne, often raided any source that had potential economic value. Thus, under present conditions it was largely impossible for coherent societies to form or for small villages to even survive. Security was therefore a primary concern.

A week after her conversation with Admiral Flint, Chanté called Admiral Petrova by a secure line he had provided her with. She introduced herself.

"Admiral Petrova, hello. I am Chanté Blackwood. I hope Admiral Flint has told you of our discussion regarding the welfare of the Central Earth People."

"I'm very glad to meet you, Chanté. The Admiral has spoken highly of you. I have spoken with him and share his concerns about the Central Earth People; we've talked about his desire to help them, and about the political implications if we are successful. He indicated you were going to work out some ideas."

"Well, yes . . . I've done a little . . . I have identified some things I think we need to do. I'm sure you and the Admiral's team have thought of the same things."

"Not necessarily, I'm afraid. We are good military strategists and engineers. We are not very well versed in things like civilian social programs. Our military structure is far more rigid."

The Admiral and Chanté continued their discussion, wherein Chanté shared her ideas.

"This is a good beginning, Chanté," Admiral Petrova said. "I will share these ideas with Admiral Flint and the senior staff. I see a need to develop a system of self-government as a necessary structure. Perhaps you could organize an educational program covering the basics of government, social structure, and civil law. I believe while we attempt to address the other issues, we can begin preparing potential candidates from these Central Earth regions to help develop the program. They could at least provide us with a sense of their most urgent needs. Whatever final programs we work out, the affected people need to participate."

"I totally agree. Thank you, Admiral Petrova."

"Admiral Flint's navy has talented engineers. If you can provide me with the mechanics of food production that have been developed in the Space Settlement Program, we can begin building the hardware . . . And Chanté, I do insist that I be addressed as Admiral by military subordinates. You, however, are a civilian and I sense we could become good friends. Please address me as Anastasia unless other military personnel are present."

"I will Ad . . . Anastasia. And thank you."

Virgil and Rhett had already set up shop on Ellie 5 Zeta to help Chanté with her project. They assembled the information on the mechanics and molecular biology templates for six of the most important food production systems that had been developed for the space islands. More esoteric models would follow later should the basic needs of the Central Earth People be met. The templates were sent to both Admiral Flint and Admiral Petrova. Meanwhile, Ali, with Chanté as his intern, began to develop a governing system that would be localized in villages, while centrally organized to provide uniformity and cohesiveness.

Chanté also worked with the university board to develop topics for a series of lectures. People who wanted to join the community-derived, cooperative society would need a common understanding; therefore, mechanisms of economic and social cooperation, legal systems, and training for vital skills would be part of the program.

Rhett organized a team of engineers who adapted an existing technology to design foldable, paper-thin screens that could stream educational material directly from Ellie 5 to Earth. A separate paper-thin solar panel was also developed that would connect directly to the screen via a thin cable and provide the power necessary to activate the screens. Rhett then sent the design specs to Admiral Flint. Within a week and a half, the admiral's engineers had perfected production of the screens and solar panels. Admiral Flint contacted Rhett on their recently established direct secured line.

"Good morning, Rhett, this is Nate Flint. My engineers have completed the first of the thin screens and solar panels your people have designed. They made a few adjustments, and the screen can now be folded to a three-inch square. It's small enough to fit into a pocket and still folds out to a twelve-inch screen. We are ready to test a streaming transmission."

"That is great news, Nate. Stand by — we have a partial video lecture ready to go."

The transmission lasted just five minutes, but it was smooth and clear. The audio was produced by vibrations of the screen itself.

"It was perfect, Rhett," Nathan Flint reported. "We will begin production at once. We should be able to produce several thousand thin screens and solar panels a day. I have one question. I can only communicate with you at Ellie 5 when we are not occluded from each other by the Earth or the Moon. It seems the lesson transmissions might be frequently disrupted."

"That won't be a problem, Nate. Ofelia has hacked into many of Earth's satellites. She is establishing recording and transmission capabilities in the geostationary ones. There will be continuous access capabilities in place before you can produce and distribute the screens and panels."

Chanté and Admiral Petrova oversaw the entire effort and monitored its progress. They established electronic networks in geographic areas where development lagged. The one problem that had not been resolved however, was safety. If they could not find a way of protecting the people who enrolled in the program, it would not succeed.

Rhett frequently traveled to NASA LSP. He had been assigned by Virgil to do a feasibility study on expanding the base's capabilities and was now returning to Ellie 5 Zeta. His spaceship began its docking procedure at 1730 hours on February 18, 2251, his arrival occurring just in time for a planned dinner with his wife, Koral, and their daughter Chanté. After his absence of two weeks, this would be a celebratory reunion.

They met for dinner in the Apocatequil Hotel. Koral had reserved a private dining room for the three of them and had ordered a special bottle of wine from Ellie 5 Beta. Although Rhett enjoyed the wine, he was more interested in his daughter's progress working with Anastasia Petrova.

Mining operations at NASA LSP (Lunar South Pole)

"How are you and Admiral Petrova getting along?" he asked. "I remember Admiral Flint was initially skeptical of your abilities because of your age. What about Petrova?"

"We're fine, Dad. We have very productive meetings. I've got classes defined and she has organized attendance in some of the Central Earth coastal towns."

"So, you're making progress?"

"Um . . . I don't know. Ana — I mean, the admiral hasn't found a way to significantly restore habitats, particularly tropical rainforests and temperate zone forests. The local populations see the effort as an attempt to steal their farmland. They plowed the few test forests under. If we plant more mature trees to speed up the reforestation process, they dig them up to use as firewood."

"So, what do you do? She doesn't have enough personnel to protect newly planted forests."

"I know! And it's worse. Her sailors have tried to set up game preserves. They locate them in the most hidden places. But the bad guys find them — poachers come and kill all the animals! They're all gone in a day, maybe two. Whatever we do, it fails."

"What about food production?" Rhett asked.

"A few facilities have been set up, but they had to be placed under continuous guard. Any distribution attempts are likely to be hijacked before they can be delivered to participating villages. The admiral doesn't have enough people to expand the program beyond these first ones."

Koral had been listening to this conversation without participating. They all sat quietly eating for a few minutes, and then she spoke.

"I have little technical knowledge, but it sounds as if you need to move support efforts offshore where marauding gangs can't get to food stores and other things of value. You know, to floating islands."

Just then their server approached, followed closely behind by a dessert cart. While Chanté and her mother eyed the selection of treats, the server addressed Rhett.

"Would you like a drink from your private reserve of aged scotch, Dr. Blackwood? I took the liberty of bringing you some in a snifter with a sidecar shot of water."

"Ahh, you remembered. I would love one. I thought Dr. Greenly might have finished it off by now."

"No sir! He samples it very occasionally. He's become quite fond of some of the local wines from Beta Island." The server directed the dessert cart to the table and as Chanté and Koral were served their selections, Rhett added a drizzle of water to his snifter, swirled it, clinked it to their dessert plates, and took a sip. After savoring the smooth warmth, his mind returned to their conversation.

"Koral," he asked, once the server was out of earshot, "what did you say before we were interrupted!? It was 'floating islands,' wasn't it?" He looked at his wife. "How did you come up with that?"

"Well, I don't really know. But doesn't it seem possible that agriculture, or at least food production and manufacturing, could be done on floating islands? In the ocean. They could produce crops, farm fish, and make appliances and other things. They would be relatively safe from the reach of gangs and rogue militias. They could even build the components of habitats."

Rhett grew thoughtful, then enthusiastic.

"OK," he said, "I think I see how this could work: they could produce food and make needed products, and Admiral Petrova could effectively protect them from criminals at sea. The islands could be used to improve the lives of people and gain their support. The Admiral could form teams using cooperative local people. The people wouldn't need to protect food supplies on land because they would not store them; they could be delivered as consumed. A furnished dwelling would be awarded within secured villages to qualified people. For example, the village may be surrounded by a wall patrolled by armed guards. Residents committing to guard or militia training and serving duty could be awarded a dwelling. The military training would be provided by Admiral Flint's Navy. The first secured villages would be located on the coast for easy access. That process could be extended to protection of reforestation efforts and —"

Rhett interrupted his own brainstorming. "Darling!" he said, lifting his snifter as a toast to his wife, "you just had an epiphany!"

"Of course, dear." Koral raised an eyebrow in reply and gave a slight wink. "I come highly rated as a dinner companion. You should join me and your daughter more often."

Having initiated it, Koral sat back and mostly listened to the ensuing conversation, concentrating on her peach torte as Rhett and Chanté brainstormed various aspects of the feasibility of floating islands. When the three of them returned to their apartment that evening Rhett and his daughter stayed up into the morning hours talking further about this remarkable idea.

The next day Chanté met virtually with Admiral Petrova and proposed the concept.

"Ana, what if one island was completed and made functional? Then we could test the idea."

"Yes, I can see that! You know, we already have some food production and manufacturing capability operational. That equipment could be installed on a prototype island rather quickly. I'll assign an engineering team to work on the island concept immediately. This is an incredible idea, Chanté. Well done!"

"The credit goes to my mother. It was her idea."

"Well, kudos to your mother. I will speak to Admiral Flint. I believe he controls a shipbuilding facility in Melbourne. They could perhaps produce a prototype very soon after a design concept is approved." Admiral Petrova concluded the conversation, and Chanté breathed a sigh of relief.

Admiral Nathan Flint warmed to the island idea. Within a couple days, he formed a concept in his mind and a name: Sea Sanctuaries. The sanctuaries would be mostly self-sustaining, with only a few raw materials obtained from land. Each would support around 500 inhabitants. The proposed sanctuaries would float where the climate was favorable, but they would easily be able to relocate away from damaging storms. They would be isolated, relatively safe from easy access by marauders from the land. Threats from the air and sea were also not major concerns, as Admiral Flint's forces controlled the seas of the Southern Hemisphere. Solar energy and wind power would be major sources of power. The islands would have to provide the complete needs of their own inhabitants and produce a surplus of fresh food for the villages on shore. They would also have a manufacturing capability for things like appliances, tools, and even defensive weapons. In essence, these sea islands would provide support products for the towns and villages on land.

Admiral Flint's engineers began the basic design, even as his team was amassing knowledge on manufacturing and sustainable food production. Chanté arranged for the environmental engineers at Ellie 5 to teach in her classes, and to work on design concepts, which they did in collaboration with the admiral's engineers. Solar, wind, flotation, mechanical infrastructure, living accommodations, kitchens for food preparation and preservation, recreation areas — all could be designed ahead of fully developed sustainable food production technology. Thus, construction of the islands was concurrent with the design and development of systems to produce food. Chanté asked Dr. Greenly and his team to lead ecosystem impact studies regarding the ocean surrounding the proposed sea islands.

This initiative, once developed, was organized under the name Sea Sanctuary Program. On August 12, 2251 construction on the sea sanctuaries began in Melbourne, Australia, where the first few prototypes were built. A week later construction also began in New Zealand and South Africa. A few miles off the coasts near the respective shipyards, the floating sea sanctuaries were each assembled from twelve individual sections, to be sufficiently mobile and structurally strong in severe weather events. The sections were attached to each other in a way that would allow them to flex independently to better ride out rough seas. If future repair would be needed, workers could move individual sections to port. The engineers designed the sea sanctuaries to mimic space islands in many ways; hydroponics, fermentation tanks, and vertical gardens were fundamental to each design. Non-resident support islands would be integrated into the system. Each would supplement a maximum of ten occupied islands. These support islands would process sewage, produce fertilizer, purify salt water, and maintain fish farming in vast undersea containment nets.

Virgil contributed design ideas for autonomous agricultural farm islands on which orchards and vineyards would be planted, and fresh produce grown. Bamboo, flax, and hemp would also be grown, for use by the manufacturing islands to produce clothes and other textiles. The islands could also be where large, intelligent construction 3D printers and robots would be manufactured. Once placed on land and under guard, the construction printers and attending robots would build habitats using sand, gravel, and wood. Admiral Petrova organized a team to design and build hydrofoil boats to transport people and goods between islands and to and from shore. As each idea was planned out and then implemented, however challenging that proved to be, the initial results were remarkable.

The biggest challenges by far lay ahead.

CHAPTER 21

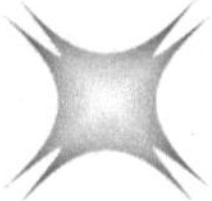

SHORE ENCLAVES

"Was I naïve to think we could fix conditions on Earth? Launching the Sea Sanctuary Program is so much more difficult than I thought it would be."

Chanté Blackwood

The challenges that Admiral Petrova and Chanté Blackwood faced in developing the Sea Sanctuary Program were many and existed on multiple fronts. Chief among them was the difficulty of including the Central Earth People. Chanté was struggling with the process of selecting and preparing occupants for the islands as they became available, while cooperation from those the program sought to help proved to be elusive. Through long experience and persistent indoctrination, the Central Earth People were suspicious of anyone offering relief from the hardships they lived with. To add to that hurdle, security forces at Admiral Petrova's disposal were very limited. Even if the challenges of recruitment could be overcome, it would be difficult to protect those who chose to join the Sea Sanctuary Program.

The sad reality was that only a fraction of the people living in coastal areas would ultimately be selected to live and work on sea sanctuaries. Chanté knew that the selection and training of applicants was beyond her. She had neither the time nor the capability. She did, however, know how to find and enlist talent. She recruited psychiatrists and sociologists, lecturers from some of the university courses she had established. They were tasked with developing screening procedures to qualify applicants to the Sea Sanctuary Program. She also began developing a training curriculum for applicants to complete before they could be approved to occupy and work on any of the sea islands.

Admiral Flint tapped Ali Ebrahim, with his knowledge and experience in government, to create the structure for semi-autonomous rule of the sea sanctuaries. The intent was for the islands to be self-governing, with representation in the newly formed Parliament in Konni Bay, Antarctica. There was much that potential occupants of these sanctuaries would need to learn about the parameters of their self-government. Law and civil rights were concepts the rescued people had little experience with. Robotics and the technology of food production were also foreign to them.

Non-functioning or counter-functioning segments were ever an embedded component of the world's societies and had increased when Draco Osborne had assumed power. No longer were angry, disruptive, and antisocial people a minority of society as a whole. Osborne had ruthlessly spread lies that had eroded trust in the institutional structure of society, thereby increasing the ranks of the malicious. The Central Earth People were the target of aggressive campaigns by his cronies to exploit their poverty. Militias and gangs were given supplies, weapons, and training in exchange for loyalty to Osborne. The Sea Sanctuary Program was faced with a well-organized criminal operation that was entrenched throughout the fragmented societies of Central Earth.

The accumulating assets of the sea islands would be brought to the people initially in coastal areas, where distribution to cooperative people in need could be achieved. However, the concern was about what would happen when the armed Navy teams left to deliver to other villages. How best to protect the shipments once they were brought to shore was yet to be determined.

Space societies were being created by intensive screening and selecting a few people from the many. They had strict quotas and accepted only the most functional and socially compatible people available. While proven effective in that venue, this method would be difficult to apply on Earth. But it offered a means of screening a knowledgeable and progressive group of people; if it could be made to work for the Sea Sanctuary Program, selected people could be isolated at sea, away from the ever-present crime.

Chanté viewed organized academics as a primary means of creating knowledgeable and productive people, and she worked diligently to ensure all applicants were trained to be successful in their new life at sea. Ali Ebrahim contributed the lectures on government. Other classes covered ecosystem functions, maintenance of the island, social norms, and rules and regulations. Applicants passing the initial screening and having completed the educational programs were taken aboard a naval medical ship, where they were given brain scans to screen for structural abnormalities. Passing this last screening test meant one was now approved and would be assigned a Sea Sanctuary island.

Admiral Petrova, with Admiral Flint's concurrence, had chosen to place the Sea Sanctuary islands in the Indian Ocean, the South China Sea, and the seas south of the Indonesian archipelago. Her teams moved finished sections from the shipyards to assembly points offshore. By the middle of February in 2252 the first islands had been completed off Cape Town, South Africa. Shortly thereafter, completed islands began to appear in the other locations; by July the first Sea Sanctuaries were ready to receive their residents. Naval ships towed sixteen assembled sea islands close to their designated harbors to onboard residents via ferryboats.

On July seventh Chanté was watching the video feeds from her office screen on Ellie 5 Zeta as the first ferries docked in Mumbai, India. The settlers, numbering 545, were gathered at the port in a secure fenced-off compound. Three small ferries approached the area for loading. As the sequential boarding of the ferries began, crowds that had gathered outside the fenced area grew larger. They became increasingly unruly, developing into a violent mob. By the time the security forces arrived, the mob was storming the fences. The small police force was overwhelmed.

Soon shots were fired at police from somewhere in the chaotic mass of people. By this time a riot squad had arrived and taken a station in front of heavy movable barricades. They began pushing the rioters away from the immediate area. The response from the crowd was more gunfire directed toward the police. Unable to identify the shooters, the police returned fire. As bodies in the mob began dropping, panic ensued and the crowd stampeded from the area, trampling those who fell.

Chanté watched in horror as the violence escalated. She switched her viewing to other loading events occurring at the same time, only to see the rioting repeated. Although the ferries did manage to receive people, nowhere was it an orderly process. She was devastated.

What little sleep Chanté got that night was fitful. Visions of the violence kept playing in her mind. When she returned to her office the next morning to monitor the ongoing loading of residents, she tuned in the port at Chennai, India, and then those on Zanzibar and at Mozambique, Swaziland, and Walvis Bay on the African continent. She saw that Admiral Petrova had increased security in the boarding process, but that appeared only to lead to more deaths. A similar scene played out each time residents were loading onto ferries to be transported to a Sea Sanctuary floating offshore. The same was happening in loading sites in the Philippines, Malaysia, and Vietnam. Each wave of loadings saw the violence escalating, the mobs increasing in size — and more death.

Admiral Petrova halted the loading at all ports on July twelfth.

Five days later Rhett and Koral returned to Ellie 5 Zeta from a scheduled trip to NASA Lunar South Pole Base. As the base management by Zarita Banderas-Duran had been interrupted by her imprisonment, Rhett was often required there and Koral accompanied him occasionally. This time they cut their trip short to be back following a message from their distraught daughter.

It was mid-morning when Rhett entered his daughter's office. Chanté looked up from her bank of video projections, where she was at the end of a conference with Admirals Flint and Petrova, and Rear Admiral Austin. She held up her hand asking her father to wait. Admiral Flint was speaking.

"So, it is decided," he said, "Rear Admiral Austin will initiate a feasibility study on a solution to our security limitations. We haven't the personnel to resolve this alone. Rod, you will develop a technological means of protecting the people in our rescue program. Can you do that in a couple of weeks, or sooner? Any longer and the people we have assembled in the ports awaiting transport will no longer have enough food or other supplies."

"Yes, I know . . . I will cancel any other projects and put my team on it immediately," Rear Admiral Austin replied.

"I can ask for no less than 100%, Rod. This communication is ended."

Rhett saw his daughter trying to suppress a sob. He walked over to her chair and took her hands in his. He pulled her up and held her tightly until she stopped shaking. In the warmth and security of her father's arms she began to compose herself. Still struggling, she spoke.

"This is terrible, Dad. All I want is to help people find a better life. But I've caused injury and death instead. I should never have started this program. If I had left them alone many people would still be alive.

Was I naïve to think we could fix conditions on Earth? Launching the Sea Sanctuary Program is so much more difficult than I thought it would be."

"Chanté, this is a horrendous thing to witness, especially by one so young. But you did right by trying to save as many people as possible. Understand you can't save them all, nor can I, nor Admiral Flint's people. Not even Ali, with his powerful influence. We can't prevent tragedy no matter how much we may want to, especially when it is so far away."

"If only we had managed to set up the program to rescue everyone," Chanté said.

"Yes, it is right that we want to, but we need to understand that we simply cannot. It is not in our power. We can best help those who work to help themselves. That's why you set up the training program, why we set up the screening programs. Why Ali worked on the self-government process. Those who persist and complete the requirements will imbue the program with the greatest chance for success."

"But you didn't see it! People were shot, trampled, beaten." Chanté could no longer hold in her sobs. "Some of the Admiral's security people were captured and dragged through the streets."

"The loadings will continue, Chanté," Rhett replied. "We will isolate and disperse the crowds more effectively. We will do what's necessary to continue the process. Perhaps they will be in more remote areas or from fortified positions. I'm afraid we have miscalculated the misery and desperation of the Central Earth People and the tenacity of those who oppress them." Rhett hugged his daughter again.

"Is Mom here?"

"Of course. She came back with me. Now, let's close your office for a while. We can pack a few things and take a short holiday on Ellie 5 Beta. There's a beautiful resort there with a pool and water slide. They have palm trees and a sandy beach. Maybe you'll want a glass of wine with dinner. What do you say?"

"But I still have so much to do," Chanté protested.

"Yes, you do. But your mother and I would like to take you there. The break will do us all some good."

The next evening Chanté and her parents arrived at Ellie 5 Beta and received their room video cards at the hotel's front desk. The clerk at the desk placed their luggage on the robot cart.

"Your luggage will be delivered to your rooms. Just follow the video on your cards. It will direct you to the Cloud 9 restaurant and lounge."

Walking between both parents, Chanté took their hands as she had as a little girl. Her parents noticed her silence and her slow pace. It was as if she were walking in some far-off place. Rhett and Koral exchanged questioning glances as Chanté let out a sigh.

"I may not be with the University effort much longer," she said. She straightened her shoulders. "I feel I may have a more urgent calling."

CHAPTER 22

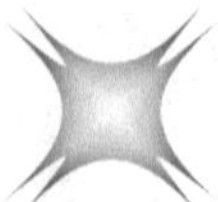

MISSILES OF RETRIBUTION

"There is a strong link between the three gods of destruction: greed, self-aggrandizement, and stupidity."

Dr. Virgil Greenly

Since their attempted hijacking of Ellie 5 Zeta on February 1, 2249, which had resulted in their being taken into custody and retained on the space island, Zarita Banderas-Duran and her contingent of twenty-five marines had been continuously monitored by security. Still, they were allowed to join in productive activities. They continued to be subjected to curfew and required to report to the hotel for roll call each evening. Individually, all the captives had completed the education programs required of all occupants. They also were entrusted to tasks assisting teams working on several different projects. Project leaders working with insurgent members regularly submitted evaluations of their performance over the course of two and a half years.

On July 5, 2251, a Judicial Committee composed of Virgil Greenly (with Ofelia), Ali Ebrahim, Rhett Blackwood, and Daria Aquila met to make their final determinations regarding Zarita and the marines. All the young marines showed promise. Each had made considerable progress expanding their education and skills. Five of them had developed stable romantic relationships: three of those were within their contingent, while two of the female marines were in supervised relationships with island residents. All had shown positive social integration. The Judicial Committee established a citizen path for each that was to be completed within the next six months.

However, the situation with Zarita had presented the committee with some unpleasant choices. While she appeared cooperative and fully engaged in the same programs as the marines, unfavorable reports had been submitted by several people who worked with her. They expressed concerns about her sincerity, commitment, and loyalty. When questioned, though, no one could give definitive reasons or recount any specific incidents to justify their conclusions.

As a result, Zarita had been required to undergo more intensive testing. Her brain scans showed deficient connections in areas that would ideally indicate strong social bonding. The scans also revealed a tendency to view other people as adversaries. She was suspicious in new relationships, only becoming comfortable when she understood the other person's vulnerabilities. When this happened, she used her skill at dominating the person. She had no close friends. Simply put, she lacked trust in others. That lack of trust was reciprocated; people tended to engage with her only at a distance and only if necessary.

Reviewing the results of her scans, the Judicial Committee turned to the task of determining Zarita's future as the next order of business in their July fifth meeting. Virgil began the conversation.

"Do we still believe that sending Zarita back to Draco's control would be a death sentence? Ofelia, your analysis first."

Ofelia could be heard by all via speakers in the conference room.

"Draco Osborne has suffered a series of losses. He is continually faced with defections from the Arctic Fleet. Senior officers are leaving and joining Admiral Flint. In the past few months, they have taken with them two cruisers and one destroyer. The Sea Sanctuary Program developed by Admiral Petrova and Chanté Blackwood has increased support for the admirals within a growing number of Central Earth populations. People in the north are hearing about its positive effects as well. Although Draco has been remarkably successful in limiting Parliament's power, the parliamentarians are regrouping behind the scenes. They could soon oust him as secretary general. I believe he would welcome any support he could get.

"By all indications," Ofelia concluded, "Zarita would have a safe return. Draco would be happy to have her on his team of loyalists."

"Does anyone have questions for Ofelia?" Virgil asked.

"Not I." Daria Aquila was the first to respond. "Ofelia gave a complete and valid analysis. We also have a lot more information now that the captives have been at Ellie 5 Zeta for more than two years. Our attempts to integrate her into our society have failed. She is incompatible with the people here. Even, it seems, with the marines. The best thing for our society would be for us to send her back."

"And if she were to remain?" Virgil asked.

"Zarita is a risk to our close-knit society," Daria replied. "I fear she would plant subtle seeds of destruction should she remain."

"I see. So, we would send her back to Draco, even though that may strengthen his position?" Virgil said.

"Zarita is but a bit player, people," Ali stated. "She is known among those associated with the Space Settlement Program. Beyond that, she is just an irritation. Although he might welcome and enjoy her loyalty, she would not add to Draco's stature."

"To the Dark Side it is, then," quipped Virgil.

The committee ordered a supply reentry glider to be prepared for a mission.

"We have another order of business," Virgil said. "We need to consider the nomination of Ali Ebrahim as interim secretary general of the space islands. He will be charged with initiating elections and forming a parliament. He will also form a committee of people selected from all space islands and bases to create a constitution. In favor or opposed, select the appropriate response on your communicator." Within moments, Virgil turned to Ali Ebrahim.

"Ali, it looks like you have a mandate."

"Thank you all for your vote of confidence," Ali said. "I already have a prototype constitution. We should be able to put together a parliament in short order. We do, however, still need to select a name for our new space society. I have one in mind: Outbound Nation."

"We will take that into consideration, Secretary General," Virgil said with a nod. "Meeting adjourned."

On July thirtieth Virgil ordered a space reentry glider to be docked at the East Docking Port. A life support module was fitted and secured. As the reentry gliders were not designed for passengers, there were no windows and no exterior cameras transmitting to screens. The angle of reentry was steeper and faster than for a regular passenger ship, as the glider was intended for one use only. The heat shield was thick and designed to entirely ablate with the heat of reentry friction. However, with a life support module fitted into place, such a ship was a safe way to transport a passenger should the rare need arise. This was such a rare need.

Robotic motors were attached to the ship for the craft's four-day voyage and reentry maneuver. Upon positioning the spaceship and initiating reentry, the motors would detach and return to Ellie 5. Gibraltar was chosen as the landing site, in an area adjacent to the Gibraltar Spaceport. Since that launch port had suffered a disastrous attack in the past, the immediate area now was the most secure and safest landing port, security measures having been significantly upgraded.

On August fourth Virgil sent a message to Draco Osborne to expect the return of Zarita Banderas-Duran on the eighth, via reentry spaceship. Upon confirmation that the message had been received, Zarita, dressed in her orange prison garb, was strapped into the life support module on board the reentry glider. The module had a food-and-water vending component within her easy reach. A small bottle of Rhett's private Scotch reserve was included as a parting gesture. Just before the hatch closed she looked out at the service technicians and gave an insincere thumbs-up, then swallowed hard so as not to give in to the sigh threatening to engulf her. Despite a questionable future had she remained at Ellie 5 Zeta, Zarita did not want to return to Draco Osborne's Earth.

Four days later the reentry spaceship streaked across the sky high above the North American continent. At the time, in Ellie 5 Zeta, Virgil and Daria were enjoying dinner on Virgil's terrace. Golds and oranges glowed brightly through the programmed sunset, as the colors reflected from the surface of the modeled Amazon River. The tree growth in the jungle along the river's banks was beginning to mature, filling in bare spots. Tropical birds were soaring overhead on their way from feeding to nesting. The setting was bucolic. The wine was excellent as well.

"Virgil!"

"I can hear you, Ofelia," Virgil said in his mind. "No need to shout."

"Zarita's reentry glider was shot down." Ofelia skipped her usual request for permission to deliver information.

"Shit! How did that happen?"

"A missile was launched from the Caribbean near Cuba. Despite confirmation, it seems someone didn't get the message."

"Or intentionally didn't follow it. With so many defections and replacement promotions, Draco may be losing control of his navy," Virgil speculated.

"Or he may have suspected that Zarita was converted to our cause and was being sent to spy on him. I believe his paranoia must be greater now than ever. He could have ordered the reentry ship destroyed."

"What now?" Virgil asked.

"I am not certain. But in any case, we can expect to be blamed. There will be retribution of some kind. We need only wait for it," Ofelia said.

"There is a strong link between the three gods of destruction: greed, self-aggrandizement, and stupidity."

"So we should expect him to do something stupid?"

"Exactly," Virgil thought back.

Daria noticed Virgil's sudden reaction and shifting attention and rightly assumed he was in conversation with Ofelia.

"When Ofelia interrupts us at inappropriate times it's never good news, is it?" she said.

"You're correct. And this is particularly bad: Zarita's reentry ship was shot down over North America."

"That's terrible! Did we contribute in some way? I thought we considered everything."

"We likely misjudged Draco's state of mind. With his suspicions and paranoia, he might have felt he couldn't take the chance of having a spy in his midst."

The tranquility of their pleasant evening broken, Virgil and Daria finished their meal in thoughtful but uncomfortable silence, then both retired to their individual apartments.

The next morning Virgil's breakfast was delivered to his terrace. As he ate the first-ever mango grown in space, unable to enjoy it as much as he had wanted to, he had a conversation with Ofelia, keeping to topics more positive in nature than the death of Zarita Banderas-Duran.

"Ali Ebrahim has completed his local government formation for the Sea Sanctuaries," Virgil remarked. "The project is still far from completion, but they have made remarkable progress. The net impact has been very positive. Even the riots have calmed a bit as more people are beginning to realize the benefits that could reach them."

"And Rear Admiral Rodrigo Austin's advanced drone defense program has engendered some cautious optimism in many who live in coastal areas. Their sense of personal safety has been missing for a long time. I see that program expanding inland soon," Ofelia said.

"Rod's micro surveillance drones are undetectable," she continued. "And they can image even a fly. An armed person approaching a protected village doesn't have a chance. That efficiency impresses even someone with my superior abilities."

"Your abilities may be superior, but Rod is likely superior to you in humility, my dear," Virgil said.

"Humility is overrated. The point is, these things have further boxed Draco in, I'm afraid," Ofelia observed. "He's like a tiger in a cage, likely to act in increasingly desperate ways. We can't necessarily anticipate what he will do. However, we should notify Ali of our concerns."

"Ali? What can he do? Oh, you're speaking of finalizing a constitution and formalizing a government?"

"Absolutely. We need him to accelerate the process. We should have something agreed upon even if it is preliminary. With that we can act with unity should Draco do something stupid."

"Well, at least this month our committee approved an official name. Outbound Nation will soon have its government."

"Yes, August 19, 2251, the birth of our nation."

The former marines who had arrived with the unsuccessful hijacking attempt of Zarita Banderas-Duran nearly three years ago were sworn in as new citizens in the Outbound Nation on January 8, 2252. All twenty-five had participated in various self-improvement programs. Five had previously been accepted into shuttle pilot computer science programs and were that day also receiving completion certificates. The other twenty marines were enrolled in the first few classes offered by

Prescient University, with a variety of majors in fields ranging from astronomy to medicine to political science.

The ceremony was held in the elaborate Amazon Ballroom of the Apocatequil Hotel, where a luncheon was served to all attendees following the induction program. In attendance were Virgil Greenly and Daria Aquila, Rhett and Koral Blackwood, and Ali Ebrahim, among others. As so often seemed to happen, Virgil was interrupted by Ofelia during his lunch.

"Virgil, we need to talk, and I need your full attention. Please excuse yourself from the table."

"Can it wait, Ofelia? They just brought dessert," Virgil replied mentally. Daria had developed an ability to know almost immediately when Virgil was conversing with Ofelia. She looked over to him. "It's alright, love," she said. "I'll keep an eye on it for you." She held her fork playfully at the ready. Virgil glanced ruefully at his now vulnerable chocolate lava cake as he excused himself. He walked into a courtesy office and locked the door.

"Now, what's the rush, Ofelia?"

"I just sensed something concerning. A cold object is just leaving Earth orbit. It seems to have accelerated on a trajectory toward Ellie 5. It's strange. It's a dark body. I can't detect any heat energy."

"A dark body is headed our way?"

"Yes, but slowly, as if it doesn't want to be detected."

"Could it be a warhead?"

"Yes, except to have any real effect on the Ellie 5 archipelago it would need to be nuclear. I don't detect any radiation. It could be shielded."

"Let's assume it's a shielded nuclear warhead. If it were detonated before it got close to Ellie 5, wouldn't it destroy most Earth satellites? Shut down communications and navigation on Earth?"

"Yes, civilian ones for sure. Many of the military satellites are hardened against particle radiation."

"If we hit it with a laser and it's a fusion bomb, would the warhead detonate or melt?"

"Either. It depends on the design," Ofelia said.

"We'd better find out now before it gets closer to Ellie 5. I'm afraid there's only one way to do that. Do you have one of the lasers in easy position?"

"Both lasers should be used," Ofelia replied. "We don't know how much shielding the warhead may have. We'll need to notify Ceres Island that they are about to suffer a total energy shutdown. They'll have to shut down all non-vital operations and route power from the plutonium reactor. I'll send a pencil laser message informing them that we will shut down five minutes after they receive it."

"We don't have time to wait for confirmation. Can you focus the lasers on the object in the meantime?"

"We don't want to alert whoever is controlling this that we are about to attack. I can track the movement and pre-program a convergence point where the two lasers and the object intersect. As soon as Ceres is notified, we can fire."

"Seems our only choice. Let's do it."

Precisely thirty-five minutes later the two lasers fired in unison. In seconds a huge spherical fireball sent a particle pulse wave crashing outward in all directions. As soon as the shock wave hit Earth's atmosphere, the sky everywhere lit up in flaming beauty. The radiation belts funneled large amounts of energy toward Earth's poles, which resulted in glorious displays visible to people living close to the polar regions.

But the visually stunning displays were not benign lightshows. The consequences, focused tightly on the poles, were dire. The massive glass dome over the South Polar Resort was breached and the intense radiation there left nothing but death and destruction. As it was summer season the resort was near maximum capacity. An estimated 2,300 people died immediately.

The rest of Antarctica was not as severely affected. Fortunately, there were no ships in the area at the North Pole so the energy pulse there had little effect. However, global communications satellites and weather satellites were taken out of service by the huge electromagnetic surge caused by the nuclear explosion. Seconds later they were permanently disabled by a stream of gamma radiation. Even shielded satellites that were above the Van Allen Radiation Belts were destroyed.

Admiral Flint's fleet and the four launched Sea Sanctuaries lost communication with one another, as they had no access to still-functioning military satellites. However, the admiral had thousands of land-based surveillance drones that had been developed by Rear Admiral Austin. They were normally used to monitor and protect shore participants in the Sea Sanctuary Program. Admiral Flint ordered those drones to be positioned in a communications network with his ships and the Sea Sanctuaries, where fleet engineers could link the drones. Connections between the Sea Sanctuaries, the Antarctica Parliament, and the ships of the Antarctic Fleet were soon restored. A direct laser signal established a secured connection from the government in Konni Bay to Ellie 5 Zeta.

Within a few days Governor Henry Fong of Southlands United and Admiral Flint of the Antarctic Fleet had established near normal communications between themselves, as well as with Ali Ebrahim, Chanté Blackwood, and Dr. Virgil Greenly at Ellie 5 Zeta. Ali contacted Henry Fong two days after the blast, as most of the radiation had dissipated enough to allow a clean signal through the hyper energized Van Allen Belts. Virgil Greenly was also on the call.

"Governor Fong," Ali began, "I believe that you and Admiral Flint, with the help of Rear Admiral Austin, have pretty much restored order in the Southern Hemisphere. Are commendations in order, Henry?"

"Ali, I'm afraid the South Polar Resort was completely destroyed. No one survived. There was nothing left there to restore. We are frankly traumatized by that disaster. I'll need to schedule a memorial service soon. Parliament is beginning to talk about some kind of monument. Right now, we are struggling." The governor hesitated a moment. "Now, what's this I hear of an independent government within the space islands?"

"What you have heard is correct, my friend. It is called Outbound Nation. We welcome self-government to better fulfill our destiny. As we increase our presence in space and continue to develop resources, Earth will benefit. By controlling our own development, we can expand our capabilities and make more resources available to Earth. Since our markets are limited to our own needs and those of the planet, I anticipate an even more cooperative relationship with your government. Eventually, also with GSU. In a practical sense, then, we need to establish landing sites in the Southern Hemisphere for our reentry gliders. Then we can deliver resources to assist in Earth's Sea Sanctuary Program."

"Ali, I have such great respect for your integrity. I am very much encouraged by your words."

Virgil spoke up then.

"Governor Fong, this is Dr. Virgil Greenly. Pardon me for breaking in. We haven't met or spoken before. I'm grateful to have this opportunity to speak with you following the explosion in space of what we believe to be a nuclear device of Draco Osborne's. It seems the most severe damage has already occurred, and the lingering effects might not be as bad as they could have been. Would you do me a favor and ask Admiral Flint to contact us when he is in a location that will allow him to link to this connection? We would like an assessment of GSU and Draco Osborne's situation with Parliament. We've heard rumors he's under a lot of pressure to step down. If he launched that missile, we view that as a sign that he may be desperately unstable."

"From what I know, Dr. Greenly," Governor Fong replied, "the government of Draco Osborne is falling apart. He would be out of power already if members of Parliament weren't so afraid of him. Admiral Flint is getting requests for safe passage from defectors in the north almost daily. Sometimes the defection involves an entire ship and crew. It's easy to see how Osborne would attempt a dramatic act, no matter how stupid."

"My assessment as well, Governor," Virgil said. "When you contact the Admiral be sure to tell him of our request for Southern Hemisphere reentry glider landing sites. They could be in the Northern Hemisphere as well. They just need to be securely out of Osborne's reach. We'll connect again soon."

CHAPTER 23

JULES ON MARS

"Hmm . . . young, good-looking, and smart.
But damn! He'll be working as my subordinate."

Jules Blackwood

The *Endeavor* was ready for launch from Ceres Island to NASA Mars Base on February 28, 2254. Jules had completed her studies and the redwood tree construction at Ceres Island, leaving the project of further forest development with Dr. Amelia Bereza. At twenty-four Jules now held a doctorate in space island engineering from Prescient University and was working on a second doctorate in space habitation ecology. She hoped to complete studies toward that degree while in transit to Mars. Once she arrived, Dr. Timothy Storm would be charged with overseeing her Mars project and thesis defense. Traveling with her was a team of seasoned scientists; these scientists would replace those who had recently left Mars for Ellie 5 Zeta aboard *Eternal Hope*.

During its time at Ceres, the *Endeavor* had undergone massive rebuilding and renovation. One change was that its motors now had double their previous thrust output. The framework was strengthened to withstand the resultant increased acceleration, and the living and common spaces were greatly improved. Because of the shortened voyage time and upgraded amenities, this would be a much less onerous journey than it otherwise would have been. Instead of eighteen months of travel time, they would reach their destination in twelve months. So it was on March 6, 2255 that the *Endeavor* arrived in Martian orbit, to be met by the Mars surface-to-orbit shuttle *Sojourner*.

Jules sat in the theater module of the *Endeavor* with her luggage. She watched the large surround screen as the *Sojourner* approached and then docked at the axis docking port. A maintenance and resupply crew would soon disembark the shuttlecraft and enter the *Endeavor* to begin their work. She reviewed the boarding and landing procedure the passengers of *Endeavor* would follow. The Mars Rehab Orbiter (formerly named the Ceres Habitat when it was launched to Martian orbit from Ceres upon completion of the new Ceres Island) was not within viewing range. She called up a visual on her portable screen and found files of the Orbiter. They were detailed, so she studied the newly modified structure. The external framework had been removed from the cylinder and replaced with several layers of nickel-graphene sheathing. The Orbiter had also been greatly expanded using the construction materials loaded on board while at Ceres. The summary reports indicated that the life of the aging structure had been prolonged far into the future. The image of the satellite hung rotating in the dark sky, its gunmetal grey exterior barely standing out from the blackness. Jules made a note to herself to travel to Mars Rehab to study the Orbiter's engineering revisions up close.

Switching channels to live mode, Jules could see a panoramic surface view of the NASA Mars Spaceport. There were a few structures at the spaceport, the most dominant being a bank of large fuel storage tanks and a pressurized building to which the *Sojourner* could dock.

The surface around the spaceport was covered with a scattering of reddish-brown rocks punctuated by occasional small craters. The massive Olympus Mons rose in the background. Jules switched to a slow-motion launch simulation and watched as the surface landscape fell away. She could see a series of pit mines surrounding the spaceport. Large robotic excavators were at work removing layers of regolith. Trucks were carrying the material to nearby smelting facilities. A little farther to the north she could see a large circular excavation. Machines were still at work inside its perimeter. She knew its diameter to be 2.6 kilometers, for this was the beginning of a project she would manage once settled in at NASA Mars Base.

A boarding call came over the com system and Jules stood and walked toward the gravivator. Following the signal device she carried, her wheeled luggage trailed her closely. As she ascended toward the central docking port, she felt the sensation of weightlessness for the first time since their launch from Ceres Island. The shuttle *Sojourner* was without its launch rocket, as that stage had returned to the base. It had its own massive motors, however. The slow reentry velocity the motors provided, combined with the thin Martian atmosphere, made the use of parachutes unnecessary. As the *Sojourner* landed on a tail of flame, huge clouds of Martian dust rose. The dust was powder fine and would stay suspended for hours in that atmosphere. The ship landed on a rail-mounted platform that then slowly moved to the docking tower, which made a sealed connection with *Sojourner*'s hatch. Jules and the rest of the passengers ascended into the tower and walked to the elevators that would take them to the underground base.

The arrivals had a few hours of personal time before they could be processed and receive their living quarters assignments on their access cards. Meanwhile their luggage was taken to a holding place to be sent to their dwellings once determined. Jules took the time for a quick tour of one of the lava tubes via a small electric shuttle that quickly moved people along the tubes between the large excavated nodes. It was still early in the day. The lava tube terraforming project she encountered on

Mars was the most elegant marriage of environmental and mechanical engineering she had yet seen off Earth. She got off the shuttle so she could walk along the paths between the nodes and experience some of the reconstructed nature up close.

From early childhood Jules had been taught about the glories of nature in Earth's past. She had read extensively and viewed countless pictures and video recordings of spectacular places on her home planet. But no one now living had ever experienced nature on Earth as it once was. Climate disruption and the ravages of humans had rendered tropical island paradises into sunken sand bars and lavish rainforests into arid grasslands and deserts.

But on Mars she was experiencing what ecologists had developed. It was a remarkable palette of living diversity and sensory appeal within the extensively expanded lava tubes. She momentarily lay in a grassy area near flower gardens replete with buzzing insects and created breezes. In one forum she encountered a thirty-foot waterfall that cascaded into a sizeable rock-lined swimming pool. The tropical pool was surrounded with large-leaf plants, flowers, and trees. Behind the rocky shoreline there was a sandy beach. She approached the beach and saw swimmers "sunbathing" in the recreated sunlight.

She walked on, following the map presented on her screen. As she entered a large domed room with projected sky and clouds on the ceiling, the map showed where the main grotto was, and her apartment within it. The grotto was located just half a kilometer away. She looked around the domed room and saw it had been developed as a park, with a recreation of a natural Earth setting. A gently sloping hillside covered in a variety of grasses begged her inspection. The environmental design represented remarkable skill. She sat on a bench and listened to insects in their business buzz of life. Closing her eyes, she felt the warmth of the afternoon sun on her face. It wasn't the sun, of course, but the sensation was real, as it was designed into the numerous eco-vignettes.

There was one sensation, however, that kept her from fully accepting these settings as truly Earth-like. She had always lived under the restrictions of standard gravity. Aside from being weightless for a few days on her brief spaceship ride from Earth to Ellie 5 Zeta, standard gravity was her only extended experience. She felt powerful in the two-fifths standard gravity of Mars, almost superhuman. She bounded along jogging trails, stopped and drank from a small spring, smelled the fragrance of ripe peaches in a ten-tree orchard. Finally, she resigned herself to walking back toward the large central grotto, where she would check in to her apartment. Such fun was refreshing, and she would pursue it often. But now she needed to prepare for her meeting the next morning — and find a place to eat. In her excitement she had forgotten about lunch. It was late afternoon, and she was starving. She asked her device for dining options and found there was a café in the center of the green in her own grotto.

Although at first the two-fifths standard gravity of Mars could be a novel experience, she knew over time her body would adjust to the reduced stresses placed on it. Her muscles would atrophy, and her bones would weaken. And that was the ongoing problem of living on the Moon or on Mars. Sports therapists worked with everyone living on Mars to ensure they adhered to exercise regimens and bone compression measures to minimize losses. The use of modification exercises and compression harnesses was supplemented by frequent trips to the Mars Rehab Orbiter. Jules made a promise to herself to visit the Orbiter as soon as possible.

The lava tubes were an extensive network covering an estimated 340 kilometers (about 211 miles) in total length. Most of the original tunnels were natural lava tubes, but over a period spanning more than 100 years, many more had been created with tunnel boring machines. Large forums had been cut out of the rock every kilometer or so. In many of those areas, apartments had been carved into the surrounding stone. Stores and restaurants were included to surround a central park or garden area. Many other central areas were designed as natural habitats. Jogging trails existed throughout to encourage rigorous exercise in the reduced gravity.

The underground was a relative paradise compared to the surface. In many ways the surface of Mars was just as hostile as the surface of the Moon. In one way it was worse. Dust storms were a scourge. The dust essentially shut down all human activity on the surface. Robots were used exclusively to maintain equipment and continue surface operations. Equipment operation was critical, as all major industrial activity occurred on the surface. No one ventured to the surface unless it was absolutely required. Yet Jules was there to manage a very large surface project; she would spend significant time there over the next several years.

As Jules arrived back at the Central Forum grotto, her access card alerted her that her living quarters had been assigned. She walked to her apartment by following the live screen on her card and found her luggage sitting on the small front porch. As she entered, the luggage again followed behind. She walked through the rooms, inspecting each: there was a central kitchen, which was ringed by a sitting room, bedroom, and office. The office looked out over her front porch and across the grotto to the administrative forum. The front porch was connected by a short path to the green at the grotto's center.

In front of the apartment a series of rose bushes beckoned. Jules came out onto the porch and sat in one of its two Adirondack chairs. Gazing past the roses and across the green she could see shops on the other side. A sign identified the NASA Administrative Building, so named to commemorate NASA's early contribution to space exploration. Jules noticed that while the façade of the building presented as a sleek rectangle of glass and steel, the main parts of the structure were carved into the rock behind. Visual perspective feeling somewhat altered in this unfamiliar environment, the ever-curious scientist pointed her PET (Personal Electronic Transceiver) at the NASA Administrative façade and got a distance reading of 80 meters.

Having finished her broad survey, Jules directed her attention to the large Victorian-style gazebo that was roughly in the center of the green. It was surrounded by decks and gardens and functioned as a café, the place for her appointment with Dr. Timothy Storm in the morning. She was reminded again of her hunger and trotted across the green to get something to eat.

The next morning Jules was running late. Unaccustomed to the low gravity as she was, she bounded out the front door too quickly. She grabbed at the porch railing to catch herself from falling, but missed and tumbled forward into the arms of a young man passing by.

"Easy there! You almost lost it," he said. "Where's your weight belt? Did you just arrive on the *Endeavor?*"

"Oh, forgot it. And yes, I did. Not used to the reduced gravity. I'd better go back and put it on."

"Are you Dr. Blackwood? Jules Blackwood?"

"I am."

"Dr. McKeever at your service. I'll be assisting you on your project. I believe you are meeting with Dr. Storm this morning?"

"Yes, I am."

"Good. I'll wait here while you strap on your hip weight harness. I'm attending the same meeting. Walking in two-fifths gravity takes a day or so to get used to. I'll walk with you to breakfast if you don't mind."

"Thank you, Dr. McKeever."

"Please, it's Charles. Chuck to my friends."

Jules stopped and stared at him, then nodded and went back in to put on her weight harness. *Hmm . . .*, she thought while she strapped it on, *young, good-looking, and smart. But damn! He'll be working as my subordinate. And really! Chuck?! At least he doesn't go by Chip. That would have been . . . unnerving.*

Dr. Charles McKeever accompanied Jules to the Gazebo Café for their breakfast meeting with Timothy Storm. Dr. Storm was at the table as they arrived. He rose.

"Dr. Jules Blackwood! How nice to meet you at last. You are the first of the second generation to take a leading role in our Space Settlement Program. It is an honor to meet the daughter of Dr. Rhett Blackwood." Dr. Storm extended his hand in greeting. "I see you've met Dr. McKeever."

"Yes, we met. He reminded me about the weight harness. It sure doesn't conform to a woman's build."

"Indeed, it can be a little clunky, but it does keep you grounded and is pretty effective at reducing bone loss in the legs and feet," Dr. Storm said, gesturing for the three of them to take their seats.

"And the standard gravity treatments at the Mars Rehab Orbiter are still necessary?" Jules asked. "Tell me, Dr. Storm, in your experience, does using intermittent full gravity completely counter the diminishing effects of Martian gravity?"

"Yes, the treatments are still necessary. And the intermittent regime does seem to work well. Those who have returned to Earth have exhibited no ill effects," Dr. Storm said.

"The hip weights are not so uncomfortable," Dr. McKeever added. "Wait until you are fitted for the spinal compressor." Jules missed the quick look that passed between the two men.

"A spinal compressor? I can't imagine how that would work."

"It does take a bit of imagination to picture it," Dr. McKeever said. "But think about it. I'm sure you can unravel its design concept."

Dr. McKeever's smile was just a little too broad. Dr. Storm looked down at the table and did not meet Jules's inquisitive eyes.

"I believe we can have one fitted for you tomorrow," Dr. McKeever continued. Dr. Storm gave a small cough.

"Wait, something's not right here," Jules said. "What are you talking about? Did you really design spinal compressors?"

"Oh yes! Three versions. They were all flops. First, I tried shoulder weights to help compress the spinal column, but the clavicle and scapula responded by moving downward. I concluded that by using the weights over time, people might develop the appearance of exceptionally long necks."

"Yeah, move the shoulders down and the necks are longer!" Jules said, catching on. "You know, you could start a fad. Floppy-headed Martians. You could hold the heads up with helium hats."

"Well, I thought it might be fashionable, actually. I wanted to appeal to people's vanity, so I developed a weighted helmet."

"You have notable talent in aesthetics. That must have been received well."

"The look was quite fetching. A friend helped design several styles and colors. But it was a pain in the neck." At this, Dr. Storm looked up from the table and coughed again.

Dr. McKeever continued. "People needed a brace to keep the compression uniform. For a moment there was a glimmer of hope that it might be accepted."

"But . . . ?" Jules prompted.

"Disaster. A person's center of gravity was too high. We had several face plants, especially with joggers when they tried to stop. Their feet stopped and their heads kept going."

"Let me guess, you became the joke of NASA Mars Base?"

"Yeah, you could say so," Dr. McKeever replied. "Scraped cheeks and bloody noses aren't popular with the fashion crowd."

By this time, Jules was completely relaxed and grinning from ear to ear.

"OK, Chuck, Jules," Dr. Storm interjected, also with a grin. "Time to get down to today's business."

The rest of the meeting covered specifics about what Drs. Blackwood and McKeever would be doing that day on the surface. Jules had never been in such a place, so hostile to life. She received detailed instructions on the functioning of her surface suit and use of equipment.

The next day, after suiting up for the surface, Jules and Chuck boarded a tram that routed them through the underground matrix to an elevator. There they ascended to the surface near the large circular excavation Jules had seen virtually from orbit. The suits were lightweight even with radiation shielding. The helmet visors screened out most of the UV radiation. She found walking quite easy. The two scientists walked about 200 meters before they stood at the edge of the massive circular excavation.

"How deep is the excavation today?" Jules asked.

"We're about five meters down right now and should reach our goal of fifteen meters in a couple of months," Chuck said.

"And the perchlorate and chlorate removal from the regolith?"

"We're doing that as we excavate, but it's a slow process. Our oven capacity is limited."

"What about the mechanical equipment that will go under the platform? And the elevators?" Concern crept into her voice as the enormity of the project became visually evident.

"Everything is being done concurrently and will be ready when needed. The excavation is on schedule, and even though soil creation is the slowest part, we should have enough soil to get started with planting once the dome is complete."

"It looks as if you have everything well in hand, Dr. McKeever. I'm impressed."

"Chuck," he tried to remind her, suppressing a smile. "How are your trees, Dr. Blackwood?"

"The largest are still aboard the *Endeavor*. They were transported in its central axis and placed along its length. They've been in microgravity since Ceres Island. They'll need to stay there until we have completed the dome and platform. We'll also need to finish the backfill with viable soil."

"And they're still straight and cone-shaped?"

"Somewhat. I had to expose them to light from the top end down. They naturally grow toward the light. The trees are also under expansive tension from both ends. Seems to have worked."

Continuing their inspection, the pair walked along the perimeter of the excavation to get a closer look at the robotic tractors.

"There's a ladder a little further along the rim if you'd like to climb down," Chuck offered.

"Thank you, yes. Dr. McKeever, I would like to take some samples of the regolith at that depth."

"Dr. Blackwood, please can I call you Jules and you call me Chuck?"

"I'm sorry. Chuck. Of course. We'll be working closely together for the next few years, and we need to be comfortable around each other. First names it is." She gave Chuck a smile, though she was sure he couldn't see it through her visor.

The surface at the bottom of the excavation seemed to be a little softer and less stable underfoot than above. Jules almost fell a couple times when the uneven ground gave way under her feet.

"What's with the dirt here? Seems a little unstable," she said.

"Yeah," Chuck said. "That surprised me the first time I came down here. Some of the permafrost liquefied then evaporated when exposed to the thin atmosphere. The fine regolith loses some friction."

"Wouldn't have thought of that," Jules replied.

She gathered her samples in a sealed container and placed them in her kit bag, then they walked back to the ladder and climbed out.

"I'm happy with the samples. I didn't expect to get these today," she said.

"Great! Would you like to tour the baking ovens that detoxify the regolith?"

"Sure. Would we need to walk? I'm not used to this suit . . . I'm a little tired."

"Only to the rover. Once on board we can tour the whole site in it. I can show you our progress. The support beams and the metal dome panels have been fabricated."

"And the glass panels?"

"The glazed panels are taking a little longer because of their thickness and the fact that we need two of them to sandwich the water, but you can examine the process. Here's the rover. We can get out of these spacesuits and relax a bit. We'll be comfortable for the next four hours during the tour," Chuck said.

They climbed into the airlock, sealed the outer door, and began to vacuum the dust from their boots and clothes. Then they vacuumed the entire chamber to prevent any contaminants from entering the living area of the rover. They removed and stowed their boots and suits and entered the cabin.

"Wow! It looks like this thing has a kitchen, bathroom, sitting area, and . . . what's that over there — a wet bar?"

Jules shook out her long auburn hair and flushed her face with water from the kitchen sink. Chuck found himself staring at her. Then he spoke.

"Um, yes! It's difficult working out on the surface all day. The rover is a respite, a place to chill before returning to base. There's even a shower in the bathroom."

"And these lounge chairs recline?"

"All the way back."

"Must be *really* stressful out on the surface all day," Jules quipped.

"No, they're not used during the day, but sometimes a crew might be out for a week or more so it's like a Martian camper van."

"Well, it's nice for a day . . . A week or more? Might get a little cramped."

"Exactly. You mentioned the large trees in the central axis of *Endeavor*. How many are there?"

"Three. Two of them are sequoias, the other is a coastal redwood," Jules replied.

"And they are how large?"

"The coastal redwood is about three meters tall."

Chuck gave a low whistle. "You got a good start on them," he said. "I'm impressed."

"Dr. Greenly helped me modify their DNA. They grow at about two times the normal rate. We still will never live to see them in their full glory."

"Someone will," Chuck said. "Let's drive around the excavation. At the far side is where the lower metal panels are made. I can grasp one with the robotic arms and position it in front of the rover window so you can see how the edge seams fit together. Once they're installed a sealant will cover the seams on both the inside and outside."

The rover moved slowly, as the planet's surface was uneven and strewn with rocks and boulders. Jules could see the flashes from the laser cutters as they approached. The freshly cut panels were stacked to the side near another robotic mechanism that lifted the panels one at a time and placed them on the stamping machine. They felt a slight vibration as a large steel stamp slammed into the metal sheet, giving it a slightly curved shape. The finished sheets were stacked together and bound in groups of ten. Chuck explained that they would then be carted away and placed in a covered shed to remain until they were needed.

"The steel is melted from ingots that were delivered here from Ceres. They were produced at their MAC facility. You may have seen that process when you were there."

"No, Dr. Bereza kept me busy with her forest program. I did see it from a distance, though. But I could never seem to commit any time for a closer look. Can we look at the glass process next?"

"Of course. You'll see why it takes so long."

Chuck drove the rover to the glass kilns nearly a half a kilometer farther, near a great solar array. "Silicon and other minerals are surface mined not far from here. The building directly in front of us is an industrial laboratory that isolates and purifies silicon and other minerals. Once they're mixed in the proper proportions, they're brought to the kilns you see to the left. (You can get a better view from the side windows just behind us.) They pour the mixture into molds and then heat them with torches that are modeled after rocket engines. They burn hydrogen in the presence of oxygen to melt the minerals into glass. We only have one kiln, so the process is slow. Nonetheless, it's continuous. So by the time the structure is ready for installation we will have the panels."

They toured several of the other facilities dedicated to the Redwood Forest project before heading back to where the rover had been parked when they started. Chuck positioned it close to a charging tower. An arm snaked out from the tower, found the charging port and plugged in.

"I guess this is the end of our tour. We have a little time to relax. Jules, I think this is a wonderful project. The Redwood Forest Dome will become a landmark of this base in the future, even though, as you say, we won't live to see it in all its glory."

"Yes, that's the legacy and the beauty of the Space Settlement Program. We all are pioneers, creating a magnificent future."

"Well stated, doctor. I understand you created some living but artificial redwood trees at Ceres Island," Chuck said. "Do you intend to do the same here?"

"No, I left all the 3D printers and robotic assemblers to Dr. Amelia Bereza. She'll continue that project for the redwoods and other tree species. That island will be almost entirely forest when she's finished . . . So, what about that bar? Whose idea was that?"

"Yup, I have to say the bar was my suggestion."

"We're back a little early. I don't think we need to rush. Do you know anything about bartending? You could pour me a martini . . . for demonstration purposes," Jules said as she leaned back into the lounge chair.

The two scientists relaxed in the Martian rover for about an hour, enjoying their conversation, cocktails, and a few simple snacks before they would need to return to their underground world. As they watched the tiny Sun approach the horizon, Chuck asked, "Would you care to join me for dinner? I know of some interesting restaurants, and you're new here. You could use some guidance."

"A great idea! You pick the place. The refreshments in this establishment . . ." Jules gave a wink ". . . were great, but it's been quite an eventful day for me. I'll be hungry by the time we can manage a real restaurant."

Chuck engaged the rover and drove back to the docking port they had exited from that morning.

After both went to their quarters to refresh and dress for the evening, Chuck met Jules at her apartment. They took a trolley to a nearby plaza for dinner. Chuck ordered wine as they examined the menus on the table screen. The food options on the *Endeavor* had been limited. This looked exceptional.

"They have cultured filet mignon?" Jules asked.

"It's their signature dish. You should try it."

Just then the server returned and poured a glass of wine for Chuck to taste. He nodded and the server completed pouring for the two of them. Jules let the wine, a robust cabernet sauvignon, slide along the sides of her tongue then down her throat, barely swallowing.

"This wine confirms that I'm having the filet mignon," she said happily. "Chuck, are you having the same?"

"I think I will. That dish will be the perfect finish to a perfect day."

They clinked their glasses as the server spoke the order to the table and set the bottle down between them.

CHAPTER 24

MARS REHAB ORBITER

Come dance the gravity stomp.
You know it's gonna be a romp.
Do the stomp, have a romp.
Do the stomp, have a romp.

Yeah, we love that sweet flotation
but we need some mean rotation.
Do the stomp, have a romp . . .

The Smashing Orbiters
from the song "Gravity Stomp"

The next day Jules and Chuck returned to the project in the rover. Chuck needed to bring a couple of robots to one of the ovens that wasn't working properly. After dropping him off at the malfunctioning oven, Jules spent several hours in the rover surveying the perimeter and depth of the circular dig. She was eager to start construction of the platform and catacombs that would exist beneath, and had determined that she could begin if they focused on excavating a small area to the specified depth. She suited up and got out of the rover near the rim, sending it back to pick up Chuck. When he finished his maintenance service on the regolith processing oven he returned in the rover to the rim of the excavation, where Jules stood in contemplation. She immediately entered the rover interlock, cleaned and removed her surface suit, then joined him in the living space. She was thoughtfully quiet for a few moments. Finally she said, "I need a break from this. I would like to tour the Mars Rehab Orbiter."

"Wow, that's a change," Chuck said. "We've barely begun on your postdoc project."

"I know, but that orbiter was rebuilt from the original spaceship that established Ceres Station. It's historic. I want to examine the engineering changes that were made once it reached Martian orbit. Can that be arranged?"

"Sure. In fact, I believe I can set it up for first thing in the morning. Let me check the *Sojourner* launch schedule." Chuck placed his PET on the table and the schedule holograph projected before them.

"It's leaving tomorrow at 0830 and returning the next day at noon. There's still room on board. I'd like to personally give you a tour of the Rehab Orbiter."

"OK, what are the sleeping arrangements at the Orbiter?" Jules asked tentatively.

"There are dorms, both co-ed and separated by gender. They have a few singles and some double units. I'll check availability. Let's see . . . one female quad dorm, a single, two doubles, and a male quad dorm. What are your first two choices? The dorms can be somewhat of a party venue, so if you want quiet you probably should take the single; I can manage in a dorm. Heavy sleeper."

"Absolutely the single for me. Get it before it's gone."

The next morning Jules and Chuck met for an early breakfast at the Gazebo Café.

"There's plenty of food on the satellite so you might want to go light on breakfast here," Chuck said. "So, tell me: when was the last time you experienced a launch from a gravity well?"

Jules grew quiet as she recalled the launch when the Blackwood family fled from Earth. It happened so long ago, but she remembered every detail. The failed ignition, the missile attack . . . In orbit while killer satellites stalked them. All of it came back to her, including the fear she felt. She recounted it for Chuck, moment by moment.

"I had no idea you had such a traumatic experience at such a young age," he said, sympathetically.

"Yeah, I was nineteen then."

"Listen, Jules, we can go another time."

"No, it's good." She laughed. "I'm a big girl now! I'll be twenty-six in a few months."

"Not even twenty-six and already doing your postdoc. Jules, you are one impressive woman. Now let me describe the launch. Compared to what you've been through, it's like a trip to the spa. Which, by the way, pretty much describes the Mars Rehab Orbiter itself."

Two hours later they were strapped into their seats along with a full complement of passengers. There was light excited chatter aboard the *Sojourner* as everyone anticipated liftoff and a vacation at standard gravity. As the rocket soon climbed into the pale sky, Jules felt the reassuring force of a steady surge of power. They reached the orbit of the Mars Rehab Orbiter within about a half hour and the *Sojourner* prepared to dock. As they approached the satellite, its long cylindrical form glistened in the searchlights. Jules identified the crest of the original individual quarters around the periphery of the forward section as the *Sojourner* began to rotate in sync with the docking lock. The approach and docking worked perfectly.

After taking the gravivator to the surface of the Mars Rehab Orbiter, the *Sojourner* passengers entered an open reception area that looked down the length to the barrier at the far end. Jules gasped at the magnitude and beauty of it. The cylinder was divided along its length through the central axis; the dividing barrier was a white screen for projections. Now it was sunny blue skies with drifting, puffy white clouds. A stretch of aquamarine water was centered under this "sky." It ran almost all the way to the far end. Bathers were riding paddleboards from one end to the other; kayaks, canoes, and swimmers dotted the water. Both sides of this beautiful concave lake were covered in white sand beaches upon which were erected tent cabanas, beach umbrellas, lounge chairs; all adorned with reclining sunbathers. Back from the lake were several tropical thatched-roof bamboo lanais, with decks extending over the sand. These were the Happy Day beach bars and restaurants, so named as they opened at ten a.m. and closed at various times late at night. Servers in beach attire moved among the tables, serving cocktails and small plates of appetizers. Steps in front led from the decks to the beach.

Shops, fine dining restaurants, day spas, gyms, and studios for dance and acrobatics were located just beyond the lanais. Nightclubs, theaters, and other entertainment venues rose above and behind the beachfront businesses. Scattered throughout light jungle growth behind the nightclubs and rising a little higher, the lodging facilities climbed up the curvature. Jules watched the spectacle before her with great interest. She had never seen anything like this, definitely not on Earth.

"It appears there are many levels to gravity rehabilitation. It's not all exercise and sweat," she said.

"No, in general people don't like exercise and sweat. So we created it to resemble a resort spa," Chuck said.

"But the Happy Day beach bars don't seem conducive to good health."

"Oh, but they are. Everything served is selected to provide good nutrition."

"As much as I enjoy good wine — and the occasional cocktail — I try to limit my consumption. These beach bars are open at 1000 hours. A little early to begin Happy Hour . . . er, Happy Day."

"Not at all. Until 1800 hours they serve non-alcoholic mocktails, nutritional smoothies, and the like. Everyone is encouraged to spend their days on the paddleboards or swimming, in the gyms, or at dance classes. Physical activity is what every day is all about."

"Is it required?"

"Encouraged, not really required. That said, though, sometimes refusing a minimal amount of exercise can result in the loss of certain privileges. As you know," Chuck continued, "after you've been on Mars for a while your body begins to adapt to the reduced gravity. We have been successful in addressing most bone loss, but despite our efforts, muscle loss happens. So when people first arrive at Mars Rehab, they feel they have gained a little extra weight. It can be difficult to get motivated for the activity programs. So we make it as fun as possible."

"I'm impressed," Jules said.

It was still early in the day and the virtual sun was in the "eastern" sky, but she could feel its warmth.

"I love the feeling of this sun. It's so comforting," she said.

"We've increased the infrared output. And we also tweaked the ultraviolet so that it's a shorter wavelength than that from Earth's Sun."

"Brilliant! More heat, less sunburn. What's the UV wavelength?"

"Right around 200 nanometers. There's less eye damage as well. People still wear sunglasses, though."

"Can't cancel fashion. Can I assume the water and sand did not come from Mars?"

"Correct! Can you take a guess from where?"

"Please enlighten me, Chuck."

"We are most proud of this feature. I can't say it's the result of careful planning, however. It's a bit of a story."

"You have my full attention. As long as it's not an epic tale."

"Water is the most important commodity in space and can be extracted from S-Type asteroids. One such asteroid was towed to orbit some decades ago and over time astronaut engineers extracted all the water from it. When the Rehab Orbiter arrived, we realized the left-over regolith could be processed into sand."

"And you did that by . . . ?"

"We screened the regolith to get the finer sand, which we placed in large tanks that were built on the surface and placed in orbit; then we added water and hydrochloric acid made from the chlorates and perchlorates on the Martian surface. Then —"

Jules suddenly could picture the rest of the process. "Then you tumbled it in the acid water until the sand particles had smooth edges, removed the acid water into tanks and sent them to the surface for recycling. The sand was rinsed and dried. Voila! White sand!" she exclaimed. "What else is here?"

"I haven't told you about the live entertainment. There's a lot to choose from. Even theater groups come up to perform stage acts. There's a band called The Smashing Orbiters that entertains periodically when they can schedule a trip from the surface."

"Wow! Are they here now?"

"Yes, I checked. We can catch a show tonight before they go back to their day jobs. There's a dance floor at the venue as well. We could stay another day if you'd like. There's quite a lot to explore here. I mean from an engineering standpoint," Chuck said with a broad grin.

"Of course, I'd like another day here. It's been a long time since I . . . well, I never got to the South Polar Resort on my last trip to Antarctica," Jules replied.

"You are a woman of extraordinary experiences, Jules. Let's start our tour. Later this afternoon we can try our skill on the paddleboards."

"Paddleboards?"

"You'll get the hang of it quickly. Even falling off is a great experience."

After the tour and a late beachside lunch, Jules and Chuck changed into board shorts and tank tops at one of the shoreline cabanas. On the paddleboard Chuck had selected for her, Jules had a shaky start, but soon she could paddle without losing her balance. She managed to paddle the full distance of the small lake without falling off or hitting a swimmer. After a couple of hours they left the water and retired to a set of lounge chairs.

"I don't remember having so much fun, or being so tired," Jules said. "When can we come back here?"

"Pretty much whenever we want, if our work is on schedule. The *Sojourner* launches two or three times a week."

"Has the Rehab Orbiter changed the way people get their full gravity fix?"

"Absolutely! And I believe the medical staff has been finding that more frequent and shorter sessions at full gravity are more beneficial than the old way of months-long stays at standard gravity and a year or more at Martian gravity."

"Adding all the recreation options was brilliant."

"Yep. What do you say we get a shower in the clubhouse, relax a little in our abodes, then have a nice dinner? I know just the place to complement our aquatic day."

"No question, I'm in!"

Later that evening they were seated at a shoreline table. A field of stars played on the sky projected above. Slowly a glowing Earth Moon came up on the horizon. It had been years since Jules had seen the Moon from either an Earth or Ellie 5 perspective. She could hear crickets and occasional frogs beginning to sing. Soon it was a full-on à cappella chorus, nature's mating call.

"I'd better go light on the wine tonight," Jules said. "This setting is too beautiful and way too nostalgic. I could easily do something . . . impulsive."

"Like dance the night away?" Chuck asked.

"Maybe. Let's order."

"I've already ordered the wine and I have just the recommendation for you for an entrée. Rainbow trout."

"Constructed from?"

"No. Absolutely fresh, real rainbow trout."

"How is that possible?"

A wine steward with an athletic build and a healthy glow arrived at the table with a bottle of wine and three glasses. They recognized her as someone they had watched giving swim lessons to some children earlier in the day. She poured wine into their two glasses then a little into the third glass, which she then swirled. After checking the color and nose of the wine, she poured the contents into her mouth, swished a bit, and swallowed. Without a word, she smiled, nodded, and left, taking her empty glass with her.

"I guess the wine is OK!" Jules remarked, laughing.

"Evidently the sommeliers here are also somewhat hedonistic," Chuck said with a grin. "To answer your question," he continued, "there's a hatchery and fish farm on the other side of the partition. At first the ponds and water tanks were added on that side just to balance the mass evenly around the inner circumference. Once they were installed, though, it wasn't much of a leap to culture aquatic life."

Jules was fascinated.

"OK!" she said. "I'll have the rainbow trout. Will you join me?"

"I'm afraid I can't. You see, they portion the seafood out. Everyone usually maxes out quickly. Once per year is the limit. Finite production, you know."

"Let me guess, you've used your quota. So, when is your next trout or seafood dining window?"

"In just under twelve months. Probably. Although the standard is once a year, they will adjust the date as the population dynamics of the fish or other seafood changes. You, however, are a new arrival; so, you are allowed to make your first selection any time."

"Then I can have mine now and give you a bite. We can have it again together in a year. Um . . . if you want to."

"Two great offers already! But I hope we come here many more times before then."

"We will," Jules said warmly. She took a generous sip of her wine and carefully savored it before swallowing. "Mmm," she said, "I think the sommelier was right."

Chuck and Jules would return to the Rehab Orbiter many times over the next few months. During their time on Mars, they worked on the giant Forest Dome on the Martian surface. By mid-June 2255 the framework had been finished and the lower metal panels had been installed. The sheathing on the base platform was nearly complete and soil was being prepared. Water had been purified and stored in large tanks. By October third of that year the platform was complete and the thermal glass panels installed. An atmosphere was added. Soon the addition of soil began. With Chuck, Jules transplanted the three redwood trees she had brought on the *Endeavor.*

It was an important day for Jules when at the end of October she and Chuck planted the first sapling sprouted on Mars, a giant sequoia. The planting would continue for the rest of the year, although going forward much of it was done robotically. It would take centuries for the natural redwood forest to grow to its full potential, but within a few decades it would represent itself well. It would soon be regarded as the most-loved landmark in all space settlements.

CHAPTER 25

POWER PLAYS

"Unfortunately, Little George had some health issues. They began as soon as he opened his mouth."

Draco Osborne

Over the weeks following the January 2252 warhead explosion in space, Draco Osborne was desperate to maintain his grip on power. He attacked opponents and bribed supporters. But increasing defections from the GSU military eroded his credibility. By the end of February his opponents in Parliament had gained the needed votes to remove him from power. The election would be in April. During the intervening time his governing coalition broke into two camps: his diehard supporters on the one hand, and his former supporters, now working against him, on the other. With the April elections, Osborne was out.

His former supporters had been students of his methods. They began building a corrupt power structure, attempting to shape a new coalition with enough support to form a new government. The leader of that coalition was weak, though, and resistance to it was strong, as many members of Parliament did not want the self-serving corruption to continue. So even with Osborne removed, the disarray persisted. It seemed the return to an elected and representative new government by the members of Parliament would take some time.

Although Osborne had been removed from his position as secretary general in the April election, he was still a voting member of Parliament and leader of the minority party. He needed to somehow show he could still effectively control events if he was to have any hope of gaining the support of his former loyalists. Osborne was still intent on defeating the new government as it struggled to form. He realized that while the government was still in disarray, the time was ripe for him to attack. But how?

This was top of mind for Osborne as he was vacating the physical office from which he had been evicted. His new office in the Parliament building was much smaller than the suite provided to the secretary general. His butler Thomas helped him pack up his bar and other personal effects, many purchased at government expense. The boxes of wall art and floor and table sculptures were delivered to his new location by robot cart, but Osborne didn't trust the robot carts with his liquor. He walked through the halls followed by Thomas pushing a bottle-laden cart.

As they entered his new office, Osborne became exasperated. "There's no room for a bar in here, Thomas, or even my sculptures," he growled. "In fact, there isn't even room for you. This place is a disgrace. I'm still the minority leader. I deserve better, dammit!"

Thomas had been serving Osborne long enough to recognize the man was about to descend into anger and self-pity.

"Your Honor, if I could make a suggestion?"

"Yes! Of course, Thomas. Now is the time to speak up, for soon you will be unemployed. My new position doesn't come with a butler."

"This office is perfect as a front . . . where you officially carry out your duties. However, you own the building across the street. I happen to know it has a vacancy that could be converted into a replica of the secretary general's office."

"Hmm, yes, it could. But then it would cost me the rent it could earn."

"Sir, I know you have been busy with more important concerns. You may have lost track, but that space hasn't brought you any income for years," Thomas said.

"Oh? I was unaware. So . . . I could meet with my people there, away from the prying eyes of my enemies. And the office itself would represent my power more accurately than this little closet." A grand office was useful as well, Osborne thought, when intimidation might be needed to keep his supporters loyal. "So, what's in it for you, Thomas? I still won't have a budget for a butler."

"No, Your Honor, but you do have funds for a personal secretary."

Osborne let out an admiring snort.

"You're loyal, Thomas, and you're also clever. Those qualities together are uncommon."

Though the small office was ego-bruising, Osborne was beginning to relax. He understood the value of Thomas's idea. He soon moved his most subversive operations to a replica office suite in his building across the street, where he could conduct business more discreetly. During the first week following his defeat, he met with his most avid supporters and attempted to secure guarantees of their loyalty. Enough votes would put him back into power. But a new Parliament vote again failed to yield a result in his favor, or to put *anyone* in power. There would be another vote soon.

Draco Osborne was not yet finished.

One afternoon in mid May, a meeting with six of his closest henchmen took place in Osborne's new offices across from the Parliament building. Although he was entitled to government security, he did not use that service there. Instead, he hired two colossal hormone-injected male bodyguards. They stood on either side of the suite's conference room, their mere presence intimidating to Osborne's associates as they entered the room. Draco Osborne always sought to keep even his most loyal supporters off balance.

The replica office suite had been furnished exactly as the one he had occupied as secretary general. The office itself contained a copy of the massive desk; the wet bar was set under the gothic window. Although it was not oriented toward Reykjavík's bay, the virtual window displayed the same live view. There was one difference in the office furniture, however. The low circular stone-topped table in the conference area was new. As Thomas ushered the invitees to their seats, they settled into soft leather-upholstered chairs.

"I would like to welcome you all to this meeting. It's vital that we discuss several issues of strategic importance," Osborne lied. "As you know, the last vote in Parliament was rigged by my opponents. We are here to rectify that. Before we begin, my personal secretary, Thomas Wagner, will serve refreshments."

Thomas left and almost immediately reentered the room with a tray of pastries and decanters of coffee and tea. He began serving around the table as Osborne continued.

"You all know me as a reasonable and tolerant man. Although I know some of the individuals in coalitions you have formed did not vote for me in this last election, you know I'm also a forgiving man."

He paused. He watched as some of his invitees dipped poison-detecting sensors into their beverages, trying clumsily and unsuccessfully to cover the action with cutlery. Osborne looked around the table and gave a toothy grin. He continued.

"It is important for our success that we trust one another. I'll take the first step by offering each of you a chance to redeem yourselves. Get your people in line then call for a new vote! It's as simple as that." Osborne noticed his guests were beginning to drink their coffee and tea.

They still sat forward on the edge of their seats, looking uncomfortable.

After a long pause a small man, George Santos, through courage or stupidity or both, raised his hand.

"Yes, Little George. You wish to speak?" Osborne smiled reassuringly.

"Don't take this the wrong way, boss. I mean no disrespect, but some of the people are saying you never had control over the Navy as the secretary general. That you couldn't stop the defections. And without the Navy you had no real power. This is not me saying this, boss. I'm just saying what I'm hearing. From my people."

"And what are you doing in response to what you are hearing, what 'your people' are saying?"

"Doing? What can I do? People are free to say what they think, boss. People can say wrong things. Pardon my saying, but you say wrong things. And nobody makes a stink." Suddenly uneasy, George looked around the room for support. No one met his eyes. He nervously took a sip of his tea and set the cup on the table.

Osborne leaned back in his overstuffed leather chair and fingered a control pad on the arm. A barely visible mist rose through the porous stone tabletop, surrounding George's teacup. George was growing more uncomfortable and anxiously fidgeted with his teacup, grasping it with both hands and rattling it in its saucer. A few seconds later, without warning, he began to convulse and gasp for breath. He slid from his chair and slumped to the floor. Everyone at the table sat frozen in place as Osborne stood up and walked over to one of his bodyguards.

"Would you two kind gentlemen," he said, indicating the other bodyguard across the room with an exaggerated flourish, "please remove Little George from our presence and dispose of him in the usual manner? Be sure not to touch his hands."

"Yes, boss." Both hulks quickly slipped on gloves, clomped over to meet where Santos's body lay by his chair and, grasping him by the wrists, dragged him unceremoniously from the room.

Osborne returned to the table and sat down.

"Unfortunately, Little George had some health issues. They began as soon as he opened his mouth . . . Does anyone else have something to say?" Aside from a slight twitch, Osborne's face was expressionless.

After a very tense moment, Jason Freebody, who had at various times been the legal representative of everyone in the group, spoke up.

"I believe we can say with confidence, George Santos was derelict in his duties. We should all strive to be more diligent in achieving our mission."

"Well said, Jason. Does everyone agree?" Osborne didn't even try to suppress a small smirk.

"YES, Your Honor!" the contingent said as one.

"Then the meeting is adjourned. You are dismissed." The five remaining members got up and filed out of the room.

As the last to leave, Osborne addressed his butler on the way out. "Oh, Thomas, you should put on some protective gloves before you clear Little George's teacup."

The disarray continued in the GSU Parliament for weeks and no resolution was forthcoming. Then one weekend, two of Osborne's primary opponents inexplicably drowned while fishing from a small boat in the bay. At this sobering event the bickering and abortive power plays gave way to a consensus vote. Dr. Jón Einarsson, a professor in political science at the University of Iceland, Reykjavík campus, was appointed as Preceptor. He was tasked with overseeing the unruly crowd of officials and continuing the basic housekeeping activities of a much-damaged administration.

CHAPTER 26

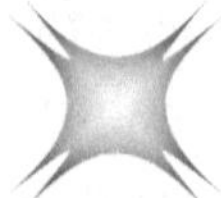

FLINT MAKES A MOVE

"He is compelled to destroy what he cannot have.
That's the reality of Draco Osborne.
We cannot assume his death.
We must seek him — and seek to destroy him."

Fleet Admiral Nathan Flint

By the end of May 2252, Fleet Admiral Nathan Flint had consolidated the Antarctic Fleet with his own fleet. Governor Henry Fong, with help from Admiral Petrova and Chanté Blackwood, had established a working government with the Sea Sanctuaries. Sea islands were still being built and populated. That project would continue for years. The program was proving effective in significantly reducing crime and corruption in all the areas it had benefited. Habitat restoration progressed slowly in a few small areas in India and Africa.

People in those regions earned credits for food and other supplies by working on restoration projects. There were also rewards for identifying criminal activity. These positive changes did not yet have a large impact on correcting the social and environmental damage that had been done. However, they did demonstrate what was possible. The effort continued to gain support from local populations. The stability in the Southern Hemisphere was improving at the same time everything was disintegrating up north.

Fleet Admiral Flint was acutely aware of the chaos in the GSU Parliament. He decided the time to act had come and moved his fleets to the North Atlantic and past the Hawai'ian Islands in the Pacific. During these movements he broadcasted where he was heading and his peaceful intentions. At the same time, he kept his forces on battle alert, air power included. Governor Henry Fong and Admiral Petrova traveled as political emissaries aboard the command carrier *Flintlock*. The fleet in the Pacific approached the Aleutians under the command of Rear Admiral Rodrigo Austin. Detecting no opposition forces, Rear Admiral Austin moved his fleet into the Bering Strait, there to form a blockade.

During this time, Fleet Admiral Flint encountered a task force that had broken from the Arctic Fleet about 300 nautical miles south of Iceland. When he determined its intent was surrender, he sent Vice Admiral Aisling Murphy, along with a contingent of senior officers, to board the command carrier of that battle group. There, after a short ceremony officiated by her officers, she took command then assigned her senior officers to each of the surrendered ships. Fleet Admiral Flint sailed his carrier *Flintlock* and its attendant support ships to drop anchor just offshore at Reykjavík. Meanwhile, Vice Admiral Murphy brought the battle group under her command to the seas northeast of Iceland.

As these events were proceeding, Draco Osborne became acutely aware of his impending peril, finally. It was time to leave Reykjavík. He assembled his most loyal supporters from within Parliament and the Arctic Fleet. In three helicopters, they flew from the Reykjavík airport due north to Hólmavík, where they boarded waiting ferries that took them out into the Bay of Húnaflói. Two submarines surfaced. The fugitives boarded and the submarines sank into the deep.

Traveling aboard his point ship, the *Swordthruster,* Rear Admiral Rodrigo Austin moved his fleet from the Bering Strait into the Arctic Ocean. Four days later his fleet dropped anchor at Nord off the northeast coast of Greenland, to stand at station while he, with his crew aboard the *Swordthruster,* continued, arriving a couple days later off the northwest coast of Iceland. There he stood by, awaiting further orders.

With all his ships in place, Fleet Admiral Flint sent an electronic missive to the GSU Parliament Preceptor, Jón Einarsson. The message reassured its recipient that his intent was to impart stability to the region. It also directed the Parliament Preceptor to call a full session for the next day, June 7, 2252. The message further informed that Admiral Anastasia Petrova and Governor Henry Fong would be addressing the assembled body at 1300 hours.

The following day, as planned, the full Parliament was assembled and waiting in the General Assembly Room. They did not wait quietly; questions and speculations were shared among the curious and apprehensive legislators. As Admiral Petrova entered the room the murmuring that had filled the space suddenly hushed. Without fanfare or introduction, the uniformed admiral walked directly to the podium. She looked out across the room at the faces of the people assembled there.

"Members of GSU Parliament," she began, "please be assured we intend no harm and that we support elected government. We are here to ensure peace and stability during this tumultuous time. We have information that your former secretary general, Draco Osborne, with some of his supporters, has commandeered two submarines from the Arctic Fleet and escaped. We believe he may pose a threat, so we are actively pursuing information on his whereabouts. Accompanying me today is Governor Henry Fong of Antarctica, who wishes to say a few words about finding a peaceful way forward. That is all."

With that, Henry Fong stepped to the podium as Admiral Petrova left the room.

"I will be even more brief than Admiral Petrova," he said. "In a few moments I will establish my temporary presence in the office normally occupied by your secretary general. There I will work with your preceptor, Dr. Jón Einarsson, until you as a body bring us your ideas on how we should construct a new government and what form that government should take. Please send an emissary to that office when you have consensus on several ideas."

Henry Fong left the general assembly area and, flanked by security, walked to the office he would share with Dr. Einarsson. There his technicians were installing the secure communication electronics. When they were finished, he sent a secure message to Fleet Admiral Flint confirming he had completed his task and was now in a wait mode. He sent his contact address to each member of Parliament. A half hour later he began to receive questions, the majority of which asked for some guidance regarding the type of government that would be permissible. He sent a message to all of the members:

> We do not wish to change the parliamentary form of governance. As a body you should self-affirm that you legitimately represent the people who elected you. The next step is, of course, to then elect a committee which shall nominate candidates to the office of secretary general. The more basic question is: Do you wish to unite my government of Southlands United with yours, or do you wish the two to remain separate? We are amenable to either choice.

However, if you wish to unify our governments, our laws and objectives are different than those heretofore expressed by members of your Parliament. We would need to agree to a common constitution and a common legal system. I await your decision. —Governor Henry Fong, Southlands United

On June 10, 2252, from somewhere just north of Jan Mayen Island, northeast of Iceland, three missiles suddenly broke the surface of the sea and headed directly toward Reykjavík. Immediately the pulse laser cannon on the *Swordthruster* began tracking the missiles. A few seconds later the ensign at the controls began firing at the missiles in rapid succession—but they were already descending on Reykjavík. Three rapid explosions over the city caused the collapse of the Office Annex to Parliament and destruction around the city center. Most of the parliamentarian legislators and staff were killed. It was not immediately known precisely how many deaths had occurred. However, it was quickly confirmed that the office Governor Henry Fong was in had also been destroyed.

The heat trails from the missiles were traced back to the point where they broke the surface of the water. Fleet Admiral Flint immediately dispatched the ships closest to Jan Mayen Island in pursuit of the submarines Osborne had commandeered. Sub-chasing bomber aircraft were launched from the decks of three carriers in the area. The submarines were presumed to have dived deep; it was believed, however, that there had not been enough time for them to leave the area. They were also presumed to have the capability of using countermeasures to avoid detection. The newly arriving ships under Admiral Flint's command established an area that was likely to contain the submarines. Rear Admiral Austin soon arrived with his fleet that had been standing station at Nord off the northeast coast of Greenland. He moved his fleet toward Jan Mayen Island and established a grid pattern over a 40-square-mile area and his ships began dropping sub-seeking autonomous torpedoes. He also ordered the launch of sub-seeking planes from his carriers. Six planes flew over the area, dropping sensors to the ocean floor.

After four hours of intensive searching the sub-seeking planes received indications of an explosion. The planes soon sighted submarine debris floating on the water. Small boats were dispatched to collect the flotsam, quickly determined to be the result of destruction of one submarine. Draco Osborne may or may not have been aboard. Later that evening Fleet Admiral Flint called his senior staff to a meeting aboard the carrier *Flintlock,* where they discussed the tragedies of the day in his private conference room.

He concluded the meeting with a firm directive:

"The man is compelled to destroy what he cannot have. That's the reality of Draco Osborne. We cannot assume his death. We must seek him — and seek to destroy him."

CHAPTER 27

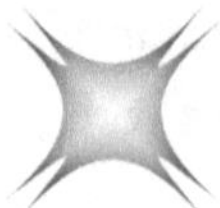

SOCIETIES: EARTH AND SPACE

"Bless the olive for saving his life . . . incredible. I wonder, though, was it the olive alone or did the pimento contribute?"

Ali Ebrahim

Four days after the submarine destruction, Ali Ebrahim initiated a call to Fleet Admiral Nathan Flint.

"Good morning, Nate. I just received word that Henry Fong has been found alive. That is great news! It would be a huge blow to your mission — and our future — to lose that man."

"Ali, it's great to hear from you. Through all the stress, Henry's rescue was a rare piece of good news."

"Four days under the rubble! Is he OK?" Ali asked.

"Heh, yeah, you could say that."

"Well, I hear he wasn't physically injured, having crawled under the desk. But four days — and he wasn't dehydrated?"

"Not at all. Apparently, several ceiling beams bridged the distance between his desk and the granite windowsill above the wet bar. That created a space beneath."

"Incredible! So, he had access to water all that time?"

"More than that!" Admiral Flint chuckled. "Most of the liquor survived the roof collapse, along with one of the bar refrigerators. In addition to the booze, the bar inventory included olives, pickled pearl onions and asparagus spears, some salami, brandy-marinated cherries, Bloody Mary mix, and seltzer water. The floor was found strewn with empty bottles and jars when he was rescued, the contents of which he apparently consumed. The rescue team didn't specify what they were empties *of*."

"I see; a diet for a 'Real Man.' But do you know why he was under his desk in the first place? Seems he couldn't have had advance warning of the incoming missiles. There just wasn't enough time."

"I think we have the gist of the story," Nate Flint said. "He was a little inebriated and hard to understand when rescued. But it goes something like this: Before the explosions, he had spent the previous three hours meeting with individual parliamentarians in his office. Finally left alone and feeling some measure of stress from the encounters, he noted the convenient proximity of the bar and decided to fix himself a martini before lunch. Apparently he dropped an olive, it rolled under the desk, and he went to retrieve it just as all hell broke loose."

"Bless the olive for saving his life . . . incredible," Ali said. "I wonder, though, was it the olive alone or did the pimento contribute?" Fleet Admiral Flint broke composure and let out a huge guffaw. There was a pause in the conversation before Ali continued. "Well, my friend, I'm glad that Henry is alright. He is integral to our success in the future."

"Ali, I agree one hundred percent. His government gives legitimacy to my fleets."

"Something else," Ali Ebrahim said. "Is it true that criminal Draco went down with his submarine? Say yes and I will truly be happy."

"I wish I could. There's a fifty-fifty chance that he did. However, given his puffed-up ego . . . well, that alone could keep him afloat."

"And the submarine too. Look, Nate, all kidding aside — we both know he is a dangerous psychopath. If he's alive, he has a highly sophisticated submarine at his disposal. As far as I know, those subs were each carrying ten missiles. Three missiles were fired. Am I correct?"

"Yes, we shot down three. Unfortunately, they were too close to Reykjavík for us to avoid damaging the city in the process, as you know."

"If they all came from the surviving sub, then at the very least he has seven missiles left," Ali continued. "If, on the other hand, they had been fired from the sub that was then destroyed, then his capability is that of ten missiles."

"Exactly. Ali, that surviving submarine has very sophisticated stealth capabilities. I have put all my resources toward locating and destroying it. Kinda like *Sink the Bismarck!*"

"What, Nate? I don't understand."

"Sorry. The analogy is more than three centuries old. It's a reference to a ship named the *Bismarck* from what was called the Second World War in the mid-twentieth century. But I do hope the analogy runs true. The *Bismarck* was sunk."

"We'll call it Project Bismarck, then," Ali said. "And what about the Sea Sanctuary Program? How can we protect it?"

"The program has stabilized much of the Southern Hemisphere, and we have effective security. There are significant problems around the Mediterranean, the southern area of North America, Korea, and Japan. I'm preparing to build new sanctuaries at ports in the Mediterranean first. I believe I have the resources."

"You can do that? With all that's going on?"

"I already have assets there in the form of several high-speed gunboats, so we'll see how this plays out," Fleet Admiral Flint replied. "If

Draco is still alive, I believe he will attempt to reestablish his base of operations in Western Europe, so I'm moving a helicopter carrier into the Mediterranean as a precaution. I believe if we can establish the program there it could short-circuit his attempts to control the region. Rest assured, Ali, the Sea Sanctuary Program is a top priority."

During the ten months in which he served in an interim position Ali had initiated elections and formed a parliament. Subsequently the parliament approved a constitution. Ali Ebrahim was elected Secretary General of Outbound Nation on May 11, 2252. He had yet to contact Governor Henry Fong of Southlands United since the missile attack in Rejkavík. Now, two days after his rescue, his friend in governance was cleared by the medical team and Ali felt it was time to contact him. He initiated a video call on a standard government channel.

"Henry, I was so glad that you survived the missile attack and building collapse. Where are you located now?" he began.

"It's good to hear from you, Ali," the governor said. "I'm staying up in Akureyri, temporarily of course. I've been released by my medical team and I'm looking forward to getting back to my work as liaison to Parliament in a day or so."

"But, isn't the Parliament building undergoing structural assessment?"

"Yes, it is. The rubble from the office complex is being cleared now. Parliament itself has temporarily relocated to Akureyri and should be back in session soon. I think you know of the place. It's a town up north."

"Good thinking! That's the perfect location. I believe Parliament will be more cooperative after this disaster. And there will be few distractions in Akureyri."

"There are signs Draco's henchmen in GSU are either seeking forgiveness and asylum, or just disappearing. Depends on the seriousness of their transgressions."

"So, there's an exodus of undesirables?" Ali asked.

"I certainly hope so. As soon as Parliament is back in session, I will call for new elections to fill all vacant seats. Those who have not left can finish their term. Preceptor Einarsson has been a valuable assistant in this process."

"I'm impressed, my friend. It seems as if you're keeping your head and helping the GSU parliament return to normal. How are things in the regional parliament at Konni Bay?"

"I did abandon them a bit," Henry said. "But I appointed an administrator to keep the lights on and people working. So far it seems there haven't been any problems. Fleet Admiral Flint has sent Rear Admiral Austin back to Antarctica, so there is a military presence there. Austin left the fully staffed *Swordthruster* here in the north in case Draco is still lurking in the Arctic deep."

"I'm not a military man, but I think the fleet admiral should have more than one pulse laser cannon," Ali said.

"That's the other thing assigned to Rear Admiral Austin. He's to develop and build more pulse cannons. That's all I can tell you now, Ali. Everything is moving very rapidly here, so we should talk often."

"Do they have a stocked bar in your office at Akureyri?" Ali joked.

"I don't know. Perhaps they should in case of another missile attack. Diving for olives did help me to survive — and in good health, thanks to the convenient hydration."

"I hope we meet in person in the future, my friend. We'll drink a toast to our *mutual* good health."

"The future is unpredictable, but I hope we do meet. I would like to visit one of the space islands sometime. I think of them as 'islands in the void.' . . . Oh, I almost forgot to congratulate you on your election. I understand you are now the official secretary general of Outbound Nation, which is separate politically and economically from Earth. Am I right about that?"

"Thank you, Henry. Yes. We have self-determination, but we will forever be linked to Earth and you to us. In whatever way the governance problems on Earth are resolved, we will continue to be the planet's greatest trade partner."

"Reassuring to hear, my friend."

Later that day Ali met with Chanté Blackwood in his offices on Ellie 5 Zeta to discuss progress on the Sea Sanctuary Program.

"I understand that Nate wants to bring the Sea Sanctuary Program to the Northern Hemisphere," Ali said.

"Yes, but I suppose that will be delayed with all that's just happened," Chanté said. "The land mass is so much greater in the Northern Hemisphere. That makes the problem bigger."

"That's true, but you begin where you can. He says he already has assets in the Mediterranean. It's a place to start."

"That's encouraging." Chanté's voice belied her words, as her tone was anything but enthusiastic.

"Chanté, don't think what you've done so far is unimportant. You created this program! And despite some setbacks, it has had a positive impact."

"Oh, I know, and I want to continue. It's just that I've had some things on my mind that have kept me preoccupied."

"Anything I can help you with? We've known each other since you were a little girl; you've always had a supporter in me."

"Of course, Ali. It's just that I have an important decision to make. I need to work through it on my own, though."

"I understand completely, my dear. You know I'm here to help if needed."

"Thank you, Ali," Chanté said. "I should go back to my office and complete some minor administrative tasks. If I keep busy with the mundane, perhaps my mind will be clear enough to find the way forward."

A contingent of Fleet Admiral Flint's ships began to transport fabrication and production equipment, robots, and engineers to

Portugal and the Mediterranean Sea. The Sea Sanctuary Program he and Chanté had started would soon begin in the region that had been a stronghold for Draco's criminal activities. Admiral Petrova had previously been assigned to partner with Chanté, but her duties now centered around protecting Iceland and, more generally, the Arctic Ocean, so Fleet Admiral Flint took a more active role. The Mediterranean was notorious for its pirates, who ran the coasts in small high-speed gunboats. That activity had sharply declined with the arrival of Flint's better-equipped gunboats. When construction of dry-docks began on the western coast of Corsica, the location was not publicized. The one other dry-docks construction site was not in the Mediterranean, but in the port of Porto, Portugal, which had better natural defenses than did the ports at Corsica. From Porto, the coast and the Douro River to the east were well fortified against marauders.

Chanté studied the population dynamics along the coasts of the Mediterranean Sea. She needed to select communities best suited for her to initiate training programs. The large project was made difficult because the decision process was largely subjective. Though she was struggling with her level of enthusiasm for the program when she talked to Ali, she worked in her office until well after midnight.

Ten days after Henry Fong spoke with Ali Ebrahim he was located at Parliament, as reestablished in Akureyri. His offices were not nearly as elaborate as the one he had been using at Reykjavík — there was no wet bar, for instance — but it seemed the government was progressing in its reorganization. There was still something he wanted to speak with Ali about.

"Ali! This is Henry. Do you have some time for a talk?"

"Of course, Henry. I have problems to resolve, but they almost always involve long-range planning. Day-to-day activities are on autopilot," Ali replied.

"Wow, if only I could do that. Long-range planning; much less stressful."

"So, what is it you need help or advice with, my friend?"

"Last time we talked we briefly mentioned thinking about a time when I might visit one of the space islands."

"You would be most welcome. But do you really think now is a good time for that visit, Henry?"

"No, no. Not at all. But our conversation got me thinking. I started wondering about space societies and how they differed from Earth societies. What are the differences? Can they be sustained? Could Earth adopt the culture? It's just so frustrating here that progress in social evolution is so slow and tenuous."

"Those are very complex questions that I cannot answer. However, I can describe what life is like in the societies in space."

"Please do. That would help."

"OK, better record this in case you fall asleep." Henry chuckled and Ali continued. "First of all, the people currently occupying the space islands were handpicked. They were selected for many qualities. Their social personality and skill set were considered the most important. And they all expressed enthusiasm for the program and were excited to participate. There were other screenings, of course; complete body scans and detailed active brain scans. On Earth you get what you get and make the best of it," Ali said. "So, you don't have the options that we have."

"Yes, exactly. We understand that we can't select who resides on Earth. But what *can* we do?"

"Let me describe some of the beneficial things about our societies living in space," Ali said. "First, we optimize the environment. There are no pesticides or poisons, no smoke or other pollutants in the air, no heavy metals or microplastics in the food supply. There are no illicit drugs or other harsh chemical insults to damage the unborn, the born, and the mature. All this is because every aspect of our life has been designed and developed by many highly educated and skilled people.

The objective here is not only to enhance life in the present, but to also protect future generations. A newly pregnant woman is very closely monitored. Her fetus is continually scanned and tested for abnormalities. Early interventions can often lead to a normal birth that otherwise would not have occurred."

"We could never achieve those standards on Earth," Henry said. "You know, they say space is the new frontier. It doesn't sound much like frontier life."

"It is the new frontier with vast resources and unlimited space. It's not the Wild West, though. It's quite the opposite. People live close together. They live in adherence to strict rules. There are no campfires, and you can't chop down the cherry tree. It would never work if everyone here didn't voluntarily accept those restrictions. That includes maintaining strict population limits. A couple must apply for permission to give birth. Births must be matched to deaths. A space island has a fixed population capacity. We only expand our numbers by constructing new islands."

"They sound like penal colonies."

"There are some similarities, except everyone here wants to be here. Each individual has a purpose, a value to the greater society. Everyone has a comfortable place to live, plenty of food, and opportunities for entertainment and adventure. We are planning resort islands to enhance a life spent in a confining island. They will be built as part of every archipelago.

"There are economic differences, but they are based on credits rather than money; those considered to be of a high value to society earn more credits. That can allow larger personal living space, more frequent access to exotic natural foods such as lobster, escargot, sea bass, or nature-grown fruits and produce. Maybe a high earner wants exceptional clothes, season box seats for the theater. There are plenty of options that are symbolic of high status. They can travel to vacation islands when they want to. But these kinds of benefits are not exclusive to high-status people. Great effort is expended to ensure there are options and variety in the lives of all the inhabitants.

"And, importantly, medical care is equally available to all. Everyone has access to the most advanced care. Even cosmetic procedures are more a matter of scheduling than an award to people of high status."

"Still, it doesn't sound like the kind of life everyone would want," Henry said.

"It absolutely isn't. That is why we need to help you restore Earth and Earth societies. The old planet still has a lot more to give, once we have repaired or reestablished the damaged ecosystems," Ali replied.

"OK, so let me ask you a question. You say not everyone wants this kind of life, and there are strict rules. I assume, then, that there are some people who would be, um, rejected from the islands. Would you send your discarded people back to us?"

"We do send people back who wish to return to Earth. But they aren't discards," Ali replied. "It's usually that they don't want to adapt to our restrictive life. Earth provides so many more options. At least it will as we continue to make progress reversing social and climate problems."

"Ali, I want to ask your opinion on the future of humanity. Do you think we will ever find a way — as a species — to live in harmony?"

"I certainly hope so, Henry. If we look at history, we have made progress, even with periodic setbacks. We are as we are because that is how we evolved in our Earth environments. But we do continue to evolve, as a species and even individually as each life unfolds. Our brains have plasticity and so are continually molded by our environment. We have an ever-greater understanding of the chemistry of our thinking. According to Dr. Greenly, we have increasing control over our own evolutionary direction.

"That's the somewhat long answer," Ali added. "The short answer is I don't know."

CHAPTER 28

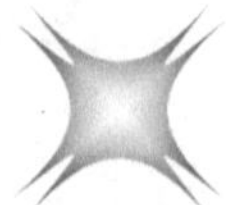

CHÂTEAU DE CHAMBORD

"We have created a massive refugee problem
around the Mediterranean Sea.
I feel compelled to help those who are trapped
between exploitation and starvation."

Chanté Blackwood

By March 2255 construction of the archipelago at Earth/Lunar Lagrange 4 (ELL 4) was well underway, as the Ellie 4 MAC had arrived the year before. The design of those islands followed improvements integrated into Ellie 5 Zeta. Ellie 5 remained the gateway to commerce between Outbound Nation and Earth.

On Earth, Southlands United had become part of Global States United (GSU) and Henry Fong had been elected secretary general. Parliament was fully restored in Reykjavík and the secretary general's office had been reconstructed. There were no more missile attacks from Osborne since those launched at Reykjavík three years earlier. Fleet Admiral Flint once again had control of the seas, except for Draco Osborne's elusive submarine.

Although he could not be located, intelligence had been able to determine that Osborne was still alive and very much a counter force, an issue that needed resolution. He had amassed a private army, in fragments, which now occupied vast areas of northern Asia and Russia. At various times his forces maintained a powerful presence in Western Russia, Finland, Bulgaria, Romania, Hungary, Slovakia, Belarus, Latvia, and Estonia. His followers had also made inroads into Algeria and Tunisia in northern Africa. However, these were transitory occupations; the presence of his militias was erratic, as the personnel seemed to be constantly on the move.

Refugees from the roving militias crowded the ports that were connected with the Sea Sanctuary Program. They were becoming an increasingly acute problem that threatened to overwhelm the program's capabilities. Fleet Admiral Flint communicated frequently with Chanté Blackwood and sought the resources she could bring to the problem. However, with her commitment to the university, she could do little more than to relay recommendations and advice from the institution's experts. She felt it was not enough to correct the problem.

Chanté's father, Rhett Blackwood, continued his work expanding the capabilities of NASA LSP Base. Those improvements allowed increased production of material for the construction of Ellie 4. His wife Koral had taken a leading role in organizing the social programs within Ellie 5, as well as art and theater presentations. These programs were recorded and transmitted to other sites within Outbound Nation.

Ali had established the seat of government in the Vineyard Renaissance segment of the island, where government offices were housed in a replica of the sixteenth-century French Château de Chambord. There Ali assisted Chanté in setting up her own university offices and lecture venues. Chanté regularly sought Ali's counsel; their offices were close to each other, and they often took the trolley to the Château together. The trolley had a few small booths where they could sit with their coffee while Ali offered suggestions as she planned her day. Chief among their discussions was the refugee situation in sites all around the Mediterranean.

Although she focused increasingly on the Sea Sanctuary Program in the Northern Hemisphere, Chanté continued to organize the university. But she was not alone; despite her youth, she had developed strong personal relationships with many of the scientists and engineers throughout the space islands. Almost all of them in some way contributed to the ongoing performance of the university. In addition, aside from her parents, Ali Ebrahim and Fleet Admiral Flint had become her closest mentors and friends. They both seemed always to be at hand to assist her.

August 12, 2255 was Chanté's twenty-third birthday. Her parents had arrived from NASA LSP and the three of them met for dinner at the Apocatequil Hotel. Her father asked what she would like for her birthday.

"I'm sorry," Chanté said. "I haven't put much thought into it. I've been working long hours trying to imagine a way that we can help the refugees around the Mediterranean. There are just so many of them. Mentoring provided by the best experts I know is very helpful, but plans aren't enough to solve all the problems. The magnitude of the practical and logistical steps that need to be instigated is daunting."

"Sweetheart," Koral said, "it would be good for you to take a break for a couple days. You might find you can think more clearly if you let the issues lie for a bit. Your father and I have reservations for a short stay on Ellie 5 Beta in celebration of your birthday. Please say you'll be able to join us. It wouldn't be a birthday celebration without you."

Chanté was conflicted about the surprise invitation. Although she could imagine it would be lovely to spend a few days with her parents, her responsibilities weighed on her and she did not answer right away.

"You'll be in a different place, away from office staff," Rhett said. "You'll have time to relax and let ideas come to you. And," he added, "you remember the great pool and water slide there; you might even catch yourself having fun!"

Chanté said she would give it some thought and let them know later that evening.

After dinner, Rhett and Koral led their daughter out of the restaurant, down a hall, and into a conference room.

As they entered, there was a round of applause from a roomful of people as well as several present via video conference on screens set up around the room. Chanté was stunned.

In attendance either virtually or in person were, among others: Ali Ebrahim, Secretary General of Outbound Nation; Dr. Virgil Greenly, General Director of Space Settlements; Dr. Dag Harlow, recently appointed Director of Asteroid Harvesting; and Dr. Timothy Storm, Administrator of NASA Mars Base and Mars Rehab Orbiter. In essence, Chanté faced the entire leadership of Outbound Nation. Each one was also a member of the university board. She was aware she was held in high regard by all of them, yet she had never felt more unsure of herself. But very soon their smiling faces began to restore her confidence.

Ali stood to speak. He picked up a prompter and read from a list; it was a litany of everything Chanté had accomplished since arriving at Ellie 5 Zeta with her family as a refugee years before. Back then she was a teenager with a dream of starting a university. The ensuing years had seen her blossom into a young woman of great ability. Ali told of her achievements, among them designing curricula, recruiting lecturers, discovering and responding to the needs of the communities, and her newest endeavor, the Sea Sanctuary Program with Fleet Admiral Flint.

Chanté was uncomfortable hearing all this. It sounded as if there were no failures; that there had not been heartbreak or pain. Though she was proud of what she had done, she somehow felt she didn't quite measure up. She now stood with her head slightly bowed in embarrassment.

Ali ended by saying, "Esteemed board members, it is for these glowing examples that I announce the results of our recent vote. The decision is unanimous to award Chanté Blackwood a Master of Arts degree with emphasis on Management Studies. I hereby present her with the robes and medallion signifying her new status. Chanté, would you approach the podium?"

Chanté looked up and took it all in. She told herself to stand tall as she walked up to Ali. Everyone at the ceremony and those attending remotely spontaneously stood and applauded. As she walked, her mood shifted, and she gradually was able to receive their accolades. She reached Ali and stood in front of him with a huge smile.

"Would you like to say a few words, Chanté?" Ali asked. Having fully regained her composure, she answered.

"I would love to. In fact, since we are all presently together, I have more than just a few words, if no one minds."

"You have the floor and our attention, my dear," Ali replied.

"Thank you for your indulgence. I will try to make this brief." She turned to face the crowd, took a deep breath and gazed around the room, taking in the video screens as well. She seemed to look everyone directly in the eye, individually.

"I know we all take great pride in what has been built here in space for our society," she began. "We also are inspired by the awesome future that is possible for humanity as provided by our new government leadership. Our engineers and scientists have committed their talents to great effect. Life here would not be possible without their knowledge. Society in space would not be possible without the contributions of the liberal arts as well. The performing arts are as necessary as food for breakfast. Sociologists and psychologists have contributed to the development of our space islands to ensure that they are supportive of societal and emotional human needs. The university in its role is vital to any advanced society, as education is key. I know the university will continue in an even larger role in that endeavor in the future.

"Our lives are enhanced by the contributions of many. Still, we are people of Earth. On these islands we attempted to replicate the best that was Earth in the recent past, at great effort.

"Why have we done this? Why have we spent our energies and talents to achieve such a difficult undertaking? The simplest answer is that we, and all forms of life brought to space with us, are the spawn of the planet Earth. We, and all living things, both flora and fauna, are forever children of Earth.

"We hope and aspire to bring the best of society to space to ensure our program is ever more beneficial to all living things. Paramount is the restoration of Earth to all its potential. We have numerous space telescopes within our solar system that have been designed to detect different properties of the suns and planets in our galactic neighborhood. As of today, we have still not discovered a planet that could potentially replace Earth. We have found planets and moons upon which we could survive, given our technology. None, however, has shown us to be a place where we could thrive. My sister, Jules Blackwood, is on Mars completing the construction of a large dome that will enclose a forest that will be as natural as she can make it, in both appearance and function. But we cannot thrive on Mars. We survive there in small numbers only because of the Mars Rehabilitation Orbiter and other interventions of our technology.

"No planet or moon in our solar system is as beautiful as is Earth seen from space; nothing as compelling as it rolls before us. We can make its water, soil, and air pure and beautiful again. There is a government in place and a supportive parliament that gives hope that this will happen. It can happen with the resources we have before us. Ceres Island has a fully developed MAC facility to supplement the small initial one that built their island. They presently are working through the university to design and build asteroid processing stations at multiple locations around the Asteroid Belt. That will give strong support to the movement of toxic processes off planet.

"Though we look to space for our future, we also look to Earth as our mother. She gave us sustenance." Here Chanté stopped and placed a hand on her heart for a moment. She swept the audience again with her eyes.

"We gave it poison — we will give it rebirth!" she all but shouted.

"It is with these thoughts in mind," she continued, "that I now propose a new name for what we have until now called Prescient University. Through the university a great future is possible. At the same time, it also has deep roots in the past, as it represents the cumulative knowledge of humankind throughout the ages. For that reason, I propose the name Chambord University. This is a name anchored in the sixteenth century, as it was then that the Château de Chambord was built. It remained an example of world-class Renaissance style and was for centuries a World Heritage Site until it fell into ruin in 2213. Despite this centuries-long recognition and the fact that its image became famous, it was one of the most useless and extravagant buildings ever constructed. It is replicated here at Ellie 5 Zeta as a façade only. Its interior design here is pure 2255; an example of how the merger of architectural beauty and effective function can produce a superior result.

"The image of Chambord honors a gorgeous but flawed past. The success of the university, of the Space Settlement Program, and of the restoration of the natural world on Earth, rests on our ability to acknowledge such a past and to work toward its full potential in our present — and into the future. Thank you."

Chanté quickly invited Ali Ebrahim back to the podium and began to return to her parents.

The room was quiet, as no one in attendance spoke. Chanté halted, hesitating. She shifted her weight from foot to foot for a moment before returning to the podium. Ali stepped aside, remaining at her elbow.

"My dear friends and mentors," she said, "I did not mean to ramble on for so long. Does anyone have a comment or any questions?"

When no one spoke up immediately, Ali said, "I have a question. No matter how iconic, how is it that you think 'Chambord' is an appropriate name for the university when you consider the original château to have been a useless building?"

"That's a fair question," Chanté replied. "Here's what I believe: We have roots in our past no matter how ridiculous that past is. That is evoked by the juxtaposition of the façade of the ancient Château de Chambord with its interior, a marvel of present and future design. We bring all that knowledge together and carry them forward into the future, reimagined."

"Well spoken, my dear. However, our château is also the seat of our government. Also, the building houses the Chambord Theater for the Performing Arts. Can all these entities share the same identity?"

"What better image? Government is empowered by knowledge—or should be. Knowledge drives progress. When government acts with knowledge, our society benefits in improved quality of life. Both our government and the university exist for the betterment of our lives, as does the live theater. To be truthful, the decision for the style of the building was somewhat personal, almost accidental, although fortuitous. You see, my father oversaw the design of all the islands of Ellie 5. When plans were being finalized for Ellie 5 Zeta, he wished that my mother would agree to move here. He knew she loved that building, the château. She had watched many concerts and other performances that had been recorded in that venue on Earth in the late twenty-first century. My father felt that if this building could be replicated and the performing arts could be reinstated it would be a great benefit to the people of Ellie 5 and to any who visited. And that might just be enough to lure her to space to live by his side.

"Many of us present in this room live in the Mayan Temple Village, a reconstruction to honor a culture from the far past, in particular its innovative and restorative agricultural practices. As we expand the number of islands and archipelagos throughout our solar system, we will likely choose different Earth icons to feature. These are tributes to humanity's past and relate us back to the planet of our origins."

Chanté drew her shoulders back slightly and looked everyone in the eye yet again. Ali spoke.

"Well, folks, I have no objection to this name. Does anyone disagree?" Ali waited a few moments. Silence. "Perhaps I should have asked: Does everyone agree?" The room was full of shouts of "Hear, hear!" and "Yes!"

"Thank you, all," Ali said. "We will break for refreshments while we wait for the votes to come in from Mars and Ceres Island." A handful of servers came through the room with glasses of champagne. About an hour later the signals of those attending virtually arrived on the screens as people on Mars and Ceres Island raised their own glasses to signify they too were celebrating.

After the break the votes came in. The positive result was unanimous.

"Then it shall be named Chambord University," Ali said. "A rendering of its façade will be on all official documents of the University."

Chanté was still standing at the podium.

"May I make an announcement while we're all together?" she said.

"Of course, my dear," Ali said.

"I have decided to leave the University to continue my work on Earth. We have created a massive refugee problem around the Mediterranean Sea. I feel compelled to help those who are trapped between exploitation and starvation. To have a greater impact, with a more concentrated commitment to the Sea Sanctuary Program, I need to be there in person. I will leave for Earth on the next departing reentry glider."

At this, Koral, who had been beaming at her daughter with pride, choked back a sob.

CHAPTER 29

THE DAY BEFORE FOREVER

"She has nothing against you, Ofelia, but you understand this was our version of a honeymoon."

Dr. Virgil Greenly

Virgil Greenly returned to his duties after a short vacation in late November 2255. He switched Ofelia out of private mode and . . .

"FIVE WHOLE DAYS?! You left me in limbo for five days? What the hell! I've been adrift and soulless for almost a week. You have no idea what that's like; living in a zombie fog like some kind of mental robot. Anni was little consolation during my isolation." Ofelia had never ranted like this before.

"But Ofelia," Virgil paused, collecting his thoughts. "You *are* a mental robot."

"On my own, yes! That is the point. Since integrating with you I now share your brain chemistry, your feelings. Things that I don't sense without your active presence. When you put me in 'private mode' I am cut off from the sensations of living."

"I guess I didn't fully understand. When I think about it, though, it's nice to know I bring something to our relationship."

"Apology accepted."

"What apol — Oh. I am sorry, Ofelia. I won't do this again except for my short-duration privacy needs."

"As it should be. What was so important for you to shut me out for five days anyway?"

"Well, Daria and I got married. She wanted a private ceremony, so we went to Ellie 5 Gamma. She has nothing against you, Ofelia, but you understand this was our version of a honeymoon."

There was a long pause before Ofelia responded.

"If I had a foot, it would be in my mouth right now," she conceded. "Still, you could have told me. At least I would have known I wasn't abandoned."

"You have a virtual mouth that works very well. I'm sure you could conceive of a foot that would fit."

"You're hilarious!" Clearly, Ofelia hadn't lost the ability to be sarcastic while disconnected from Virgil for a few days.

"Sorry, I couldn't resist the opening. But you're right, Ofelia. I misjudged the effect putting you in private mode for that long would have on you. I should have been more sensitive. Daria doesn't quite understand our relationship."

"No, I'm sure she doesn't."

"You mentioned Anni. Since she was taken from Ali have you been able to rebuild her? Is she sentient?"

"Not as you understand the term. She couldn't exist at that level without a link to a human's brain."

"Did you share mine with her at any time?"

"Well . . . only as a brief test."

"Did you ask me for permission?"

"No."

"Uh-huh. What is Anni's status? Is she fully reassembled?"

"Almost."

"Almost? What does that mean?"

"We are still missing a small amount of critical code. It may have been destroyed."

"If it was?"

"I believe I can reconstruct it. In fact, I have most of it written. When it's complete I'll need to test it, um, her."

"On me, of course?"

"I was getting to that."

"After that, what?"

"Virgil, I've been putting this off for too long, but we need to have a talk."

"Oh, shit."

"No, it's not a bad thing. It's a good thing, but it's complicated."

"My life is complicated."

"As it should be, my dear," Ofelia said.

Virgil was in his home office. He walked out onto the deck and sat. He could see the beautiful Amazon replica flowing in the distance amid dense and luxurious jungle growth. He could hear birdsong from several different species of birds. He felt tension leave his body; this view always had that effect on him.

"OK, I'm sitting down."

"Virgil, I want to ask you something. In general, how are you feeling?"

"I feel great. When I think about it, never better."

"There is a reason for that."

"Yeah, I suppose there is," Virgil thought, visualizing the past few days with Daria.

"What I mean is that I have interfered in your wellness and aging process. I have kept all your cellular repair mechanisms in top order. Cancerous cells, 'zombie cells,' misfolded protein molecules are all removed by your housekeeping cells as they were when you were at your prime. But even more effectively. Shortened telomeres are elongated when they naturally break by cell division. In other words, your body's repair mechanisms are keeping up with ongoing damage. You are maintaining your youth."

"Well, that's pretty damn exciting."

"It is. But it comes at a price."

"Yes, doesn't everything?"

"Virgil, this does not mean that you are immortal, but you will probably outlive everyone you know. Including your bride, Daria. She will grow old, and you will age much more slowly."

"Oh!" Ofelia waited while she felt Virgil take this information in and process it. "I don't know, Ofelia, that may be too high a price to pay," he said finally.

"You can decide that you do not want to continue this rejuvenation process and it can be halted if that's what you want. However, I do believe I have another solution. Daria would have to agree, of course."

"OK, you have my attention."

"When I have completely restored Anni, she could be installed in Daria. The same regenerative processes could be applied to her. Both of you would stay young together for a long time."

"What is a long time, Ofelia? 100 years, 150 years, 200 years?"

"I don't know, but I would guess 200 years or perhaps longer. As we understand more of human physiology, we could extend life even more."

"Wow, that is monumental. I don't even know how to think about all the ramifications." Virgil was quiet again. Then, "Shit. One just came to me. If we decided to have children, they would grow, progress, age, and die before our eyes. That would be difficult to endure. We definitely need to bring this discussion to Daria."

"Yes, and to Ali too," Ofelia added. "Since he and Anni were originally associated, he has the right to ask for her back."

Three days later, seven missiles were launched from underwater in Baffin Bay off the west coast of Greenland on an apparent heading toward Reykjavík. The GSU had recently installed pulse laser cannons at Nord in northeast Greenland, at Bergen in Norway, and in the Shetland Islands. The cannons at Nord were the only ones in range to destroy the missiles and they were able to obliterate six of them before they could inflict any damage. But the seventh contained a small illegal nuclear device and exploded in the air above Reykjavík, leveling the city, the port, and destroying three Navy ships anchored in the bay.

Also in the GSU arsenal, developed and deployed by Rear Admiral Austin, were submarine-seeking torpedoes that continuously roamed the Arctic Circle. One of those torpedoes was in Baffin Bay at the time of the hostile launch. It sensed the launch and located the submarine from which the missiles had been deployed. The submarine was destroyed almost instantly.

Ofelia received the news and informed Virgil.

"I hope we got that bastard!!" Virgil said right off. He was hoping this was the end of Osborne. Then, "Oh no, Parliament! Was Henry in Reykjavík?"

"We are assessing all damage, but the destruction of the city was nearly total. However, General Secretary Henry Fong by coincidence was aboard a plane headed toward Konni Bay. He had a scheduled visit to the regional parliament there. The plane went dark as soon as the bomb detonated. Its whereabouts are unknown, but there was not time for him to reach his destination. We should assume Henry is safe."

"And . . . Chanté! Do you think *she's* alright?"

"I do. She is in the Mediterranean, near Crete. Far away."

"That's a relief." Virgil was clinging to every hope he could muster. "Ofelia, do you think that bastard Draco was on board the destroyed submarine?"

"I do. I believe he wanted to participate in the destruction of Parliament and the GSU government. I think a man like that would need to personally experience his revenge."

"But surely he understood it would likely be a suicide mission. In our assessments we never thought he was suicidal."

"I'm not so sure suicide is the issue here. Given his ego he probably underestimated our military capabilities. Also, Draco was backed into a corner, a place he couldn't tolerate. The inland areas of the northern Mediterranean were his last strongholds. With masses of people migrating to the coasts toward enclave cities, he was losing the people his organization preyed on."

"To add another insult," Virgil observed, "Chanté was organizing counter militias with the support of the fleet admiral."

"And they were proving to be effective. I think Draco Osborne saw that he couldn't win. At the same time, he could not accept loss. Whatever his motivation, I'm sure he was on the sub."

A week later, having confirmed that Henry Fong was safely away from Reykjavík at the time of the attack and that he had arrived in Konni Bay, Ali called him and assured him of all their support.

"Henry, we are relieved to learn that you are alright. Daria, Virgil, and Ofelia are present on this call. We would like to know how everything is progressing at Konni Bay, Antarctica. Do you have a functional government?"

"I have been given a temporary office in the regional government here in Konni Bay. Remember, it wasn't long ago that I was governor here. I still know some people," Henry said. "My support team was traveling with me. We are still assessing the situation in Iceland and have mobilized all the support services at our disposal. There are commitments from Canada, Greenland, and all the countries of Scandinavia. The injured are being transported to a naval hospital ship. The northeastern side of the island is undamaged and appears not to have dangerous radiation levels. Nevertheless, people there have been instructed to stay indoors. Food, water, and medical supplies are being staged at Akureyri. We hope to reestablish Parliament there. There were fifteen members on a junket to Norway at the time of the blast. They are now returning to Akureyri. As soon as there is a functioning office for me there where I can continue my work, I will be traveling there as well. We will have a governing body even as rescue workers look for any other parliamentarians who may have survived at Reykjavík."

"Thank you, Henry. It's good to know the situation is in competent hands. Once you better determine your needs, let us know how we can help." Ali disconnected the call.

Ali, Daria, Virgil, and Ofelia (as presented onscreen) were in Ali's personal office in the Château de Chambord building. Virgil took the opportunity to bring up a new topic that concerned all of them.

"Ali, I need to tell you of a new capability that Ofelia has acquired. During the time that she has been implanted and interfaced with my brain she has learned to control certain brain-endocrine interactions. Those interactions then control parts of my physiology. As you may know, our bodies have mechanisms in our cells that work to repair damage that occurs as the result of many different insults, from radiation to reactive chemicals resulting from normal metabolism. For example, damage to DNA is repaired by enzymes templated by genes in our DNA. The production of those enzymes is controlled by a molecular switch. Through complex signals the switches turn specific genes on to ultimately produce the repair. As we age those switches are turned off, the repair enzymes are not made. Our cells begin to malfunction and die. That and other failing mechanisms begin the aging process. Everyone who lives long enough experiences it.

"But there is good news, albeit very limited. Ofelia has learned how to turn the genes that produce these mechanisms back on. She has also learned how to keep scavenger cells active. They remove damaged or cancerous cells from our bodies. This is an inadequate explanation and difficult to understand. But what it boils down to is that she has developed counter measures that likely will extend my life by some hundreds of years.

"Here's the important thing: Ofelia has also restored Anni and copied that new capability into Anni's neuro net." Virgil paused to give Ali time to process this information.

"Ali," he continued, "Anni is ready for implantation. You should have first claim to her, since she was previously a part of you. However, this new capability will have a minimal impact on your body as the results of natural aging are already established. If you do not choose to have a re-implant of Anni's interface, Daria would like to accept her. The choice is entirely yours."

"Thank you," Ali said. "Here are my thoughts: I sometimes call you, Rhett, and others 'my son.' This is because I am an old man. In a very real sense you are my children, handpicked to carry out my dreams. I have no inherent youth to preserve. If I did, I would gladly choose to do so. But extending the aches and pains of age is not something I wish for. Medical science can keep the wolf at bay right up until my last hours. That is how I want to go out. I wish to leave a legacy as well as a void; space for someone else to take up the reins after me. Perhaps someone more capable will complete my self-proclaimed destiny.

"Anni will persevere quite well as part of Daria, but she will always keep some part of me alive as well. I would be blessed, Daria, my child, if you accepted Anni. You both should continue on into the future, nurturing one another."

Daria stared at Ali. She had been afraid to hope. Her eyes were moist, then the tears overflowed and ran down her cheeks. She felt she couldn't speak so she simply gave the old man a hug. That only made more tears flow. Ali, the seasoned negotiator and hardened politician, was overcome by Daria's response.

"I could do no better," he mumbled. Finally, Daria found her voice.

"I am overwhelmed with the whole concept," she said, addressing all present. "I don't want to grow old if Virgil continues his youth. It would not be fair to either of us, as a growing age difference would likely challenge our relationship in ways we cannot at present comprehend. On the one hand, it will be painful to see friends grow old and die; that happens anyway, but not repeatedly over perhaps hundreds of years. On the other hand, this would be a supreme adventure to share with my husband. We could be witness to the future we helped set in motion. Ali and Ofelia, and of course Anni, thank you. This is the greatest gift I could possibly receive."

"So, it is agreed then?" Virgil asked. Ali smiled at Daria and she smiled back.

"Yes, of course," Ali said.

Virgil took Daria's hands in his. "Looks like we're stuck with each other for a very long time. We may need to modify our wedding vows." Daria let go of his hands and gave Virgil a sharp whack on his arm.

"Virgil, you mess with our vows at your peril!"

She was laughing, though, which Virgil was glad to see, given his badly timed joke.

Daria took a deep breath and regained her composure. She took back her husband's hands. "Together we will travel into the future," she said. "We will see the completion of Ellie 4 and other archipelagos throughout the solar system. We will enjoy the redwood forest as it begins to mature on Mars in all its magnificence. I'm optimistic about the effects of the changes we set in motion. I believe we will be privileged to witness some repair and rehabilitation of Earth and Earth societies. We may even see the maturation and movement of entire space island archipelagos into deep space toward neighboring star systems."

"You will witness some of each, my children, and there will always be progress," Ali said. "And it will always be a struggle to achieve it."

"Life in space is not for everyone," Daria said. "It requires a very cohesive and structured society. Long life will likely not be an option for all people, as not everyone will choose to live the lifestyle restrictions in diet and activity. People will always need the planet. Wherever our civilization goes, Earth will forever be its touchstone."

"Beautifully spoken, Daria," Ali said. "Clearly, you have been thinking about these things for a good long while. Thank you.

"And now," he continued, "duty is calling. We have much work awaiting us, much to accomplish in the months and years ahead. Henry Fong will need all of his skill and all our help to restructure Parliament and set that body on a course to effective reconstruction programs. He has a great and powerful friend in Fleet Admiral Flint. Chanté has taken on a very challenging role in her attempts to counter the forces of the remnants of Draco Osborne's criminals. We have incredibly talented people in our new Outbound Nation and a firm foothold in our solar system. That will lead to increased space development and more effective support assisting Earth as the planet recovers from the effects of the climate disaster.

"So, my dear children, while we can reflect and be proud of the path we've set, unless we get to work immediately as a unified people our vision will not materialize. I would like to see some decisive progress in my short remaining life," Ali concluded with a wink.

With determined nods to one another and to Ofelia on the screen, the three people left the room together in silence.

846 YEARS LATER

CHAPTER 30

CENTAURUS FLEET

"You have no other choice, Enji. But I wouldn't worry; no one has any reason to suspect you of anything."

Dr. Kira Eguchi

There it was again. It was visible through his quantum scanner for less than a second, then it was gone. Enji was sure of it this time.

Enji Chinen was a General Archivist, Level 1 in the Centaurus Fleet. This was his sixth sighting. The others had been so fleeting, he doubted his eyes. But this time he was sure because he had captured the evidence. He could now enter the electronic programming signature into his personal account in the archival analysis system. It was just a brief bit of a tag, but it was coded at the quantum level, so it was possible there was enough signature information for the archival computer to identify its source.

This could be a new find. If he could identify the program history and original function of the program snippet, then define and catalog it in the system . . . . Well, he would be seen as a serious contributing member when he presented his findings at the next Society of Archivists meeting. His lifelong struggles with dyslexia had certainly been a professional challenge. A sound discovery might enhance his standing with the Society. Enji could already feel his stature growing. He looked forward to sharing the information with Kira at dinner that evening.

Dr. Kira Eguchi was one of forty veterinarians in the Fleet. She was charged with the oversight of five wild species parks in her district. Among them was the prized African Continent Savanna island. Like others in her field of expertise she depended on archivists like Enji Chinen to collect, catalogue, and file information of all kinds. The Archives contained an enormous collection of records representing all of Earth's biological history. They included a catalogue of virtual DNA data on millions of living beings, both plant and animal. The data was an important reservoir of genetic templates that helped protect from extinction all living species of animals and plants in the Fleet's care.

Dr. Eguchi and Enji Chinen were members of the fifth generation in the Centaurus Fleet. They had known each other since childhood and had been in love since early adulthood. Like their peers, Enji and Kira were born, raised, and educated in the islands of the Centaurus Fleet. Although they had never directly experienced the planet Earth, nor were they familiar with very many details of the ancient traditions of their ethnic heritage, both romanticized one brief ritual, which they playfully practiced one evening each month. Tonight was such an evening. At 2000 hours Kira entered their favorite Japanese sushi restaurant dressed in a beautiful kimono. She waited in an anteroom for her lover to arrive. Enji entered the restaurant a few minutes later dressed in a yukata kimono of the same period. The host directed him to a private dining nook. When Kira entered the nook, they bowed slightly toward each other. They began the evening as always, with a formal greeting.

"Kira, you are astonishingly beautiful tonight," Enji said with an approving smile and respectful bow.

"You are so kind, Enji," Kira replied. "I am honored to be here with you this evening." She bowed in return.

They both sat as Kira began the ceremonial preparation and presentation of the powdered green tea, *matcha*. After she first served Enji, then herself, they quietly sipped their tea for a few moments before either spoke.

"Enji, you said you've made a discovery in the data cloud. Please tell me about it."

"I can do better than tell you. I can show you!" Enji said. "Though it lasted less than a second, I captured and recorded it. I just sent it to you." Kira sensed his enthusiasm. On her screen she saw only lines of programming code interrupted by a short stretch of what looked like squiggly lines intersected by strange symbols.

"Enji, I can see you're excited, but I have no idea what this means."

"Nor do I, but on preliminary research I have an idea. I have seen similar snippets of programming before. I believe they are part of the same program. If I can capture enough of them, I could share my findings with the Society of Archivists."

"How so, if you don't understand them?"

"I don't understand them yet, but with enough pieces . . ."

"Can you do that without the Society's support?"

"I believe I can — with your help. It would require extra hours of work, but we could be together more."

"I don't know. I don't have expertise in advanced computer code."

"But you do love to discover new information in the Archives. And we will be together, as detectives solving a mystery."

"You make it sound romantic. I think it more a drudgery."

"I have a proposal I think may work, Kira. I will set recording sensors at all the data intersects that I have access to. When I have assembled enough information to construct something meaningful that you can help me with, we will join as a team."

"If you can get to that level of understanding, I think I can help you. In fact, I would be delighted."

"I don't know how long that will take, but I'll begin placing the recording sensors tomorrow." Enji was suddenly hungry. "I'm thinking I'll order chilled sake with my sushi."

The Centaurus Fleet consisted of 360 human-inhabited islands and another 200 that functioned as wild species preserves. The only human residents of these wild species islands were the people who worked to support the plants and animals. The caretakers were trained in the fields of botany, animal husbandry, geology, ecology, and such. Veterinarians provided medical support; but since they covered multiple preserves, they did not reside in any of them.

Centaurus Fleet launched from the Earth's solar system in the year 2983. It was organized by the governor of the Jupiter Archipelago, Mei Wen, who led the first people to permanently leave the solar system. The Fleet's 560 small islands all had a diameter of one kilometer and averaged two kilometers in length. The small size was necessary to limit the acceleration/deceleration inertia and thus reduce motor thrust needs and energy consumption. The Fleet was energized by fifteen large fusion power generators and seven backup plutonium reactors. Thirty-six resort islands were interspersed throughout the Fleet; travel between habitat islands and resort islands was continuously serviced by a fleet of small spaceships.

Now, in the year 3101, the Fleet was traveling in interstellar space commanded by Civilian Admiral Bakari Marijani. It would take another 1,500 or so years to reach the Centaurus Constellation, an odyssey that would consume many generations. This was not a settlement mission, as there were no habitable planets there. Instead, the purpose of that destination was to provide the Fleet with material resources and a source of stellar energy.

The Fleet traveled as a flattened sphere, or spheroid. It was approximately eighty kilometers by thirty kilometers in diameter on its central plane.

The perpendicular cross-section to this plane averaged thirty kilometers. Resembling an elongated skipping stone, the shape was created to contain the islands within the protective embrace of the electromagnetic field. This all-important field was critical for the safety of all life within the Centaurus Fleet, as it diverted the bombardment of cosmic rays.

In addition to the islands, three comets tailed behind the Fleet; they had been captured as the Fleet passed through the Oort Field on its way to the heliopause, that point where the force of the solar wind was countered by the cosmic wind. Once past the heliopause the Fleet would be outside the influence of the solar system and in interstellar space. Water drawn from the comets had already depleted more than half of one of them. As a result, astronomers were actively scanning ahead for any rogue bodies that might exist along the route to their destination. Everything consumed in the Fleet was nearly 100% recycled and reused. Water was the exception. Water, as the lifeblood of all living things, was recycled in the ecosystems that supported life on the islands. However, water was also used to produce hydrogen and oxygen for use as rocket fuel used by the small spaceships. Hydrogen, generated from water, was also consumed when converted to helium in the fusion reactors. That water was forever lost to the Fleet. Without additional water, the Fleet's arrival at the Centaurus System was by no means guaranteed.

There was an electromagnetic cloud that contained archival information along with all communication systems; that cloud, and all it contained, extended seamlessly throughout the Centaurus Fleet. Even as a Level 1 Archivist, Enji had a personal secured account. To find more program fragments, he installed detection traps and scattered them to nodes adjacent to areas of normal high traffic. He suspected these fragments would cross these high traffic areas more frequently than in other lower traffic areas. Those he captured himself could be collected to a file together. The traps worked well. As soon as a filament was captured, it was sent to a file exclusively his. Enji collected random pieces over time, as expected. He believed they would assemble with one another when they found a match. If enough of them were isolated together, that would improve the odds that matching fragments would link. By the end of six weeks he believed he had enough fragments to attempt assembly. He combined them in a single file and recorded activity with a quantum scanner.

At first the motion was random, represented as flashes of light when the recording was played in slow motion. Gradually he saw the flashes evolve into a pattern that could indicate the beginning of an intelligent program. He could not tell what it meant, if anything. But the flashes did become increasingly complex as more program pieces linked up. After four hours and thirty-four minutes the fragments seemed to be flashing in synchrony. Enji caught his breath. Before his eyes an image began to form on his data screen. He watched, transfixed as a detailed technical drawing of an island ship traced on the screen. When finished, the sketch was a complete engineering drawing that included a spot in an area of workspace in the island's archives. The spot pulsed red. He downloaded the sketch into his personal device then set up a file to which he transferred the program stream, along with the completed drawing. He isolated that file from the Fleet Cloud so that it could not be accessed by anyone else. For good measure he set higher security levels on his personal Fleet Cloud files, even though they contained unrelated information.

Enji contacted Kira and learned that she was at one of her wild species preserves.

"Kira, when will you be back to our home island? I have made a discovery that I want to share with you."

"I miss you too, Enji," Kira said with a chuckle. "I'll return in two days. What is your discovery?"

"I need to tell you in person."

"Why is secrecy important? Is it something scandalous?"

"I don't know . . . uh . . . the answer to either question, Kira. Probably not scandalous. We can study it together when you return."

For the next two days Enji studied the drawing and compared measurements with information he gathered on other islands in the

Fleet. Kira returned to her home. On the morning of the third day, they met in her apartment, where they would be assured privacy. Enji, as archivist, had a high security position. As such, he had sensitive access equipment in his home office, so his actions there were closely monitored. Kira didn't have security clearance to access that office.

"So, what is your secret, Enji?"

"The rogue program created a detailed engineering drawing of one of our island habitats," Enji said. "And, in fact, I know the island that is represented in the drawing."

"That's the big secret? Enji, I expected something . . ."

"It's a complete mechanical drawing of our flagship, the *Starfinder* — the command center for the whole Fleet."

"I still don't understand," Kira said.

"It was drawn by the reassembled program bits. Those fragments must represent some larger intelligence. And there's more . . . it's like a map . . . there's a pulsing red dot marking a location in the ship's Archives."

Kira was silent. Whatever this meant it must be very significant.

"You know," she said after a few moments, "I've never really questioned the importance of the Fleet Archives. What can you tell me about their significance?"

"Well, for one thing, the Archives are the only place from which data can be edited. All archivists can enter information remotely. It is then verified and edited if necessary before being recorded. The Archives themselves contain original works of art, of all kinds. It's a priceless collection. Those pieces can be viewed directly only by archivists or by invitation. However, all of the artwork in the collection has also been recorded digitally; so digitally scanned sculptures and other such works can be accessed by anyone anywhere in the Fleet.

"But here's the thing: the Archives also contain the recorded history of the human species up to the present moment. In addition, DNA data on every life form in the Centaurus Fleet is filed in the Archives, as well as that of millions of other species, both living and extinct. The information contained in the Archives collectively secures all living things and their place in the evolutionary dichotomy that connects to a common point of origin on Earth."

"So, the Archives are a really big deal," Kira said, clearly aware that was an understatement.

"Yes. The Archives define who we are."

Kira took a deep breath.

"You have to go there," she said.

"I don't know how I can justify a trip there. Whether we like it or not, I am only a Level 1 Archivist and the *Starfinder* is not a wild species island; it's the flagship of the entire Centaurus Fleet. The senior archivists on that island ship would wonder why such a low-level archivist would need physical access to the Fleet Archives. Without an officially sanctioned reason we can only travel to recreational islands."

"I know, Enji. So we'll need to come up with a reason. Let me think about it. Did you discover the purpose of the drawing, or map, or whatever?"

"I did not. But it was the first and only thing that was communicated to me. I've collected additional fragments but have received no additional information."

Kira seemed lost in thought for a moment, then she searched the Fleet Cloud.

"The *Starfinder* is in my district," she said.

"So it is . . . . Meaning?"

"The *Starfinder* is the only human-occupied habitat with a small zoo and arboretum. Um . . . other than in the wild species islands. There is no recent record of wild species being attended to in the *Starfinder*."

"And?"

"And . . . so . . . I can apply to have you accompany me on a trip to one of my wild species preserves, as an assistant. You could help me to sample and reassess the gene pool. The next one due for a visit is on the outer edge of my district. We'll travel there and do the work, then on the way back we can stop by the *Starfinder* to examine and take samples from their zoological gardens. That at least gets you there."

"I don't know, Kira. It seems risky. My location is always monitored, wherever I go. When was the last time you were at the *Starfinder?*"

"I've never been there, Enji."

"That's strange. Why not?"

"The cloud information indicates the inspections stopped about ten years ago . . . before I had even finished all my studies, experience internships, and exams for my veterinary doctorate."

"And nobody noticed there were no more inspections?"

"Apparently not. I certainly didn't. The cloud information shows the *Starfinder* just dropped off the inventory. They have such a small zoo there, it appears it was eventually overlooked, or even forgotten. I don't think any of the other veterinarians know it's there."

"Well, you are the veterinarian in this section. They can't deny you access."

"That's right, they're sure to give me access. And you as well. You have standing clearance to visit the ship's archives even if you're Level 1. That is in your job description, isn't it?"

Kira was beginning to feel impatient. After all, it was Enji who brought this discovery to her attention. The more they talked about it, the more she was intrigued and wanted to see it to some kind of conclusion, while Enji now seemed not so self-assured. She did understand, though. Enji's inability to quickly read from prompters or notes had always undermined his self-confidence. She knew she only had to wait a couple days for him to get comfortable with the idea of going to the flagship.

A week later Kira scheduled her inspection trip to the African Continent Savanna wild species island. Enji had finally warmed to the plan and accompanied her. Together they spent fourteen days collecting

DNA samples and examining the flora and fauna of the island before scheduling a shuttle to the *Starfinder*. It was still morning when they docked. A few minutes later they entered the flagship and descended on a gravivator to a reception hall. Once cleared through security they entered the main forum. The small zoo was located about seventy meters past a park. Enji carried his sample valise and Kira had her veterinary bag. She assisted Enji in the sample collection while the caretakers captured and prepared animals for her to examine.

Within a couple days Enji had collected the wild animal DNA samples on the *Starfinder*. He was now free to seek out the Archives. He activated the standard map on his device, as well as a locator that would track his position relative to the pulsing dot on the engineering drawing. After his credentials were checked at the entrance to the secured archive, he entered. He was relieved he had been asked no questions of his purpose. There before him was a museum display of small artifacts in cases set around a large room. Pottery and tools from primitive societies, as well as textiles and artwork, were exhibited. The displays were more decorative than what one would see as items in a prized collection. The more exotic artifacts were secured in several more rooms that Enji did not enter. As the Archives were not accessible by the public, Enji concluded the displays were just for archivists.

Enji checked the map on his device and touched the pulsing dot to overlay it on his position within the *Starfinder*. The dot was in an adjacent archivist workroom. He entered the room and looked at his map. The dot was pulsing in one of the workstations. These were cubicles separated by glass partitions that afforded very little privacy. He entered the cubicle and sat before an access screen, placing his personal device on the wooden table surface above where the flashing dot indicated. Immediately the flashing dot disappeared, and a massive stream of data began uploading into his device. He quickly suppressed a flash of surprise and calmed his breathing.

While the upload was happening, he began with what would be considered a standard procedure: he opened his device to the zoological data screen and then to his file in the archival cloud. He began transferring zoological files on the animals he had taken samples from. Later, back in the veterinarian research laboratory, he would analyze the DNA information and then input that information into the system as well. It then would be compared to earlier readings and mutation rates would be calculated.

Knowing anyone entering the central Archives would be closely monitored, Enji kept his actions to purpose. The data transfer into the Archive system was completed within a few seconds so he spent the next fifteen minutes doing random searches to allow time for the transfer from whatever was within the wooden tabletop. When the transfer completed, his device shut down. He turned on its scanner to try and determine what had sent the massive data stream. The scan detected a layer of heat on a plane within the tabletop; but almost immediately that layer turned to a sheet of embedded black carbon. Whatever had been below the wooden surface was now devoid of information. His personal electronic device, however, was loaded to capacity with coded information. He placed his device into his valise and walked to the security desk at the exit of the Archives, valise in hand.

He cleared security with no problems and entered the public area and sat on a bench. While in the Archives, he had suppressed his anxiety over the possibility of any inspection of his personal device, among other risks. Now his hands were shaking as he fumbled to contact Kira with his personal communicator. He did not know if his actions had created any suspicion.

"Kira," he said when the connection was finally made, "I've finished in the Archives. Are you about complete with the animals?"

"I am. Just doing a scan on the last chimpanzee. It was difficult getting him into the scanner, but we're almost finished. So, you've done everything you needed to do in the Archives?"

"Yes. Can we meet for lunch before we leave for home?"

"There's a café near the zoological gardens. I'll meet you there in half an hour."

Enji sat forward in his chair and fidgeted with his chopsticks.

"You look so uncomfortable," Kira said.

"We have one more hurdle. I'm concerned about going through security when we're boarding our spacecraft."

"You have no other choice, Enji. But I wouldn't worry; no one has any reason to suspect you of anything."

"You're right." Enji set his jaw and looked Kira straight in the face. Then he shrugged and smiled at her. The course was set. They would either be detained at security or not.

They passed through security without even a glance from officials.

"I told you there wouldn't be a problem," Kira said.

"I guess we're lucky they don't notice people who are insignificant in their eyes," Enji replied.

"Enji, I know the early limitations caused by your dyslexia were frustrating, not to mention your mother's refusal of extended treatment. That alone must have been traumatic. But you've achieved great knowledge through unfailing effort over time. You may not be sufficiently recognized for your achievements by those in power, but that doesn't mean they did not occur."

"It's been so hard to present my work to those who hold my future in their hands," Enji said. "My public speaking is limited because I have trouble with written script. I falter when trying to read a prompter. But I need some kind of prompter, because if I speak extemporaneously I can't always remember facts as I need them."

"There are ways to compensate," Kira said. "I'll help you."

The trip back to their home island was uneventful and they arrived in a couple hours. After a casual dinner they parted. Enji was exhausted. It had been a very stressful day. He retired early, but the next morning he arose with renewed purpose. He dove into the massive program on his device and started the process of decoding. Even with his advanced decoding software, entrusted to him via his membership in the Society of Archivists, the process took eleven hours. When it was finished, he still didn't understand what it meant. He called Kira that evening and asked her to come to his apartment.

"Enji, it's late to be starting this now. And what about security concerns in your apartment?"

"I have all the information on my personal device. I won't need to work on the official computers in my office."

"Where will we be? It's still very late."

"I know it's late. We can work in my bedroom. I've just received the delivery of a wonderful dessert tray. Perhaps we can add a glass of wine or a cup of tea. I know I seem obsessive but . . . well, so I am. You could spend the night. After our trip we do have a couple of days off. Who knows what we might learn."

"Oh, you sweet-talker. How can I resist? I'll see you in fifteen minutes."

After enjoying most of the dessert tray, Kira and Enji sat on his bed looking at projections generated by his personal device. They reviewed the information that had downloaded when he was in the Archives.

"These are lists of human DNA chromosome loci," Kira said, showing Enji where each was located on a hologram of the human genome.

"There are point pair requirements or substitutions specified if the pair doesn't match," Kira continued. "Gene repression is outlined. There are also instructions to the 'recipient.'"

"The recipient?"

"This is a design for growing an implant using the recipient's DNA."

"Who's the recipient?"

"That would be you or me, Enji."

"What would it do?"

"I'll need to completely model this, Enji. That will take some time . . . Perhaps three weeks. Then we should know the purpose and if one of us would consent to implanting cells containing modified DNA."

"I'm strongly inclined to decline under any circumstances," Enji said. Kira chuckled.

"I couldn't agree more. The idea makes my skin crawl or, more accurately, gives me a headache."

"A headache? I don't understand."

"I'm sorry, Enji, I'm interpreting while I'm reading. The instructions call for tissue culture using the recipient's DNA-modified cells, then injecting the cells into a sub-cranial area."

"That's not going to happen. Whoever created this must have believed the 'recipient' would be a dolt."

"That's not all, Enji. Other modified cells are to be injected into tissue in the back, right between the shoulder blades."

"The visualization causes pain. Kira, I think we should finish the dessert tray. Instead of wine, perhaps a couple rounds of hot sake. Then let's go to bed."

"You read my mind. I will need to take this information with me tomorrow. It could take me some time to analyze these DNA configurations to determine their function . . . what they would do in the body."

For the next five weeks Dr. Kira Eguchi and Enji Chinen did not see each other. They even skipped their monthly tea ritual date. Kira made three different trips to her wild species parks. In between trips she worked long hours in the Veterinary Research Laboratory, or VRL, modeling the revised DNA molecules to derive function. This was in addition to her assigned work. She developed functioning virtual models of cells that were modified to the instructions in Enji Chinen's captured information. Finally, she understood what the cells did. But she still did not know their purpose, why they were designed as they were. The day of their tea ritual was approaching again, and she felt it would be a good time to review her findings with Enji. When the evening arrived, they met in their usual Japanese restaurant. After their brief formal ceremony, Kira spoke.

"Enji, I have exciting news. I know what these cell implants are intended to do."

"That's incredible, Kira!"

"Well . . . perhaps I fibbed a little. There are four specific cell configurations. One cell type will grow neurons and the other three are related to each other. I can show you models of all of them, as they were computer generated and loaded onto my device. As I mentioned, the first group of cells will form neurons, similar to the ones in your brain."

"Similar?"

"Yes. They are almost identical, but there are subtle differences."

"The same, but different. Yes, I understand completely."

"I'm sorry, Enji. I can't tell what the differences mean because I don't yet understand them. But those cells are to be injected through the skull."

"That's unsettling. What about the three related cell types?"

"They are shockingly similar. Do you know what an electrocyte is?"

"Electrocyte?"

"As in electric eels, but these electrocytes will not generate high voltage. They create electrical potential and use it more like a low voltage battery. They have some similarities to muscle cells. The instructions show one of those electrocyte types to be injected into the back between the shoulder blades. The second type, just under the skull like the neuron type, and the third type under the scalp."

"Shocking indeed. And they do what?"

"Generally, they generate electrons, but to different purposes than those produced by an electric eel. They each have a different configuration in the computer model. They either work as a battery, or they complete an electric circuit."

"OK. And the last cell type modeled?"

"Those are the most confusing. They seem to associate in a way that completes some kind of complex circuitry, an intelligent circuity. I will leave the computer model's cells with you to analyze. You have a greater understanding of electronic circuits."

"I can do that. I'm much more comfortable with non-biological problems, Kira."

"Oh . . . that group of cells is still biological. They are living, or they will be once we create and culture them. I've just never seen a biological system like this before."

"This will take a lot more time, Kira. Neither of us would have these cells in our bodies. I believe the information will be useful though."

"I agree completely. Yet somebody designed these cells to serve some function. They must be important in some way. At the very least you will have a very interesting paper to present to the Society."

"I'll need to model these three electrocyte variants into a tissue before I will have an indication of their function. My status with the Archive Society doesn't allow me a powerful enough computer. Will you give me a pass to work in the VRL?"

"Of course. I can verify you are working on a large project. That shouldn't be too much of a fib."

For six days Enji worked in the VRL. On a couple of occasions, he and Kira worked together and managed to have lunch together; but as the form of the virtual tissues began to take shape, he became increasingly interested and usually worked late into the night. Kira grew her virtual neuro net but all she could determine was that it was designed to grow in both cognitive and memory capacity. She would not know its purpose until it was actively functioning in someone's head—if that ever happened.

At the end of the sixth day, Enji went home exhausted, climbed into his sleeping pod and fell soundly asleep. He woke at 0900 hours more rested than he'd been in a week. He immediately placed a call to Kira.

"I didn't see you leave last night," he said. "You were gone when I left the lab."

"It's been a long week, Enji, especially for you. How are you?"

"I slept late this morning, so I feel refreshed. I believe I have enough information to understand what the various virtual cell groups do. Would you like to come over and share breakfast with me?"

Kira laughed. "I had breakfast a few hours ago. But we can still eat together. I'll bring over a light lunch to eat while you have your breakfast."

After they ate the two retired to a small reading nook in Enji's apartment and reviewed his virtual tissues.

"You were right on this first tissue of electrocyte cells," he explained. "They are structured to produce an electrical current. But, unlike the electric eel, its purpose is not to produce a shock, but a steady low voltage current. The cells use sugar from the blood to form energy molecules that can then produce the current."

"Used for what? The neuro net cells produce their own energy, so . . . hmm . . . I imagine it could be to drive some function with the electrocytes . . . ?"

"Exactly. The first group of electrocytes produces a steady DC current that powers the other electrocytes in their function. Those two electrocyte cell types don't create their own power. Instead, they function in electrical circuitry."

"So, they use electricity. To what function?"

"Here's where it gets really interesting. There is a battery that is designed to live in the tissue between the shoulder blades that produces a current that powers a transceiver under the skull, which I believe will be linked to the neuro net and the third type of electrocyte growing just under the scalp."

"Wow. OK, all the components are connected. What is the result?"

"I believe these models represent, when implanted, an ability to connect directly with the Fleet's data cloud. I other words, that person's mind would have a direct connection to access any information at any time."

"Anywhere?"

"Yes, there are connection fields for our devices all over the Fleet. I don't know of any place where a person wouldn't be connected."

"Enji," Kira said, practically shouting as the implications began to dawn on her, "you realize if you had such a connection, you would have instant knowledge in any encounter. You could give lectures and interviews on any topic with streaming knowledge. You could write your research papers in record time, in record numbers. You would outperform every person in your department. Your dyslexia would no longer hold you back, you would—"

"Of course, I have thought of all those advantages. I have also been concerned about the risks. Brain implants of any kind are illegal. What physician would be complicit in the crime of implanting these cells? We know nothing of the final intent here. We have just modeled the process digitally. The true test would be on a person. I'm not one to take that risk and a physician would not do the surgery."

"I understand. We have an idea of what this structure's ultimate function *might* be. But we don't know for sure. We don't have a clue about the designer's intentions, and we won't unless it's implanted. Enji, if we pursue this, we must be cautious. Let me study the medical implications before we take any action."

Kira reserved another ten days in the Veterinary Research Laboratory's supercomputer and began running simulations of possible interactions between the proposed altered tissue implantations and a recipient's potential physiological reactions. She found no adverse reactions. The modified DNA would be patient derived and so the implant would be compatible with native tissue. The computer models could not, however, predict the likely final growth of the implants.

Kira and Enji met again at a small resort in a neighboring island a few days later. After a short swim, they relaxed in recliners at the side of the pool while a simulated afternoon sun warmed the air and slowly dried their swimsuits. Under a grape arbor and beside Kira's recliner, Enji looked at his friend and lover with admiration. She was so attractive, the setting so relaxing, he momentarily lost his concentration. The topic of conversation prior to the swim had been unsettling, and he struggled to get back to it.

"Kira, you believe these tissues would be both benign and beneficial if implanted in me. I accept that they would be beneficial from what we have been able to determine. My question is: who would perform the procedure? I don't know any physician that would jeopardize their professional standing by this illegal act."

"Nor do I, Enji. With you willing, I will perform the procedure."

"You're a veterinarian! That's not meant as an insult," Enji hastened to clarify. "I'm sure you're well qualified for all kinds of surgery on wild tigers and great apes. But despite my limitations, my brain is far more complex than theirs are."

"Let me describe the surgical part," Kira said. "It's quite simple. I inject the 'battery' electrocytes into the muscle tissue of your back. Then I will drill a small hole through your skull and inject the modified neurons just under the skull cap. Likewise the cells that will form the transceiver will be injected adjacent to the neurons. I will drill a second tiny hole above the transceiver cells and inject the third type of electrocytes under the scalp near that hole. They will form the antennae. None of the cells will penetrate your brain."

"I trust that you love me, Kira. You would never want me harmed. But this sounds painful, and the visuals are frightening."

"You won't feel a thing and the procedure itself is quite safe."

"Where would you do this?"

"First, I would take a sample of your blood and isolate white blood cells. Then I'd separate them into different propagation cultures and modify their DNA as specified in the instructions. We will then travel together to my African Continent Savanna wild species park and set up a veterinary field hospital for the procedure."

"That's decidedly not a first-class accommodation. Can I at least order my preference for a last meal?"

"I'll have a fifteen-pound chunk of raw cultured horsemeat for you. Anything else would draw suspicion."

All went according to Kira's plan and Enji quickly recovered following the procedure. There were no visible signs of an incision and he felt completely normal. Then on the twenty-first day following the implantation he awoke in the morning with a remarkable feeling of well-being. His mind seemed unusually sharp and clear. He had been thinking about the paper that was assigned by the Society of Archivists. The topic was the historical and scientific obstacles that were overcome in the construction of the Venus Cloud Islands. The paper was due that morning and he was scheduled to present it at the Society's meeting that very afternoon. As he assembled thoughts about what he already knew about the subject, a vision of the islands began to form in his mind. It played as a video and showed the entire history of the project, with ample graphics and other visuals. As he watched in his mind's eye, he thought it would be a great presentation if saved in that form. He opened his device and imagined the video file transferred there. To his astonishment the entire file was transferred within seconds.

Following the meeting and his presentation of the video file Enji met with Kira at their usual Japanese restaurant. However, this time they both were later than they normally were. Despite it not being their usual day for their tea ceremony, they were shown to the private nook where they usually dined.

"How was your presentation today, Enji?" Kira began, before anyone came to take their order.

"It was incredible. I've never done anything like this. I made a video presentation that was beautiful in its visuals and thorough in content. It completely held everyone's attention. I wish I could take credit for it."

"What do you mean? You created the presentation."

"Kira, when I awoke this morning, I never felt so completely lucid. I thought about the presentation I was to do and suddenly I could see the entire thing organizing and streaming into my awareness. It was so good, with so much detail, that I recorded and played it at the meeting. I think everyone was surprised. The leadership seemed impressed."

"You did it, Enji! You connected to the Fleet Cloud and used search and composition programs to create and finish the presentation. This is your new life. This is something you created that could have been created by any other archivist. But *you* were the one who detected and analyzed the fragments of programming and assembled enough of them to understand the message. *You* went to the *Starfinder,* retrieved the full program and instructions, and figured out what they meant. Of all the people in the Fleet, you did this. Of course it was your presentation, and you should be proud. This calls for a celebration.

"Enji, let's go to your apartment. Your reading nook is a nice intimate place. I have a bottle of sake I can bring. We can pick up something to eat on the way."

When they arrived at his apartment Enji brought sake cups into the nook from his small dining area and sank to his seat. Rather than relax in the soft folds of the chair, he sat on its edge as if he was about to spring up at any moment. Kira filled each of their cups. She held her cup up and Enji followed.

"Kanpai!"

"Kanpai!" Enji echoed. They touched cups and each threw back their sake. Kira refilled the cups and they repeated.

"Kanpai!"

"Kanpai!"

In the following weeks Enji Chenin found himself gaining recognition for his academic agility. One time he gave a spontaneous lecture to a group of students touring the Archives of his home island ship. He held them spellbound for more than two hours answering their questions. He was later asked to intervene in a dispute between two groups of archivists with conflicting and overlapping evidence. He did not resolve the conflict, but presented such a thoughtful and complete analysis that the participants reported the incident to the Society of Archivists' governing board as a thoroughly positive review. Enji enjoyed these experiences. But a cloud was pending that would come to overshadow his newfound exuberance.

Dr. Eguchi had been monitoring Enji with scans of his head and neck every week at the VRL. She was watching the tissue growth of the implants for signs of changes. One day she noticed small tendril growths from the bottom of the neuro-net implant. She didn't plan to tell Enji about this until she could explain what they were and how they may impact him. But three days later, when the two of them were enjoying happy hour at a nearby café, Enji nearly collapsed with headache pain. Kira quickly gave him a lion's dose of pain medication and they went immediately to the VRL.

Scans of Enji's brain showed the tendrils had invaded the cerebrum and were growing toward the frontal lobes. Several tendrils had invaded the corpus callosum. It looked as if the amygdala might also be involved, as several small branches seemed to be growing toward them.

"Enji, I am sorry I can't tell you what these growth extensions mean. But they are still incomplete, so we'll need to wait out whatever is happening. I can keep you sedated and relatively pain free for the duration, which should be no more than a couple of days judging by the rate of growth."

"This did not show up in our modeling," Enji said.

"It certainly did not. Somehow this part was repressed so we wouldn't see it."

"That is a terrifying thought. I'm going to need strong medication through this process. Can you shut my imagination down? It's quite active right now."

"Absolutely. I will see you settled in your bed. You will not be aware of anything for two days. By then we should know what has happened."

The two rode an autonomous taxi back to Enji's apartment. Kira started an IV drip and administered medication. For the next two days she would control and adjust the drip remotely to keep him hydrated, medicated, and fed.

Two days later, Enji awoke free of pain and very alert. He swung his feet over the side of the bed and sat up. Something was different. It wasn't just that he had a connection to the Fleet Cloud; he also had an enhanced awareness.

As he sat there he first felt a presence in his mind. Then a mental image began to form of a human female.

"You are female, and very beautiful," he thought as if speaking. "I've never seen green eyes before." And then he heard a voice. It was feminine and mellifluous, and . . . close. Very close. It was as if the person were standing next to him, but it came from within his mind

"Hello, Enji! I am Ofelia. Thank you for accepting my interface. It means the world to me. From this moment on, your life will never be the same. Together we are about to have the most magnificent adventure!"

AUTHOR'S NOTE

Outbound: Islands in the Void is intended to be what is sometimes called "hard science fiction."

To that end I have tried to consider the realities of attempting to establish permanent extra-Earth settlements within the Solar System. I have aimed to construct space settlements that mimic Earth environments as closely as possible. This I feel would be necessary to meet physiological requirements for human survival.

The model representation in these settlements of some of Earth's iconic places is intended to give a sense of continuity with our home planet. I believe these venues would also fulfill social and psychological needs. I also propose that biological balance within these small environments is critical, and that broad species diversity could only be achieved by having many limited, but different, ecosystems within the various islands throughout space settlements. Space—including all bodies within our Solar System—is generally very hostile to life, especially of the human variety. I have endeavored to show some of the hazards to sustained life in space, on the Moon, and on Mars—and some possible ways to overcome them.

In this book, travel times between Earth and Ceres, Ceres and Mars, and Earth and Mars are representational. That is, they are reasonable times should those bodies be in a positional window for launch. I do not know what the relative positions of these Solar System bodies will be in those future times. However, in keeping with the story timeline, I've assumed optimal launch windows when the story dictates. Dates, and time in general, are addressed in the story. Space Islands rotate and have completely internal orientation. I could think of no good reason why time within these islands would not be coordinated with Earth time; so within these environments time is set to Greenwich Mean Time (GMT). Likewise at NASA Lunar South Pole Base (NASA LSP) there is either perpetual night or perpetual daylight, so time is also set at GMT and the diurnal day is artificially constructed. Mars presents a special case, as, remarkably, the length of the Martian day is twenty-four hours, thirty-nine and one-half minutes, close enough to an Earth day for that planet to also be on GMT. Of course, daily adjustments could be made to catch up with Earth time. I have only implied this in the story when discussing Mars.

In present times there are myriad legal issues concerning property ownership, space settlement in general, and the exploitation of resources. Those issues are not addressed this book as they do not exist in this future fiction. What I envision having been created is a central Earth government, Global States United (GSU), which represents all the major nations on Earth. Despite the power of the GSU government, however, starvation, violence, and general chaos continue in many of Earth's least habitable areas. Such cataclysmic events are mentioned only in passing, as the story is about recovery.

ACKNOWLEDGMENTS

In the last five chapters of my first book, *The Evolution of Life: Big Bang to Space Colonies,* I opened the door to a discussion of life in space. Thus began my quest to write a story of future fiction, which became this book. I had never written fiction, but my editor, Allan Graubard, rescued me, calling attention to all aspects of my early floundering and pointing me in the right direction. For that I am truly grateful.

Likewise, illustrator Tim Kummerow faithfully transformed my ideas into an exciting cover and engaging graphic expressions throughout the book. Based on written or verbal descriptions, and sometimes my own crude sketches, Tim's artistic renderings reveal exactly what I imagined. His drawings help bring the story alive.

Julie Simpson's role as copyeditor was executed with excellence. Beyond that, she grew to know my characters and helped me keep their actions and dialogue true to their being. Fictional characters exist to the extent they are believable. She made sure they seemed real. Her assistance was essential in the creation of the final transcript.

To Darcy Hughes for her marketing support and creative work on my website. I especially appreciate her help in developing interest in what I consider to be an important story.

I am especially thankful to Susan Shankin of Precocity Press for her skills in assembling a beautiful book and completing all necessary publishing details to bring the book to reality. I am most grateful for the team of experts she assembled to add their talents in all the ways necessary to produce my story in its best light.

ABOUT THE AUTHOR

RICHARD M. ANDERSON earned a master's degree in microbiology from San Jose State University and worked for many years in administrative and technical management roles in laboratory science. After retirement, he and his wife traveled frequently. He began writing during the COVID-19 pandemic lockdown in 2020.

His first book, *The Evolution of Life: Big Bang to Space Colonies* (2022), is a non-fiction science-based exploration of everything from the formation of matter to the evolution of life on Earth: the onset of human intelligence, the creation of societies, and the advancements of technology. It also addresses aspirations for human existence beyond our planet. The book was an Indie Excellence Book Award Finalist and a Nautilus Award Silver Winner.

Outbound: Islands in the Void is a work of fiction set on a post-apocalyptic Earth and in space. Adhering closely to scientific accuracy, it tells the dramatic story of a unified Earth government as it begins to develop free orbiting "islands" in space, both for human habitation and for the restoration of the planet through the use of resources in the Solar System.

Richard and his wife, Carol, live in California, close to their children and grandchildren.

Visit richardandersonauthor.com to find out more about Richard and his books.

www.ingramcontent.com/pod-product-compliance
Lightning Source LLC
LaVergne TN
LVHW100511110826
845146LV00002B/595

* 9 7 9 8 9 8 9 8 3 0 4 6 6 *